I0608686

DREAMER'S SYNDROME

MARK BOUSQUET

More great SF, Fantasy, and Pulp Adventure
from White Rocket Books

Sentinels:
  When Strikes the Warlord
  A Distant Star
  Apocalypse Rising
Van Allen Plexico

Voices for the Cure
Edited by James Palmer

Non-Fiction:

ASSEMBLED! Five Decades of Earth's Mightiest
By the Jarvis Heads of AvengersAssemble.net

DREAMER'S SYNDROME

MARK BOUSQUET

WHITE ROCKET BOOKS

Dreamer's Syndrome originated as an online serialized novel for Frontier Publishing, though the site ceased publishing new material before the novel was finished. The author would like to thank all of the people associated with Frontier for their support and editorial contributions and wishes all of them continued success in all their endeavors.

This is a work of fiction. All the characters and events portrayed in this book are either products of the author's imagination or are used fictitiously.

DREAMER'S SYNDROME

Copyright 2008 by Mark Bousquet

Cover art and book design by Van Allen Plexico for White Rocket Books

Cover Design Consultant: Anthony Schiavino

Title font (Wolf's Bane) by Dan Zadorozny of Iconian Fonts

All rights reserved, including the right to reproduce this book, or portions thereof, in any form.

A White Rocket Book
www.whiterocketbooks.com

ISBN: 978-0-6151-9245-1

This book is set in Times New Roman.

First printing: February 2008

0 9 8 7 6 5 4 3 2 1

For family, friends, and storytellers everywhere.

Chapter One
Do-Over

Austin McNamara woke up dressed as a pirate.

He didn't notice this at first because he had slept in the nude and never thought to look down at what he was wearing. He was vaguely aware that he was wearing clothes, but on nights when he and his girlfriend, Kelly Reed, didn't have sex (which, he was pleased to say, was actually on less nights than not despite their having been together for over two years), he wore boxers and, if it was cold, a t-shirt.

So it was that Austin McNamara awoke, yawned, stretched, and was surprised when he went to scratch himself and found his hands blocked by a pair of pants. His eyes still closed, Austin tried to remember if he and Kelly had had sex the night before. Yes, he thought. They definitely had. He had sat on the couch and watched *The Prince of Tides* with her without complaining once. Frickin' Barbra Streisand, he thought. How could Nick Nolte whore himself out to star in a movie with Barbra Frickin' Streisand? How could the man who made *North Dallas Forty* and *48 Hours* make a fucking movie with Barbra Fucking Streisand?

Somehow, Austin had made it though the whole movie without once making a smart-ass remark, without once wondering out-loud (out-loud being the key) why Nick Nolte would make a movie with Barbra Streisand, and, most importantly, he hadn't – not once – made any attempt to check out the score of the Red Sox game. Not once. Of course, they had been in Chicago last night and it was pouring in Chicago and he was pretty certain there would be a long rain delay if not outright cancellation but he didn't know for sure and that drove him nuts.

When it came to girlfriends in this regard, Kelly was the best one he'd ever been involved with. She actually liked to go to Fenway and knew enough about baseball to not have to ask Austin what was going on. She loved to go to the games, and didn't mind watching them on TV, just so long as Austin didn't try to watch every inning every night. Usually he'd watch an inning or two, then let Kelly watch an hour of broadcast TV, then come back to the game for the end. It was a workable arrangement, and Kelly really was a great girl, which is why he was able to put up with missing a few innings a night now and then.

Even if that meant watching *Friends*. We all have to make sacrifices, he'd told himself every Thursday night at 8 for two years.

Nothing drove him nuttier than people who didn't follow baseball on a regular basis and then showed up on the couch at the end of the season or in the playoffs and ask questions like, "Why are they getting so angry?" or make comments like, "They really shouldn't swear on the field. Kids are watching."

Or the worst: "It's only a game."

Austin had long ago taken a solemn oath to never date a woman who said, "It's only a game," or "It's just a game," or "It's not life and death." Or really, any variant of that. He'd dumped three girls in his lifetime because they'd uttered those sentiments, and he always felt better after doing it. It was one of the small "codes to live by" he'd come up with.

Kelly had never said it. In fact, he was so terrified that this perfect woman might say it at some point, even though she seemed like exactly the kind of woman who wouldn't, that he mentioned the code to her. She thought him quite mad, but Austin felt a little better that she knew it, even if she did think he was a bit crazier because of it.

Austin rolled over so that his face was pointing in Kelly's direction. His eyes were closed. He liked it when Kelly was the first sight he saw in the morning. He never told her this because it seemed like kind of a dorky thing, but he liked doing it. Her breathing was even, meaning she was still asleep.

The question of why he was wearing clothes even though they had made love was gone from his mind.

He opened his eyes.

Saw Kelly's peaceful face. Brown hair. Flawless skin. He felt good. Happy. Noted that her left arm was tucked under her pillow and her right hand was tucked beneath her face. She really was beautiful, he thought. Made a mental note to tell her this more often. The sad, dorky, pathetic truth (he was using his friends' adjectives) was that he was honestly, truly, deeply (he was using Kelly's friends' adjectives) in love with Kelly Reed and, because of that, he sometimes actually forgot how beautiful she was.

This is what angels must look like, he thought. And then she wrinkled her nose, scratched it, and rolled towards him, onto her stomach. He saw her back. He thought this:

"What the hell?"

She was wearing a light blue evening gown. Not just any evening gown, either. Very fancy. Kinda puffy. Silk, he thought. Whatever it was, she hadn't been wearing it the night before. He was positive about that. She disliked wearing evening gowns, which was too bad because she looked great all made up. Kelly was a jeans and t-shirt girl. Out-doorsy. Never wore a dress unless she had to. He couldn't imagine her ever wearing this ... this ... Snow White looking, poofy monstrosity.

"I must be dreaming," he thought, rubbing his eyes. Getting out of bed, Austin stumbled to the bathroom to splash water on his face. As the water ran down his face, he looked in the mirror, and things got a whole lot weirder. It took a moment for him to comprehend what he saw, but when his mind had processed the image his eyes had brought it, this is what he said:

"Why the hell am I dressed as a fucking pirate?"

"Well, this blows a whole in your theory that the humans can't comprehend us, doesn't it, Gabriel?" Raphael asked, holding up a copy of the morning paper.

THE BOSTON EXAMINER
HOLY HECKFIRE!
ANGELS TO MAKE DREAMS COME TRUE

Cover Story by Jessica Jenkins
THE SKY – In a revelation sure to have far reaching implications, angels appeared above the skies of the world yesterday to announce that they were granting everyone's childhood dream.

That's right. No more getting up at dawn and working eight hours at the factory. No more sweeping floors. No more cubicles.

At least, that's how it's supposed to work. Whether it happens or not, of course, we won't know until tomorrow. In fact, when you read this story, you should know whether the angels were able to fulfill their promise, or whether it's just a large hoax.

"I think it's a publicity stunt," said Austin McNamara, a twenty-eight year old associate professor of Literature at Northeastern. "We'll find out tomorrow this is some stupid new Microsoft product. Angels XP."

His girlfriend had a different take. "I'm doing what I've always wanted to do," said Kelly Reed, a twenty-six year old naturalist painter/photographer from Cambridge. "So I imagine tomorrow won't be much different."

That remains to be seen, of course.

No one is certain exactly how the change will occur. The angel Azrael, when asked about this, replied, "Humans! You always have to know everything, don't you? Just relax. Go home, have a good night's rest, and when you wake up tomorrow you'll have your dream job. You don't need to know anymore."

What some experts say is most surprising is how nonchalant most people appear to be taking the news that angels really do exist. "It's disappointing," Father Thomas Otten said, his old eyes still locked on the sky, "but people cannot be forced to acknowledge any religion. All we can ask is that people use the angels' gift to become better people."

Asked if he had any doubts about the veracity of the angels' identity, Father Otten replied, "I have no doubts. Those were authentic angels in the sky yesterday."

"No, they weren't angels. They were aliens, man. Big albino aliens with big black eyes," said Potato Johnson, 30, of Durham, New Hampshire.

Such disputes over exactly who was in the sky yesterday only fuel to the confusion and that confusion, according to Psychology Professor Sheila Watson, carries with it a potential danger. "I think people are nervous. They're not sure what to believe about what they saw. The truth is, it all depends on tomorrow morning. If we wake up and nothing has changed this event will quickly be forgotten. If, however, as preposterous as it sounds, we wake up tomorrow as ... I don't know, astronauts and movie stars ... I don't think anyone can predict what will happen."

As for this intrepid reporter, when I was a child I wanted to be a bird. A dove, to be exact. We shall see what will become of me.

"Do you know what upsets me most about that story?" Gabriel asked.

"That Azrael let himself get interviewed?" Raphael asked.

"No," Gabriel shook his head. "The part about how the people down there on Earth weren't really all that fazed by our announcement. Maybe if they had remembered the part about God it would be different."

Raphael clasped his fellow angel on the shoulder. "Do not get depressed, old friend. Let us see what the world does today." Raphael looked at Gabriel with concern as the older angel's frown did not disappear. "What is it?"

Gabriel sighed. "I've been put in charge of the Reorganization."

Raphael winced. "Ouch."

"How about you?"

"Princes and Princesses," Raphael replied cheerfully.

"Lucky you," Gabriel sighed. "I guess I better be going. Lot of work to do. Wish me luck."

"Good luck," Raphael said, then added. "One more thing. Lose the sighing. It makes even rational, loving people want to punch you in the mouth."

Gabriel nodded, offered a half-smile. "Gotcha." He looked down to the world below and said softly, "It's not all going to be fun and games, you know. Even now, it's not all happiness." The angel pointed to the paper. "That reporter, Jessica Jenkins."

"Has she turned into a dove?"

Gabriel shook his head. "But a lot of others have. In the bargain, however, they've lost all rational thought and free will. They're just animals now."

"That's awful," Raphael remarked, heart-broken.

"There are some, of course, who wanted to be a bear who could talk, so there's some talking bears and what-not, but it will not be easy for them."

Raphael frowned. "Do you think God knew—"

Gabriel shook his head. "I don't know. He must've."

"We need to find Him."

"We can't. You know that. We've tried since He left and we just do not have that power."

The two angels stood in silence. Around them in the white city in the clouds, angels bustled to fill their new duties. "What did she become?" Raphael asked after a moment. "The reporter. Miss Jenkins."

Gabriel shook his head. "Hers was not an easy childhood. I fear she will not live through this experience well. Not all dreams are pleasant ones."

Jessica Jenkins' head was buried in her hands, but they could not hold back the tears. She knew she shouldn't have lied in the paper, and partly blamed what had become of her on that lie. Call it Catholic guilt. "If I had just left it alone!" her mind cursed, but she knew, deep down, that wasn't true. When angels come and change the world, there is no place a lie can hide.

She picked her head out of her hands and looked around at her surroundings. It was hot – everything was hot: the sun, the beach sand, the water. It was an island Paradise, in the middle of some ocean. Had she come here under other circumstances, it would be a dream vacation. But she had not come here under other circumstances.

Jessica had been placed here by the angels, fulfilling the overriding dream of her childhood …

To be alone. To be as far away from her mother as possible. To never have to rely on anyone for anything.

"I can't believe this!" Kelly Reed held her dress in her hands and squeezed tightly. "What the hell am I supposed to be? Snow White? Sleeping Beauty?" She looked over to Austin, "I swear to God if you say Cinderella I will pummel you into submission."

Austin threw up his hands and took a step back, chuckling softly. "You look sexy."

Kelly flipped him off. "You look like a waiter at a fish shack."

Austin laughed. "Come on, Kelly. This is absurd. Think about it," he said, moving towards her. "It's completely ridiculous. I mean, angels, aliens, the fairy godmother … whatever it was that caused this … it's just … absurd. It can't mean anything at all."

Kelly ran her hands through her brown hair, and wrapped her arms around her boyfriend. "You're right. You have to be."

"Of course I'm right," he smiled, kissing her forehead. "I'm always ri-owwww!" His hand came up to rub his head. "Something hit me."

Something squawked.

Kelly and Austin looked over to their couch. On the back of the couch, a green parrot dug its claws into the leather and looked at them. "Shiver me timbers! Squawk!"

Austin was nearly speechless. "You have got to be kidding me."

A voice from the window said, "Sorry about that. We had to train them awfully quickly."

"Austin," Kelly said, taking his arm in her hands, "there's an angel in our window."

The angel stepped in, folding his wings behind him. "Name's Azrael." He looked the two of them over, nodding. "Nice outfits. All we angels ever get to wear are robes and these glorified diapers." Austin and Kelly noted the angel was right. He wore sandals, shorts and nothing else. His alabaster skin and silvery hair seemed to light their entire apartment. "Princess and Pirate. Very nice choices."

"We didn't have a choice!" Kelly blurted.

"Sure you did," Azrael replied. "You just made it twenty years ago."

"You son of a—"

Austin clamped a hand over her mouth. "Dude, angel or not, watch it." He let Kelly go.

"There will be time to make changes," Azrael assured her. "But we needed the dreams of innocents to make this work, not the dreams of adults. Much too complicated with adults. Anyway," he smiled, "here are your Dream Fulfillment Packages."

Austin and Kelly each took an envelope, looking confused.

Azrael leaned towards them and lowered his voice. "They're instructions, really, but Dream Fulfillment Packages sound so much better, wouldn't you agree?" Azrael clapped his hands a few times and turned to leave. "Oh, one last thing," he said, turning back to face Austin. "Parrot's name is Mollug. Stupid name, but you picked it."

"Mollug?" Kelly asked as the angel jumped out of their window.

"It's Gollum in reverse," Austin mumbled. "I was five! I didn't know any better!"

Kelly smiled and shook her head. She ripped open her envelope and read the instructions. Austin alternately looked from her to Mollug and back. "What is it?" he asked.

"Bad news."

"What?"

"It says here I've got to report to the Providence airport by tonight."

"Providence? Yikes. That is bad news."

Kelly crumpled her letter and tossed it at him. "You're a moron. Don't you get what this means?"

Austin winced, "That you're going to hit me again?"

"Read your instructions," she said, turning away to look at the parrot. "I'm guessing you're not going to Providence."

Austin skimmed his note. "Nope, I'm headed for Port Gloucester. Supposed to pick up a ship there and sail for the open ... seas." He looked to Kelly and saw she was chewing on her lower lip. "Aw, hell," he said, holding her tightly to him. "They're splitting us up."

"What if we just ignore the instructions?" she asked, her head buried in his neck.

Austin shook his head. "Read the bottom. Says we're all required to do this. If we don't, the angels will come get us. Says there will be time later to ... to sort things out."

They held each other close as the parrot behind them shredded the top of their leather couch.

Potato Johnson had been laughing since shortly after opening his eyes this morning. He couldn't believe his luck. He was in the top room of an ivory tower that reached up into the clouds. All around him, gold coins, rubies, gems, pearls, treasure chests dotted the large room.

He looked down at the letter that sat atop his wooden desk and read it again.

Attention Potato Johnson,

While it is, of course, impossible to make you the richest man in the world (since so many had the same dream), we can assure you that there is no one on Earth richer than you, though there are several thousand with just as much wealth as you. Specific to you, of course, is this shimmering ivory tower. As per your dreams, we have placed this tower near the Atlantic coast of New Hampshire. Best wishes on living out your dreams.

Signed,
The Angel Juramel
- The Angel in Charge of Wealth and Power

"Power," Potato thought, tossing gold coins into the air. "I should have dreamt of power, too."

Former Psychology Professor Sheila Watson had never been more overjoyed. She owed all of this to the kids who had picked on her as a child. The ones that had called her fat and stupid and ugly. The one who told her she was uglier than the ugliest Halloween witch.

Sheila remembered the Halloween from when she was eight. She was in the third grade, and it had been a brutal week at school. It seemed more kids than usual had been making fun of her, and with more anger than they ever had before. Sheila had come home from school and watched a movie with a mean, ugly, evil old witch in it. Then another. And another. She had made a decision through her tears that night – if this is what the other kids thought of her, then this is what she would become. (Although she always had hoped she'd turn out beautiful.)

Time had soothed that bitter little girl, of course, and but it had not erased it. Sheila was drawn to psychology just because she saw it as a way to have power over others. Once she understood why those kids picked on her, they lost their power over her. But now …

She stood on a platform high above the ground, looking out at the Atlantic Ocean. Behind her, a menacing castle. Behind that, the Maine countryside.

A kingdom for her to rule.

Troubled was the mind of the priest.

Father Otten was a priest yesterday when the angels came and he was a priest now after the Reorganization.

Something, he knew, was wrong. He could not believe this was God's will. Something was most definitely wrong.

He intended to find out what it was.

Chapter Two
The New World

Father Thomas Otten looked out over the small sea-town of Port Gloucester, Massachusetts with a frown. Under his right arm was a folded over copy of this morning's *Boston Examiner*. Distubing article by Jessica Jenkins. Not only was it a lazy story – most of the people interviewed were people she knew personally – but that bit about the dove was almost assuredly a lie. In his left hand was a cup of water where a cup of coffee should have been, but there was no coffee to be had this morning.

Father Otten believed that a priest should be a member of the community in which he lived. He believed this for two reasons. The first was so the community would see him as an active participant, and so he could know as many members of the community as well as possible. The second reason was that he felt it was important to give back financially to the community; every week hundreds would come to his parish and donate their money. The amount was never great, but it was steady, and while other parishes around the state would see their financial support rise and fall like the stock market, the parishioners in Port Gloucester were as steady as the seas at high tide that lapped at the shores of this small town.

Every morning, then, Father Otten would walk out into the town and buy a cup of coffee at the Ocean's Kiss Diner. Linda McLachlan owned the Ocean's Kiss – had owned it for thirty-nine years and never failed to open. Back in '64, her father, a fisherman, had gone to sea and not returned. Fourteen years later, in '78 she'd lost her husband, also a fisherman, to the sea. In '87, she lost one of her sons to these same waters. Thomas had presided over the funerals of both husband and son. In his thirty years here, he'd presided over too many funerals of those lost at sea. Despite – or perhaps because – of all this, Linda was still here. She was born here, raised here, lived here, and would die here.

Or so everyone thought.

"Where's Miss McLachlan?" Father Otten had asked the angel posting a CLOSED UNTIL FURTHER NOTICE sign on the door of the Ocean's Kiss.

"Gone," the angel replied pleasantly without turning around. "Her childhood dream was to escape."

"Where to?" Father Otten asked.

"Anywhere but here," the angel replied, smoothing a piece of tape over the edge of the sign. The angel turned to face Otten and a look of surprise came over his face. "Oh! A priest. There aren't many of you left, you know. Lots of astronauts and firemen, but not so many priests. You're very important, you know."

Father Otten ignored the angel. "Where is Miss McLachlan gone to? Where have you taken her?"

The angel rubbed his chin. "Nebraska, I believe. Someplace far away from the ocean."

An anger that had been simmering deep inside of him bubbled to the surface. "How can you do this? Her whole life was here. I don't care what her childhood dream was, Miss McLachlan's whole life was-"

The angel raised his hand. "Sorry, Father, but it wasn't our call. It was God's. Now, please, I must be going. Blessed is the Lord."

Father Otten narrowed his eyes as the angel flapped his wings and leapt into the sky. "It should be beautiful," he thought, watching the angel flap his wings, "but it just feels wrong."

His anger rolled back like the receding tide, replaced with a sense of unease.

"So ..."

"So."

Austin McNamara stood face-to-face with his girlfriend, Kelly Reed, beside her car in a Dunkin Donuts parking lot. The store was closed. Every store was closed, they'd noted. Few people, it seemed, had dreamt of growing up and serving coffee and making doughnuts. Kelly's head rested on his shoulder and their hands were intertwined. She was dressed as a Princess and he as a pirate; their wistful childhood dreams made manifest in a time and place that was never part of that dream. Austin's parrot, Mollug, sat on top of the car, watching them with a dispassionate eye.

"This is good-bye," Kelly said, her words mumbled into him. "It's so stupid. All of it."

"I know," Austin said softly. "It doesn't seem possible ... the whole world is on the move today, moving to fulfill their childhood dreams."

"I liked my life," Kelly said, pulling her head back to look Austin in the eye. "I liked being a naturalist-photographer-slash-painter. I liked living with you."

"You did?" he asked, feigning surprise.

"Don't be an ass this morning," she said, smiling weakly.

Austin shook his head, looking to a column of pirates walking down the road behind Kelly. "Kelly, listen, this is all ... whatever it is ... it'll work out."

"How do you know?"

He kissed her forehead. "I don't. It's just ... there's never any guarantees in life. There's no guarantee that while you're off doing your photography thing that you won't get attacked and killed by a pack of wild mallards. Or that three hot young nymphic Nordic coeds wouldn't burst into my office one day looking for help with their papers, willing to do anything to repay my assistance. I mean, one thing could lead to another and the next thing you know-"

Kelly kissed him to shut him up. "I'm the best woman you'll ever get. Don't forget it."

Austin smiled, and wrapped his hands around her waist. "I won't."

"Heck, this is all too strange to last, isn't it? We'll probably be back together before we know it. Didn't Raphael say there would be a time to make corrections?"

"He did. Heck, we'll probably be separated for less time than we were last year when you took that assignment in New Zealand."

Kelly smiled, kissed him lightly on the lips, then pulled back, frowning. She leaned to the left to look past Austin,

"What is it?" he asked, looking at her with concern. His ears caught a sound. "Is that a horse?"

"Er ... yes."

"Greetings, milady!" a rich voice boomed down to them. "Is this pirate causing you consternation?"

"Listen, pal," Austin started, letting Kelly go to turn around, "this is my ... girlfriend." His words trailed away as he looked up at a guy whose dream must have been to be Prince Charming.

"Whoah," Kelly whispered beside him.

Looking down at them was what looked like a rugged Prince on a horse. The large, handsome man pulled the reins on his horse, bringing the massive steed to a stop before them, then swung down off of it. He took Kelly's hand in his and kissed it. "My lady," he said softly. "Are thoust in need of saving?"

Kelly blushed. "Um, no … it's just Austin."

"Her boyfriend," Austin added, though neither Kelly nor the stranger looked at him.

"My name is Frederic Kornell," he announced, bowing low.

"Are you a Prince?" Kelly asked, a light blush still upon her cheeks.

"Nay, my lady," he replied, straightening himself. "I am a ranger, a defender of the weak who roams the countryside, and calls no castle home, nor man King, nor woman Queen."

"That was your dream?" Austin asked. "That's a pretty advanced dream for a ten year old kid."

Kornell looked to Austin and smiled. "Would you like to see my Dream Fulfillment Package assignment papers?" he asked, reaching inside his vest to remove a roll of parchment. Frowning, Austin snatched the parchment from him. He had a bad feeling, the same feeling he got anytime he met anyone that Kelly showed any interest in. The truth was he knew, really knew, that Kelly was the best thing that had ever happened to him. He loved her. Flat out. They'd dated long enough that he no longer lived in total fear that she would leave him, but there was a voice in the back of his head that never totally went away. The guy she dated before him was a tall, handsome Wall Street-type who played left wing at Harvard. The *Boston Examiner* had named him Boston's Most Eligible Bachelor two years in a row. Austin knew he wasn't a bad catch, but, as one of his ex-girlfriends – *Examiner* reporter Jessica Jenkins – kept telling him, "You can't compete with Brad Regent. Why Kelly stays with you when she could have him back at any moment is a wonder to us all."

"Let's see what this parchment says," he mumbled, unrolling Kornell's assignment paper and pushing Jessica's insult to the back of his mind.

"You are a Princess?" Kornell asked Kelly.

"I am," she replied, smiling up at the tall, handsome man.

"Though I am a ranger, and not a Prince, I have been told to head to Providence with the Princes and Princesses," he said, beaming a heroic smile down to Kelly.

"Why are you a ranger and not a Prince?" Kelly asked, wanting to keep the conversation going.

"My mother always called me her little Prince Charming," Frederic explained, smiling regally. "My father hated it. Said Prince Charming was a sissy mama's boy. Told me I should want to grow up and be a Black Panther."

Kelly looked confused, but smiled anyway. "Um ..."

Kornell chuckled. "I thought he meant Black Panther, the superhero. When he saw me dressed up in that costume at Halloween he went postal. 'Kids today!' and all that. Superheroes were sissies, he said."

"He said that a lot, it seems," Kelly said, her smile growing.

"He did," Kornell replied. "Told me real men were rangers. I had no idea what a ranger was. Of course, he meant Army rangers, but I was afraid to ask for a clarification. My mother told me it was like a Prince, except that he wasn't out for himself, or his kingdom, but for those who needed help."

Austin interrupted them. "You have got to be kidding me!" He held out the parchment and pointed to the written text. "Your dream was to be a 'ruggedly handsome ranger'? What ten year old thinks like that?"

The taller man grinned. "Never actually knew what that meant, to be honest, but my mother said that's what a ranger should be, so that's what I wanted to be."

Austin looked at him skeptically. "You did turn into a mama's boy."

"Austin!" Kelly erupted, punching him in the arm.

"Ouch!" Austin yelped, rubbing his arm. "You hit me."

"You were being a jerk."

Kornell laughed, "It is quite alright, my lady."

"Stop calling her your lady," Austin snapped.

"I'm a ranger," Kornell replied. "Every woman is my lady."

"Not this one," Austin said.

"Stop it, Austin," Kelly ordered. "He's just being polite."

Austin looked at her, suddenly not wanting to let her out of his sight, even for a minute. He had a sudden, awful gut-wrenching premonition of his own heart breaking.

"And you know I hate it when you're possessive," she finished.

"Yeah, yeah," Austin said, shrugging. He looked to the ranger. "Sorry."

Kornell smiled politely. "Think nothing of it, Austin." He offered Austin his hand.

"Yeah, yeah," Austin repeated himself, shaking Frederic's hand.

It was then the angel Raphael floated down to stand with them. "Let's pick up the pace, mortals. You," he said, pointing to Austin, "get to the docks. You need to be assigned a ship. And you two," he turned to Kelly and Frederic, "need to get to Providence."

Austin let out a sigh of relief. There was no way the ranger could keep up with Kelly – Frederic had a horse, Kelly had a car.

"Take the horse," Raphael said. "It'll get you there quicker."

"Excuse me?" Austin asked. "The horse is quicker than the car? What," he asked, turning to Kornell, "did you dream about the world's fastest horse, too?"

Raphael answered for the ranger. "We've enhanced the abilities of certain animals to help get everyone where they need to be. We want the Reorganization done as quickly as possible. You'll find your parrot has an extraordinary vocabulary. But it won't last. Angels can't be everywhere, of course, so we've built 'helpers' into the system to answer questions for you." The angel turned to look at the parrot. "Isn't that right, Mollug?"

"Squawk," Mollug replied.

"See?" Raphael remarked proudly. "Brilliant bird."

"What was so brilliant about that?" Austin asked.

"He said 'squawk'," Raphael replied, as if it were obvious.

"All parrots squawk," Austin said.

Kelly, Frederic, and Raphael all sighed.

"What?"

Kelly shook her head. "It said 'squawk,' Austin."

"And?"

"It *said* 'squawk,'" Frederic repeated. "It said it."

"Yeah, yeah, I heard it," Austin said, growing angry and confused in equal parts. "It squawked. All parrots squawk."

Raphael looked at him with concern, then turned to Kelly. "Is he always this dense?" he asked her.

"Most of the time."

"Honest to God, what the hell is the big deal about a parrot squawking?"

Kelly touched his arm lightly. "Parrots *squawk*, Austin. This parrot *said* 'squawk.' It *said* it. It didn't squawk. It said 'squawk.' It would be like a dog saying, 'bark-bark,' instead of actually barking. Do you understand?"

Austin shook his head, focusing on the parrot. "Am I stupid, or are they crazy?"

"You're stupid, I'm afraid," Mollug replied.

Austin shook his head, hating life. He felt Kelly kiss him on the cheek, whisper her good-bye and then move to join Frederic by the horse. "I don't want to part like this," he said numbly, watching the ranger pull her up onto the horse's back. "I feel weak and humbled and pathetic. I feel like the world is out to get me. That's not me, Kelly. I'm a good guy, most of the time. Sure, heck, I like to joke around, but ..." his voice trailed away. He didn't know why he let those words get out, they only made him feel weaker, more humbled, and more pathetic.

Kelly positioned herself behind Frederic, her arms wrapping around the ranger's waist. "I don't want to say good-bye, either," she said somberly. "You don't think enough of yourself, Austin. If you were a weak, pathetic man I wouldn't have anything to do with you."

Austin turned to Raphael, feeling a panic rise up inside him. "How do we contact each other?"

Mollug squawked. Or said, "Squawk." Austin wasn't sure, and didn't care.

Raphael shook his head, looking at Austin with concern. "With your cell phone, I'd imagine. You do have a cell phone, don't you?"

"Oh, yeah," Austin answered, reaching down to fell the familiar weight in his pants pocket. He looked up to Kelly. "I love you, Kelly."

"I love you, too, Austin," she replied, smiling. "Don't worry. We'll get back together as soon as we can. Never fear adventure. Heck, you've written enough papers on all those heroic myths you can't get enough of. It'll do you good to have an adventure on your own – instead of just reading and writing about the adventures of others."

Raphael clasped his hand on Austin's shoulder. "These things tend to sort themselves out, Austin. Enjoy your time as a pirate. It is an incredible gift we are giving humanity, a chance to live out your childhood's dream. If, in time, you find you do not like it, you can, of course, do something else. But now is the time for dreams. You are a man of books, but a man should not be content to experience life only through words. Have an adventure, Austin. Test yourself to see if you are equal to the protagonists in all those books you've read over the years." Raphael turned to look up at Frederic and Kelly, "Ride to Providence, ranger. I shall meet you there shortly."

Frederic nodded to the angel, then turned to Austin. "I wish you well, Austin."

Austin nodded, but had no words. His eyes were locked on Kelly's. "I've always hated saying good-bye to you," he said softly. "I'm always afraid you'll never come back."

Kelly smiled sadly. "And I'm always afraid you won't be home when I return. With my luck, Jessica Jenkins' dream was to be a pirate, too."

Raphael looked surprised, then shook his head. "You have nothing to fear about Miss Jenkins," the angel said softly.

"Why?" Austin asked.

"She's on the other side of the world, stranded on an island paradise. Completely alone."

"Good," Kelly said, with more hatred than she intended. She smiled at the hurt look on Austin's face. "I love that hurt puppy dog look. I'll see you soon, lover."

"Yeah," Austin said, then watched Frederic dig his heels into the side of the horse and ride off with his girlfriend. Austin watched them until they rounded a corner, then turned to the angel. "I hate this."

Raphael smiled. "Mysterious ways," he said, then took to the sky, leaving Austin alone with his parrot.

Sheila Watson's official title was Duchess of Kent Harbor, Maine. A part of her disbelieved it, of course – the whole world was still slightly disbelieving of what was happening – so she had taken her Dream Fulfillment Package assignment paper and hung it on the wall, so any and all visitors to her Throne Room could read the Heavenly Proclamation.

Her castle was tall and black and menacing. She wondered what it would look like from the ocean that pounded on the nearby shore, thinking it so awful than no sailor would dare plot a course for this shore.

She had thought none would dare live within sight of this castle, but that, she found, was not the case. To her north was the town of Kent Harbor, and they had already sent emissaries to her with a tribute payment, as per the orders of the angels.

"They are the people who live under you," the angel Juramel said to her as they walked through the silent, stone halls of the Black Castle. Juramel was the angel in charge of Wealth and Power and he was, as were most angels, making the rounds to meet as many humans under his care as possible. "While your dreams did not specifically contain a small, port city town for you to rule, we have taken the liberties of combining certain dreams."

"They wanted to live under a Duchess?"

Juramel smiled thinly. "No, nothing as dramatic as that. Merely that there were those who dreamed of being fishermen or firemen or actors ... jobs that depend, to some degree, on a community for support. Fishermen need a community to sell their wares and actors need an audience to perform before, after all. Tucked inside your dream was the inference of control and power, so you were given a community to rule. How you rule them is, of course, up to you to decide, just as it is up to them to decide how they shall act under your rule."

They walked in silence for a few moments, moving out of the front drawbridge and into the warm afternoon air. Sheila's castle was located on a hill – to this side, a short rolling field of green and a deep forest beyond. On the opposite side, the castle sat on a cliff, overlooking the Atlantic Ocean. "Tell me something, Juramel," Sheila implored. "What did you do with those whose dreams were ... less than honorable, shall we say?"

Juramel frowned. "We were duty bound to make those dreams a reality. Most of them, at least. There were some who dreamed dreams so horrible we could not let them loose on the public. But others ..." the angel stopped and looked hard at the forty year old woman. "Your dreams were not pleasant, Sheila Watson. You dreamt of revenge and power and bringing pain to those who caused you pain. You dreamt of being wicked. We have provided you with the means to achieve this, but whether you seek to make those horrible dreams real ..." The angel shrugged, letting his thought go unfinished. "There are those who dreamt of being superheroes. We shall give them the opportunity, but what they do with it is up to them. Just as it will be up to you to determine if revenge is truly what you want."

Sheila shook her head and leveled her gaze at Juramel. "I don't believe it. What if revenge is truly in my heart? What if I want to bring pain to the people of Kent Harbor? The angels will fly in and stop me."

Juramel shook his head, his gaze dropping to the wet grass beneath his feet. "We will not. We are forbidden from interfering in the world of man unless God instructs us to interfere. Think back," he said softly, "to all the horrors you know have been brought onto this world. Think of the genocides inflicted upon the Jews and American Indians. Think of the Crusades. Think of the millions of children abused." Juramel sighed sadly, "No, Duchess of Kent Harbor, we will not interfere." The angel brought his silver eyes to bear on Sheila. "I should tell you that among the people of Kent Harbor are many of those who tormented you as a child. Not all, of course, for some had dreams that brought them elsewhere. But there are some."

Sheila felt the hand of anger close in tightly around her heart. "You lie."

Juramel shook his head. "I do not. Think of it either as test or opportunity, Duchess, if it allows you a better night's sleep. But they are there, in that town below us. Revenge is only a stone's throw away."

Austin was shuffled forward amidst a crowd of pirates towards the docks of Port Gloucester. Five hundred pirates, he'd heard someone say. Looked about right, he thought. Mollug sat on his shoulder. Almost every pirate around him had a parrot on his shoulder.

"Squawk," Mollug said.

"That's getting old," Austin snapped. "Wise-cracking sidekicks are overplayed."

"Sorry," Mollug replied in its characteristic parrot-speak. "It's just … well, try and put yourself in my shoes. Those damn angels have given me this big vocabulary to assist you in the Reorganization. But once you find your way, they take it all back. What should I do? You don't really want to discuss philosophy, do you? You'll be too busy worrying about that ruggedly handsome ranger stealing away your girlfriend to want to discuss Platonism's views on morality. So I figure, my only real shot is to play the comedic role. Maybe you and the angels will find enough in that to want to keep me around. No one wants to keep around a philosopher parrot."

Austin looked at Mollug with a very confused look on his face.

"What?" the parrot asked defensively. "You'd rather I squawk?"

"Um … can I have a moment to think about that?"

"I knew it," the parrot said, shaking his head.

Austin softened. "Hey, look, I'm sorry. It's just … I'm sorry. Okay? Let's just make the most of this – I promise we can talk about philosophy when we get a chance, okay?"

Mollug turned its head back. "Really?"

"Really."

"You're not just saying that?"

"I'm not." Pause. "On one condition."

"Name it."

"Don't call Kornell 'ruggedly handsome,' okay?"

"That bothers you that much?"

"Yeah."

Mollug blinked a couple times. "Why?"

"He reminds me of Kelly's ex-boyfriend. Except … well, taller and nicer."

"And more ruggedly handsome?"

"You're pushing it," Austin said dryly. "The one thing about Mr. Flipping Most Eligible Bachelor Brad Regent that drove Kelly nuts was that he was, without question, a major league jerk."

"Sorry."

Austin let it go at that, turning his attention to the scene around them. Still looked like the same amount of pirates, but they had come to stand on the docks themselves now. Before them, three large wooden ships were moored to the docks. At the top of each ship, the Jolly Roger flapped lazily in the breeze. The would-be pirates around Austin chatted each other up, but Austin was glad none had tried to engage him in conversation. He could hear excitement and fear and confusion in their voices and he wasn't sure to which camp he belonged.

"Austin!" a voice called to him from somewhere in the crowd. "Austin McNamara!"

Austin turned around, seeking out the speaker, but in the crowd of pirates he couldn't discern who it was that was yelling at him. "Over here!" That doesn't help, Austin thought, turning around and around until he spotted an older man waving his arms as he politely made his way through the crowd.

"Father Otten!" Austin said, reaching out to shake the man's hand. "What are you doing here?" The priest took several deep breaths as he clasped his hand on Austin's shoulder. Some of the pirates around them cast sideways glances at them, but Austin ignored them.

"So … glad I caught you," Father Otten said, straightening himself. "I thought I saw you pass by the rectory." The priest looked Austin up and down. "When you were a child you told me you wanted to grow up to become a doctor."

Austin shrugged, smiling. "Didn't think the Catholic Church would think too kindly about piracy."

"We don't," Otten replied, letting a small smile play out across his face. "But that is neither here nor there. Something is wrong."

Austin laughed. "Of course something is wrong. The whole world's been turned upside down. Wait – you're still a priest? That's what you wanted to be when you were a kid?"

"Yes," the priest replied. "It is all I have ever wanted to be. But that is not important. Listen to me, Austin. Something is wrong. I can feel it. This does not feel like the actions of God."

Austin turned away from the priest. "I don't know, Father. Who else has this kind of power? And look, up there, at the angels. What are they, if they are not angels?"

Otten narrowed his gaze, his brow furrowing above his eyes. "I believe them to be angels."

"So ... they're angels, but they're not acting in accordance with God's will?"

"Yes," Otten nodded, not taking his eyes off the flying angels. "No ... I'm not sure." The priest turned back to Austin. "I feel a great unease in my heart. Just, please, whatever happens, keep an open mind. You were always a most skeptical student. Right now ... that skepticism might come in handy. Promise to visit me when you return to this port. We will talk ... compare notes."

Austin nodded. "Father, I-"

"Pirates, welcome!"

All eyes turned towards the docks as an angel descended onto the bow of the middle ship. Like all angels, he wore sandals and briefs as the only covering for his alabaster skin.

"My name is Berathon!" The angel's voice boomed out over the docks as he folded his wings behind him; unlike the almost airy voice of Raphael, Berathon's voice was a powerful low rumble. "Before you are three pirate ships to which you will be assigned: *Puritan, Plymouth Rock,* and the *Cottonmather.* I have your assignment upon these parchments!" he cried, holding up three rolls. "Before this, however, the angel Gabriel will speak to you. Look to the sky!"

All eyes did as Berathon ordered, and they saw Gabriel's face shimmer into view.

"Good afternoon, residents of New England," Gabriel said politely. "My name is Gabriel, and I am in charge of the Reorganization of Humanity. I am speaking to you today from the White House. I want to let you know something about how this new world works. As you can imagine, more than one person dreamt of being the President of the United States. There were several thousand, in fact, but of these, only 172 remain. The others were willing to take other positions. So, you see, there will be an opportunity to move around. It will just take a little time to get to all of you. The 172 Presidents of the United States are in charge of your country, though there are many smaller, regional rulers. Throughout New England there are many dukes and duchesses, lords and ladies. The easiest way to remember them is thusly: a Duke or Duchess is a regional ruler, while a Lord or Lady is merely someone whom has acquired wealth or property. There is one main ruler for New England. Believe it or not, there was one human who dreamt of being King of New England. I know. Who dreams likes this? And yet, someone had this dream and we are duty bound to honor it. For those in this region who dreamt of being in the Navy or Army, of being policemen or firemen, you will serve this new King. Princes and Princesses of the region will be members of his Royal Court, though you will be given regional castles in which to live. Dukes and Duchesses will take some of the Princes and Princesses into their castles. The King's Castle is located in Boston, of course. We wish you all success in this new endeavor. And now, I present to you the King of New England, His Highness Bradford Regent!"

Austin felt his stomach drop through the docks.

"Oh, hell," he mumbled. Kelly's ex-boyfriend was his King.

"Why are you upset?" Mollug asked. "You should be thrilled that guy is the King of New England."

"Why?" Austin asked. "That guy's a jerk."

"Exactly," Mollug replied. "And since you're a pirate, your duty is going to be to rob the King blind."

Austin blinked several times and felt his world brighten. "Good point, Mollug." He ignored the stern stare of Father Otten. "Suddenly, I feel very good about the horrible things I'm about to do. Read the ship assignments!" Austin called out to Berathon. "We've got some pirating to do!"

"Hurrah!" the pirates cheered around him, and the angel Berathon unrolled the first parchment. "First ship, the *Puritan*! Listen well to the calling of names, pirates! Let us start this new adventure off on the right foot!"

Austin and the pirates cheered their approval as Father Otten slowly retreated through the crowd.

He would not sleep well tonight, or any night, for a very long time.

Chapter Three
The First Night Feast

The New World was taking form.

This was evident to Potato Johnson as he looked out across the horizon from a room at the top of his Ivory Tower. His stronghold was in the middle of a thick forest, in the shadow of the White Mountains in north central New Hampshire. It was the Tower – and behind and below him were the riches – given to him by aliens during the previous night, fulfilling his childhood dream to be the richest man in the world. Everyone, the aliens said, were having their childhood dreams filled.

By the look of the forests around him, it seemed to Potato not everyone wanted that dream brought to life.

The sun was setting on this, the first day of the New World, and the forests were occupied by those who rejected the new way of things. Potato had started to notice them hours earlier as a family of five exited the woods into the circular clearing around the Ivory Tower. Potato had watched and listened, as the mother and father (dressed as an astronaut and cop, respectively) hurried the three young children along on their path to the White Mountains. "We must get to the Mountains," the father had said over and over, sometimes pleading, sometimes full of anger – like when one of his sons had asked what the Ivory Tower was.

"Never mind that Tower!" the father spat, looking upon the gleaming tower as if it were the cause of all the changes in the world.

Potato watched the family move across his vibrant green lawn and back into the woods, and then he turned his eyes outward, scanning the forest in all directions around him, watching and listening. More walked through these woods – *his woods* – with every passing hour to the total of forty-three people in all. He watched as fires were birthed, then quickly extinguished.

"The angels will see you!" he had heard one voice ring down into his valley.

"Fools," Potato thought. "We do not have these gifts from angels, but from a vast and powerful alien race." Let those who were dumb enough to do so believe in a supposed all-powerful entity who had created the universe; Potato could see that these "angels" were aliens as clear as day.

The thirty-year-old man, for the first time in his life, thanked his parents for something: the rejection of religion. He'd grown up as the son of two eternal hippies—hence the name Potato; if he had a dollar for every time someone asked him what his real name was, and he had to reply that Potato was his real name, he wouldn't have needed the aliens to give him all of this gold to be the richest man in the world. His father had become a successful businessman completely by accident. Rejecting not only God but capitalism, it was Potato, while a home-school-taught teenager (his parents didn't believe in schools, either) that had convinced his dad that when he was driving around selling his home-grown vegetables, they would be "helping" people out by delivering their goods for them, too. A small fee, to cover gas only, of course, wasn't too much to ask, and the people were more than willing to pay. It had grown from there. His father had never been all that thrilled with it, but Potato had taken over as much of the business as early as he could. Business school really wasn't an option for him, which was fine – he was getting all the experience he needed directly at "Peace, Love, and Shipping."

Potato had changed that to PLS Delivery at the first chance.

He might not know much about corporate financing or IPOs, but Potato knew people. People who were interested in shipping items locally didn't give a damn about Peace and Love; they wanted Quick and Cheap.

And that gathering enclave of "mountain folk" had his mind racing. Surely there was some way he could use them to his advantage. The question Potato needed an answer to wasn't how to get them to do what he wanted, but what he wanted to use them to accomplish.

Austin McNamara stretched his sore back, trying to block out the pain in his hands. He'd been a pirate, an official pirate, for about five hours.

It sucked.

Completely, wholly, unarguably, sucked.

After parting with Father Otten this morning, Austin's name had been called to the roll of the pirate ship *Puritan*, a large, beautiful ship docked between the *Cottonmather* on the left, and the *Plymouth Rock* on the right. The large crowd pleasantly jostled and maneuvered through itself to get to the three ships, and Austin had hit the deck of the *Puritan* feeling better than he had in a long time. He wasn't quite able to push aside the image of his girlfriend riding away on the back of a horse, her arms wrapped around a "ruggedly handsome" ranger's waist, but he was able, at least, to calm his rampaging fears about it. Even Mollug, his downtrodden philosopher-parrot, seemed in a good mood.

It felt, Austin thought pleasantly, the sea breeze now warm and inviting, like the perfect start to a perfectly good adventure.

The other pirates seemingly felt this too, and each new addition to the deck of their ship was greeted with a loud, "Ahoy!" from the assembled crew basking in the warm autumn sun.

"It's interesting," Austin had said to Mollug, "how the dream made real changes."

"How so?" the parrot asked.

"When we fantasize as kids, we do it from a kid's point of view. Things tend to be simpler, more romantic. I want to be a pirate, I had believed as a kid, but ... well, look over there. I had never dreamed of serving on a ship with a dude who clocks in at 350 pounds-plus."

Mollug did something that passed as a chuckle. "Do you even know port and starboard?"

"Sure," Austin replied, "Port is left- no, it's right." He furrowed his brow. "No, it's left, definitely left."

"Are you sure?" the talking parrot asked.

Austin frowned. "No."

"It's left," Mollug informed him. "Starboard is right. Bow is front and stern is back."

"I knew that," Austin snapped with a smile.

All that had been five hours ago, before their Captain had arrived: Captain Ezekiel Crumb, United States Navy.

"Yer not done mopping that deck!"

31

"Yes, sir!" Austin snapped to attention, as his mind was yanked back to the present. In truth, he couldn't remember much of anything Captain Crumb had said today, but he was certain that there was yelling.

A lot of yelling.

Almost all of it coming from Captain Crumb.

Austin remembered some of the content as he slapped his mop back onto the deck, but the past few hours were lost in a pain-induced haze. His hands had been rubbed raw by all the wood and rope he'd grabbed and pulled all afternoon.

"I've got my eye on you, McNamara!" Captain Crumb yelled from right behind him.

"Yes, sir!" Austin said, feeling more like he was on board one of Crumb's Navy ships rather than on a pirate ship. Crumb's old eyes were full of a raging intensity that spooked Austin. They always seemed to be looking at everything. Austin was thrilled when he heard Crumb stomp past him and up the short stairs leading to a smaller deck above him, knowing that his own back would gain at least a momentary reprieve from Crumb's stare.

"Listen well, my sea dogs!" Captain Crumb bellowed.

"Jack Palance," Mollug whispered in his ear.

"What?" Austin asked.

"Who the Captain looks like," the parrot replied. "Looks like Jack Palance, mixed with a bit of Robert Mitchum – before his face got too droopy – and that guy who got shot in *Dallas*."

"City or TV show?"

"TV. What was his name?"

"Larry Hagman," Austin replied, looking at Mollug skeptically. "You're a very strange parrot."

"Crew of the *Puritan*!" Captain Crumb boomed out over them as the pirates all shuffled forward towards Austin's position near the rear of the deck. "You are a miserable lot, but I declare this ship to be sea-worthy! Huzzah!"

"Huzzah!" the crew cheered back with something less than full enthusiasm.

"Soft!" Crumb bellowed, his rough hands tightly gripping the wooden railing before him. "Yer too soft, but that will change. Listen well to my words; you have put in a hard day's work and that is good, but I require more of you. It is not only your bodies I want sharp, but your mind, as well. I will not have an ignorant crew aboard my ship. There are 107 of you aboard the *Puritan*. You will find the number of sleeping bunks sufficient for only eighty of you.

I fully expect some of you will quit." Crumb leveled his gaze on the aforementioned 350-pound-plus man who was wheezing rapidly and loudly. "I'm talking about you! As big as a truck and as soft as a doughnut! It's lucky I won't ask any of you to pull your weight because you don't have a chance, Private Fat Ass!" Crumb leveled his steely gaze on the rest of the crew. "This ship, the *Puritan*, is a schooner. It was favored by pirates of the Atlantic. She's fast, maneuverable, and has more gun power than it appears. It's not one of them fancy Spanish galleons, but she'll do the job. If you're disappointed, well, hellfire, if you're panting and wheezing after cleaning this ship, think of how you'd feel after cleaning a ship twice as large!" Crumb leaned back, allowing a smile to creep across his face. "If we were on a brigantine, let alone a galleon, you'd be working all night and miss the party!"

Crumb let his words sink in, watching his crew exchange confused glances. "That's right, sea maggots, the angels on high are throwing a party tonight, something they're calling the First Night Feast. Supposed to breed joy or some other new age crap." He paused, let a wide smile spread across his face. "All I know is there's going to be all the free beer I can drink! Who's with me?"

"Huzzah!"

"I can't hear you!"

"Huzzah!" they exploded.

"Head for town, boys! Do the *Puritan* proud!"

"Milady, I give you Providence." Frederic Kornell swung down off his horse with a flourish and motioned with his hand to a large castle in the middle of a modern city.

Kelly Reed shook her head. This was the most ridiculous thing she'd ever seen. Milling around the city of Providence, Rhode Island were what looked to be several hundred refugees from Walt Disney cartoons of the 1950s. Men and women in (to Kelly) ridiculously overdone costumes – pastel silks, white lace, golden tiaras, glimmering jewelry – moved through the city streets of this old city.

"Beautiful, is it not?"

Kelly and Frederic looked up to see an angel floating down to meet them. "The angel Raphael," Frederic greeted. Raphael was the angel in charge of Princes and Princesses. "It is our pleasure."

Raphael smiled warmly, his feet touching down on the concrete sidewalk gently. "Princess Kelly and Ranger Kornell, so nice to see you. Welcome to Providence." Raphael bowed slightly, motioning to the glistening white castle behind him. "The Castle Providence." He leaned in close, dropping his voice to a whisper. "The angels built this overnight. Had to tear down a block of office buildings, but no one was scheduled to work there anymore. It all-"

"You've made Brad Regent King of New England," Kelly said, sticking a finger in Raphael's chest.

"Why, yes," the angel replied, taken aback at the hostility, "we have."

"Why?"

"Well, my dear, that was his dream."

"Interesting," Kelly said, leveling her gaze, "that the angels would willingly give power to someone who dreamt of power. What part of the Bible talks about coveting power as a good thing, again?"

Raphael scratched his hairless chin. "Power is neither good nor bad, milady. Power is. It is what one makes of it that causes it to be good or bad. Power may be what allows a Hitler to bring evil to the world, but it is also what allows Roosevelt to bring that evil to an end. There have always been people in power. What we have done is simply to rearrange who has that power."

Kelly shook her head. "Not buying it. Coveting power, especially at such a young age as you angels have used as the 'dreaming point,' can't be a good thing."

Raphael looked to Kornell, then back to Kelly, a smile upon his silvery face. "Ah, but there's the rub. The dreams of a ten year old have been filtered by the experiences since. Take yourself, Ms. Reed. You dreamt of power, for what is a princess if not a woman of power? You may not have dreamt of ruling the world, or commanding an army, but a princess is a woman of privilege, and that means you wield power, whether overtly or discreetly. You have the benefit of wealth."

"That's different," Kelly replied, hating the fact that her argument was wavering.

"Is it?" Raphael asked, smiling pleasantly. "Why? Because you would never horde that power over anyone? Because you would only use your power for good? How do you know until you have wielded power what you would do with it? Do you know that when Woodrow Wilson was elected President of your United States he entered office preaching that domestic concerns were more important than international concerns? Yet by the end of his two terms he was a staunch internationalist. Power changes you, just as love or hate changes who you are. You are concerned that King Regent will be bad for New England because …?"

34

"He's a jerk," Kelly said flatly.

Raphael titled his head to the side, "Ah. I see. You have a personal problem with him. That's not exactly an objective stance, is it, Ms. Reed?"

Kelly turned to Kornell. "He's a jerk. Full of himself like you can't believe. Greedy. Arrogant. Thinks he's God's gift to women."

Kornell raised his hands slowly, indicating he wanted no part of this discussion.

"He also donated $100,000 of his own money to various local charities," Raphael revealed. "Perhaps his singular, personal relations with you are not truly exemplary of the whole of the man?" Raphael opened his wings wide, preparing to leave. "I can assure you, Ms. Reed, that those humans who truly desired to do great harm and bring great evil into the world have been removed."

"To where?" Kornell asked.

Raphael flapped his large wings gently, his body rising slowly off the ground. "To a place to which no human can journey," he informed, flapping a second time. "Now, I beseech you, Ms. Reed, give the New World a chance. In one hour the First Night Feast shall begin, but in thirty minutes you, and all the Princesses, have a meeting to attend inside the Throne Room of the Castle Providence. Please do not be late."

Kelly and Kornell watched Raphael ascend into the darkening sky, a frown upon her face to match the smile upon his.

"I don't like this," she said as Raphael arced to their right, heading into the highest tower in the Castle Providence.

"Methinks the lady worries too much," Frederic chuckled, turning to her. "My mother once told me that if God had intended for everything to go our way, He would have put each of us in charge. That's not how life works." The ranger placed a gentle hand on her shoulder. "Haven't you ever wanted to help people, Kelly? Well, now you have that chance. You're a Princess. Raphael was right. Being a Princess brings with it access to wealth and power. What was it you did, again, in the Old World?"

Kelly sighed. "I was a naturalist-photographer. Sometimes painter."

"So you were an environmentalist? You cared about the animals of the forest?"

"Yeah."

"Think of what you can do for them now," Kornell implored, letting his hand lightly rub across the back of her Princess-gown.

"You'll be able to protect them like never before." He looked down at her and smiled, "And there's no reason you still can't photograph them, or spend more time painting them."

Kelly frowned, "Yeah, I guess. I mean, I think you're right."

"Even if I'm wrong," Kornell chuckled, pulling his hand away and motioning to the white-stoned castle that towered above them, "there's time to change. The angels have promised us that. All, it seems, they're asking in return is to give this New World a chance."

Kelly shot him a harsh look. "Okay, okay. I get it." She noted that Kornell's expression looked like she had slapped him, so she made a point to soften her stance. "You're right, Frederic. There's no reason not to give this New World a few days."

Kornell smiled, "Good. I'll see you tonight, at the First Night Feast."

"Where are you going?" she asked as he moved to his horse.

"I've got to take Alfred here to the stables," he replied, patting the horse.

"Alfred?" Kelly asked. "You named your horse Alfred?"

Kornell smiled back at her, taking the horse's reigns in his hand. "Batman's butler. I watched that show constantly as a kid. Adam West was my kind of superhero."

Kelly slapped her forehead playfully, thinking of Austin's parrot, Mollug. "You boys and your stories. Just promise me one thing, if you and Austin ever run into each other again, don't mention that you named your horse after that TV show, okay?"

"Why?" Kornell grinned.

"He hates that show," Kelly stated emphatically. "Hates it."

"He likes his Batman grim-and-gritty, is that it?"

"Seriously, Frederic," she implored. "Save yourself the half-hour rant. I made the mistake of buying him the George Clooney movie on DVD for Christmas a few years back. It wasn't pretty."

Frederic laughed, "Understood, milady." He bowed low to her, putting on a show. "Your command is my will. I shall remember your words, and heed their warning. Until tonight, then," he said, rising to his full height.

"Until tonight," she smiled in return, and then turned to look at the Castle Providence. She sighed, but kept the smile upon her face. "Austin always said, no party with free booze can be that bad of a party." She hiked up her dress and started up the stone steps. "Let's hope the angels were smart enough to stock the bar with plenty of vodka."

"Did he pass out already?" Austin asked, nodding to the 350-pound plus man in the corner. Austin deposited four mugs of beer onto a wooden table and dropped in beside Theodore Levenson's lifeless body. The two men who shared the table with them smiled, reaching for their beer. Across Theodore's back, three parrots sat and watched, all them looking bored beyond their capabilities.

"Hell no," Hector Ladrone smiled. "Teddy's asleep. All that work today on the ship took its toll on the big fatty."

"Must you call him that?" Carl Yesek asked, taking a huge pull off his beer. "Blech. What is this stuff? Didn't they have any Heineken?"

Austin grinned. "Captain Crumb said Heineken's not pirate beer. Pirates drink the cheapest brew in the joint."

"Intolerable," Carl shuddered, pushing his beer away.

Austin and Hector laughed, clanking their large glass mugs together. The four newly-minted pirates sat against the far right wall inside the local pub, as members of the pirate crews of the *Puritan*, *Cottonmather*, and *Plymouth Rock* milled about, drinking and eating to their hearts content, all courtesy of the angels and the First Night Feast. The pub was an old, dirty building, and its interior was mostly untreated wood, with dull yellow lights scattered around the room on the walls.

"So what's your story, Austin?" Hector asked. "What were you before the angels came and reconstructed the world?"

"Associate Professor of Literature," Austin replied, taking a big bite out of a cheeseburger. "Woo?" he asked through the beef and bread.

"Auto mechanic," Hector replied with a deep satisfaction. "Two years out of high school and I'm making $50,000 a year."

"You mean, you *were* making fifty grand a year," Austin replied. "All that money won't do you any good now, will it?"

Hector frowned. "Why not? Won't the angels roll over our bank accounts?"

"No," Carl shook his head. "I asked Berathon – the alien in charge of Pirates – about that this morning. My wife and I had just come into some money – her mother had just passed away and left us the bulk of her estate – and I was wondering how I could access it. The angels told me I couldn't. Which, of course, raises the larger questions about this New World's economy. My guess is that all of the world's wealth has been seized and redistributed in order to make the New World work."

Hector shook his head, "The big questions make my head hurt. Every time I think of- wait. Did you say Berathon was an alien?"

Carl winced through another sip of his beer. "Yeah. Creepy looking, too – even for a white headed, big-black-eyed—"

Hector wasn't buying. "He's not an alien. He's an angel. I talked to him and-"

"Listen, Hector," Carl replied, turning in his seat to face the man half his age, "they're aliens. Only aliens could have the technology to pull something like this Reconstruction off."

"God doesn't need technology," Hector replied sharply. "Besides, how would the aliens know what we all wanted to be when we were ten years old?"

"How would God?" Carl asked back. "Haven't you read Genesis? For all the talk that He's omniscient, He doesn't know that Eve has bitten the apple, or Cain has slain Abel, for that matter, until well after the fact. Until he's specifically told. By humans. I don't think-"

"Guys, guys, enough!" Austin implored, reaching across the table to pat Hector on the back. "Whatever our benefactors are – angels, aliens, men in black, smurfs – they told us we would all see them differently, according to our own belief system. Seems to me that it doesn't matter who they are or how they did it, because it's already done."

Hector started to protest, then stopped. He looked at Austin and shook his head. "Of course it matters, Austin. Not just as a matter of faith, either. I'm a mechanic – figuring out how things work is how I operate. I might not thrill to the big questions, but I love unpacking all the little questions."

Carl nodded, "I agree with young Mr. Ladrone. I'm a biochemist. I want to know exactly how the aliens," he looked to Hector, "or angels," then back to Austin, "did what they did. I want to know- oof!"

A short but muscular man was knocked into Carl's back, causing Carl to drop his beer. The three parrots on Theodore's back flapped their wings as beer was splattered up onto them.

Theodore kept snoring.

"Watch it!" the squat man shouted as Carl picked his face up off the tabletop.

"Watch yourself," Hector challenged, rising to his feet.

The short man looked up at Hector as he folded his thick arms across his chest. "You got a problem?" He looked around the table at Carl, Theodore, and Austin. "Looks like we got us a table of pussies right here. What ship do you sissy boys crew on? It's either the *Plymouth Rock* or the *Puritan,* cause it sure as shit ain't the *Cottonmather.* Whatchoo gonna say to that, boy?" the man asked, reaching up to put his finger in Hector's chest.

Hector didn't back down. "I just found out that all the money I've been saving these past two years is gone," he said slowly. "Did you know that? Did you know the angels have taken everyone's money?"

"So what?" the squat man replied. "We're pirates, we'll steal some more."

"Oh, I know that," Hector shot back, smiling. "I'm just talking. Wanted to give you a chance to back down."

They were beginning to draw the attention of the pirates around them. Conversations were stalled as eyes refocused and bodies repositioned themselves.

"Why would I want to back down?" the short man asked.

"Because if you don't," Hector drawled, "me and my friends here are going to kick your teeth in. No one-" Hector looked around the room, raising his voice, "and I mean no one, pushes around any member of the *Puritan* crew unless they want the rest of that crew to come calling." He smiled down at the *Cottonmather* pirate. "So what's it going to be, shorty?"

Hector's answer was a chair to the back of his head by a second *Cottonmather* pirate.

The short man grabbed the front of Hector's shirt and pulled him down to his level, then slammed his fist upwards, breaking the young man's nose.

Austin jumped to the side as Hector's body slammed into the table, sending the glasses of beer flying. "Oh, hell," he groaned as the chair-wielding pirate smashed his fist into Austin's stomach.

Sliding down the wall, Austin watched, through blurry eyes, as the bar erupted into a brawl. "If Kelly could see me now," he mused, hitting the floor.

Kelly reached for another Cosmopolitan, and stopped. She wasn't stopping her hand precariously above the drink because she had a sudden thought that she should stop drinking. No – that thought had entered her mind three drinks back and had been violently dismissed. At the moment, Kelly's hand was being stopped because, well, while six Cosmos might be a few too many Cosmos, it was not a few too many drinks in total; there was a whole table full of alcoholic drinks for her to sample, and she intended to sample.

Looking left and right, the table seemed to stretch 100 feet in either direction. Kelly found the drinks much, much more appealing than the scene that was going on behind her – the First Night Feast. Five hundred Princes and Princesses, she had been told. Five hundred. Ninety-five percent of them looked like her – stepping straight out of *Cinderella* or *Snow White* or *Sleeping Beauty* and into the New World. There were some Jasmines and Little Mermaids, but not too many. All in all, it reminded her of every sorority mixer she'd avoided attending in college.

There was a voice in the back of her head cautioning her against picking up any new drink at all that wasn't labeled "water" but Kelly ignored it. She knew she was drinking too much, but, as Austin would say, "Everyone needs to get their drink on now and then."

Tonight was as good a night as any.

Better, in fact.

Reaching for something called "Electric Lemonade," Kelly knew that the voice of Austin in her head was a controlled one. It was the "voice of Austin" she wanted to hear right now, the one she would've heard back before they were dating, the one who was always just slightly to the left of nervous, willing to encourage or tolerate her behavior because he didn't want to risk pushing her away.

Had Austin been here, the authentic "voice of Austin" would've said something like, "Hey, enough's enough, Kell. Save some for the alcoholics."

While Kelly was dribbling Electric Lemonade down the front of her gown, Frederic Kornell stood across the great hall, just inside an arched doorway. He leaned his back against the white stone blocks of the Castle Providence and watched Kelly intently. She was everything he had ever wanted in a woman – beautiful, smart, independent-minded ... he had been wondering since the moment she wrapped her arms around him on his horse and they left her boyfriend behind, if the angels hadn't delivered her to him on purpose. Love at first sight, his father had warned, was nothing more than a sign that a man needed any woman, not that woman.

Kornell considered his father's advice appalling about just about everything. Especially women.

The ranger pushed the thought aside; he wondered what his mother and father were doing right now and hoped the angels had done something his mom had never been able to do – separate her from her husband.

Frederic was pulled out of his thoughts

"Hey handsome, care to dance?"

He looked down, expecting the voice to be directed at him, but it wasn't. Stung ever so slightly, the ranger turned his attention back to Kelly.

She was gone from the table.

A sudden, sharp panic hit him and he looked around the room wildly. She was nowhere. 'Calm yourself,' his mind blared at him in his father's voice. Taking a deep breath, Frederic scanned the room slower, looking for dresses first, and faces second. He scanned the table of drinks first, because that's where she'd spent most of her time. Starting at the far end, his eyes moved quickly down the far wall.

There she was.

Pain stabbed his chest.

She was with another guy. Some Prince Charming wannabe who had his arm around her, leading her outside. 'God,' he thought, 'she's all over him, all sloppy drunk and ...

"... and almost unconscious," he finished aloud, feeling an anger well up inside of him. The same anger he felt as a child every time his dad came home late, stinking of liquor and deceit.

Frederic's hand went to his side to find his sword, then slipped out the doorway and into the back gardens. Kelly and her kidnapper were moving straight for the large fountain that dominated the courtyard ... then they were past it and into the wooded and shrub-filled gardens beyond. The ranger swore, but moved quickly in pursuit. At the edge of the gardens, the kidnapper ended his charade, picking Kelly up into his arms and pushing quickly for the unlit areas of the gardens.

Frederic gave a quick glance over his shoulder, looking for guards or cops, but found none. It would be up to him, his heart hammered.

His first night as a ranger and he was already fated to save a damsel in distress. That it was Kelly, the object of his twelve-hour crush, made it all the sweeter. It wasn't that he intended to steal her away from Austin, but if she, of her own free will, decided to leave him for a "ruggedly handsome ranger," well, Frederic wasn't going to stop her.

As he pushed into the darkness, he wondered if, now twenty-five, he'd finally know what it was like to kiss a girl.

"No!"

Kelly's voice rang out from ahead and to the right. Frederic quickened his pace, unsheathing his sword as he searched through the row of shrubs to his right for a glimpse of Kelly and her attacker.

Slap!

Frederic paused dead in his tracks as the shrubs parted to reveal a small clearing. Kelly was surrounded by five men. They pushed her back and forth, tugging and ripping at her dress. An instant, damp sweat broke out over the ranger's flesh. The sword in his right hand suddenly felt as if it were a hundred pounds.

Five attackers.

Five.

He was only one.

Frederic shook his head. *Why? Why more than one?* Panic was beginning to creep in around the edges of his body as one of the men slapped Kelly hard across the face.

Move! his mind screamed at his feet, but his feet stayed firm.

The idea of being a hero, saving damsels in distress, was a lot less appealing now that Frederic saw the cost one had to risk. Five men. How could he beat them?

Sissy! his father's voice screamed in his mind. *My son is a god-damned sissy!*

"The hell I am," Frederic whispered. He took a couple of deep breaths, then made to step into the clearing-

Only to see a Prince emerge from the other side, yelling, "Stop that!"

Kelly's five attackers turned quickly on the intruder. The man who had abducted her grabbed her by the arms and held her in place as the other four attacked the intruder, viciously beating him down.

Frederic's momentary surge of courage left him. The visage the angels had created for him was revealed as nothing more than a mask. Inside, Frederic was still the chubby kid whose mom did everything for him, who fought all his battles for him, who never pushed him to do anything. Frederic Kornell suddenly wanted the world back the way it was. Wanted to be back pushing a broom at the high school where he was a janitor, wanting to be as far away from here as possible.

He wanted to be back dreaming the fantasy instead of being forced to live it.

The intruder, the man who'd been brave enough to step in and try to save Kelly was being pounded into unconsciousness. Blood covered him, the ground, and the men who were administering the beating.

And still, Frederic couldn't move to help.

Fear choked him, dropped roots from his feet deep into the soil. He could neither move forward nor back. All his posturing to Kelly was just that – an act, cultivated during his late nights alone, dreaming of bedding this pop princess or that actress after beating up a druggie rock star or lecherous politician.

Courage, he was discovering at the worst of all moments, was not something one could thrust upon oneself. It was not something to be bestowed. It didn't come with the costume or the new body or the Dream Fulfillment Package. The angels could change the world, could change the surface and function of humanity, but it was still up to people to make the choices, to take the actions, to determine who they really were.

Frederic was a coward. A lamb dressed as a bird of prey.

And Kelly Reed was going to pay the price for it.

Chapter Four
The King of New England

"How the hell can a man sleep through a bar fight?"

Hector Ladrone shook his head at Theodore Levenson as the two men emerged from a bar and into the warm autumn New England night. Ted shrugged an apology, already wheezing from the short walk through the bar and to the exit. Pirates from all three ships stationed at the Port Gloucester docks – the *Puritan, Cottonmather,* and *Plymouth Rock* – emerged from the bar, all of them showing some sign of the fight they'd just been engaged in.

Austin stood next to a telephone pole, waiting for Hector and Ted. At his feet, the fourth member of their little group, Carl Yesek, sat on the ground, his back against the pole and his head buried in his hands. His right boot was off and blood was pooling beneath his bare foot. "Hector, over here!"

Austin winced as he waved his left arm. He'd spent the first part of the brawl sitting on the floor with the wind knocked out of him. When he did get up – in order to help Carl – someone had broken a bottle of Bud across his upper left arm. Austin ran his right hand over the slight gash and found it was still bleeding, though not as profusely as it had been.

"Carl alright?" Hector asked, coming to stand near them. Ted was a good four steps behind him, waddling along.

"Winded more than anything," Austin replied. "He did step on a rather big piece of glass, though. Went right through his boot."

"Bad?" Hector asked.

"Ever see *Die Hard*?" Austin asked back.

"Ouch," Hector winced. The twenty-year old former auto mechanic reached down and slapped Carl on the back. "You fight pretty good for a skinny scientist, Carl."

Carl took his head out of his hands and looked up. His face was sweaty and pale, "I didn't have much of a choice, did I?"

Hector laughed, "Guess not. Christ, Teddy," he said, spinning on the overweight man, "can you wheeze on someone else for a bit?"

"Sorry, Hec," Ted wheezed.

"Oh hell," Austin said, "look who's coming."

The four men turned to see the short, stocky man who'd started the fight with them in the bar walking towards them with a group of six pirates behind him. "Look who it is," the stocky pirate taunted, "Paco and the Nerds. I seem to remember you promising you were going to kick my teeth in, chump."

Hector replied, "If one of your *Cottonmather* buddies hadn't punked me from behind, I would've."

"Why don't you try it now?" the stocky man laughed.

Hector made a point to look down menacingly on the smaller man. "Tell your girlfriends to leave, and I will."

Before a response could be given, a hard gust of wind bore down on them, followed by a commanding voice. "That will be all, gentlemen." The crowd looked up to see the angel Berathon staring down on them. The angel, dressed in a silver tunic, hovered above them, his arms crossed and his wings beating slowly. "As the angel in charge of Pirates in this New World, I command you back to your ships. There has been enough violence for this night." Berathon turned his eyes directly on the stocky pirate, "That is an order, Samuel."

The stocky pirate grumbled, but led his crew away, leaving the angel with Austin's crew. When Samuel's group had rounded the nearest corner, Berathon dropped to the ground.

"Thanks for the assist, Berathon," Austin said, letting out a deep breath of relief. "We didn't want-"

"Silence, human," Berathon snapped, turning hard on Austin. It was unnerving to hear such harsh words coming from such a light voice. "Any night other than this I would have gladly let him rip out your throat. Look at the four of you," he scoffed. "A mechanic, a professor, a biochemist and," he turned to Ted, "an internet gambler. You are pirates now, gentlemen. I suggest you start acting the part, or else you shall soon hear the horns calling you to the Gates."

Kelly Reed felt the strong hands that bound her let her go – two seconds before her face smashed into the grass. She was vaguely aware of a struggle going on somewhere around her, and vaguely reminiscent of …

She vomited into the grass before her face, and all her thoughts went with it.

In the bushes, not more than twenty feet away, Frederic Kornell watched. He had been unable to do anything but watch through the whole sordid affair. Well, he tried to tell himself, he had followed Kelly out here, and he had intended to stop the man who'd abducted her, but that was before he reached this spot and saw that there wasn't just one abductor, but four more associates.

The angels had turned Frederic into a "ruggedly handsome ranger," but the truth was that before the angels had remade him into his childhood dream he was a thirty-one-year-old overweight janitor at a local high school. He'd spent nearly every night since he was twelve dreaming of "this girl" or "that woman," but he'd never actually kissed a real one. So while Kelly, Austin, and everyone he'd met today seemed embarrassed about being transformed into their childhood dream, Frederic stood alone. He loved the New World. He'd been dreaming the same heroic dreams since he was a kid. If anything, it actually felt natural to now be the person he'd always imagined himself to be in his fantasies. "All I need," he had thought a hundred thousand times in his life, "is the chance to be who I want to be."

This was his chance.

He was acutely aware that he was blowing it.

Frederic was discovering that there was a big difference between being a hero in a dream where one never gets hurt and being one in reality where physical harm seemed a certainty. The scene before him revealed four things of note:

1: Kelly Reed, his fantasy-at-first-glance-girl, laying face down in a puddle of her own vomit,

2: Kelly's would-be rescuer lying unconscious on the ground,

3: Kelly's abductor and his four accomplices standing over the would-be rescuer, alternately kicking and spitting on the unconscious man, and

4: A new rescuer emerging through an opening in the shrub wall, charging hard. Dressed in what looked to be a very expensive business suit.

The latest man brave enough to do what Frederic was too cowardly to attempt rushed in hard, knocking the closest attacker in the back hard, sending the man hurtling into another attacker and knocking both of them to the ground.

Frederic watched as the hero kicked the man on his left and, all in one motion, spun and slammed his fist into the stomach of the man on his right.

"How dare you abduct that woman!" the hero yelled at the original abductor, before rushing him and decking him square in the face. Two of the other attackers were on their feet and jumped the hero from behind, but the hero – in a move Frederic had accomplished in his dreams (and only in his dreams) a thousand times – grabbed both of their heads and slammed their faces together, knocking them both to the ground.

"Whoah," Frederic thought. In the back of his mind, he noted how his emotions had run from total fear to abject awe within a minute – and both conditions caused him to be rooted to the ground, unable to do anything but watch.

"Stand back, or I'll kill the bitch!"

The original abductor had fallen to his knees behind Kelly, using her as a shield between himself and the hero. One of his hands tugged hard on her hair while the other had wrapped itself around her throat. Kelly was choking, vomit running down her face, and her eyes were all over the place. Frederic wondered if she even knew what was going on.

One of Kelly's attackers rushed the hero from the side, but the hero stepped casually back, tripping the attacker over his foot. "Let her go!" the hero yelled to the abductor. "If you harm her I swear I'll hunt you down and kill you like the dog you are!"

Frederic thought, "Damn. Good line."

Four of the attackers were lying on the ground, unconscious or rolling in agony. This mysterious hero in an Armani suit, whoever he was, had single-handedly come in and defeated all four of them with ease. Frederic wanted desperately to be jealous, but he was too impressed for jealousy to stand a chance. This guy was saving Kelly. All that was left was the original abductor, who was now dragging Kelly to her feet and backing away from the hero …

Backing up towards the hidden spot where Frederic stood.

Swallowing, Frederic felt his adrenaline surge, and the sword that had felt like five hundred pounds of immovable steel now seemed to shed its weight with every pounding beat of Frederic's heart. The earth allowed his feet their freedom and Frederic found himself taking a step towards the abductor, then another, and another.

"I'm getting out of here, and I'm taking this bitch with me!" the abductor screamed.

"The hell you are!" the hero yelled and lunged forward, running towards them.

"Ah!" the abductor yelled, dropping Kelly to the ground. The man spun on his heels and ran away from the approaching hero as fast as he could.

He made it three steps.

A look of total surprise washed across his face and he looked down to find himself impaled on the end of Frederic's sword. "What ... who ... ?" he asked, then fell backwards, sliding off the sword and hitting the ground.

Frederic was too stunned to move anything but his eyes. He looked down to the blood that dripped off the end of his sword, down to the ground to see the bleeding abductor grabbing his stomach, then slowly across the ground to see Kelly, looking up at him with a stunned recognition, and finally up to the hero who looked, Frederic thought, somewhere between happy, surprised, angry, worried, and stunned.

"Are you harmed, Princess?" the hero asked, coming upon Kelly. He knelt down and gently took her into his arms. "Did these men cause you- *Kelly*?"

"Thass me," Kelly slurred, her eyes fluttering and vomit spitting out of her mouth. "Do I know you?" she asked, her eyes trying to focus on the hero.

"I would be wounded if you did not," the hero smiled lovingly.

Kelly seemed to gather all that remained of her will and focused her eyes on the man that held her in his arms. When they had centered and focused, recognition rippled across her face. "Brad?" she asked through the fog of alcohol. "Brad Reeeeeegent?"

"The one and only," Brad smiled.

"Aussstin would be sooooo pisssssssed if he could seee thisss," she slurred. Her eyes seemed to float for a few moments until she spied Frederic standing there with his bloody sword. "Fred'ric! You sssssaved meeee!" She reached up to touch Brad's face, "Fred'ric saved me. He's a ... a rangerrrrr," she finished, then fell unconscious.

Brad sighed. "Never could hold your liquor." He laid Kelly gently on the ground, and then rose to his feet, his gaze boring into

Frederic's. "Thank you for your assistance, good ranger," Brad said stiffly, moving across the grass to shake Frederic's hand.

"Nothing to it," Frederic lied, feeling a ripple of shame wash through him. "Are you …?"

"Yes," Brad replied, nodding. "I am the King of New England, and your deeds here shall not go unrewarded."

Frederic said nothing, his mind more concerned with hoping the man he'd accidentally stabbed would somehow make it out of this alive. Death suddenly seemed all too real and Frederic wanted no part in it.

"Asshole," Ted wheezed as Berathon took to the midnight sky, leaving Austin's group among the few remaining stragglers.

Hector looked down at Carl. "Are you telling me, Mr. Agnostic, that what we just saw was not an angel?"

Carl looked up, his foot aching. "Of course not. That was an alien."

"You didn't see the wings?"

"What wings?" Carl asked, pulling on his boot.

Hector shook his head, turning to Austin. "What did you see? Alien or angel?"

Austin held up his hands, "Hey, don't involve me in this. They said we'd see them as whatever we believed in. I know you two have some need to know why and how this is all happening, but I don't."

"Bah!" Hector spat, turning away from them. Teddy and Austin reached down to pull Carl to his feet and the four of them started walking back towards the docks where the *Puritan* awaited them.

Austin shook his head. "I'm just more concerned with what Berathon said is all, Hector. We're *pirates* now," he emphasized, jerking his thumb back towards the bar. "Pirates. What just happened in there is the way things are going to be from now on. Are you ready for that?" With a devilish smile upon his face, Austin looked around at Hector, Carl, and Ted. "Are any of us? Heck, a bar brawl is a nice story to put in a memoir some day, but that's no longer the exception for us. That's the way it's going to be."

"Not really," Teddy replied. "We'll be on ships most of the time, won't we?"

"I wasn't being literal," Austin explained in a tone he usually used with his Freshman Comp classes. "I was talking about the fundamental shift in lifestyles we're going to have to come to grips with. Heck, Carl here was complaining because we couldn't drink Heineken. You think Captain Crumb is going to stock the galleys with imported beer?"

"Why not?" Carl asked, limping along beside them. The streets of Port Gloucester were nearly deserted, and the closer they walked toward the docks, the more they noticed that a fog was rolling in. "We're pirates, right? Let's steal some in every port we're in."

Austin gave the older man a weak smile, "That'll work for the next few months, but what happens when all the imports run out? How many people out there do you think were dreaming of being brewmasters when they were ten?"

Hector shook his head. "So, what? We should give up?"

"No," Austin replied, looking at the fog around them. "Not at all. Just that we've got to take Berathon's advice." He stopped as they rounded a corner and looked at Teddy. "Take his advice literally, at that. We've got to start acting like pirates."

Teddy wasn't convinced. "Eh, I don't think I'm quite ready to rape and pillage, Austin. Don't think I ever will be."

Hector added, "Let's hope none of us are ever ready for that." He looked to Austin, "Come on, man, let's get back to the *Puritan*. I'm tired and sore." The young man looked around at the others, "And I ain't old and broken down like you guys, neither. You three must really be hurting."

Carl nodded. "I agree. Let's get back. My foot is killing me and we've likely got another long day swabbing the decks for Captain Crumb to look forward to tomorrow. Weatherman said it's supposed to hit 90 along the coast. No breeze." Carl winced as he applied pressure on his injured foot. "And since it's the last weather report we're likely to get for a while, I say we pay it proper respect and-"

"Hang on," Austin said quickly, an idea coming to him. "I grew up in this town, you know." He pointed to a building down the street. "My first job as a kid was in that store down there. Flynn's Hardware. Come on. I've got an idea."

Without waiting for a response, Austin jogged across the street on a diagonal path towards Flynn's.

"He would have to jog," Teddy whined. "Doesn't he know he's got a fat man and a scientist with a busted wheel to think about?"

Hector smiled, "Survival of the fittest, Teddy," and ran after Austin.

Ted and Carl looked at each other. Carl asked, "You're an Internet gambler?"

"Yep," Teddy said, trudging across the street.

"Any good?" Carl asked.

"Doesn't really matter now, does it?" Ted asked. "Can't imagine there's even going to be an Internet to gamble on. Too bad, too."

"Why's that?" Carl asked, shuffling alongside the man nearly three times his weight.

Teddy couldn't hid his disappointment, "You know how many kids in this country grew up dreaming about being a pro athlete? Two days ago there was, on average, thirty professional teams in all four major sports: baseball, football, basketball, and hockey." The gambler stopped in his tracks. "Today? I'd be shocked if that number didn't increase tenfold. Damn, I wonder if there's an angel in charge of gambling," Teddy thought wistfully as he started moving again.

Carl added, without turning, "You mean an alien in charge of gambling."

"Carl," Teddy said pleasantly, catching up, "don't be a fucking prick."

"Sorry," Carl said apologetically as they came upon Hector and Austin.

They stood in front of a glass window. A hand-painted sign on the glass read:

Flynn's Hardware
A New England Tradition Since 1842

"Seems a shame," Hector said. "Place has been in business for a hundred and sixty years and now it's gone."

"Don't shed any tears for this place," Austin said harshly. "The Flynns have always been more interested in their own well-being than anyone else's." Austin reached to his belt and removed his pistol. "Jerk." He brought his arm up suddenly and blasted the window, putting several small holes in the glass. The other three looked shocked, nervously looking around as the store's alarm rang out.

"What are you doing?" Carl asked in a nervous, tittering voice.

Austin looked at him and smiled. "Acting my part." Noting the concerned look on their faces, he did his part to waylay their concerns. "Guys, we're pirates. I'm sure if our talking parrots were anywhere to be found, they'd tell us this was God's plan." Austin caught himself, and turned to Carl. "Or the Alien Leader's Plan."

Hector pulled out his pistol, took aim at the glass window, and fired. "That's a good point, Austin." He turned to Carl. "What do you hear when the angels-slash-aliens say, 'God'? Do you hear, 'Alien Leader'?"

Carl frowned. Slowly, he reached down, removed his own pistol and fired a third shot into the storefront. "I hear 'God'."

"Shouldn't you hear something else?" Hector asked, not bothering to hide his smile.

Carl shrugged. "Yeah. I suppose I should."

Frederic Kornell stood in a hallway on the upper floor of the Castle Providence. Around him, a small group of the King's Guards stood waiting for their king. Before him, an open door into an elegant bedroom. Through the doorway and across the room, Frederic watched as the King of New England, Brad Regent, gently placed an unconscious Kelly Reed onto a large, ornate bed. A small group of handmaidens stood nearby, watching attentively.

Frederic wondered if these women dreamt of being handmaidens or something else, like nurses, that the angels converted.

"You will spend the night with her," Regent ordered them. "If any harm shall come to her ..."

"We will watch her with all due care," the head handmaiden said, bowing slightly.

"I am certain you will, handmaiden," Regent said formally, then leaned in to whisper something Frederic could not hear.

The clanging sounds of approaching metal on stone caused Frederic to turn away as the Captain of the King's Guards approached. He caught Frederic's eye. "The bastard you gutted will survive."

Frederic nodded, relieved, though he took care not to show how relieved he was. There was no point in any of the King's men thinking him soft. The ruse made him sick, but the obvious care and concern the King showed for Kelly – combined with the ruthlessness he showed on her attackers – gave Frederic the impression that he could stow his feelings away for a better moment. His insides were tortured – while he wanted Kelly's abductor brought to justice, that justice didn't involve killing. Frederic was firmly anti-death penalty, whether it was death at the state's hands or his own.

"A shame," the King said, exiting the room and shutting the wooden doors behind him. "The bastard deserved death for abducting the Princess."

52

Frederic, his mind as emotionally exhausted as it was, wondered why Regent was being so formal. Kelly was an ex-girlfriend, an ex, according to what he'd heard from Austin and Kelly this afternoon (*Was it only this afternoon?* he wondered inside the wondering), that Regent still desired. So why the formality?

King Regent turned to Frederic, "Ranger, the kingdom owes you its thanks. Come, dine with me."

Frederic coughed nervously into his hand. "With all due respect, it's late and I—"

Regent smiled, clasping his hand on Frederic's shoulder. "Please, good sir, do not refuse a King's hospitality. It is late. I have spent the day traveling my kingdom, meeting too many lords and ladies and princes and princesses to remember. What I desire most, at this moment, is to dine with friends, but," he cocked his head toward the bedroom door, "it appears the one person in this castle I know is asleep."

"Forgive me, my king," Frederic replied, bowing slightly, calling upon all of his mother's hospitality. "It would be an honor to dine with you."

Regent smiled. "Excellent. Guards," he ordered, "show this ranger to the dining hall. Bring us bread and meat and wine." The King looked to Frederic. "I will join you in a moment, but first I must have a word with the Captain of my Guards."

"Of course, sire," Frederic replied. He turned with the other guards and moved down to the hall's end, where a curved staircase awaited them. His thoughts turned to ponder how quickly some had adopted the formalities of the positions they now filled. Take Regent, he thought. Sure, his costume is all-wrong (wearing a business suit and not a king's robes nor crown) but he moved and sounded like a king out of an old fairy tale.

As the staircase curved back, Frederic's eyes could look up and view the King talking with his Captain. The vagaries of sound in a Castle brought several words of the King's voice to Frederic's ears.

Words that gave him pause.

The words, all from the mouth of King Regent, were:

" ... arrived with Kelly on horseback ..."

" ... she thinks he saved her ..."

" ... not in my plans ..."

and

" ... public flogging ..."

Wonderful, Frederic thought, though he wasn't a hundred-percent certain what they meant. But as the day seemed to be turning for the worse, he figured it wasn't good news for him.

"Someone wanna tell me why we're robbing the hardware store?" Carl asked as he moved through the now completely smashed front window. He needed to shout; the store's alarm was wailing even louder now that the window was smashed in.

Austin moved quickly to the alarm's keypad next to the door. He punched in a five-digit code and was mildly surprised when the alarm stopped. "Wow," he said calmly. "He never changed the code. I haven't worked here in over ten years."

Carl was still looking nervously around. "Austin, why are we robbing the hardware store? I thought you said money doesn't matter anymore?"

"Untrue," Austin replied. "We can't access our bank accounts for cash, but hard currency might still have value. We're not here for money, though." Austin looked around the small store, at the rows of tools and brushes and household appliances, but it wasn't until he looked to the backroom that a wistful smile came over his face. Was it really ... ten, eleven years since he first touched Jessica Jenkins' breasts in that very back room?

"What are we here for, if not for money?" Hector asked. The shelving units in the store were short enough that they could look at each other's faces wherever they stood in the store.

Austin walked to the third of four aisles. "Paint." He turned to see who was closet to the near wall. "Teddy, grab some brushes."

"Why?" Teddy asked, though he was already moving to grab them.

"If we're not strong enough to be pirates with our bodies, we can still be pirates with our brains."

"Can't we just take the cash?" Teddy asked. "That should be pirating enough for Berathon, shouldn't it?"

Austin was busy reading the colors off the paint cans, and answered without turning. "Take the cash from the register if you want. Hell if I care."

Concerned, Hector came over to stand by Austin. "You okay with us robbing the store you used to work in?"

Austin shrugged, picking up two cans of white paint. "The guy who owns the store now is my age. Johnny Flynn. We went to high school together. Both of us worked here, but it was his dad's shop, you know? Johnny's dad, for some reason, paid me more. Not a lot, maybe twenty dollars more a week. Stuck in Johnny's craw, though, so he started lifting money from the register." Austin handed a can to Hector. "Mr. Flynn found out the register was short and Johnny blamed it on me. Went so far as to plant money in my jacket pocket. You believe that shit? I got fired. Worse, my parents made me pay back Mr. Flynn for all the money Johnny had taken. Around 500 bucks. So, no, I don't care if you guys rob the store blind." Austin smiled as he handed a second can to Hector. "I know it's morally wrong and all that," he shrugged, "but how's that saying go? Yo-ho-ho, a pirate's life for me? I'm not saying I'm ever going to be okay with raping and pillaging, of course, but a little revenge thievery? I can live with that."

"Your life, bro," Hector replied, smiling. He looked down at the two cans of paint. "Uh, Austin, you gave me a can of pink paint."

"That I did," Austin replied.

To their right, at the back of the showroom floor, Teddy raised a hammer above his head and started smashing the cash register.

Hector watched the gambler lay into the register, then turned back to Austin. "Say, where do you think our parrots have flown off to?"

Austin looked to the smashed-in window, half-expecting Mollug to be sitting there. "Good question. Probably went back to the *Puritan*."

"Yeah," Hector said unconvincingly. "That's probably it."

King Bradford Regent closed the doors of the main dining hall behind him and turned his gaze to Frederic Kornell, who stood at the far end of a very long, wooden table. On the table before Frederic were two large plates of roasted pork, boiled tomatoes, and steaming, sliced potatoes. "Excellent," the King said, removing his suit coat and loosening his tie. "I'm famished. Before we eat, however," he said, coming to stand three chairs away from Frederic and in front of one of the plates of food, "let's finish our business. I owe you a great deal of thanks for assisting me with Kelly's attackers."

Frederic couldn't hold the King's gaze. "I ... uh ... you really saved her. I just happened to show up at the last second."

"Kelly thinks you saved her," the King said pointedly.

"She's drunk," Frederic said quickly. "She won't remember anything in the morning." He stared into the King's hard eyes, feeling trapped, then added quickly, "I'll be sure to tell her who she really has to thank for her safety."

"Thank you," Regent replied dourly. "But you're probably right. She won't remember much of anything that happened tonight." He frowned down into his plate. "Come, let us eat."

Frederic gave a quick nod and sat down at the head of the table, then thought better of it. "My apologies, King, but the head of the table is yours."

Regent waved his hand aside, sitting down at the plate to Frederic's left. "No need for formalities at this hour, ranger." The King forked his pork and sawed a large chunk off with his steak knife. "Tell me, how is it that you know Kelly? The Captain of my Guards told me his people noted you had words with her earlier in the day. Is this true?"

Frederic felt like a trap was being laid for him, but saw no reason to lie. "She rode with me from Port Gloucester this morning."

Regent's hand paused just as it was to deliver the pork to his mouth. "From Port Gloucester? Do you know her well?" he asked casually, then shoveled the meat into his mouth.

"No, sir," Frederic replied, still not touching his food. "It was a coincidence we met. I was riding through town when I saw her arguing with a pirate."

Regent chewed his food slowly, then asked, "Was the pirate's name Austin McNamara?"

"It was."

Regent dropped his fork on the table with disgust. "The man is a clown."

Frederic wasn't certain about how to respond to that, so he decided it was a good time to try the boiled tomatoes.

"He stole her from me," the King said, his eyes glaring out the window, "like a thief in the night. It is not surprising to me – not at all – that he's become a pirate." Regent turned his gaze back to Frederic. "I need for you to do me a favor, ranger."

Frederic swallowed, feeling the trap about to be sprung.

"I want you to escort Kelly to Kent Harbor," he said, his eyes hawkish in intensity. "It's in Maine, though not far up the coast. She has been assigned, along with two other princesses and four princes, to take up residence there. As you may have noticed, Kelly, for all of her fiery independence, has a problem with alcohol. She does not drink often, but when she does … well, as I said earlier, she does not hold her liquor well. I am afraid that tonight's display will not leave her ideally suited for travel."

Frederic couldn't help but feel relieved. The idea that he'd get to spend a few more days with Kelly ... wonderful! "Of course, your majesty."

The King nodded. "Excellent, ranger. There are not many I can trust, but I feel, by the warrant of your deeds this eve, that you can be trusted to protect Kelly's life with your own."

"Of course," Frederic repeated, sitting up straighter in the chair, trying to push the memory of his earlier stage fright from his mind. "But ... what about the princes in her traveling party?"

"I do not know any of them," Regent replied, "and so I cannot trust them." The King reached over to his suit coat that was laid on the table, and dug his hand into an inner pocket. He withdrew a stack of hundred-dollar bills and tossed them to Frederic. "That should cover your expenses." The King rose to his feet, "Just to be clear, ranger. Should any harm come to her, your life will not be safe in my kingdom."

"I understand," Frederic replied, feeling suddenly very unsure of himself.

The King clapped his hands together and two women emerged from the side entrance, dressed like Princess Leia from her time in Jabba's Palace. Which is to say, dressed in not much at all. "Kornell, I am told these women very much wanted to meet you." Regent turned to the two women, "Is this true?"

"Yes, King," they giggled, their dazzling eyes drinking in Frederic's body.

Regent turned back, a thin smile spread across his lips. "Enjoy your stay in the Castle Providence, ranger. You have earned your rewards." The King let his thin smile become full, "Just remember that you ride at noon tomorrow. Do not be late, no matter how entertaining the women are."

Frederic watched, stunned, as the Princesses approached him. This can't be happening, he thought, over and over. It must be a trick, his mind insisted, but when, for the first time in his life, the lips of a woman touched his own, his mind's complaints no longer held any sway. The women seemed to effortlessly lift him out of the chair and before Frederic even realized he was walking, the women had led him out of the room, leaving the King alone.

"Can we trust him?" a voice asked the King.

Regent turned to see the Captain of his Guards enter the room from the servant's door. "I believe we can, yes."

"Can we trust the women?" the Captain asked gruffly.

Regent shrugged. "Trust them to do what, Captain? They know nothing of our plans, and they actually do want to sleep with the chicken-shit bastard." Regent eyed the Captain carefully, "Are you certain of your intelligence? What were those costumes the women were wearing? They seem familiar."

"Princess Leia outfits," the Captain explained. "I ran a full check of the ranger down at the police station. The angels haven't bothered to shut it all down, yet. Then again, who knows if they ever will? What's important is that it's running now. I have a full work-up of Frederic Kornell being put together by my officers, but with the preliminary information I was able to ascertain that he spent, if you can believe it, nearly three thousand dollars last year alone in Star Wars memorabilia on eBay." The Captain smiled. "My guess is that he'll be more than satisfied with any woman who crawls into his bed, let alone those two fine-looking sluts. Beyond the geek crap, he spent a surprisingly staggering amount of money on porn."

"Kelly believes he saved her," the King grimaced, his hands slamming down onto the table.

The Captain shrugged. "She's drunk. She won't remember anything in the morning. We'll just tell her you saved her and she'll believe it."

"Not her," Regent seethed. "Not with the history between us."

The Captain tried to hide his discontent. "You do realize, of course, you are the King. There are plenty of women who would-"

"Spare me!" Regent spat, flipping his plate of food over violently. "I'm not as easily satiated as that fucking ranger. Do you think I love Kelly Reed? Please, Captain. Do not mark my actions through some misguided lens of love. Her boyfriend stole her from me. Austin McNamara is the object of my ire. Kelly is merely the pawn. I want her to want me, Captain. I want her to choose me so that I may take her as a trophy before throwing her back." Regent felt his fury growing with each passing second. "Where were your men?" he asked, turning to point his finger at the Captain. "You were supposed to have the entire area secure so that I saved her myself!"

The Captain shook his head. "He was right on her heels. There was nothing we could do that wouldn't have attracted attention. I'm telling you, it was plain luck he stabbed the abductor at all. Kornell didn't do anything but stand there and watch. And shake in fear. The only thing he did tonight that impressed me was in not pissing his pants. Trust me, he was terrified." The Captain tried to calm the King. "Do no worry, sire. I have a plan."

"We wouldn't need your plan if you had followed mine!" Regent shouted.

"Nonetheless," the Captain continued, "hear me out. I assure you, Kornell won't be a challenger for Ms. Reed's affections by the time they reach Kent Harbor."

"Shh!" Austin ordered his two giggling compatriots, Carl and Hector. The three of them were in a small boat, pulling alongside the *Cottonmather*. Their ship, the *Puritan*, was docked in between the *Cottonmather* and the *Plymouth Rock*. Teddy, whom they deemed too heavy for the small craft, was playing lookout on the docks on the other side of the pirate ship.

"Are you sure about this?" Hector asked, looking nervously up towards the ship's deck.

"You got a better plan for getting back at these assholes?" Austin asked, smiling. "We're no match for Stocky Samuel and his crew in a fight of brawn, but I'm rather certain we've got him beat by a country mile with our brains."

Hector met Austin's smile with one of his own. "Sounds good to me. Hand me a bucket of paint, Carl."

Floating high above them, unseen by anyone, were the angels Berathon and Enimon. "Painting a ship?" Enimon, the angel in charge of astronauts, asked his pirating counterpart. "Disappointing, Berathon."

"Give them time," Berathon replied. "Out of all the pirates docked in the three ships below us, these four are the only ones still engaging in mayhem. There is hope for them. Let us see just what it is they paint on the hull of the *Cottonmather* before we pass an ill judgment on them." Berathon turned his eyes from Austin's mischief to his fellow angel. "But that is not why we are here, is it?"

"No," Enimon answered somberly. "Bad words float through the clouds of heaven, old friend."

"Concerning Gabriel." Berathon's words were a statement, not a question.

"One close to him doubts the veracity of God's last message to us."

Berathon's eyes opened wide. As certain as he was that this meeting had to do with Gabriel, the veracity of God's word was not the subject he anticipated discussing. "How could this be?"

Enimon shook his head. "It is too early to tell, Berathon. We must keep this completely secret, even from the others that we trust.

This rumor cannot be allowed to spread. All we have, so far, is the doubt of one who is close- eh? What's that noise?"

Before the words were out of Enimon's mouth, Berathon shot past him, diving quick and hard to their left. Enimon watched as Berathon grabbed two parrots in his hand.

"There's one more!" Berathon yelled to Enimon. "He's headed for the *Puritan*!" To reinforce the severity of what they faced, Berathon raised his hands up to show his angelic brother the two parrots. Without a word, Berathon squeezed, crushing the life out of the two birds.

Enimon nodded and materialized a mystical bow and arrow. Finding the third parrot, Enimon fired the all-white arrow across the midnight sky, where it tore viciously through the front of the parrot's neck.

Mollug fell to the deck of the *Puritan* with a sickening thud.

Chapter Five
Ex-Parrot

"Where the hell have you four sorry sons-a-bitches been?"

The sun was just coming up over the horizon as Austin McNamara, Hector Ladrone, Carl Yesek, and Teddy Levenson dragged themselves onto the deck of their pirate ship, the *Puritan*. The ships were docked starboard side running parallel with the shipping yards in what was, until yesterday, a commercial dock specializing in fishermen and whale-watching tourists. To the *Puritan*'s fore, the *Cottomather* and at its aft, the *Plymouth Rock*. The four newly-turned pirates were sore, aching, and tired, but with a feeling of accomplishment.

Not even Captain Ezekiel Crumb's growling face could spoil their mood.

"We've been pirating," Austin said, noting how the other three fell in behind him. 'Looks like I'm playing leader today,' he mused silently.

"That so?" Crumb asked, pulling himself up to his full height and slowly crossing his arms across his barrel chest. Behind him, many of the remaining crew members stretched and yawned as they emerged onto the deck from their cramped sleeping quarters. About twenty pirates of the 107 housed on the *Puritan* were sleeping at various spots around the deck, the *Puritan* with quarters enough for only eighty crewmen. "How, exactly, have you four been pirating?" he asked, the last word spit out with a smirk, sounding like, 'pie-ruttin.'

"We robbed a hardware store," Carl said, almost bemusedly, like he was still struggling over what he believed less: that they'd robbed the store, or that they'd gotten away with it.

"Oh?" Crumb asked. "Well, then, maybe we should let you four be the captain of this here ship since yer such big badasses and all."

"Blow it out your ass."

All of the air on the deck of the ship was sucked back into the lungs of the crew and an uneasy still settled down onto the deck. Austin, Hector, and Carl turned slowly behind them to see Teddy, all 350-plus pounds of him, sweating, wheezing, and pale, but standing straight and staring daggers into the Captain.

"What did you say, fat ass?" Captain Crumb asked menacingly.

"I told you," Teddy replied, "to blow it out your ass. And when you're done doing that, check out the hull of the *Cottonmather* to see our execution of Austin's plan."

Crumb took a deep breath, sucking on his teeth. "Mathers!" he shouted.

As the person everyone assumed had to be Mathers hurried down off the wheel of the ship to stand by Crumb, Austin thought for a second that a localized vacuum was about to be created right in front of them. The crew, who had yet to let out their collective deep breath from Teddy's comment, seemingly found enough lung space to bring in even more air.

Mathers, to everyone's surprise, was a woman.

A very attractive woman wearing a very tight pirate's costume.

"I'm in love," Hector whispered over Austin's right shoulder.

"Who isn't?" Carl whispered back.

"Yes, Captain?" Mathers asked, coming to stand to Crumb's left.

Crumb eyed Austin's crew carefully as he gave Mathers his order. "Lean over the side. Tell me if you can see the hull of the *Cottonmather*."

Mathers nodded and walked across the deck to the port side of the schooner ship. The small group of pirates that stood in her way parted to make way for her, their eyes staring at her with varying looks of surprise, lust, and anger. All eyes on deck but two pairs stared longingly at Mathers' backside as she leaned over the railing. The two dissenting pairs of eyes belonged to Captain Crumb and Teddy Levenson, whose eyes were reserved only for each other.

Returning to Crumb's side, Mathers announced, "I can see the hull's been painted. Looks pink, but it's hard to determine with the rising sun."

Crumb nodded. "We were going to head back into town this morning," he said, loud enough for all to hear but with no effort given to shouting. Crumb had one of those voices that just seemed to command attention, whose orders just seemed to find everyone's ear that needed to hear what he had to say. "But it seems Mr. McNamara and his crew have done some *pie-ruttin'* while they were supposed to be sleepin'. So, instead of going in and rustling up the last good breakfast you yellud-bellied cowards," he looked to Teddy, "and random tub of fat were likely to get in a good long while, we're going to set sail and check out what these here *pie-ruts* have spent their night doing."

Crumb spit tobacco on the deck. "And it better be damn good because except for Hector here, all of you were a damn embarrassment in the bar fight last night." Now, Crumb did raise his voice. "Set sail for open waters!" The crew exploded into action, a feeling of nervous excitement rushing through them. Crumb leveled his gaze at Austin's crew. "You four are staring at cleaning the deck. Alone. I better be impressed."

At his side, Mathers looked on with a wicked smile in her eyes. She reached for the pouch at her side and handed it to Crumb.

"Oh yeah, I almost forgot," he lied. He tossed the leather pouch to Austin. "I believe this is yours."

Austin caught the pouch easily. Hector and Carl crowded him to see what it was as Austin opened the cover flap and reached inside, pulling out a writhing, feathered object.

"Mollug!" he gasped.

The parrot was in rough shape and Austin wasn't sure how the bird was still alive. Mollug's throat had nearly been ripped out and the bird's green feathers were pinned to his side by a leather strap, keeping the bird from taking off. He was in shock. Mollug's eyes were wild, panicked, and his feet kicked and clawed at anything, everything, and nothing. His mouth moved as if to squawk, but no sounds came out.

"What happened?" Austin asked the bird.

"It fell on me," Mathers said from right in front of Austin, her words empty of emotion. He hadn't heard her approach and her words startled him. "I bandaged its throat and tied it up to settle it." She held up a bloody piece of cloth, "Just took it off before you came aboard. Needs to be redressed."

Austin felt sick to his stomach. He thought of Stocky Samuel, the pirate that had started the bar brawl and, it seemed, had chosen

Hector and Austin as his mortal enemies. "Who would do this to a parrot?" Austin asked.

No one answered.

The King of New England dined with the angel Gabriel inside the Castle Providence. The night's sleep had served him well; his anger at Frederic Kornell for mucking up his choreographed capture and rescue of Kelly Reed had cooled. Brad Regent recognized that while the ranger was a new rival in his attempt to steal Kelly back from the man who'd stolen her from him, Austin McNamara, it was still Austin who drew his main ire. Kornell, he felt, could be controlled.

And people who could be controlled were worth keeping close.

If only the rest of New England was so easy. He'd spent the previous day visiting castles in Worcester, Massachusetts, Hartford, Connecticut, and here in Providence, trying to get to know the people who would live under his rule. In his life in the "Old World," Brad was an investment banker. A successful one at that, but nothing he'd ever experienced prepared him for ruling a six-state region.

In front of him, a bowl of his favorite cereal, Fruit and Flakes, barely touched. The fruit chunks and corn flakes were as engrossed in their surrounding skim milk as Brad Regent was in the reports that Gabriel had handed him only minutes earlier.

"Troubling," Regent said, frowning.

"Indeed, it is," the angel replied hurriedly. Gabriel was the Angel in Charge of Reorganization. Everything that happened, in one way or another, fell under his jurisdiction. Regent found Gabriel to be a professional necessity and personal annoyance. The King of New England needed Gabriel's help in setting up his new kingdom (the angels had built Castle Providence, and many other castles throughout New England, overnight), but he found the angel to be a nervous, worrying sort. The King's investment company had employed several men and women like Gabriel. None of them lasted, and if they did, none of them brought in the commissions or clients the company needed from them to stay employed.

Why such a creature had been placed in charge of a world-wide reorganization was beyond Regent's imagination.

"Four hundred thousand?" Regent asked skeptically.

"Plus another seven hundred and fifty-two," Gabriel added. "Transients. People who have refused to accept God's Gift, and reject the beauty of the New World for the darkness of the forest. Many of them are families."

Regent's right hand – the hand with the spoonful of milk, flakes, and blueberries – paused half-way to his mouth. "That brings up an interesting point, Gabriel. What's happened to all the children?"

The angel coughed. "The children?"

"Yeah," Brad said, turning to look hard at the standing angel. "The kids. Where are all the kids?"

"They have been incorporated into the New World," the angel said without strong conviction.

"Where?" the King pressed. "I've seen teenagers running around, but no *kid* kids. No infants. No toddlers. No one, I'm guessing, who hasn't hit puberty, yet. Am I right?"

Gabriel turned to the window, letting out an anguished sigh. "Children cannot fend for themselves, King Regent. They are being cared for."

"Where?"

Gabriel chose his words carefully. "I ... I am not at liberty to tell you. Rest assured, they are being taken care of. They want for nothing."

"How did you convince parents to give up their kids?" Regent asked. The conversation thrilled and terrified him – just how far did the angels go to reorder the world?

"They were given assurances," Gabriel said softly. "They were shown the ... the Caring Lands."

"The Caring Lands?" Regent asked, the term striking him funny and odd and dangerous. "Did you get that from a Care Bears movie?"

Gabriel shook his head. "I don't know where it came from ... it was all I could think of on short notice. We angels have never been good at naming things already created. That was God's specialty."

Regent leaned back in his chair. He was enjoying this. "I thought that was Adam's specialty?"

Gabriel rolled his eyes. "Adam? If everything were up to Adam, humans would still be trying to figure out how to start a fire. Adam," he scoffed, "like all prototypes, might best be categorized as a successful failure. He wasn't such a disaster that God declared humanity a failed experiment, but he wasn't successful enough to go it on his own. Speak no more of him," Gabriel ordered, but to Brad it sounded more like pleading. The angel detected this, and said quickly, "I must be going. Be on the lookout for the transients, King Regent. They may reject the way of things, but they need to know

65

we will help them become a part of this new society. All they need to do is ask." Gabriel gave Brad a quick nod of his head, then extended his wings. "Good day to you."

"Likewise," Regent replied sourly. He turned back to the reports – names and locations of the transient population. This was not what he had in mind when he was a child and dreamt of being King. Brad dreamt of dragons to slay and damsels to be saved; he fantasized about leading armies into glorious battle, meeting dwarves and elves and killing orcs and goblins.

Paperwork played no role in those childhood dreams, unless they were ancient scrolls that foretold prophecy or held maps of hidden paths through dark forests. But this ... this was drudgery, the kind of grunt work he had been saddled with every day at his office. He wondered what could be done about those who wanted no part of this world; who lived, it seemed, in open rebellion. *If Kelly was here*, he thought, *she'd probably accuse me of wanting to kill them.*

That was nonsense. Brad was pro-death penalty (and Kelly was adamantly anti-death penalty), but that didn't mean he wanted everyone who broke the law rounded up and put to death. "Typical Liberal overreaction," he scoffed. Rounded up, sure, but just because someone was for the death penalty, he'd tried to tell Kelly time and again, didn't mean they were for random slaughter.

Brad scooped another spoonful of cereal into his mouth. How long would it be until all the boxed cereal in the world was gone?

"Maybe I'll just push all the transients into New York state," he mumbled.

His thoughts were interrupted by a knocking at the door. "Enter!" he called.

The door creaked open and the Captain of the King's Guard entered. "Good morning, your majesty."

"Good morning, Captain O'Malley. Please, join me." Regent watched as the forty year old man walked the short distance across the small dining room to take the seat opposite him at the round table. Wallace O'Malley had been a state cop in the Old World and was now a state cop, of sorts, in the New World. "It was all I ever wanted to be," he had told the King upon meeting him. He had come from a family of civil servants: policemen, firemen, and general town employees dominated his family tree. Regent took to the man immediately. He was loyal, disciplined, and saw the New World as an opportunity to fix the problems of the legal system as he saw them. "Too much power in the courts," he had groused, "and not enough power with the cops on the street." Brad had been surprised to learn that this twenty-year veteran of the state police had thought about running for political office when the Reorganization hit. He was even more surprised when O'Malley put on the silver armor afforded to him by his position. Regent had O'Malley pegged as being unwilling to give up his regular cop's uniform.

Captain O'Malley motioned to the papers Gabriel had brought with one hand as his other stroked his fumanchu mustache. "Something I need to be aware of, sire?"

The King shook his head. "Not now. Later, after this entire business with Kelly and the ranger is concluded." He took a bite of cereal then dropped his spoon back into the bowl with disgust. "Soggy," he mumbled, pushing the bowl away. "What's the latest?" he asked, rubbing his suddenly-throbbing temples.

Captain O'Malley cleared his throat. "Ms. Reed is still sleeping in her quarters, though she is showing signs of life. The handmaidens report she vomited several times over the course of the night and she will, almost certainly, be hung over this morning."

Brad nodded. "She'll be a hellcat to deal with," he said from memory. "The ranger?"

"Frederic Kornell is sleeping in his quarters, the two sluts having worn him out," O'Malley reported. "One of the two Princesses he took to bed is still sleeping beside him. The other," he let a small smile just tug at the corners of his mouth ever-so-slightly, "was, at last look, rummaging through the ranger's belongings, looking for something to steal. We were quite correct in our assessment of the ranger. His performance was, to put it plainly, pathetic."

"His performance?" the King asked.

"Yes, sire," O'Malley replied. "It was, in all likelihood, his first time with a woman. The two women spent just as much time with each other. His stamina was-"

Regent blinked, leaned forward. "How do you know what his performance was? Have you already talked to the women?"

O'Malley was taken aback at the King's words, and proceeded cautiously. "No, sire. We watched them."

"You watched them?" Brad asked. "Having sex?"

O'Malley nodded. "We have a tape, if you'd like to-"

"You taped it?" Blink. "You taped them having sex?"

"Of course," O'Malley replied. "Would you like to see it?"

"Not really, no," Brad answered, leaning back in his chair, his mind trying to wrap itself around what O'Malley was telling him.

"It's standard police procedure to place a suspect under surveillance," O'Malley informed him. "I surmised that you would want to know everything about Kornell. Was this a mistake?"

"No, no, of course not," Regent said quickly. He was uncomfortable with what O'Malley had done, but decided he wouldn't question his actions. For now, at least. He made a mental note about O'Malley's methods and filed it away. "Tell me about Kelly's abductor."

"I was going to see him now," Captain O'Malley said plainly. "Would you like to accompany me?"

The King nodded. "Yes. Yes, I would."

Austin stumbled into Captain Crumb's office, Mollug in his hands. He couldn't quite understand how this had happened or who could be responsible. It could be worse. Hector and Teddy's parrots hadn't even returned, so it looked likely that someone probably shot them. *Target practice after a drunken bar brawl. A way to relieve tension.* Whatever it was, Austin felt oddly horrible about the incident. It wasn't like he'd grown that attached to the bird – he'd only met him yesterday – but there was something about the fragility of the parrot's plight that struck him deep. Mollug was his responsibility. The bird, just like the rest of the world, had been reordered by the angels. Austin began to wonder where the bird had come from – a pet store? A forest? Someone's home?

For the first time since the Reorganization, Austin felt a growing anger at God and the angels for what they'd done.

Austin placed Mollug back into Mathers' leather pouch, and hung the pouch gently from a peg along the wall of Crumb's cabin. As he pulled his eyes away from the pouch and towards the cabin door, the pistol at his hip felt very, very heavy.

He felt a sudden, violent stab of longing to talk to Kelly.

Frederic Kornell placed a tray of breakfast food in front of the hung-over Kelly Reed. Kelly mumbled her thanks as Frederic slid into his chair opposite her. Of all the princes, princesses, rangers and guards that sat in the castle's cafeteria, there weren't two people feeling more wildly different this morning than Frederic and Kelly. The ranger gleefully shoveled scrambled eggs and sausage into his smiling mouth, and Kelly did little more than push her fresh fruit slices around her plate.

The embarrassment of his failure to save Kelly the previous night was pushed into the back of Frederic's mind, replaced with the soaring triumph he felt at his tryst with the two princesses. He couldn't deny that he'd failed Kelly, but in the end, she was safe (if hung-over) and he'd finally had sex.

Honest to goodness sex. With two women! Two!

It was hard not to feel good after a night like that, he grinned, taking a big gulp of orange juice.

He wished he knew where he'd misplaced the stack of hundred dollar bills King Regent had given him, though.

King Regent and Captain O'Malley exited the back of the King's white stretch limousine. O'Malley scowled at the quickly gathering crowd of princes, princesses, shopkeepers, and cowboys that rushed over to greet the King.

Regent, for his part, waved and smiled at the throng, but quickly moved with O'Malley to the door of Tonelli's butcher shop. Inside, several of the King's guards mingled with the local authorities. The King's guards, similar to their Captain O'Malley, wore silver armor, while the local authorities wore the (until yesterday) standard cop uniforms of the Providence police force.

"Cowboys?" O'Malley asked roughly, staring back out the window.

King Regent nodded. "The angels flew them in from Western Europe this morning on a 747. They're moving out for Oklahoma later today. Now," he said, his face turning serious, "where's Kelly's abductor being kept?"

"In the back, sire," O'Malley answered, motioning towards the door behind the counter.

Regent looked at the meat in the cases around them. "I don't want this to go to waste." He pointed to a handful of local cops, "Package this meat and deliver it to the airport. There's a fair amount of traffic being moved through here by the angels and I don't want those people going hungry if we can feed them for free."

The local cops gave the King a bemused smile, as if to say, "Do it yourself."

The King ran his hands down the front of his Armani suit. "Captain O'Malley?" he asked, his eyes staying locked on the local cops.

"Yes, sire?"

"Did you know that Providence is getting their own professional football team?"

"I did not."

"Then I am sure you were not aware that, as we speak, their cheerleaders are gathering at the airport."

"That a fact?"

"It is, Captain. The angels told me that we can expect forty to fifty cheerleaders arriving today. If the local authorities are unable to pack and move this meat, and then, of course, guard the cheerleaders from any unsavory types, order your men to complete this task."

"Of course, sire," Captain O'Malley replied. As the King and he moved into the back room, O'Malley noted that the local cops were already moving to package the meat. *Not how I would've handled it,* he thought, eyeing one of the locals and purposely running his hand over the hilt of his sword, *but I suppose it works.*

"Come along, Captain," the King called and O'Malley followed. O'Malley wasn't sure what to make of the King. He didn't like how Regent still wore a business suit instead of a king's robes. Seemed wrong. If he had to wear a suit of armor as Captain of the Guard, then the King should have to wear robes. The King had told him he was an investment banker in the Old World. Whatever the fuck that was. That was the world that existed off the ground, in the high-rise towers around Boston. Wallace O'Malley hadn't been welcome in that world and wouldn't have wanted any part of it even if he had been. His life was on the street. Twenty years a city cop. A beat cop. Always a beat cop. The penalty he paid for an early infraction. The Commissioner had let him keep his job, with the penalty he'd never rise through the ranks. Too risky. Secrets never stayed buried.

Of course, O'Malley thought as he motioned for the two King's Guards standing by the meat locker to open it, Old World secrets no longer meant shit. The angels had placed him next to the King of New England. "Why?" he'd asked.

"Because," Ocilael, the Angel in charge of Law Enforcement had replied, "things have a way of working out."

O'Malley wasn't sure what that meant, but didn't see any reason to argue against the one, big promotion he'd spent the past two decades dreaming of receiving. Whether that was part of some divine plan or coincidence … O'Malley didn't like to deal in hypotheticals and so he brushed the thought aside.

Save that for the Brad Regents of the world.

The guards pulled open the meat locker and O'Malley and King Regent stepped inside to find five men, all of them princes and all involved in Kelly's abduction, waiting for them. The man who had seduced and abducted her lay on a bloodstained table, the abductor's blood mixing with the dried blood from the meat that had been spilled on this table in the Old World. The abductor's eyes were closed and for a moment the King thought him dead.

"How is he?" the King asked, seeing the abductor's chest rise and fall.

"He's fucking stabbed is how he is," one of the princes said sharply.

Too sharply for O'Malley's liking, but this was the King's show so he marked it in his mind and filed it away.

"I thought no one was supposed to get hurt," the agitated prince continued. Regent and O'Malley, two men from different parts of Old World Boston, both marked the man's nervous undertones. This was a man who could not be trusted, they both knew, their differing backgrounds nonetheless bringing them to the same assessment.

"You were told there would be risks," Regent said calmly, drawing on his experience dealing with angry clients in the Old World. "He will be compensated."

"How about me?" another prince complained, stepping forward to show Regent and O'Malley his bandaged nose. "You broke my nose."

Regent waved the prince's concerns away. "There's plenty of money in the kingdom's coffers to-"

"Just what the hell is going on anyway?" Prince Broken Nose continued. "I agreed to let you beat me up to impress some girl, but I didn't know you were planning on drugging and kidnapping her. That's messed up."

"Quit your fucking whining."

All eyes in the room turned to the prone man on the table. The abductor had spoken. "If there's anyone who ought to be whining, it's me, and you don't hear me bitching." The abductor held his stomach where Frederic's blade had penetrated deep and tried to sit up. He winced, unable to rise more than half way. With his left eye still closed in a wince, the abductor opened his right eye to stare down the King. "Don't just stand there, Brad. Give me a fucking hand."

The King took several quick steps towards the abductor. O'Malley thought the King was going to attack the man who'd insulted him, but that didn't happen. Regent placed his left hand under the abductor's back and with his right he reached in front of the wounded man to pull his legs off the table, making it easier for the abductor to sit up.

"Thanks."

"You look like shit," the King said, his face graven.

"Well," the abductor said, grimacing, "I was run-through with a goddamn sword. Who the hell was that guy? What was he doing there?"

"Failure of security," the King said quickly, noting the abductor's eyes glance to O'Malley and feeling O'Malley's eyes boring into the back of his skull. "Local cops," the King added quickly. "Not the Captain's men." It was a lie, but it should calm both of them.

"Whatever," the abductor shrugged. "Just get me out of here. Why the hell are we in a meat locker anyway?"

"We didn't want to put you five in with the gen pop at the city jail," O'Malley said quickly.

Prince Broken Nose inserted himself into the conversation. "We were read our rights. We're not really under arrest, are we? We were doing what you told us to do!"

Brad turned to the four men in the corner, putting on his banker's smile. "It's all a formality," the King said. "We need it to look legit-"

"To cover your ass!" Broken Nose accused.

O'Malley had about enough, stepping between the King and the four princes. "Enough of this. You knew the deal going in. Harass the girl, let the King beat you up and save her, be carted off to jail for a night's stay. Oh yeah," O'Malley sneered, "and be paid ten thousand dollars apiece."

"So we can go?" Broken Nose asked, though with a bit less ferocity.

"In due time," the King said, coming forward to place a hand on O'Malley's shoulder. "There were complications. There was," he turned back to the abductor, "a witness. We need to wait until he's out of town before we can let you loose. And yes, yes," he added quickly, a dull throb coming into his brain, "you will be compensated for it."

"Brad," the abductor said in a low, serious voice, "you didn't come here to touch base. We've known each other too long to fool me. You've got bad news you want to deliver. I can see it just behind your eyes. A dark cloud getting darker. Like that time senior year in college when you wanted to tell me you caught my girlfriend cheatin' with that prick from DTD. So give it to me straight. What's the deal?"

Brad eyed his friend carefully, then nodded once. "You're right." He glanced over his shoulder to Captain O'Malley. "Take those four back to the Castle. Put 'em in the dungeon. Cover their faces."

O'Malley nodded, and led the four princes outside, leaving Regent alone with the abductor.

The King watched them go and when the door was closed behind them he moved to stand in front of his friend. "Before I tell you what needs to be done, rest assured that you will be compensated."

The abductor snorted. "Come on, Regent. Money don't mean shit to me. You know that." He ran his hand through his short, dark hair than scratched his stubble. He looked disgustedly down at what remained of his prince costume. "These are some fucking sissy clothes, man. If my teammates could see me now ..."

"It's in the public's eye," Brad said dourly. "What you did. The angels don't have the newspapers and television news working, yet, but your actions are the talk of the street. Lot of people have seen your face, Catlin. A lot of people."

"And?"

"And a lot of people, even in this New World, aren't going to be so forgiving of a guy who abducted a princess." Pause. "They might not want that guy playing for their pro hockey team."

"Hey," the abductor accused, "the angels said we could be what we wanted. I want to be a pro hockey player."

Brad shook his head. "All the angels can do is put us in position. It's up to us to see what we do with that chance." Brad didn't mention to his friend that he knew that while the Jim Catlin sitting in front of him might want to be a hockey player, the ten year old Jimmy Catlin dreamt of being one of them metal things from *Battlestar Galactica*. Cylons or something they were called - Brad had never been a big television watcher. The angels had come to him, knowing (as they seemed to know everything) that the Jim Catlin of today was not the kid who dreamt of killing people, and knowing that the two of them had a connection. They offered Catlin to be placed under the King's guidance, and created a cover story around one of Catlin's lesser dreams of power, which they "interpreted" into making him a prince with the promise he could try his hand at being a pro hockey player once a few weeks had passed and the major work involved with the Reconstruction was over. It was that, or Catlin could end up locked away, wherever the angels had isolated the "really bad people" as Gabriel called them. Brad didn't want that for his friend. For anyone, really.

The King placed a hand on his friend's shoulder. "Look. The press isn't up and running strong, so I'm sure we can ship you out west. I'll do whatever I can to cover your tracks."

Catlin nodded. "You're playing me, Brad."

Brad shook his head. "I'm not. I'm laying it out. You can't play in New England." Beat. "But right now, you're not even thinking of playing, so stop bullshitting me. I know what you want. You know what you want. Admit it, and I'll make it happen."

Catlin ran his hand over the bandaged scar. "I want the fucker who did this to me. Remember the beating we put on that guy who fucked my girlfriend? This is going to be worse. So much worse."

Regent nodded, held in a smile. 'Typical Jim Catlin,' he thought. 'The more things change, the more people stay the same.' Catlin's never-ending quest for revenge against someone, somewhere, was what fueled him as a minor league hockey player. His inability to ever get past that revenge was probably what kept him in the minors. 'Or maybe,' Brad thought, giving his friend some credit, 'that sense of injustice was what enabled him to even make it as a professional. God knows he's not that talented.' Their friendship meant the King could trust Catlin, but it was Catlin's personality that made him perfect for this assignment. In a few days, he'd set Catlin loose on Kornell, and Kelly could see the ranger revealed as his true coward self.

"Well?" Catlin prompted. "Are you going to say it or am I going to have to guess."

King Regent locked eyes with his friend. "You going to have to undergo some punishment before you get your revenge on Kornell. The public needs to see it, to know that there's going to be law and order in this New World. More," he said, motioning to the dingy room around them, "than this."

"Name it."

"Public flogging."

"What?" Catlin groused, his face making an expression like he'd just eater a rotten egg.

"Jail time takes too long and doesn't deliver the message with full authority," King Regent explained. This much, at least, was true. He'd thought long and hard overnight about the role law and order needed to take, and had consulted with the angel Ocilael. "It's too early for a trial. No one wants to sit in a court of law and hear this case. The frivolity of last night was replaced this morning with the impatience for the princes and princesses to get to their new homes. The populace was already in a foul mood and they want to see justice."

"So you're going to flog your best friend?" Catlin asked, equally believing and disbelieving his friend would do this to him.

Regent nodded. "We'll mute the lash, of course, and we'll administer only ten blows. Enough for the public to get the idea." He offered a half-grin. "The more you could scream, the more effective it will be. We don't have to give the public blood if you give them anguished screams."

Catlin rubbed his face with his hands. "This is so screwed up. You're asking me to take a dive."

King Regent nodded. "Just remember that when this is done, you'll get your shot at revenge. Frederic Kornell is yours to do with as you will. Kill him if it makes you happy."

Catlin brushed the thought aside. "Yeah, right. Kill him. I'm getting publicly flogged for the bastard stabbing me. What will you do to me for-?"

King Regent reached into his Armani suit and removed a black mask, tossing it to Catlin. "Simple plans are the best. If no one sees your face, no one can accuse you of shit."

Catlin looked at the mask, then up to his friend, a man who was now King, who commanded this entire region. He nodded. "You're the boss."

King Regent nodded. Indeed he was.

"Austin McNamara," Captain Crumb shouted amidst the roaring laughter of the *Puritan's* crew, "you just might make a good pirate, yet!"

The *Puritan* had moved into open waters off the docks and the crew looked back to witness the prank Austin, Hector, Carl, and Teddy had played on the *Cottonmather*. Austin and the three others smiled, basking in the glow of their fellow pirates' affection. Mollug wasn't forgotten, but Austin was able to enjoy the moment. Looking back at Stocky Samuel's boat, Austin couldn't help but feel a sense of pride as the roaring laughter swelled around them.

The port side of the *Cottonmather* had been covered in graffiti, bright pink letters proclaiming, "PLYMOUTH ROCK RULZ!" near the front of the boat and "REAL MEN AIN'T MIDGETS!" near the back. Austin hadn't been crazy about that last phrase, but Hector had done it on his own. Carl's phrase was in the middle of the hull, and it had surprised both Austin and Hector, who had no idea what kind of insult the forty-something biochemist would paint.

Carl had painted, "SUCK IT, SISSY BITCHES!"

"Sissy bitches?" Hector asked. He'd wanted to ask it since Carl painted it.

Carl shrugged. "My neighbor's kid used to say it all the time. What I can't figure out is why we gave the *Plymouth Rock* all the credit."

Mary Mathers appeared at Carl's shoulder. "Because we get all the laughs, and the *Rock* gets all the retribution." She turned to Austin, her long blonde hair tossing naturally and seductively. "Well played, Austin."

Captain Crumb silenced the crew, his eyes peering through a set of binoculars. "Something's happening on the deck of the *Cottonmather*. I think they've realized what's been done to their ship. Let's see now what they do about it."

All but two of the crew obeyed the Captain's orders. The two who did not: Teddy Levenson, who stared daggers into Crumb's back, and C.O. Mary Mathers, whose sparkling eyes watched Teddy as the wheels of opportunity spun eagerly inside her head.

"Ready, milady?" Frederic Kornell asked a still hurting Kelly Reed. They were in the large stables of the Castle Providence. Frederic's left hand pulled the reins of his horse, Alfred. Around them, horses stood in stalls doing horse things.

Kelly scowled at him. "What's got you so chipper this morning?" She eyed the horses with a deep hatred, convinced they were munching and scratching and whinnying just to annoy her.

Kornell shrugged, keeping his secret. They walked slowly towards the exit, staying clear of the stable workers. "Amazing," Frederic said, "that some people dreamt something so simple as to work with horses."

At the end of the stables, a group of three princes and two princesses waited for them.

"Kelly Reed?" one of the princesses, a middle-aged brunette, asked as they approached. Kelly nodded. "Excellent. I'm Georgia. Georgia Mulrooney. You must be the ranger," she said to Kornell.

"I am," Frederic said, giving her a short bow. He turned to the other princess and did a double take at the beautiful young redhead. It was one of the women from last night. "Ma'am," he said breathlessly, giving her another bow.

She giggled as a sheepish grin came to Frederic's face. For his life, he couldn't remember her name, only that this was the princess that was up and gone before he awoke this morning. He nodded to the three princes.

"We need to hurry," Georgia said. "There's going to be a public flogging in the city center in twenty minutes. If we hurry, we can watch it as we ride past."

"Public flogging?" Frederic asked, his stomach turning at the thought of someone's punishment being turned into a public spectacle. "Who? For what crime?"

"We don't know his name," the redheaded princess said, her eyes popping wide in excitement. "But they said he abducted some princess last night." Her eyes glanced to Kelly, whose own eyes perked up, and then locked with Kornell's. "And then some brave hero ran him through with his sword."

The fog began to lift from Kelly's mind. "Come again?" She looked to Kornell. "Is she talking about you?"

"Indeed," the princess smirked. "This brave hero saved an abducted princess."

Frederic coughed nervously, his eyes avoiding Kelly as shame came creeping into the corner of his heart.

The crew of the *Puritan* watched with nervous anticipation as the *Cottonmather* made its way away from its moorings and headed out to sea.

Headed, they noted, directly toward the *Puritan*.

"Are they coming for us?"

"They're coming for us!"

"How do they know?"

"They can't!"

The nervous whispers grew louder and more frequent as they watched the equally equipped schooner unfurl its sails. The sails caught the easy morning breeze, flapping majestically above the deck. Austin felt a sense of dread sink through him. The *Cottonmather* was coming for them. The distance between the ships and the sheer size of the schooners made the wait drag out, fraying nerves slowly and steadily. It was Hector's "midget" comment on the hull, he guessed. Samuel must've seen it, or been told about it, put two-and-two together, and convinced their captain to come after them. His mind went to Mollug, wondering if it was even remotely possible that Stocky Samuel was responsible for the parrot's injury.

He thought of Kelly, and how she used to smile at him when he was being ridiculous. Closing his eyes, he thought, *God I miss her.* He wondered if the *Cottonmather* would dare fire on them this early into their career as pirates.

"Calm your nerves!" Captain Crumb roared above the nervous chatter, his eyes locked on the *Cottonmather*. "The *Cottonmather* doesn't have us in her sights." He pointed. "Watch. And remember, pirate ships don't have forward guns. They have side-guns."

"Side-guns?" Austin asked, his eyes searching out across the water. His eyes noted that the *Cottonmather* had their gun ports raised. He drew a line across the water with his eyes. "Oh, hell," he said, understanding what was going to happen one second before thought became reality.

The *Cottonmather's* cannons fired and the thunderous booms cracked the ocean air as white and grey smoke rose in sharp, violent clouds from the ship.

The *Cottonmather* was firing on the *Plymouth Rock*. The first sea battle had begun.

Austin was acutely aware he had caused it. He watched, stunned, as cannon balls ripped into the *Plymouth Rock*, splintering and shattering the wooden hull of the schooner.

'People,' he thought, 'are going to die. And it's going to be my fault.'

Stocky Samuel stood on the deck of the *Cottonmather*. Unlike the rest of the crew that was busy firing upon the *Plymouth Rock*, Samuel's eyes were locked out towards the horizon, where the *Puritan* rocked gently in the Atlantic waters. The Captain might have been fooled about who marked the side of their ship, but Samuel wasn't.

It was the four misfits: Austin, Hector, the nerd, and the fat boy.

Across the waters, he sent out a mental promise.

"I'm coming."

Inside a leather pouch, madness tugged at the mind of the parrot Mollug, battling with fear for control. There were no rational thoughts in the parrot's angel-enhanced mind, just a repeating sequence of images: of the angel Berathon crushing two fellow parrots in his hands, killing them, of the angel Enimon firing a psychic arrow across the night sky, tearing through Mollug's throat, and of the words between the two angels that Mollug had overheard, words that worried that the angels were being misled.

In the face of God's word being potentially false, Mollug's mind believed madness might be the safest road to travel.

Chapter Six
New World Consequence

The crew of the *Puritan* stood upon the deck of their ship and watched in mortified horror as, across the waters, the *Cottonmather* obliterated the *Plymouth Rock*. Yesterday was the first day of the New World, the day the angels came to Earth and turned everyone into their childhood dream. The crews of the three pirate ships of Port Gloucester came from all over New England. They individual crewmen were as diverse as any group of men from across the six northeastern states would have been, though they had one common bond. They were pirates. They shared this dream as children, whether that childhood was ten years or fifty years in the past.

The angels had offered this massive change to the status quo of the world as a gift from God.

To the crew of the *Puritan*, the gift was beginning to look rotten.

The little laughter that now remained, following their prank on the *Cottonmather*, was nervous and skittish.

The *Cottonmather's* retribution had come hard, fast, and looked destined to be complete. Cannon after cannon was fired from the *Cottonmather* towards the *Plymouth Rock*, which was still moored at the docks. It was a sitting target, unable to move as the *Cottonmather* took it apart, one cannonball at a time.

"Twenty-five shots," Captain Crumb mumbled in horrified awe to Mathers. "She got off twenty-five shots before the *Rock* was able to get off her first." The ex-Navy captain shook his head slightly, trying to stay in command of his externals as his internals churned.

Off to Crumb's right, Teddy Levenson saw the small crack in the visage of the rough old man and it made him smile. The rest of the crew might buy into what Crumb was selling, but Teddy wasn't. He'd been thinking back on those childhood dreams of his. *Treasure Island*. That's where his idea of pirates came from. That's the kind of pirate he wanted to be now. The kind that tore out a page of a Bible and made a black circle on it and left it for the victim.

The smoke from the *Cottonmather's* canons was so intense that it had begun to cloud the vision of the *Puritan* crew. The breeze pushed the smoke cloud towards the *Puritan* and to some of the crew it felt like the cloud brought death with it. Members of the crew began coughing as the acrid smell seered its way into their lungs and eyes.

"Should we assist the *Plymouth Rock*?" Carl asked.

All eyes turned to the former biochemist, then to Captain Crumb. "No," Crumb answered, his voice rough and old. "We're heading for deeper waters." His eyes met Carl's. "We're pirates, Yesek. Pie-ruts. There's no reason for us to get involved in the business of other pirates unless it's for our benefit." Crumb looked around at his hundred-person crew with a look of almost sadness. He looked like he was about to say something, then lost himself in a memory.

In front of the Castle Providence, an ancient-looking structure built two nights previous by the angels and situated in the middle of a modern city, a crowd gathered. There was to be a flogging, retribution taken for the abduction of a princess.

At least, that's what the intended function was to relay. The crowd, instead of calling for blood for harm done to one of their own, stood and waited in the fall sun with an expectant, almost cheery air about them.

Looking down at them from a window high above the castle's front steps, King Brad Regent stood in an Armani suit, a deep frown trying to make itself permanent upon his young, athletic face. "They look like they're waiting for a festival performance of Shakespeare, not a public flogging!" he fumed.

Behind him, the Captain of the Guard, Wallace O'Malley, stood calmly. "They'll get the message, sir."

"And what if they think it a game?" Brad raged, spinning on O'Malley.

O'Malley patiently answered, "Well, sir, seems to me you'll get what you want either way. If the crowd acts like it's a game, if they fail to be horrified by the beating, then we plant that bug in your friend's ear. Get him even more pissed off than he already is. Tell him we saw Kornell in the crowd, laughing at him." Pause. O'Malley kept his cold eyes locked onto the King's. "And then we set the abductor loose."

Brad calmed himself, nodding slowly. The truth was, his mind was already on to other things. He wanted to steal Kelly away from Austin, sure, but this entire King of New England business was already starting to wear thin. He started to look down at the crowd and quickly changed his mind, looking out over the city. All that he could see was his to rule.

He thought of the 400,000-plus transients living out there somewhere – men, women, and children who had rejected the angels' gift. Schemes and emotions began to intermix in the king's mind – the elaborate game he'd created to "rescue" Kelly from an abductor, all in an attempt to try and steal her away from Austin mixed with the business end of his position: the transients, the allocation of princes and princesses throughout his kingdom, paying off the abductors, and, worst of all, ordering the public flogging of a friend to satisfy the concept of "justice."

Jamming his hands into his pants pockets, Brad felt a pang of envy towards the transients. They had no responsibilities except … what? Was it dangerous out there for them? It didn't look like they were high priority on the angels' list. Wasn't that why Raphael had visited yesterday? To dump the transient issue into Brad's lap? Why weren't the angels taking care of them?

Inside his right pocket, the fingers of his right hand wrapped themselves around a small object. A sense of shame rose up inside him and he removed the object so that he could stare at it.

"Sire?" Captain O'Malley asked as he began to wonder if Regent had the guts to be King. A leader needed to be solid, unbending. There were moments when it appeared to all come together for Regent, but then there were times like this, where the King disappeared into his own thoughts.

Times like this worried O'Malley. He didn't want to be stuck as the right hand of a weak ruler. The former beat cop had waited his entire career for a promotion like the one the angels had given him – he wasn't about to blow it on a 30-year old kid who couldn't stick to his guns. The cowardice of local politicians and senior officers is what had led Wallace to consider running for public office himself.

Hell, O'Malley mused, *if he can't keep himself on track, I sure as hell don't mind doing it for him.*

The King turned around and showed the object to O'Malley. It was a cell phone. "Kelly's," he announced, placing it in his palm and offering it to O'Malley. "I took it off of her when we put her to bed."

"Why?" O'Malley asked, though he could guess at the answer. *You're a fucking pussy.*

"Didn't want her to be able to contact Austin," Regent replied sheepishly. "Or him to contact her." He shook his head. "Silly."

O'Malley couldn't agree more, but he wasn't about to voice that feeling.

The phone still extended in his palm, Brad took a step towards his Captain. "Return it to her. Tell her we found it on the floor of the bedroom."

O'Malley kept his tongue down and grabbed the phone. He nodded to his King, but thought a different tune to himself: *Geese will shit golden eggs before that bitch gets her phone back.*

While not averse to making the occasional romantic gesture (as his three ex-wives could all attest), Wallace O'Malley's mind was solidifying around the belief that Kelly Reed was a hell of a lot more trouble than she was worth.

Their carriage was like something out of Cinderella. With large, spoked wheels that stood six feet tall, a thick wooden body painted black with golden designs intricately painted onto the exterior, a shimmering red, cushioned interior, the carriage that would carry the three princesses and three princes to Kent Harbor, Maine was, like much of the New World, a gift to humanity from the angels.

"We're supposed to ride in this thing?" Kelly Reed asked, her hangover beginning to lessen, if only slightly.

"We are," Georgia Mulrooney, a princess in her mid-forties, replied. "Isn't it wonderful?"

Kelly decided it was best that she didn't answer. No need to make enemies before the trip had even started. Instead, she turned to look at her traveling companions. Besides Georgia and Frederic Kornell, there was a buxom redheded princess who eyed Kornell as if he were an object she desired to possess. Kelly decided instantly that she hated this princess, and the severity of her assessment (coming as it was through the slowly regressing fog of a hangover) shocked her. Why should she care if another woman looked at the ranger as dinner?

Because he saved your life, a voice said from inside her head.

Did he? Kelly asked back.

Don't you remember?

No. Kelly shook her head. *No, actually I don't.*

Funny side-effect of drinking too much alcohol.

I didn't! Kelly shot back. *I drank a lot. More than I should have, but ...*

But what? the voice pressed.

But not so much that I should've blacked out.

Then how do you suppose you ended up being dragged off into the woods by a stranger? What would Austin think about that?

"Austin," Kelly said aloud.

"No, no," Georgia said beside her. "Kent Harbor, honey. We're headed for Kent Harbor, not Austin. I don't even think there's an Austin, Maine. Did you mean Augusta? Thank God we're not going there. Augusta is a dreadful place. My husband loves it, but I can't stand it."

Kelly flashed a concerned-looking Frederic a look – *Help!*

The young redhead came to her rescue instead. "I'm Samantha Dixon," she said, her voice undercut with a sly, southern drawl.

"Kelly. Kelly Reed," Kelly replied, nodding her thanks.

Samantha turned to the three princes that stood behind them, at the front of the carriage. They were attempting, with only a small amount of success, to rein two of the horses to the carriage. All of them were dressed identically in white and red outfits that looked as if they had come from the same amalgamated Disney movie that most of the princesses had been born from. "Next to useless," she confided, dropping her voice, then shot her eyes to Frederic, who was busy patting the mane of his horse, Alfred. "Unlike him." Samantha brought her eyes back around to bear on Kelly, and the sheer energy sparkling in them gave Kelly pause. "Is it true? Did he save you?"

Kelly scratched her head. "I ... I think so. I'm not sure. I was pretty drunk."

Samantha nodded knowingly. "Party girl. I like it."

Georgia, feeling left out, interjected nervously, "Oh, you two will be the death of me. If my husband knew about this ..."

"You're married?" Kelly asked with more force than she had intended. "What happened to your husband?"

Georgia gave Kelly an odd look. "What happened to him? My dear, you sound like some tragedy has befallen him. The angels have let him become that which he always wanted to be."

Samantha asked, "And that would be ...?"

Georgia giggled, an odd look for a middle-aged woman. "Elvis."

"Elvis?" Samantha and Kelly asked.

"Elvis," Georgia repeated. "Elvis Aaron Presley."

"That is so hot," Samantha nodded enthusiastically. "I'd love to fuck a rock star."

Kelly rolled her eyes. Elvis. If Austin had turned into Elvis she would've broken up with him on the spot.

"How are you feeling?"

Kelly turned to see Frederic coming up behind her. She was glad he was here, though she found it disconcerting how he kept stealing glances over to Samantha. Did they know each other? "Better," she said. "Head's clearing." Kelly kept her eyes locked on Frederic's face until the ranger turned his focus back to her. When she had his attention, she spoke in a low, serious voice. "I hear I owe you thanks for saving my life. I don't remember-"

Kornell turned immediately away. "You were really out of it."

"Apparently so," she replied, biting her lip, noting he neither admitted or denied the claim. "I didn't think I had drunk that much, but-"

"I think you were drugged."

"What?" she asked, stunned.

Frederic gave her a quick shake of his head. "Later. Right now, we've got to get going. Kent Harbor's a long way off." The ranger looked to Samantha, then over to the three princes who'd apparently figured out how to attach two of their horses to the carriage. "Let's mount up. I want to be clear of the city before the public flogging is over." He forced a smile he didn't mean. "Mom always said it's the wise man who beats the traffic. I figure she never had horse-drawn carriages in mind when she said it, but if the saying fits ..."

Kelly gave Kornell a weak smile, and turned away as Samantha came over to flirt with him.

The first sea battle of the New World raged behind the *Puritan* as the pirate ship made for deeper waters. Austin stood on the deck of his ship, feeling lost. Around him, the crew made itself busy fulfilling Captain Crumb's orders. Austin had no drive to join them. There were men dying because of the prank that he'd put in motion. Mollug was severely injured. The New World suddenly felt a whole lot bigger, and darker, than it had the night before. The bar fight they'd been in seemed almost innocent now.

Looking back through the acrid smoke, Austin watched the *Cottonmather*'s cannons rip the *Plymouth Rock* to kindling. How many men were aboard that ship? How many lives would be on his head?

"McNamara!"

"Huh?" Pulled out of his thoughts, Austin was yanked around by the *Puritan*'s Commanding Officer, Mary Mathers.

"Are you deaf? Captain Crumb wants to see you in his quarters," the mid-thirties, attractive blonde informed him. "Now."

"Yeah, sure," Austin mumbled. His eyes drifted back towards the front of the deck, to the door to Crumb's quarters. "Doesn't matter how old you get," he said to the C.O. without turning, "it still sucks to get sent to the Principal's Office."

Mathers grabbed Austin's elbow. "What are you talking about? You think Crumb wants to yell at you? I'm half-worried he's going to give you my job."

"Why would he do that?" Austin asked, turning to look into a pair of angry eyes. "We're heading for deep waters. Missing his big final breakfast treat or whatever he was complaining about."

Mathers stepped in close, squeezing his elbow in a tight grip. "Listen to me, McNamara," she said, dropping her voice to a harsh whisper. "There's more things going on than you and the rest of the crew can see. I've been with Crumb nearly from the start of the New World. The aliens are riding him hard. He thinks they're angels, of course, but they're aliens. 'Make 'em pirates,' they tell him. 'Show them the truth about what they wanted to be.' They scare me," she said as her eyes danced around, looking like she was certain the aliens would suddenly be standing there before them. Mathers turned back, leaning in close enough to allow Austin an olfactory swim in her expensive perfume. "Especially Berathon. There's something dark about him." She let go of Austin's arm. "I don't scare easy. Believe me. I put my last boyfriend in the hospital when I caught him cheating. But," her voice dropped even lower, "the aliens … there's something wicked about them."

Austin studied her face and made a snap judgment. *This was the kind of woman who always got men to do whatever she wanted.* He heard Kelly's voice scold him inside his head. "Don't be an ass."

"Fair enough," his own mind answered back as Mary Mathers stood before him, waiting for his reaction. "Why are you telling me this?" Austin asked her.

"The Captain's waiting," Mary replied, stiffening her back.

Austin nodded. *If that's how you want to play it …*

He walked across the deck to the Captain's quarters, feeling Mathers' eyes on his back the entire time.

"Are you ready for this?" the King asked his best friend.

"I am," Jim Catlin, Kelly Reed's abductor, replied.

The King and his accomplice stood just inside a hallway off the main entrance hall of the castle. They had a moment's privacy before the flogging. Neither of them wanted to walk out onto the front steps, but this is where the activities of the past day had brought them. Private plans that now demanded public actions. The public, Regent believed, needed to see that criminals would pay in the New World.

Or at least in New England.

"Jim, I'm sorry."

Catlin nodded. "You and me both."

"The ranger is yours."

Jim sucked on his teeth, then turned to face his friend-turned-King. "Answer me a question?"

King Regent nodded.

"Are you letting me kill Kornell because you want him dead, or because you're trying to make me happy?"

Brad took in a deep breath and exhaled slowly. "Both."

Jim scoffed. "All of this over Kelly Reed. Kelly Fucking Reed."

Before Brad could respond, Captain O'Malley walked into the hallway. "It's time," he stated plainly.

Catlin eyed the rope the Captain carried and held out his arms so O'Malley could bind them together. "I suppose it wouldn't do me any good to ask for a pardon?" Catlin asked without a smile.

"Sorry," Brad answered.

"Right," Kelly's abductor said, turning to O'Malley. "Let's do this."

Captain Crumb sat behind his desk, his fingers brought together before his face, his eyes staring Austin down hard. *This is worse than the principal's office.* Crumb looked old – old as the weather, as Austin's dad used to say – but with an intense thoughtfulness. Austin didn't know whether to react to that thoughtfulness with fear, sorrow, or respect, so he did what he always did in a situation that unnerved him.

He played stupid.

"Mathers said you wanted to see me, Captain?"

Crumb nodded, his eyes never leaving Austin's.

"Er ... I'm sorry about making us miss breakfast-"

Crumb waved the apology away with an angry flourish. "To hell with breakfast. You can see with your own eyes what would've happened to us if we'd gone ashore. We'd have come back, bellies full, and been ripped to shreds by the *Cottonmather*. The quicker we get clear of them, the better. We're not ready for the likes of them."

"Will we ever be ready, sir?" Austin asked, the numbness returning to him. "We're not killers."

Crumb took a few short breaths, his fingertips drumming against their opposite numbers. Austin could tell the old man was measuring him. Crumb, at the last, nodded once. "Guess I passed," Austin mused, wondering if that was a good thing or a bad thing.

"You're right," Crumb said slowly. "You're not killers. Thing is," he said, leaning forward over his desk, "I think the crew of the *Cottonmather* are killers."

Austin agreed. "Looks that way when you stand on the deck and look back at what they're doing to the *Plymouth Rock*."

Crumb shook his head, but instead of the reprimand Austin was certain was coming, the Captain's voice was tired, almost depressed. "Not what I meant." Crumb slowly rose to his feet – every action the Captain made in his office looked slow, deliberate. The wild, expressive persona that Austin and his crewmates had experienced on the deck was absent here, in the privacy of Crumb's quarters. "What I mean, Austin, is that I think they're killers. I think, in the Old World, they were bad people."

"What do you mean?" Austin asked.

Crumb moved around the left (from Austin's point-of-view) corner of his desk. "Did you think only the goody-two-shoes got a ticket into the New World?"

Austin had to admit that he really hadn't thought much of the question before now. Everything was happening so fast that there wasn't any time to think, only to react. "But why would the angels let people like that into the New World?"

Crumb stopped shuffling his feet and placed his knuckles down on the desktop. "The better question is, 'Why wouldn't they?' There was a lot of evil in the Old World, Austin. The angels never stopped it before. Why should they stop it now?"

"Because this is the New World," Austin replied. "This is God's gift to humanity."

Crumb nodded. "To humanity. Not to the people He deemed 'good.' To all of us. Or most, anyway." Crumb picked his knuckles off the desk and started to move along the wall to Austin's left. "I asked Berathon, the angel in charge of Pirates, what he wanted me to do with you folks. I figured this was akin to an amusement park ride. I'd show you how to sail, take you out to sea, maybe fire off a few cannons at the open water." Crumb reached his destination, a birdcage that held a pouch. Austin's heart skipped a beat; that was the pouch that held Mollug. "I didn't think this world was real. Thought it was a big game of dress up." Crumb shook his head as he reached inside to remove the pouch. "I was wrong."

Austin swallowed, his eyes glued to the pouch,

" 'Teach them how to be pirates,' Berathon told me," Crumb explained, opening the pouch. "Real pirates. Show them there's a price to be paid for everything. 'Even dreams?' I asked. 'Especially dreams.' " Crumb's hand gently reached inside the pouch to remove the bound and bandaged parrot. A small piece of brown cloth covered the bird's head. " 'Teach them,' the angel said, his voice colder than the North Atlantic in January, 'what it means to be a pirate. Or I'll do it for you.' "

Austin felt weak as Crumb handed a catatonic Mollug to him. "Berathon threatened you?"

"Here's what I think, Austin," Crumb said plainly. "I think the *Cottonmather* is Berathon's assurance that all of you learn the consequences of being a pirate. I think that damned ship is coming to kill us and I think the angels want them to try."

"But ... why?"

Crumb turned to the small window, looking out at the rolling waves of the Atlantic Ocean. "That is a question I would very much like an answer to, Austin."

Austin stroked Mollug's feathers, careful to stay clear of the hood that covered the bird's eyes. "But ... what do we really know? I don't mean to be disrespectful, Captain, but most of what you've said is just speculation."

"I'm a military man," Crumb explained patiently. "Been one since the day I turned eighteen. Can't escape it, even in retirement. I think like a military man, Austin. When the angels come and reorder the world, we all ask why. My answer to that question is in military terms."

"You think the angels are going to attack us?" Austin asked, not believing it.

"No," Crumb replied, shaking his head. "If the angels wanted us dead ..." He let the words trail off.

"Then what?" Austin pressed.

Crumb chose his words carefully. "I think they're testing us. Now," he added quickly, "I can't prove that, and I don't know it to be true, but something about all of this smells rotten to me." The old man pointed to Mollug. "I think that bird might know something."

"Mollug?" Austin asked, looking down at the hooded, catatonic parrot. Austin had believed it was the pirates they'd been in a fight with at the bar – the so-called "Stocky" Samuel and his crew – that had done this to Mollug, but thinking it now, Austin could see that it didn't make sense. If Samuel had been the one that harmed Mollug, it had to be a random act of violence, didn't it? Samuel couldn't really tell which of the hundreds of parrots flying through the air was Austin's, could he? Austin looked up from Mollug to find Crumb's weary face staring back at him. "What could Mollug know?"

Captain Crumb walked towards the room's door. "When I close this door behind me," he said without turning around, "take the hood off the bird. Say nothing to me about what you hear until I ask you. Say nothing to anyone, including the three you hang around with. If I catch wind you've disobeyed this order," he threatened, turning around to face Austin just as his hand grasped the door latch, "I'll gut you myself. This isn't the time to take chances."

Austin nodded (wanting to ask, "Then why are you taking a chance with me?") and waited until Crumb had left him alone with his parrot. Taking a deep breath, Austin removed Mollug's makeshift hood.

Mollug's eyes shot open and they began to frantically search back and forth, back and forth, up and down, almost bulging right out of his head. He squawked in a panicked series of yips and Austin could feel the parrot's heart racing wildly beneath its chest. "Mollug!" he said in a demanding whisper. "Mollug, what's wrong?"

Mollug's body appeared to seize as it went stone-cold rigid in Austin's hands. The parrot's eyes closed, then reopened, looking at Austin but seemingly focusing on some unseen object behind its keeper. When it spoke, the words chilled Austin's spine, though Austin wasn't exactly sure why. He just knew that it was bad. Really, really bad.

Mollug said, in a squawk that was more a whisper than a shriek, "Bad words float through the clouds of heaven. Bad words float through the clouds of heaven. Bad words float through the clouds of heaven."

And on and on, repeating the eight-word sentence until Austin had heard enough and replaced Mollug's hood over its head. What did those words mean? Had Mollug heard them from someone? From who? The angels? Was it possible?

Mollug fell silent and still and Austin stood there, in the Captain's quarters, sweating, feeling the deep, powerful waters push and suck at the *Puritan*.

Austin felt very small and very, very afraid.

"Isn't this exciting?" Samantha Dixon cooed from inside the horse-drawn carriage.

Beside the well-endowed redhead, the slightly overweight, middle-aged Georgia Mulrooney nodded in excited agreement. "Look, there's that wicked man now. Oooh, I hope they beat him good!"

Sitting opposite the two women, Kelly wasn't as thrilled. Diverting her eyes from the massive crowd that jammed itself in front of the Castle Providence, she focused instead on the plush, bright-red interior of the carriage. One of the dirty little secrets about herself, Kelly knew as she ran her hands over the cushions, was that as much as she loved the outdoors, she thrilled at the rare occasion to be pampered.

Just so long as it didn't become suffocating.

It was hard not to think of Brad as her eyes took in the interior. It was all so reminiscent of Brad's world – limousines, formal events, high society, the best of everything. King of New England? It made sense. Brad hadn't been so rich he could afford to buy whatever he wanted, but was well-enough off that he could fake it. "I don't have to be the richest man in Boston," he'd told her on more than one occasion, "just the richest investment banker." If only he'd spent as much time on their relationship as he did trying to impress other people. One of the trappings of wealth, Kelly believed, was that it didn't take long for something to be taken for granted.

Including girlfriends. Brad spent all his time on the hunt. He was a great guy to date while he was trying to win her over, but once he did ...

"Oh, Kelly, look," Samantha beamed. "They're starting the flogging."

Kelly glanced out across the crowd to see the man that supposedly abducted her standing at the top of the steps of the castle. His hands, bound together, were hoisted above her head by a winch. Behind him, a man in a black hood and silver armor, raised a whip and struck down hard on the abductor's back. "ONE!" the Captain of the Guard bellowed beside the administer.

Samantha giggled, Georgia gasped, and Kelly turned away. She felt guilty and hated herself for it. The man had abducted her, planned to do who knows what to her, and yet as she sat here in this luxurious carriage, she hated the viciousness of the state's retribution. *Of Brad's retribution.* What was wrong with jail time? And why wasn't there a trial?

Typical Brad. Everything had to be done at once and to the nth degree.

The cracking of the whip extended over the appreciative crowd and Kelly turned to look out the opposite window, where she found Frederic stealing a lingering glance at Samantha. "What the hell was with these two?" she wondered. Turning her attention to their other traveling companions, she noted that one of the princes rode behind the ranger, his eyes watching the public beating. The other two rode up front, their horses responsible for pulling the carriage. Kelly could hear them arguing over the map the King had given them, trying to figure out how to read it. She hoped they'd figure it out soon; the map held their course to Kent Harbor.

"At some point," Kelly told herself, her head once again starting to throb, "I'll have to learn their names."

For now, though, the naturalist painter/photographer-turned-princess sank back into the large cushions of her seat and closed her eyes, wanting to be at Kent Harbor as soon as possible.

And wishing, honestly truly wishing, that Austin was there to greet her.

Above the crowd, back in his high-perch, Brad Regent's eyes looked not at the public beating of his friend (though he had noted that someone had already disobeyed him; it was to be a *flogging*, not a whipping), but at the carriage that carried Kelly Reed away from him, and the ranger that rode beside the carriage. The ranger that had mucked up Brad's plan, that had run Jim Catlin through with a sword, that had caused all of this to go public.

For that, Frederic Kornell would have to pay. Brad didn't do it out of malice; he did it out of a business-honed practicality. Catlin would want revenge, so Brad would give it to him to keep him happy, the way he'd given a younger associate a corner office to make up for slashing the woman's salary. Brad didn't hate Kornell, but Catlin did, and Catlin was a valued business associate, and Catlin was being whipped right now because of Kornell's interference.

As he watched the carriage make its way through the city streets, Brad was glad to see it go. He was glad to see Kelly moving away from him, out of his life. It all seemed to be too much of a hassle right now. He'd keep tabs on her, and, when the time was right, steal her back from Austin, but right now she was a distraction he didn't need.

"TEN!"

Captain O'Malley's voice rang out across the crowd, bringing Brad's attention back to the scene below him. Catlin's back was raw with blood, and he hung, proud but limp, in his bonds.

At least this was over, the King of New England sighed to himself. Once he saw Catlin one last time, Regent could be done with Kelly, done with the abduction plot, done with Providence.

Or so he hoped. There was still the matter of the four princes he'd foolishly brought into this abduction plot. He hoped – he *sincerely* hoped – O'Malley paid them off. Whatever amount they were asking for was well worth paying.

"Did you feed him the line?" Mary Mathers asked.

Captain Crumb nodded. "You disagree?"

"It's not the C.O.'s place to disagree."

"Damn straight." Pause. "But …?"

"Can he be trusted?"

Crumb raised a pair of binoculars to his eyes, stared hard back at the *Cottonmather*. "It's not about trust. It's about expectations. What you need to understand, Mathers, is that the angels don't want us to play pirates. They want us to *be* pirates."

"Yeah," she said impatiently, "and you think they're yanking our chain."

"What I think," Crumb answered, dropping the binoculars, "is that the angels are keeping things from us. Makes me want to know not just what, but *why*. That parrot's the key."

Mathers nodded. "Yeah, but you never explained why."

"The wound at its neck," Crumb explained slowly. "Whatever made that wound, it wasn't any weapon I've ever seen. Like I told McNamara, I'm a military man. I've been looking for threats for over fifty years. There's a threat here of some kind. We just need to ferret it out."

"So why Austin? Just because it's his parrot?"

"No," Crumb said, looking to the door to his quarters to see a shaken Austin emerge. "Because of expectations. Can't you smell it on him?" he asked, turning to the younger woman. "He's looking for an opportunity to play hero."

Mathers cocked her head. "Doesn't look like a hero. Kinda scrawny."

Crumb wouldn't budge. "If there's one thing to keep in mind in this New World, Mathers, it's that looks don't mean shit."

King Regent entered the cell of Jim Catlin, signaling the guards to leave them alone. Brad had spent the last twenty minutes steeling himself for this encounter. This wasn't friendship; this was business. Catlin lay on his stomach, eyes facing away from the door, his back cut and raw from the whip. "You look like shit," Brad said without humor.

"Fuck you too, buddy."

Brad walked around to Catlin's front and showed him an obviously full hockey bag.

"That my equipment?" the former (and hopefully, future) hockey player asked.

"In a manner of speaking," the King said.

"I ain't in the mood for games."

Brad dropped the bag to the floor, where it landed with a loud thud. "Funny thing for an athlete to say." Without waiting for a response, the King of New England reached into his suit coat and removed a map. "This is the route I've ordered Kelly's group to take to Kent Harbor. You know everywhere they'll be. What you decide to do – or not do – is up to you."

Catlin motioned to his bloody back. "And I'm supposed to believe you'll let me kill Kornell without getting punished?"

Brad nodded, kicking the hockey bag. "Tell me why you never wanted to play goalie?"

Catlin let out a humorless chuckle. "'Cause no one knows what the goalie looks like. Hard to get laid when the chickies don't know who you are."

"That's the way to think, Catlin," the King said. "Good luck."

Down the hall, Captain O'Malley entered the small cell that held the four other princes involved in the abduction and harassment of Kelly Reed. O'Malley also carried a hockey bag; his was full of gold coin. King Regent had ordered O'Malley to pay these men off to shut them up.

O'Malley knew that anyone low enough to have their silence bought was a second dollar figure away from having it bought back.

The Captain dropped the hockey bag on the floor and unzipped it, revealing the gold coin beneath. Without looking at the four princes, he announced, "Whatever you can carry is yours, boys. Dig in."

O'Malley stepped back as the princess greedily stepped forward. While their attention was locked on the gold, O'Malley's attention was locked on them. None of them saw the Captain of the Guard's hand move to the hilt of his sword. Had they, they surely would've expected O'Malley to remove the sword and attack them with it. O'Malley would've, for a moment, disappointed them.

His hand slid past the hilt of the sword and to the small of his back, where his police-issued handgun waited, taped to his armor. O'Malley freed the gun, brought it around, and made certain that the four princes never spoke to anyone about the King's abduction plot.

"That," he thought, looking down at the four spasming bodies, "is how you guarantee silence."

King or no King, Wallace O'Malley wasn't about to let Brad Regent fuck up the New World for him.

Austin McNamara stood on the deck of the Puritan and looked, for the final time, at the *Plymouth Rock*. He would have stood and watched the *Cottonmather* rip the *Rock* to shreds all afternoon and long into the night, the remnants of his Catholic guilt rooting him to the deck.

He was spared, however, by one simple, incontrovertible fact: the *Plymouth Rock* no longer existed. Austin watched, his eyes barely able to make out the sight at this distance, as the *Rock*'s main mast sank beneath the waters of the Atlantic Ocean.

In his heart, Austin knew Captain Crumb was right. The *Cottonmather* was coming for them.

Chapter Seven
Nemesis Hunting

The three pirate ships of Port Gloucester, Massachusetts were identical in their construction. The overall length of the *Puritan*, *Cottonmather*, and *Plymouth Rock* was just over ninety-five feet, with a deck-length of sixty-five feet, and a rigging height of seventy feet. Three masts bore three large sails, and each schooner could reach a top speed of ten knots under ideal conditions. The wooden vessels were designed to hold crews of seventy-five, though each had roughly a hundred pirates to begin life in the New World.

Berathon was the Angel in Charge of Pirates and knew the intimate details of every pirate ship in the world. He knew the schooners of the North Atlantic, the Galleons of Spain, the sloops favored in the Caribbean and southeastern United States, the Mediterranean Brigantines, and the junks of the Pacific nations. He knew the positives and negatives of the Merchant Carriers, the Dutch Fleuts, Frigates, Corvettes, and the East Indiamen. He knew the European Naval ships that would come after the pirate vessels: Snow, Sloop, and Man O' War. The angels were, after all, the first architects, and had enormous pride in their work.

If one could view both the alabaster face of Berathon – floating high above the Atlantic Ocean, just off the coast of Massachusetts as the bottom of the sun touched the horizon – and sight below him - the sinking of one of his ships, the *Plymouth Rock* – one could not be blamed for assuming that it was the *Rock*'s demise that caused the stern, grim visage that clouded the angel's face.

One would be wrong.

Berathon cared little for physical possessions. The *Rock* had been destroyed by the *Cottonmather*, after all – one of his creations destroying another caused pride and grief to cancel the other out.

Nor was he able to muster any grief for the eighty-seven who had already died in the first battle between pirate ships in the New World. With Heaven as a reward, what was there to grieve about? And for those who had Hell in their future, Berathon had nothing but contempt. To grieve for them was to grieve for Lucifer himself.

No, it was not the destruction nor the deaths that caused Berathon to look down on the waters of the Atlantic Ocean with a concern. Berathon had been in a foul mood since his talk with Enimon the other night, where his fellow angel had told him there were rumors circling that God's letter was a forgery. The thought was almost too large to comprehend. The power needed to complete such a forged document was incalculable; not even Lucifer, Berathon believed, would undertake such a plan. *Unless ...*

The angel shuddered, not wanting to complete the thought, but his mind was not listening to his heart.

... Unless God isn't coming back.

There it was. For days, Berathon had kept his mind from formulating that thought, but his mental walls of defense had finally fallen. God had been missing for a few centuries, ever since the incident with the rock that had caused him to leave Heaven and walk amongst his creations. When He left, He left with only a letter. When He sent word to reorganize the world, again His method of communication was a letter. If the recent letter was a forgery, the implications were staggering, including the possibility that the *first letter* was a forgery as well. If that was true ...

The angels, Berathon knew, needed to find God. *If only it were possible ...*

God had modified his original design of the angels in such a way that they could not find Him if He didn't want them to find Him. In one of the relatively few truths to be found in the Bible (Berathon viewed the New Testament the way Batman fans viewed the Joel Schumacher films), Earth was, actually, built in seven days. The fallacy, of course, was that God built the world, when really it was the angels that had done most of the grunt work. Which was fine, of course; Berathon and the vast majority of the angels were honored to serve the Lord.

Too honored, perhaps, since the angels hounded God repeatedly to make certain everything was created exactly as God imagined it. God needed a break, and re-engineered the angels so they couldn't see Him so long as He didn't want to be seen. Berathon had always wondered about the re-engineering. Couldn't God just disappear if He wanted to? Why the need to actually re-engineer the angels' physiologies?

The angel shook his head as his eyes spotted movement on the deck of the *Puritan*. God was a different deity in the old days. Berathon wondered how many Christians had ever read the Old Testament and noted that God was not only far from omniscient, but prone to incredible bouts of anger and depression.

Berathon pushed the thoughts aside as his target sauntered across the deck of the Puritan.

It was time Berathon had a talk with Austin McNamara about the current whereabouts of a certain parrot.

"What pirate story, exactly, was the one where they were eating chicken parm?" Carl Yesek asked pleasantly as his fork speared his plate's chicken and his knife began to slice into its surface. Austin, Teddy, and Hector smiled as they sat on the elevated aft deck of the *Puritan*, each with a plastic plate of spaghetti and chicken covered with a pepper and mushroom sauce and sprinkled heavily with parmesan cheese.

"*Treasure Island*, I think," Austin said, forcing a joke and chuckle through his already forced smile. The former Associate American Literature Professor was trying to keep the storm clouds that he felt gathering around him from his three friends. (*Friends? I've known them for what, two days? How well do I really know them? Can I actually call them friends?*) The New World had gotten off to a thoroughly rotten start when Austin was separated from his girlfriend, Kelly Reed. That, at least, had been manageable. Due to their jobs and professional obligations, they were often separated for days at a time, sometimes even as much as a week. As much as he loved her, as much as he wanted to be with her, the aching loss hadn't set in yet. Wouldn't, he believed, for another few days. Everything else … that's what was bothering him. He could accept, as some cruel twisted fate (he was a Red Sox fan, after all, so dealing with cruel twists of fate was not uncommon to him) that his girlfriend's ex, Brad Regent, was now King of New England. *Why not?* he figured. If he could suddenly be a pirate, why not have a King of New England?

Austin stole a glance behind them, back out across the waters to where the *Cottonmather* followed in their wake, feeling trapped between the proverbial rock and a hard place. The *Cottonmather* was the rock that was bothering him. Austin and his three friends had played a prank on the *Cottonmather*, painting rude sayings on its hull. It was meant to embarrass, to get a laugh. In response, the *Cottonmather* had destroyed the *Plymouth Rock*, sinking the moored ship right at the Port Gloucester docks and killing God knew how many of its crew. Austin turned back towards his friends, looking out over the deck of the *Puritan* towards the quarters of Captain Crumb - the hard place that was holding him here, waiting for the *Cottonmather* to come and smash him. Austin's mind was troubled greatly by his conversation this afternoon with Crumb. Crumb believed the angels weren't acting as benignly as they let on; that the angels were using the New World to test humanity, but for what ultimate purpose he didn't know.

Bad words float through the clouds of heaven.

The words Mollug, Austin's injured parrot, repeated hysterically. Austin had left Mollog, restrained and cloaked, in Crumb's quarters four hours ago, yet his mind was still in that room, hearing that phrase repeated in the parrot's wild squawking over and over and over.

"*Treasure Island?*" Hector asked. "I hate that movie. They made us watch it in third grade one day when we got stuck in school because of a snowstorm." Hector chewed on a piece of chicken. "Now, *Pirates of the Caribbean...*" He flashed a thumbs-up sign. "That's a good movie. I'd rescue that chick any time."

Carl nodded, chewing thoughtfully. "It's not a bad movie, but I found it to be a bit ridiculous. Pirates shouldn't be fearless and fun, they should be fearless and dangerously desperate."

Austin twirled spaghetti with his fork. "What about you, Teddy?" he asked the large man. "Got a favorite pirate movie?"

Teddy smiled, "*Cutthroat Island.*"

The other three looked at him blankly.

"Never heard of it," Carl admitted.

"Me neither," Hector shrugged.

Austin cocked his head to the side, thinking. "Is that the Matt Modine movie?"

Teddy grinned, "You bet. You haven't lived until you've dreamt of being pirated by Geena Davis."

The four men settled into a relaxed conversation, finally coming out of the fog the day had placed them in. Austin believed their relaxation had something to do with the food, but also something to do with the setting sun. The night blocked the *Cottonmather* from their view and while Austin expected their thoughts would turn nervous again tomorrow if the *Cottonmather* was still there, for now, it was out of sight and out of mind. He wished he could talk to his three friends about his conversation with Crumb, but Crumb had explicitly forbidden it. Austin hated that he'd been dragged into this … what, this "mystery" … "conspiracy" … by their Captain.

"How's your parrot?" Hector asked. "Can't believe the other two still haven't come back."

Austin gave his spaghetti an extra few bites, thinking of how to phrase his answer. "Mollug's fine," he lied.

"If he's fine," Teddy asked, "why's he being kept in Crumb's quarters?"

"I mean, he's injured," Austin added quickly, "but he's recovering."

A commanding voice interrupted them. "Your parrot could be replaced."

Their eyes turned upwards to see Berathon floating down to them, his wings blotting out the full moon and casting an ominous shadow across their faces. Austin felt his stomach tighten as the angel landed beside them on the deck. "I could have a new one here for you in the morning," Berathon said to Austin.

"Um, no thanks," Austin said, gulping down the food in his mouth, thinking of Crumb's warning about the angels. "Mollug should recover."

Berathon held Austin's gaze for a second too long, before shrugging. "The parrots," he announced to the other three, "have been, on the whole, a tremendous disappointment. Two of you are missing parrots, too, I understand. Is that correct?" He didn't offer to bring them replacements.

Teddy interrupted, "Why don't you just fix Mollug?"

Berathon turned his head haughtily towards Teddy. "Excuse me?"

Teddy wiped his mouth with the back of his hand and set his empty plate down. Austin rolled his eyes as his stomach sank; Teddy was the kind of person who just seemed to get off challenging authority. "You heard me," Teddy continued. "Why don't you just fix Mollug instead of replacing him?"

Good question, Austin couldn't help thinking.

Berathon's face tightened, then relaxed. "The world does not work that way. We cannot simply fix things with our power. Humanity must solve its own problems."

"But you'll replace it?" Teddy asked, enjoying poking at the angel.

"Replacing it is within our charge," Berathon replied, his voice becoming cool. "Fixing it is not."

Austin could feel, rather than see, the angel's agitation, and decided he didn't want Teddy pushing Berathon any further. Not after Crumb's pondering that the *Cottonmather* was crewed by a band of criminals that were coming to destroy the *Puritan*. Austin figured the best place to be with the angels was any place but their bad side. "That's okay, Berathon," he added quickly, shooting Teddy a look that told the large man to let it all drop. "I'll keep Mollug. I've become rather attached to him." Austin waited for the angel's response, but when Berathon had turned the focus of his gaze from Teddy to him, the angel still remained silent. "Er," Austin stumbled, hating the silence, "what did you mean when you said the parrots were a disappointment?"

A look of disgust flashed across the angel's face. "Talking animals," he groused. "Ridiculous. Let me state for the record that if it were up to me, Walt Disney would be rotting in the Sixth Level of Hell."

"Are you being literal?" Austin asked. "Are there really nine levels-"

Berathon shot Austin a disgusted look. "Oh. That's right. You're a *literature* professor." Berathon made the word sound dirty. "Angels aren't always literal, Mr. McNamara. You would do well to-"

The voice of Captain Crumb cut across the deck, drawing all the attention aboard the *Puritan* to him.

"Something I can do for you, Berathon?"

The angel turned, contempt written across his face. "There is. Assemble your crew. There is a truth to be revealed this eve."

Jim Catlin couldn't sleep. His back ached, his flesh torn apart by the stinging whip. Each slicing of the flesh was punishment for … what exactly? Getting caught? Hell, Catlin reasoned, all he was doing was following orders. It wasn't his fault that ranger, Frederic Kornell, witnessed what happened. It was Kornell's, or the cops, but Regent couldn't punish Kornell because then the King's plan would come out and everyone would know the King of New England's first act was to come up with some idiot plot to impress a girl that wasn't, in Catlin's mind, worth impressing.

Kelly Reed. Fucking Kelly Reed. She'd never been anything but a pain in everyone's ass. Let McNamara have her, for all Catlin cared.

The door to his cell clanged open, but Catlin could only half-heartedly turn around. He was still on his stomach and every turn, no matter how slight, caused the wounds to offer up a fresh flow of blood. Expecting dinner – he hadn't eaten all day – he was disappointed to see that it was the Captain of the Guard, Something O'Malley, dressed up like a tin can soldier and carrying a small black duffel bag.

"Get up," O'Malley ordered.

"Fuck off," Catlin shot back, in no mood to take orders from Brad's guard dog. Catlin turned away, letting his wounded back settle into its relaxed position. It took less than two heartbeats to realize turning your back on Something O'Malley was an unwise move.

O'Malley tossed the duffel bag across the stone walled cell, letting it drop with a smack onto Catlin's back.

"Fuck!" Catlin roared, spinning around and off the bed, leaping to his feet. He came up quick, fists first, ready to return the pain to O'Malley.

Before his eyes had even focused through the pain to turn the three blurred images of O'Malley into one coherent image, he caught O'Malley's left fist across the jaw. He spun hard, dropping with a thud onto his cot.

Phrases like, "Get up and I'll knock yer ass out," and "Try it again tough guy and your mouth will look like yer back," shot through O'Malley's mind, but he kept his mouth shut. Too many cops thought they were continuously on a cop show or in a movie and couldn't wait to talk tough when they had some helpless perp in their sights. O'Malley wasn't into wasting words, didn't particularly care to hear his own voice. Threats just delayed the inevitable, made the victim's anger boil just beneath the surface. That was the kind of anger that fed on itself, that plotted revenge, and waited for its opportunity to strike back.

If Catlin got up, O'Malley would knock him back down. Speak with the fist, not with the mouth, and let the victim determine for himself when he'd had enough.

Catlin wiped the blood from his mouth and stayed seated on his cot. He'd gotten his ass kicked once today and saw no need to repeat the beating. "What do you want?" he groused.

"I want you gone," O'Malley replied with indifference.

"Brad said to stay here until I was healed."

O'Malley raised an eyebrow. "You don't want to get started hunting down the ranger?"

Catlin grimaced. "Maybe you didn't see me get whipped this afternoon."

O'Malley wasn't impressed. "Maybe you don't really want to get Kornell."

"Fuck you," Catlin spat.

"You look in the hockey bag, yet?" O'Malley asked, nodding to the large equipment bag that the King had brought his friend. Catlin shook his head. "It's a suit of armor. Black. Sword included."

Catlin looked sideways at the former cop. "Are you fucking kidding? Brad expects me to wear a suit of armor?" The former pro hockey player looked O'Malley's silver armor up and down. "No fucking way."

O'Malley nodded. then softened his tone. "Hard to move in armor until you get your legs. You want revenge, plain and simple, right? You're not looking to wear the armor long term?"

Catlin shook his head. "I just want to kill Kornell, then I want to play hockey."

O'Malley nodded, using techniques learned interviewing suspects and witnesses to bring Catlin to his side. "That's what I thought. I told Brad the armor was a bad idea," O'Malley lied. The Captain of the Guard nodded to the duffel bag that lay on its side on the cot. "In there's all you need. Dark clothes. Kevlar vest. Two Glock 17s. Twenty ammo clips. Black mask. Cell phone. Take the map from the hockey bag, then put the rest of the bag in the back."

"In the back of what?"

"Your new vehicle."

"Vehicle? You mean I don't have to ride a horse?"

O'Malley shook his head. "There's only a limited supply of gas, so we might as well use it while we can."

"Thank God. I hate fucking horses." Catlin was warming to the Captain. "What kind of vehicle is it?"

"Hummer. I've had my men confiscate thirty cars and park them out behind the horse stables, in the abandoned McDonald's parking lot. Keys are in the duffel bag. The King gave you a map of the route he ordered Kornell to take." O'Malley eyed Regent's friend carefully, hating that the King had left it to someone else to tie up this loose end. That was O'Malley's job. "When the ranger is disposed of, call me on the cell phone. Numbers programmed in." O'Malley purposely failed to mention that the number Catlin would call was the number of Kelly Reed's confiscated cell phone. Even in the New World, O'Malley saw the value in protecting one's ass.

The conversation made Catlin's back feel a hell of a lot better.

"I've got a doctor coming to wrap your wounds," O'Malley said plainly. "You'll need to rest when you're done, but if you leave within the hour, you can catch them on the main road."

"Main road? What road is that?"

"I-95."

Catlin couldn't believe it. "You sent them up 95? In a horse and carriage?"

O'Malley nodded, allowed himself a small grin. "Feel like getting started?"

"Get that fucking doctor in here. Now. Kornell's dead by midnight."

Kelly Reed slumped on her plush red seat inside the large, black, horse-drawn carriage. The sun was going down and a deep need for sleep was beginning to creep up on her. Her hangover had never fully left, and the click-clacking of the horses' hooves on the highway pavement kept a dull throbbing ever-present in her head. Of course, possibly even more aggravating than the horses' hooves was the incessant prattling of her two traveling companions – Samantha Dixon and Georgia Mulrooney. She'd asked Kornell twice if they could pull over and get some aspirin, but he had rebuked her on both occasions. "I'll send one of the princes to get you some later, when we've stopped for the night," he'd told her.

Unfortunately for Kelly, Kornell was in no more a hurry to stop for the night than he was to relieve her headache.

Jim Catlin was not a thinker, yet there was something about the scene that struck him as so odd that it was worth thirty seconds of contemplation. He was standing in a McDonald's parking lot, full of confiscated cars, dressed in a solid-black military uniform, behind a medieval castle. His friend was the King. This afternoon, he'd been publicly beaten.

At this moment he was opening the door of a brand new, black hummer, ready to track down and kill someone.

And it was all possible because of the angels. The freakin' angels.

For the first time in his life, Jim Catlin wondered if maybe he should've paid closer attention at Catholic school.

Austin stood near the portside railing as the crew of the *Puritan* crowded onto the deck, facing the elevated aft platform where Berathon stood between Captain Crumb and Commanding Officer Mary Mathers. He felt like bad news was coming. It was the angel that addressed them, which made his feeling grow even worse.

"I sense an unease in you," Berathon addressed them from above. "No doubt the cause of this malaise is the *Cottonmather*'s destruction of the *Plymouth Rock*." Berathon let a slow murmur work its way through the crowd as the crew nodded and mumbled their agreement. "To this I can say but one thing." Pause. "What did you expect?" A louder murmur, a dangerous mix of anger and surprise rolled through the 107-man crew. "You are pirates, after all, and you must take the ill with the pleasant. We have not freed you from consequence in the New World, merely allowed you to assume the role you desired as children."

The murmuring grew louder and a few newly-turned pirates shouted a few complaints – "We didn't ask for this!," "Who are you to do this?," "Fucking aliens, man! Go back to space you freak!" – when Berathon's head was turned the other way. The angel let the insults roll up over the deck at him for a half-minute, then raised his hands, bringing the murmuring down below the sound of the hull slicing through the waters of the Atlantic Ocean.

"You take our gift and throw it back at us?" he asked with only a hint of anger in his airy voice. Off to the side, Austin thought the voice contained disappointment, not anger, but he didn't know how many of his fellow crewmen would hear the angel's words in that tone. Berathon continued, his voice imploring rather than scolding, "You have been given the greatest opportunity since Adam and Eve. You have your dream handed to you, and yet you complain that it is not good enough." Berathon looked heavenward, saying a silent prayer to calm himself before turning back to the crew. "Forgive me. It is not my intent to anger or frighten you. I have come to reassure you."

"Bullshit," Teddy Levenson whispered beside Austin.

"Shhh," Austin scolded him. "I want to hear this."

Berathon announced, "While it is important that you realize we have not freed you from consequence and obligation, I fear that today's actions by the *Cottonmather* – dictated, as they were, by the actions of four of your own – have left you with an incomplete view of piracy. I cannot read your minds, but as an angel I can read your hearts, and I sense the confusion and anger. I sense that a good number of you are doubting the path your childhood dream has now placed you on. This is not wise. Behind you, the *Cottonmather* stalks you as a hunter stalks its prey. Mark my words, the *Cottonmather* is coming for you, to do to you what it did to the Plymouth Rock."

So much for not scaring us. Austin sighed.

"You are not ready to face them," Berathon continued. "You do not yet know what it means to be pirates. You need to learn."

"How?" Teddy shouted. He pointed to the center mast, "We don't even have a jolly roger flying yet!"

Berathon turned his golden eyes to the largest pirate aboard the ship. "You are correct, Mr. Levenson, and if you'd listen but a moment, I will tell you how to rectify that."

He'd taken to calling himself "Stocky Samuel" because, it seemed to him, any pirate worth his own shit had a nickname. Blackbeard. Bluebeard. Captain Jack Sparrow. The sun had almost fallen completely below the horizon. It was the kind of sight, made all the more possible to Samuel because of where he stood, on barrel in the forward deck of his ship, that people said was beautiful.

Samuel stared hard at the horizon for several minutes, searching for what was beautiful about it, but was left unimpressed. Just looked like the sun going down – a sight he'd seen a thousand times.

No, the sight that was, to Samuel, truly beautiful, was the distant image, tracking northeast, of the *Puritan*. Austin and his three buddies might have fooled Captain Lazarus (*I hate to admit it, but that's a damn good pirate name*), but they hadn't fooled Sam. Samuel's original problem had been with Hector, but he could see that Hector wasn't anything more than a sidekick. Muscle to the softer leader, Austin.

Not that destroying the *Plymouth Rock* wasn't fun, of course, just that it delayed Sam's vengeance. Samuel never liked his attention diverted. It was his single-mindedness that had helped him amass a small fortune from his petty thievery.

Two days before the angels came, he'd fenced a larger-than-expected haul. Twenty-thousand dollars. More money than he'd ever had. And now ... he didn't know if it was worthless or not, but he was damn sure the jewelry he'd stolen and sold was worth more in the New World than the paper bills he'd taken in exchange.

He looked out across the waters, following the wake of the *Puritan*. It wasn't until after the *Rock* had sunk that Captain Lazarus listened to Samuel's assertions that the *Puritan* was to blame.

"Well, then," Lazarus had said, a sparkle in his fifty-something eyes, "I guess we'll have to go get them next. Set a course!"

So they did.

"I'm coming," Samuel grumbled to himself, his eyes locked on the *Puritan*, and as he spoke an idea popped into his mind. He turned quickly, looking over the crew, his eyes searching for a parrot.

Berathon held the attention of every man and parrot aboard the *Puritan*. They looked up at him, in the costume of pirates, but without the feel of pirates. Their faces were mostly soft, slightly rounded, or alternately too young or old. They were, on the whole, too clean-shaven. They didn't yet smell foul, though many, accustomed to showering every morning, felt as if they were dirty. They would soon learn, Berathon knew, but he wondered, for not the first time, how fair the Reorganization of the Old World into the New World was for humanity. They had no training, no real warning. How would the angels react if they awoke tomorrow and found themselves humans? Was "pirate" any more foreign or shocking a concept than "angel" to humanity?

"As you will remember," he began, "in time you will all have the opportunity to turn to whatever life you so choose." What he didn't tell them was that the angels had added that provision on their own, as a safeguard against a rebellious humanity. "You must spend a few days as pirates, however, long enough that you gain the full experience of what it means to be a pirate, so that you may make an informed decision. You have experienced, if only at a distance, one of the primary horrors that you will face as a pirate – a battle at sea. You now know that death is possible.

"Now ... now you must face a challenge of the pirates so that you may taste the thrilling joy that piracy can bring a person."

Berathon reached to his belt and removed a large scroll. He tossed it into the air, where it seemed to magically unroll. As all eyes were on the scroll, Berathon reached behind him to steal the large knife off of Crumb, then hurled the blade at the map. The hunter's knife caught the map in mid-air and drove it twenty feet through the air to imbed itself into the mast at center deck.

"A treasure map," Berathon announced. "Find the treasure and you'll find your Jolly Roger."

Captain Crumb strode forward. "McNamara, tell us where we're headed."

Austin gave the Captain a "Why me?" look, but held his tongue. The crowd parted to let him move from his standing spot at the portside railing to the center mast. Austin felt the eyes of the crew on him, but kept his gaze forward, not wanting to know what their eyes held for him. Were they expectant? Afraid? Angry ... and at whom? Berathon? The Captain? God? Him? Austin brushed the speculation aside as he came upon the map.

The treasure map was large, bigger than he'd expected, maybe a good two feet long and foot-and-a-half wide. The map itself was made of what looked like thick parchment, and hand-drawn with exacting detail in a green ink.

"Well?" Crumb asked, eager and demanding.

"It's a map of the New England coast," Austin replied, looking at it. "From Rhode Island straight up to Maine."

"And our goal?"

Austin noted that their destination was marked, as he had assumed it would be, with a big, bright red "X." He turned from the map, looking over the crew and up to the elevated aft deck where the Captain, Berathon, and Mary Mathers stood waiting. "New Hampshire," he said confidently. "The town of Durham, near the border with Maine."

Berathon's gold eyes seemed to blaze into his very soul. "Is your target the entire town, Mr. McNamara?"

Austin turned back, looking closer at the "X" and noting the thin tower drawn next to it. "No," he said, turning again, relating the inscription he had read under the tower, "our target is the Ivory Tower of Potato Johnson, the wealthiest man in the world."

Jim Catlin slowed the Hummer down to a cruising speed of 40 mph. O'Malley had told him he should come upon the carriage at around 10 p.m. He checked the clock on the Hummer's dash and saw that it read 9:54. He felt calm and it unnerved him slightly. Catlin had the same feeling wash over him that he had at the end of blowout hockey games, when he knew the coach would put him in just to get in a fight with the other team's goon. It was almost always in the last minute, but scoring in hockey rarely came all that rapidly, so with about ten minutes to go, Catlin would start to focus on the opponent. There was rarely any confusion about whom he'd be fighting – since it was almost always someone he'd fought with before. He let everything except his opponent fade away: the crowd, the score, the game, his teammates ... only his coach's voice could break through the tunnel vision of remembrance as Catlin went through a mental catalogue of his opponent's fighting techniques, the injury report, the league gossip ... anything that he could use to get an edge in the fight.

That's what he was doing now, only this time he intended to kill his target, not beat them to within an inch of death.

At his side was the dossier Captain O'Malley had given him on Frederic Kornell. Spent a lot of money on porn - *Maybe I'll rob his apartment when this is over* – and Star Wars. Fucking geek.

Taking his hands off the wheel, Catlin reached for the black ski mask and pulled it over his head. Next came the black goggles. These he slung over his head and let hang around his neck. He'd put them on when the time to fight came.

Ready for action, he depressed the accelerator.

Potato Johnson looked at the handful of men, women, and children who stood before him, all of them transients that had taken up residence in the nearby hills.

"Have you gotten the items I desired?" he asked the man who passed for their leader.

"We have," the man – father to three motherless children – answered, motioning to a small pickup truck. "All of the Twinkies we could find. About three hundred boxes."

"Well done," Potato replied, giddy at the notion that these people had come begging to him for help. Not that was disappointed; he figured it was only a matter of time before the transients came to steal his gold and jewels. The quicker he could draw them to his side, the better. "You have kept your part of the bargain, and I will keep mine. You may sleep on the ground by the tower. I trust you have taken camping equipment from the stores?" The leader nodded. "Excellent. You may sleep here and I will provide for you. The nights are still warm so there should be no problem sleeping outdoors. When it turns cold, if you have kept up your end of our arrangement, I will allow you to sleep in the guest quarters. In return, you will assist me in building fortifications around the Ivory Tower and protect me should your fellow transients try to steal from us."

Potato smiled, "I believe this is going to be the beginning of a very fruitful relationship. Strength, as they say, in numbers."

Not ten miles ahead of Catlin's Hummer, Frederic Kornell began to get an uneasy feeling in the pit of his stomach. Since the sun had gone down the confidence he'd gained from his threesome last night had begun to erode. He glanced inside the carriage to the two women who were, at this moment, at the center of his universe. On one side, sleeping restlessly, was Kelly Reed, the object of his current crush, the kind of woman he'd always dreamt of marrying. She was the perfect girl who could turn the rogue monogamous. (Because in all of Frederic's daydreams, he'd never settled down before having lots and lots of meaningless sex. He wondered, from time to time, which of the two scenarios—crazy sex or solid marriage—was more improbable for a lumpy janitor.) Across the carriage from her sat the object of his current lust, Samantha Dixon, a fiery Southern redhead, and one member of the previous night's threesome. The manipulative one of the two, Frederic recalled. (And he'd spent much of the day recalling everything that had happened last night.)

"Man, when are we going to stop?"

Frederic turned away from the women to one of the other three princes that rode with them. The other two sat atop the carriage, their horses pulling the ornate vehicle forward towards their ultimate destination – Kent Harbor, Maine.

"Soon," Frederic replied, wishing he'd exited the highway at the last stop to find lodging. "Next sign of lodging, we'll stop."

"Are there even going to be any hotels open?" the young prince asked from his horse. Frederic had asked – and forgotten – the young man's name three times already and didn't want to go through it again. He was among the youngest people he'd seen in the New World, so far, young enough to still be in high school. As for the other two princes, well, as Kelly had remarked to him earlier, "I'll learn their names eventually, I suppose, but for now it's the Young Prince, the Blonde Prince, and the Normon-Osborn-Haired Prince."

"I mean," the Young Prince continued, "I don't think a lot of people dreamt of running hotels, you know?"

"The King assured me the rooms were on an honor system," Frederic explained. "First come, first serve. All doors lock from the inside only."

"Sweet," the Young Prince gushed. "Can we get a room with a hot tub?" He nodded back to the carriage. "You can have the old one; I'll take the other two. The redhead kinda looks like Linds-"

"Silence!" Kornell snapped as he jerked his horse around. *What was that sound?*

"What?" the Young Prince asked.

Frederic didn't respond to the Prince; his reply was for the two princes driving the carriage. "Get the carriage off the road!" he ordered. *It's a car! Gotta be, and coming fast!* Frederic's breathing quickened.

"What?" the Blonde Prince shouted back. "Get it off the road? Why?"

"Do it!" Frederic hissed, reaching for his sword. Inside his gloves, his hands were already wet, as if they oozed sweat instantaneously.

"We can't," the Blonde Prince spat back. "There's a guard rail here."

Frederic wheeled his horse around, his face stone cold. "Get to the center!" he ordered, his voice as harsh as he could make it. He fought to keep the panic down, but he knew he was failing. There was no reason to assume what was coming was dangerous, but if he could get the carriage off the road and into the grassy, concaved center between the divided highway, he wouldn't have to worry about an accident. "Go on!" shouted again when he saw the hesitation.

Samantha stuck her head out of the carriage long enough to ask, "What's going on out there?"

The approaching vehicle was close enough now for the two princes riding on the carriage to hear its approach. Looking back down the highway there was a slight bend off to the right, hidden from view by a cluster of trees. Frederic and the Young Prince's eyes were locked on the bend as the carriage moved, too slowly, to the safety of the center. The appearance of headlights coincided with a chill wrapping itself around Frederic's spine.

Panicking, his eyes darted to the carriage, still straddling the highway. "Get on the median!" he yelled.

"They can't!" the Young Prince shouted back. "The horses won't get on the grass!"

"The horses won't get on the grass?" Frederic replied, disbelieving what he was hearing. "They're horses! Why won't they-?"

"I don't know!"

Frederic glanced down to the bend and saw a vehicle roar into view. From this distance he couldn't make out the car's identity, but he could tell it was big and moving fast. Some kind of SUV or large truck. "Find out!" he ordered, pushing his horse forward one second before he wondered just what the hell he was doing. He didn't really intend to stop a truck with a horse, did he? *No, but if I can get down far enough into the vehicle's headlights, if I can get into the driver's line of sight, he'll slow down.*

Won't he?

The headlights of the vehicle washed over Frederic and his horse, causing two reactions in the ranger. One, he became, for the second time this week, paralyzed by his own fear. Two, he was glad to note that his brain hadn't stopped working. He saw that the vehicle – a Hummer, he believed – wasn't slowing down. In fact, it seemed to be speeding up. To his left, he noted the guardrail – if he could get his horse to jump the rail, he'd be safe.

Or safer. But if he did …

His horse, Alfred, struggled forward against Frederic's hard hold on the reigns.

Frederic stole a glance behind him to see that the carriage still hadn't moved off the highway.

"I've got to wait until the last second," he told himself. He didn't know why the driver of the Hummer wanted to hit him, but he apparently did. "And why not?" his father's voice burst into his mind. "Look at what's around you – a dark road, no signs of life, no cops. Perfect place for a joyride hit and run! People love to kill, boy. I learned that in the army. Give a man a gun and promise him no retribution for his act and a man will kill without pause."

Frederic ignored his old man and did his best to steady Alfred in place. The Hummer was coming, boring down on him. "Wait, Alfred … wait," he pleaded, trying to gauge how much time he had. If he waited until the last second, the Hummer shouldn't have time to swerve back over and hit the carriage.

"It's off!"

"What?" his head snapped back towards the middle of the road.

"The carriage is in the clear!" the Young Prince shouted. "Get off the road."

Frederic turned to look to verify the Young Prince's words and when he did he relaxed his grip on Alfred. The horse was in no mood to wait another second, and took a powerful stride towards the guardrail, leaping over it and into the clear. In the saddle, Frederic jerked his head around this way and that, trying to see the road.

The carriage containing the princesses was, indeed, on the far grass. Just in time, too, he noted, feeling himself relax as the Hummer was almost upon them. Alfred backed up away from the road and Frederic let him, glad the danger had been avoided. The carriage was safe, he was safe-

But the Young Prince was not. The Young Prince sat upon his spooked horse, which bolted up the highway, away from the Hummer.

It was a noble, but failed attempt.

Frederic watched as the Hummer zoomed past his location, past the carriage's location, and ran down the horse that carried the Young Prince, smashing into the horse's hind legs with a sickening thud and sending horse and rider spilling across highway I-95.

"My God …"

The excitement over Berathon's words was wearing out, as the crew of the *Puritan* began to head below decks to turn in for the night. Austin stood alone on the elevated aft deck, his thoughts troubled. Berathon had come for Mollug. There was no denying that fact in Austin's mind. The angel had come to try and get Austin to give Mollug to him.

"Why wouldn't he just take the bird?" Austin asked himself, but he knew the answer. If Berathon had just taken Mollug, it would've raised suspicions. The young man looked back across the deck, to the small crowd still gathered at the treasure map.

"Are we ready to be pirates?" he asked aloud, to no one in particular.

He hadn't expected an answer, but one came anyway. "Beats the hell out of me."

Austin looked behind him to see who had spoken to him, but there was no one there.

"Over here, dummy."

Austin looked to the starboard rail and saw a parrot sitting with a parchment rolled to his leg. "The fat guy told me you were Austin McNamara. Is that true?" the parrot asked.

"It is."

"Good," the parrot replied. "I've got something for you. Take this parchment off my leg, would you?"

Austin did as the parrot asked, removing the string that held the small role of parchment in place. As soon as it was free, the parrot took off into the night sky. "Read it, lame ass, it's for you."

His fingers unrolled the parchment as his eyes searched the night sky for the parrot. "Full moon," he mumbled to himself. "Night for crazies." He looked down to the parchment and felt his blood freeze in his veins. The message was short and to the point, scrawled in black ink:

"I'M COMING. SLEEP WITH ONE EYE OPEN. – STOCKY SAMUEL"

Chapter Eight
The Morning Between Ranger and Pirate

Frederic Kornell rolled away from Samantha Dixon and out of bed. His whole body ached. Rising to his feet, he gingerly touched the left side of his rib cage. Nothing felt broken, but it didn't feel all that healthy, either.

A single, slender beam of sunlight streaked into the room, cutting the bed in half and drawing a line across Samantha's slim back. The light touched, ever-so-briefly, her flowing red hair. Frederic rubbed the back of his neck, his hand rubbing across a line of dried blood, causing the scabs to flake off his skin and float aimlessly towards the carpet.

He forced himself to turn away from the gorgeous college student and walked towards the bathroom. A long hot shower might help him find some perspective. There was a part of him that was ashamed at what he was doing with her. Frederic knew that the two nights he'd spent with Samantha were only possible because of the New World, because he'd been transformed into a "ruggedly handsome ranger" by the graces of the angels.

Entering the bathroom, he caught a glimpse of himself in the mirror and flinched. His face was bruised and swollen. No, he knew, there was no way a girl like Samantha Dixon would have had anything to do with a fat high school janitor who still considered his mother the greatest woman he'd ever met. Frederic turned away from his own image, knowing Samantha was sleeping with a lie.

"She is, isn't she?" he whispered to himself. "This," he looked down at his body, "isn't me, is it?" The ranger reached for the nozzle that sent hot water pouring into the small tub. Wasn't he still himself? Wasn't this image the image he'd always had? So was it still wrong to sleep with a woman who wanted him for physical reasons when he now had the physique she wanted? "So many questions," he mumbled.

"About what?"

Spinning quickly, Frederic saw Samantha standing naked in the doorway. "Uh, nothing," he offered weakly.

"Nothing?" she asked, yawning, stepping inside.

"What are you doing?" he asked, reaching for the shower curtain to cover his own nudity.

Rubbing the sleep out of her eyes, Samantha replied, "I gotta pee."

"Oh," Frederic replied, as if the thought that beautiful women ever had to do such a thing had never occurred to him. "Let me, er, step outside."

Samantha looked at him through her hair that had fallen in front of her eyes as she sat down. "A thoughtful ranger, even at ten in the morning."

"It's ten o'clock?" Frederic asked, panic jolting through him.

"Yep."

"Shit."

"I hope you're not giving me an order."

"What? Oh. No. God no. It's just … we've got to get going."

"Why?"

Frederic felt a storm cloud roll up inside him as memories of the previous night (pre-Samantha) came rushing in. "He could come back." Beat. "The abductor."

Samantha gave him a wry smile. "Not after what you did to him, stud."

Frederic swallowed. Everywhere he looked, a lie stared back at him.

"Where are you going?" Samantha asked as Frederic made his way to the door. "You don't have to leave." She glanced at the tub, filling with hot water. "Join me."

Frederic didn't look back as he shook his head. "Gotta check on Kelly and the Young Prince."

"Don't forget to put on some clothes!" Samantha called after him, wondering if she should start to consider Kelly Reed a rival for the ranger's affections, and what she'd do if Kelly became the competition.

In the outer room, Samantha could hear Frederic following orders and throwing on some clothes and hoped his eyes didn't spy what she'd hid under the bed.

Despite everything he'd been through in the past few days, Austin McNamara thought it was the most amazing morning he'd ever experienced. The sun was bright on the Atlantic Ocean this morning and the sea breeze was stiff and warm. Everywhere Austin looked there was the ocean. It was glorious. His back ached from sleeping on-deck, but the pain seemed to vanish a little more with every breath he took of the salt air. Combined with the excitement at what they were about to do – pirate a rich man's treasure – the entire crew seemed to be alive.

"If this was a movie," Austin thought with a grin, looking out at the bustle of activity, "the crew would burst into song any minute now."

The gloom that he felt was still inside him somewhere, lurking on the distant horizon of his thoughts, but Austin did his best to push them aside. There was something dark happening in the world, and, as unbelievable as it sounded, his parrot, Mollug, had something to do with it. Perhaps it was the situation with Mollug – the sheer unbelievability that a talking parrot held a key to unlocking something dark and mysterious – that helped Austin to feel better this morning, or perhaps it was that the *Cottonmather* was nowhere to be seen this morning.

For the first time in this New World, the morning sun brought with it a sense of hope instead of confusion or fear. Why not enjoy the New World? Wasn't this exactly the kind of adventure he'd always read about? The kind he'd spent hours dreaming about as a kid when he'd take a blank notebook and fill it with stories? And if there was something sinister in the plans of the angels, wasn't he glad that he was involved, at least peripherally, so that he could help determine the outcome?

Austin nodded. Yeah, he was, and while there was a somber quality to what was happening, would he really rather be sitting in a committee meeting instead of on board a pirate ship?

Not a chance.

"Someone's happy this morning."

Austin turned to see Captain Crumb's C.O., Mary Mathers, walking up the stepladder to the elevated aft deck. He shrugged, but the smile stayed on his face. "Perfect morning."

"You were raised in a fishing town, right?" Mathers asked.

"Yep," Austin nodded. "Port Gloucester born and raised. You?"

"Brattleboro, Vermont," Mathers replied easily. "Not an ocean in sight. So, what, this is some nostalgia-trip you're taking that's giving you that goofy grin?"

Austin shook his head. "Not really. Never woke up on a pirate ship."

Mathers laughed easily and Austin's image of her as Crumb's stone cold lackey began to fade – if only for a moment. "What do you make of everything?" she asked, her voice dropping low and serious. "Of this fool's quest Berathon has us undertaking?"

Austin gave a short sigh, determined not to be pulled into this conversation any deeper than he had to. "Dunno. I'm not really sure how we're supposed to figure out whatever it is Crumb's worried about. I mean, we're dealing with angels-"

"Aliens."

"Regardless," Austin continued, looking out over the waters. "All we can do is wait and see, right? There's no way to spy on the angels or aliens. Getting into a spaceship isn't much easier than getting into Heaven, is it?"

Mathers cocked her head to Austin. She looked at him quizzically for a few moments, then let a small smile creep across her face. *Crumb is right about you*, she thought, feeling a sudden connection to the man that she began to feel was more important than any of them realized. "It's going to be one hell of a day. By the way," she said, turning her body now to face him, "you've been put in charge of one of the raiding parties."

"What are you talking about?"

Mathers saw Austin wince and let her smile grow wider. "The raid on Potato Tower. Crumb's decided on a two-front attack. You're leading one of the raiding parties." She punched him gently on the side of his arm, "And I've got the other one. Be careful, McNamara," she teased, turning to walk away from him, "if you do to well I might think you're after my job."

Frederic didn't bother putting on a shirt as he exited his hotel room, needing to get out of the room to quiet a rising panic attack.

He took in several deep breaths as he placed his hands against the hallway wall. Lie upon lie. His running theme for the New World.

Samantha's words: "Not after what you did to him, stud."

Lies.

What does she know? Didn't she see what had happened?

Frederic made his way to the staircase; Kelly and the Young Prince were staying in a suite upstairs. The Young Prince had wanted a room with a Jacuzzi. The hallway and staircase were, thankfully, empty; the memories of last night were providing Frederic with more than enough company …

The Previous Night

Frederic Kornell sat upon his horse behind a guardrail on Interstate-95, looking out at the carnage. In the middle of a two-lane highway, a horse whinnied in pain as it lay crippled, its back legs smashed by a Hummer. Ten feet away from the horse its rider, a prince (Frederic was embarrassed that he hadn't even learned the prince's name), lay on his stomach, his left leg twisted awkwardly away from his body. The prince had been thrown from the horse when the Hummer crashed into it and from where he sat upon his horse, Frederic couldn't tell if the prince was alive or dead. A few hundred yards up the highway, the black Hummer that had caused the accident was turning around and coming back at them.

The ranger's heart pounded. Was it an accident? Was the driver coming back to help? Was he coming back to finish the job?

The driver of the Hummer hit the accelerator. It turned to the right and Frederic felt its headlights wash over him as they centered themselves back on the highway, finding the injured horse.

Frederic tried to swallow. Couldn't.

The Hummer picked up speed.

Frederic found he was frozen in place. His horse, Alfred, wasn't, and when the horse took several nervous steps backwards, moving deeper into the woods, the ranger didn't stop him.

The voice of Frederic's father screamed in his head: "You're a goddamned pussy!"

Frederic didn't argue with his father. He never had. Not even when- *no*.

Frederic pushed the thought aside.

119

The Hummer swerved to its right, towards the other side of the highway and its headlights left the horse and focused instead on the body of the unmoving Young Prince.

"I should move!" Frederic's panicked mind yelled. But he didn't.

Not even when his eyes noted movement at the edge of the Hummer's headlights. Not even when his mind processed that the movement was Kelly Reed, exiting the carriage and running towards the Young Prince, trying to save him before the Hummer arrived.

The Present

Captain Crumb stood on the elevated aft deck, looking down at the 107-man crew of the *Puritan*. The rising sun was at the Crumb's back, sending his shadow down across the newly-created pirates. The Navy lifer looked down across their faces, wondering if they realized what the day would bring, wondering how many of them wouldn't make it back to the ship by sundown. Crumb wondered, most of all, if they were truly ready to become pirates, and if they realized just what that would entail.

It was time to find out.

The Previous Night

Alfred wouldn't budge. Frederic kicked the side of the horse, but Alfred did nothing more than whinny in protest and shuffle in place. The irony was not lost on the ranger – finally willing to put himself in danger, his horse wanted no part of jumping the guardrail and saving the Young Prince or Kelly from the oncoming Hummer.

"No!" Frederic yelled, once again a non-involved witness to a scene that should have included a heroic ranger.

Across the highway, Kelly Reed gave no indication she heard Frederic's yell, nor any fear at the headlights that grew brighter and brighter with each passing second. Kelly made her way towards the unmoving Young Prince as the Hummer bore down on the prone body.

"Plenty of time," she mumbled to herself, trying to believe it. Behind her, she could hear the shouts of the two princes from atop their carriage to get out of the way. *Some help they are*. She moved up the small incline to get on the road surface, then tripped over her dress, slamming her knee onto the pavement. Groaning instead of swearing, she pushed herself back to her feet and shuffled forward.

Looking into the headlights to locate the Hummer, Kelly's eyes reflexively winced at the too-bright lights. As her head turned slightly to the right to minimize the glare, the Hummer's engines roared wildly.

Kelly knew she wasn't going to make it.

Across and back down the highway, hidden in the dark, Frederic Kornell had come to the same conclusion – Kelly wasn't going to make it.

Imagine, then, his surprise when Kelly kept moving forward.

The Present

"You expect us to get into that thing?" Carl Yesek asked, looking at the landing boat they would need to go ashore.

"Apparently," Hector said, scratching his head and glancing towards the shore that was now within rowing distance. The two new friends stood near the starboard railing, watching as the landing boat was lowered down into the water. Behind them, the crew of the Puritan alternately milled about, waiting to board, or performed their ship duties.

"Teddy's pissed he isn't going," Carl said passively.

Hector nodded. Though they had empathized with Teddy's desire to go, they were secretly glad he wasn't coming. Friend or not, the last thing either of them wanted was a 350-plus pound guy weighing them down.

Only half the crew was going on the treasure hunt Berathon had arranged for them; Crumb was keeping the other half behind to protect the ship. Berathon had promised the *Cottonmather* was headed south, towards Long Island sound, but Crumb wasn't about to "leave my ass bent over and unguarded." Hector stole a glance back at the elevated deck, where Austin stood with Crumb and Mary Mathers.

Carl noted the glance. "Wonderin' why Austin gets to run this enterprise?"

Hector nodded slowly. "Yeah. Ever since Mollug was injured, he's been spending a lot of time with Crumb. Saw Mathers hanging around him earlier, too."

"And that bothers you?" Carl asked, running his hand through his thinning hair.

The former auto mechanic thought on it a moment, then shook his head. "Naw."

"Really?"

Hector let the question go unanswered.

The Previous Night

"What the hell do you think you're doing?"

Inside the mind of Kelly Reed, the question repeated itself. With each subsequent interrogation, the voice of the speaker changed. At first, it was her own voice asking. Then Austin's. Then her mother's. Then Frederic's. Then Brad's. She pushed them all away.

Her knee was numb, and with the numbness came a return of flexibility. Once again she was running, her hands holding up her "Snow White" gown. Thankful she'd taken off her high heels in the carriage, Kelly began to think she just might make it to the Young Prince.

The Prince wasn't moving but Kelly knew/hoped/prayed he was alive. His head was hanging off the side of the road, on the small grassy incline of the median, while his legs were out in the road. Just a few more steps …

Across the highway, Frederic cursed his inability to act.

Atop the carriage, the Blonde Prince and Norman-Osborn-Haired Prince thanked God it wasn't them lying in the road.

Inside the carriage, Georgia Mulrooney rubbed the bump on her head she'd received when the carriage veered off the highway, knowing this was somehow her husband's fault.

Next to the carriage, Samantha Dixon began to walk in the direction opposite from Kelly, her eyes locked on something she found much more interesting – the reason the horses wouldn't, at first, move off the highway and onto the median.

Behind the wheel of the Hummer, Jim Catlin bore down on the prone body he earlier had thought was Frederic Kornell, furious that he'd hit the wrong person but willing to compromise. Kornell was somewhere close by and Catlin would flush him out. When he turned the Hummer around and started back towards the prince he'd hit, Catlin thought a direct assault on the victim would bring Kornell to him.

He was wrong.

Someone was coming towards the downed prince, but by the dress Catlin could tell it was one of the princesses. The glare of the headlights reflected off the princess's shiny, blue and purple dress, hiding her identity.

Until now.

Catlin swore as the headlight angle changed just enough for him to figure out who was foolish enough to rush towards and oncoming Hummer.

Kelly.

Of course.

Kelly Fucking Reed.

For a half-second, Catlin entertained the thought of running this bitch over and doing Brad Regent a favor. Then remembered his friend was not only King of New England, but had given him the okay to go out and murder the ranger. His "best" friend had also dragged him before the public and beaten because Catlin was caught doing something Regent had instructed him to do. Gritting his teeth, Catlin pushed his back into the Hummer's driver's seat, feeling the welts on his back sting and pulse blood.

No, killing the crazy bitch wouldn't be allowed.

"What the hell?" Almost disbelieving what he was seeing, Catlin almost acted too late - the crazy bitch was jumping towards him,

Swearing, almost on top of her, Catlin jerked the wheel to the left and felt the Hummer's passenger-side wheels thump over something. Panic shot through him and he slammed on the breaks, his eyes locked on the rearview mirror. He couldn't see anything, so he removed his goggles.

Nothing. He saw nothing. Slamming his fist onto the steering wheel, Catlin reached for the gun on the passenger seat and hopped out of the Hummer. "If I killed her," his mind raced, then let the thought hang in the night air as he started to walk back up the highway.

The Present

"What do you think you're doing, fatty?"

Teddy Levenson turned from his spot at the railing of the elevated aft deck to stare into the eyes of Captain Crumb. "I'm going with them," the 350-plus pound man said defiantly.

Crumb guffawed. "No you're not." He jerked his thumb to a mop and bucket to his left. "Go mop the deck like the good fat ass you are. That's your job. Do it."

Levenson grunted, turned his back on the Captain, and began lowering the seventh landing boat into the water. "Watch me, old man."

"Fine," Crumb grunted. "I should've sent you, anyway. There's no chance you'll come back."

"Oh yeah?" Teddy asked, turning again. "What makes you so sure I can't handle myself?"

"For one thing," Crumb laughed, playing to the crowd of pirates that were now watching them, "your tubby face is already beet red and your wheezing is strong enough that Aeolus is worried you're coming after his job."

The pirates laughed at the Captain's joke, but Teddy ignored them. There was no reason to play to a crowd of morons.

"Go ahead, Levenson," Crumb waved his hand. "Go play pirate if that makes you happy, but you know and I know that you don't have the balls to come back."

Teddy stared daggers into Crumb's back as the Captain moved towards the ladder that would take him back to the main deck. "Fuck this," Teddy thought. "Fuck him and fuck all these assholes. I'm off this motherfucker!" Breathing hard, like a bull ready to charge, Teddy saw the laughing pirates around him in slow motion. "I'm outta here!" he screamed.

"Told you you'd never come back!" Crumb yelled back without turning. "No room on my ship for fat assed pussies! Don't know why the angels ever sent me a goddamned fatty," Crumb continued to mumble as he turned to go backwards down the ladder. When he did so, his eyes met Teddy's as his feet dropped him down, one step at a time. Even though Crumb was still fit for a man in his 70s, he needed to be careful walking down the steps. Step pause step pause … all the time his eyes locked on Teddy's. "Why don't you jump overboard and do everyone a favor?"

Something inside Teddy snapped. His whole life people like Crumb had been riding him. No more. Not in the New World. Not when he was a pirate. "Jump?" Teddy sneered. "That's the first good idea you've had, you sanctimonious pile of shit."

Crumb paused, sensing Teddy had gone past a line he wasn't likely to come back from. In his decades in the Navy, Crumb had seen it a dozen times. Being out at sea for months wasn't easy. Stable men could snap. Unstable men …

Unstable men did things like Teddy Levenson was about to do.

A primal scream unleashed itself from Teddy's throat and he ran towards the Captain, only halfway down the six-foot ladder. The crew was too stunned to do anything but watch as Teddy lunged at Crumb's exposed chest. In his mind, Teddy's dive was an athletic lunge, like a puma attacking its prey. In reality, it was little more than a belly flop. Teddy's hands grabbed at Crumb's face as the heavy man's weight followed behind with great force.

Captain Crumb fell backwards towards the deck with Teddy following, falling just above him. Crumb knew he was in trouble when his hands failed to grasp the ladder. His mind, decades of naval training at the call, could only think of one thing to do – hit the deck and roll like a bastard.

"Aaaaaiiiieeeeee!" Teddy screamed, his face an enraged red.

Crumb's lower back hit the deck. "Roll!" his mind screamed. His body reacted, but too slowly. The Captain of the *Puritan* made it to his side, when Teddy Levenson landed on top of him. Crumb's seventy-year old ribs cracked like kindling as 350-plus pounds tried to knock him through an unmovable deck. All of the air in the veteran's lungs was shoved violently out of his body as unconsciousness tried to rush in.

"You were right, old man," Teddy wheezed into his ear. "Jumping was a hell of an idea."

Austin jumped from his landing boat into the ocean and found himself knee deep in the warm surf. "Everyone out!" he called again, turning to see the other four men in his boat hadn't followed his first order.

They'd come to shore in six boats: ten men to four boats and five men to the remaining two. Austin had the lead with three and Mary Mathers the lead with the other three. Mathers, to no one's surprise, had already gotten her three boats ashore. Austin could see her standing smugly on the beach and turned away to see Hector and Carl, who he'd placed in charge of the other two boats, ordering their crews into the water.

"Let's go, Mr. McNamara!" Mathers called joyfully as Austin struggled to lug his boat onto the sand. "We've got gold to find!"

Austin couldn't hold back a smile. "Yeah, I suppose we do, Mrs. Mathers," he called back as the boat was run aground.

"That's Ms. Mathers," the blonde woman replied, showing Austin that her hands were free of rings as the younger man came up to stand next to her. "I'm not the marrying kind," she grinned wickedly, giving his arm a playful squeeze. "Now, tell me again why we've landed in Maine when our target is in Durham, New Hampshire?"

Austin looked at her sideways. "Thought you were from Brattleboro? Don't you know your New England geography?"

Mathers shook her head. "Not really. My mother's family was from upstate New York, so when we traveled, we traveled west, not east."

Nodding, Austin said, "Right, then. Durham is right over the border. Probably a 20, 30 minute drive from here. The beach," he looked down to his feet, "makes for a convenient landing point. Plus, it's in the open. Crumb wanted a landing point that was in the open so no one snuck up on us."

"Someone meaning the *Cottonmather*?" Mathers asked, looking past Austin to see Hector and Carl pulling their boats ashore. In the near distance, the *Puritan* waited for their return. *Is someone lowering a seventh boat?* she wondered.

"Yeah," Austin replied. "Can't say I blame him. Never can be too careful."

Mathers turned away from the ship and to the fifty-man crew that gathered around them. "Only one question left to ask," Mathers said to Austin.

"What's that?"

"How did you plan on us getting to Durham if it's a half-hour away?"

Austin couldn't help the smile that came easily to his face, though his own unique brand of Catholic guilt made him at least pretend to be bothered by what he was about to say. "York Beach is a vacation town, Ms. Mathers, which means," he said, pointing behind her, "that there's likely to be a lot of SUVs and trucks we can use to carry our haul sitting unattended in the parking lot of the big hotel behind you. Maybe even an RV or three."

"Mr. McNamara," Mary Mathers drolled, "I do believe you mean to have us steal a car or two."

Austin grinned. "Yo, ho, ho, a pirate's life for me," he said plainly.

Around them, the fifty newly-created pirates shouted their approval.

"I just hope, for your sake," Mathers grinned to Austin, who found himself momentarily lost in the older woman's blue eyes, "someone knows how to hotwire a car."

"I'm sure-"

"What the hell is Crumb doing?" Mathers asked, interrupting Austin and pointing out at the *Puritan*. "He's lowering another boat."

The Previous Night

In the glare of the oncoming Hummer, Kelly Reed leapt forward, aiming for the median on the other side of the Young Prince. As her body flew over him and down onto the slight incline of the median, she grabbed the prince's tunic, using her weight to pull him off the highway.

Her desperate move had almost worked.

Almost.

She landed with a thud in the grass and pulled on the prince as hard as she could. Her yank had managed to get only part of him off the highway when the Hummer whizzed past. Kelly felt vomit rise up from her stomach as the Hummer smacked into the prince's right leg, sending his unconscious body tumbling away from her.

Kelly swore to herself as she scrambled along the moist grass towards the prince. Horrified as she was with what had happened to him, the jolt from the Hummer had caused his body to spasm, as if he'd been knocked awake instead of unconscious. Kelly reached him in a few moments and with one look the vomit that had threatened earlier now boiled up and over. She was glad for the excuse to look away.

The Young Prince was in a bad way. His left leg was twisted awkwardly – definitely broken – and his right pant leg was soaked through with blood. Kelly wiped the vomit spittle off her mouth with the front of her hand as she turned back around. *At least he's moving now.* The prince was coughing up blood as his head rocked back and forth wildly in the grass.

Kelly placed a hand on his chest, trying to calm him.

"Is he dead?" a voice from the highway above her asked.

"No," she said, turning to look up at whom she assumed would be one of the other two princes. It wasn't. Instead, she looked up at a man dressed from head-to-toe in black, holding a gun in his right hand. Surprising herself, she felt no panic. *Must be the adrenaline.* "You're the driver of the Hummer," she said.

"I am."

Something in his voice ...

"What do you want?" Kelly asked. "Why did you-?"

127

"Shut the fuck up, bitch," the man grunted.

"Please," Kelly said, knowing it would do no good but trying to buy herself more time, "this man needs help."

"He would. I just ran the fucker over with my car."

Do I know you? Why does that voice sound like I should know who you are?

"Where the fuck is Kornell?" Catlin screamed.

Kelly said nothing, but inside her head, she thought, *That's a very good question. Where the hell is Frederic?*

Across the highway, Frederic Kornell was fighting a losing battle against irony. When he'd been in position to attempt to save Kelly from her abductor, fear had frozen him to the spot on which he stood. He had been a coward. Now ... now when given a chance at retribution, to once again save her, his fear urged him forward.

His horse, however, wanted nothing to do with a Hummer and stayed rooted to the ground.

Frederic had watched Kelly dive out of the way, had watched the Hummer's brakes slam on, bringing the large vehicle to a halt, had watched a man dressed in black exit the Hummer and walk back up the highway.

Towards the location of Kelly and the Young Prince.

Fear and panic had begun to crowd in on him and he dared do nothing beyond sitting here, on his horse, and waiting. The back and forth in his brain between want and fear, between helping and getting hurt, caused the body to freeze. With each step the man in black took, Frederic became a smaller and smaller man in his own mind. The ranger – the Old World janitor who spent his days and night daydreaming of being a hero and rescuing some gorgeous damsel in distress – started to believe he would, once again, be nothing more than a witness to Fate.

It was then he saw the object in the attacker's hand. The world slowed to half-speed as his father's voice barged into his mind, "You're a goddamned pussy! Huh? What the fuck are you looking at?"

"Dad," Frederic's voice choked out, as the world slowed to a blur, "don't."

"Don't what, *pussy?*"

Frederic was nineteen years old. He was standing in the kitchen of his parent's apartment. The floor was cheap linoleum and covered with the remnants of a dinner his father didn't want: spaghetti, sauce, peppers, onions, Wonder Bread, margarine, milk. A pot was overturned. Milk oozed down the wall where his father had thrown his glass, just after hollering, "Is this skim fucking milk?"

"Don't, dad," Old World Frederic pleaded. "Don't."

There was one other thing on the floor that shouldn't have been there, but unlike the spaghetti and bread, it wasn't unused to being on the floor. Frederic's mother.

"Frederic, honey," she said, her voice quivering as blood dribbled down her chin and onto her lime-green shirt, "never you mind this. Go on and do your homework."

None of them wanted to mention the handgun that Mr. Kornell held in his hand.

"Homework?" his father yelled, his right hand shaking the gun at his side. "A nineteen year old boy shouldn't have homework! A nineteen year-old boy should be off becoming a man! He should have a job! *He should be in the army!*"

"Dad ..."

"I'm not your dad," Mr. Kornell challenged. "No son of mine could be such a goddamned pussy. Look at me, *son*," he sneered. "I just hit your mother. I just hit your cunt of a mother and I'm standing here with a gun in my had ready to kill this useless bitch for serving me spaghetti two nights in a fucking row and acting like I'm crazy for even thinking she could do such a thing. And what do you do? You stand there like the fucking pussy you are, the worthless fucking pussy that can't even protect his own mother. You don't deserve a mother!"

"Where the fuck is Kornell?"

Frederic was jolted out of his remembrance at the shouting of the attacker; the memory had transformed him. All the regret from that moment, all the heartache, poured out of him at that moment, at the sight of the handgun and the danger it represented for Kelly. He was afraid, yes, but no longer beholden to it. Barely understanding what drove him, Frederic jumped down off of his horse and started running. He leapt over the guardrail as his heart threatened to pound right out of his skull.

Passing the Hummer, Frederic's right hand reached for his sword and in a flash it was raised high over his head. "Aaaaaaahhhhhhh!" he yelled, five steps from the attacker.

The attacker turned, gun drawn, and Frederic brought his sword down with all the might his New World body and Old World mind could conjure forth. His goal was the attacker's wrist, which he intended to sever.

He missed.

Fortuitously.

The sword cut deep into the handgun, forcing Catlin to lose his grip. The gun rattled across the highway and Frederic and Catlin stared at each other. "You're a dead man!" Catlin yelled and connected a punch on Frederic's jaw, spinning the ranger around, with Kornell's sword joining Catlin's gun on the pavement.

Frederic had never felt such pain in all his life. His whole jaw burned with pain and his hand went directly to his face. "Ow!" he yelled.

"Ow?" Catlin asked. That anyone in a fight would say "Ow" was, to Catlin, unthinkable. There could be no doubt as to what Kornell was doing. "You mocking me?"

"No, I-"

A second punch. This one a left to the gut, doubling Frederic over.

Frederic knew he was in trouble. There was no way he could stop this guy from doing whatever he had come here to do.

"That's because you're a goddamned pussy!"

Thanks, dad.

Catlin stood over the ranger and dropped his right hand down hard on the ranger's collarbone, knocking Kornell to one knee.

"Why?" Frederic choked, more concerned what Kelly and Samantha would think of him as opposed to the beating he was taking. In a weird way, he hurt a little less with every blow, as if the pain was spreading out over all of his body instead of being concentrated in one spot.

"Why?" Catlin asked. "Because you got me flogged, you sunuvabitch!"

"Huh?" Frederic asked, looking up. He got only a glimpse of the ski-mask-covered face before another blow (a left uppercut) knocked him backwards onto the highway.

Stars. He saw the starts of the night sky winking down at him. The angels, it seemed, had arranged the New World specifically for this moment, where the entire universe could look down on Frederic Kornell and laugh. Frederic's view became blocked as the attacker moved above him. "I'm going to kill you for what you did to me."

"What did I do?" Frederic asked through watering eyes, not bothering to get up or attempt to get away.

The attacker reached to his left shoulder and pulled on a Velcro patch, removing the Kevlar vest and dropping it to the ground. The entire time his eyes were locked onto Kornell. "This is what you did to me," the attacker raged, lifting his black shirt off his body to reveal a torso wrapped with an ace bandage.

"I don't know what you're talking about," Frederic choked.

Slowly, Catlin unwrapped the beige bandages. With every rotation, as the wrap that was against Catlin's back came to the front, Frederic saw more and more dried blood. When the wrap was completely off, Catlin dropped the bandage down onto Kornell and turned around.

Frederic gasped.

Catlin's back was raw and oozing blood. It looked like he'd been … whipped.

Everything fell into place for the ranger. "You're the abductor," he said as Catlin turned back to look down on him. "You're the guy who kidnapped Kelly."

"Fucking right. But you fucked our plan up."

Shit. Frederic looked around for his sword, but it was back near the grass. On the other side of his attacker. *Shit shit shit.*

"What plan?" Frederic asked, pushing himself back across the tar as he tried to keep from going hysterical.

Catlin didn't answer as he took a step to stay over Kornell. Frederic could tell the man was smiling beneath the ski mask.

"Whose plan, then?" Frederic asked, trying to buy time and solve the puzzle at the same time. "Who were the other abductors?"

"There was only one abductor," Catlin grunted. "Me. The others were-aaargh!"

Kelly Reed had entered the fight.

Frederic looked up to see that Kelly had slapped the flat side of his sword across the attacker's back. Catlin's body reared up as the pain shot through him. Kelly wasn't finished. Frederic could see in her eyes that he was not the only one who had something in him snap this evening.

"You kidnapped me?" She brought the sword around again, slapping his back a second time and covering the blade in blood. "You're the one who kidnapped me? Who the hell are you?"

Catlin grunted through the pain, spinning around. "Don't you remember, you drunk bitch? Of course not. You never could hold your alcohol, especially after I spiked your drink. You were too drunk to recognize someone you knew." Catlin grinned beneath his mask. "Put the sword down and I'll let you live."

Kelly kept Frederic's sword between them, staring hard into the eyes of her abductor. Who the hell was he? Why did he seem so familiar? Why couldn't she remember what he looked like? Did she know him? Wasn't he just a frat pretty-boy? Isn't that why she talked to him at the First Night Feast? Because he was so unlike Austin? Why couldn't she remember?

She asked, but she knew why. *Too much alcohol.*

Catlin wasn't done talking. "I never could figure out why-." He stopped himself and shook his finger at her. "Almost said too much."

Kelly felt a deep rage burst over from someplace deep inside her. "Frederic, no!" she yelled.

Spinning to the side, Catlin looked down to the ranger to see what Kornell was attempting.

Kornell wasn't attempting anything.

Kornell was, in fact, even more surprised at Kelly's outburst than Catlin. The two men's shocked eyes met each others and Catlin knew, a full second before it happened, that Kelly *Fucking* Reed had outsmarted him.

The sword sank into his shoulder and pain followed right on its heels. Catlin, stunned, looked at the sword, then traced it back down it's length to the hand that held it, then up the arm to the face of the woman who had cut him. "Fucking bitch," he spat.

Kelly pushed the sword in deeper. "Who are you?"

Calling on the last of his strength, Catlin pulled away from her and turned to run back to the Hummer.

Neither Kelly nor Frederic followed. Kelly watched the abductor escape, her whole body feeling numb. Frederic watched Kelly watch the abductor escape, then pushed himself to his feet. "Kelly," he said softly as the Hummer's wheels screeched to life, reaching for his sword. Putting one arm around the young woman's back, Frederic took the sword from her. "It's over."

His father gave him only a moment's peace as the Hummer's taillights grew fainter in the distance.

"You know goddamned well it isn't," his father grunted from the kitchen of twelve years past. He stood over the body of his dead wife, and pointed the gun at his son. "Get out of my sight, pussy. I don't want to see your fat face again until you're ready to finish this. Stop crying and go. Go!"

The Present

"Oh, shit."

Frederic stood in the open doorway of Kelly's hotel room, feeling more depressed than shocked or panicked. The room was empty and a trail of dried blood led out of the room and down the hallway, toward the far elevator bank. A note had been taped to the door. It read:

Frederic,

The Prince – his name is Saul – needs medical attention. I know you told the other two princes to look for medical help while we brought him up here, but they were back in the hotel after only twenty minutes. I had to take him. His leg was even worse than we thought once I cleaned the blood off. I would've told you, but I figured you were busy. With Samantha. This couldn't wait.

Kelly.

Kelly Reed left Saul Stein moaning in pain in the back of the carriage as she ran into the second hospital she'd come across since leaving the hotel. Hope turned to despair as she called out for help and received no response.

Austin looked around the Trading Post and was more than a little surprised at how eager his fellow pirates were to rob the store blind. The Trading Post sold outdoor equipment and clothing for tourists, campers, and hunters. They'd stopped for what Mary Mathers had called a "practice run."

"Glorious, isn't it?" she asked, suddenly beside him, as they watched fifty pirates steal and destroy the store.

"It's almost scary how much they're enjoying this," he confided.

Mathers looked at him sideways. "We're pirates now, Mr. McNamara. Stealing is what we do."

"Yeah, I know that, but ..." Austin let the words trail away as he watched Hector swinging wildly from the antlers of a stuffed deer head. The twenty year-old former mechanic had supplanted his pirate costume with a bright orange hunter's cap and was howling like Ric Flair.

Mathers nodded. "But you're surprised at how easily they've taken to criminality?"

"Yeah."

"Don't be," she replied, smiling. "It's not criminality that's driving them."

"Then what is it?"

She turned to him, her eyes sparkling with excitement. "It's freedom. Freedom from morals." She placed a hand on his shoulder, making Austin feel instantly uncomfortable. "Tell me, Mr. McNamara, can you accept the pirate's life? Can you live free from morality?"

"Of course," Austin shot back without thought. He was arguing just to argue, taking the opposite position simply because he didn't want Mathers' accusation to stick.

"Really?" Mathers asked, letting her hand run down his chest. "Maybe I'll let you prove that later tonight – if you survive the day, that is."

Austin wanted to knock her hand away, but didn't. Something inside him wanted to see the scenario play out, even if the moral part of his brain knew it was nowhere good. "What are you talking about?" his mouth asked as his brain scolded him. It was one thing to be a passive passenger, but something else entirely to actively push the issue forward.

Mathers stopped her hand at his belly button, then let it rotate so that her fingers were pointing towards the floor. She said nothing, but smiled, teasing him with nothing more than the idea of the possibility of her hand moving a few more inches south.

This time, Austin did push her hand away and moved past her, deeper into the store. "Tell your crew to steal some winter parkas. It gets cold on the ocean."

"You're learning, Mr. McNamara," she teased towards Austin's back. "There's no place for morality aboard a pirate ship."

Teddy Levenson lay on his back on the beach, panting as he had never before panted. Rowing in from shore, alone, was a hell of a lot more physical work than he'd done in years. Maybe ever.

He thought of the crunching of Crumb's bones when he'd landed on the Captain and began to laugh.

Teddy felt free, and freedom was a wonderful, wonderful thing.

The Previous Night

Samantha Dixon's eyes were locked on a peculiar object on the side of the road. It was, she believed, the object that had kept the horses from leaving the danger of the highway for the safety of the median. Later, in the comfort of a warm bed and in the afterglow of sex, when Frederic would relate the story of what happened to him, Kelly, and the abductor, the ranger would find it hard to believe that Samantha had missed the entire episode.

"What happened?" he'd ask. "What could be more interesting than a crazy guy trying to kill us?"

"Georgia hurt herself," she'd respond, telling a half-truth.

But half-truths are also half-lies. Georgia was hurt, but it wasn't Georgia that held her attention. It was the thing that lay five feet off the highway in the tall grass. A thing that was, put simply, a million times more fascinating than a crazy guy in a Hummer.

It was a dead angel.

Samantha stared at the being for several long minutes, mesmerized by the alabaster skin, by the silvery hair, but especially by the broken wings. One of the angel's eyes had been ripped out, but there was no blood. Unless the silvery liquid that had crusted over the eye was blood.

Off to her left, the Hummer roared past, reminding Samantha that there was an entire world beyond the sight of the angel that lay dead in the grass before her. Knowing she needed to get back, but half-believing the angel would disappear the moment she turned her head, Samantha, on impulse, reached down into the grass and pried an object the size of a large book from the angel's hand.

It was a harp.

A harp that was about to make Samantha Dixon a very popular princess.

Chapter Nine
Yo, Ho, Ho! A Pirate's Life for Me!

The cool noon sun beat down on an unmoving body, and two living bodies. All three bodies were alabaster in color, the color of angels.

Raphael, the angel in charge of Royalty, frowned, "I had forgotten the sorrow of such a sight."

"In truth, Raphael," Juramel, the angel in charge of Wealth and Power, replied, "I have never laid eyes upon one of our bodies devoid of its soul."

The two angels looked down at the soulless corpse of their fellow angel, Enimon, his skin already starting to burn away where the sun touched it. Instead of turning to flame, the angel's body flaked away in shimmering white flakes that floated heavenward. "We should alert Gabriel at once," Raphael asserted, his eyes not leaving Enimon's corpse.

Juramel nodded. "Ocilael, as well."

Raphael pried his eyes away from Enimon to challenge Juramel. "For what purpose? It is Gabriel who is in charge of the Reorganization."

Juramel shrugged and looked down the highway to hide his discontent. "Ocilael is the angel in charge of Law Enforcement, Raphael."

"We have never had to police ourselves, Juramel," Raphael insisted.

"When was the last time we had a need to?" Juramel replied. "Tell Gabriel, by all means, but Ocilael should be told." Juramel narrowed his eyes and lowered his voice. "The angels have no secrets, Raphael. If Enimon's death was an accident, the angels will know. But if it's not an accident ..."

Raphael wouldn't hear of Juramel's accusations. "Murder? Preposterous. Who could kill an angel but another angel? No angel would commit such an atrocity."

"Do not be so foolish," Juramel scolded, his voice terse and eyes on edge. He grabbed Raphael's shoulder and pulled the angel several steps away from Enimon, as if the dead body would tell the world Juramel's thoughts.

"Juramel?" Raphael blurted. "What is the meaning of—"

"God's word has been compromised."

Raphael's body jerked to attention. He could find no words to voice his shock and disbelief at the information Juramel had relayed to him.

Juramel continued in a somber whisper. "There are rumors circulating that the letter ordering the Reorganization received from God was a forgery."

"It cannot be-"

"Have you seen the letter?"

"N-no, but few have," Raphael protested. "There is no reason to distrust Raphael or the others. There is no reason for any angel to distrust any other angel."

Juramel looked past Raphael to Enimon's body, then back to his fellow angel with a doubting expression. Raphael offered up his hands in apology, then turned back to the corpse. A troubling thought tried to form in the back of his mind, but he couldn't force it to coalesce into an actual concern. He watched the columns of sunlight, dispersed through a nearby tree, gently eradicate the alabaster flesh, saying a prayer for his fallen brother. The horror of the scene could not be missed, Raphael realized, and he was foolish for seeking to keep Ocilael – or any angel – from seeing or learning of this sight. 'Too much time with the human Royals,' he mused, ashamed at himself. 'I'm starting to think like them already.' One of Enimon's eyes had been ripped from its socket and both of the angel's wings were broken. Several of his white feathers were moving across the grass, scattered by the gentle breeze. Something beyond the obvious was wrong, but what was it? Raphael narrowed his eyes, concentrating, reliving the past few moments, and with the clarity of a thunderclap, a deep concern was suddenly brought into focus. The rumor of Juramel. Where had it come from? How had Juramel-?

"Raphael," Juramel said in a cold voice. "Enimon's harp. It's missing." Juramel stomped past Raphael and knelt beside the body. "Humans," he sneered, turning his head to make eye contact with Raphael. "Not even Lucifer himself would steal an angel's harp. Do you see what the humans do with our gift?" he asked, turning back to Enimon's corpse. "They spit it back in our face."

Raphael stared hard into the back of Juramel, wondering if his fellow angel was playing a game, or if he really believed that humans could slay an angel? As convinced as Juramel apparently was that a human had slain Enimon, Raphael was equally convinced it must have been an angel. Further, he believed, the forgery of God's word and the death of Enimon had to be connected. But how? Was Enimon killed because of something he knew about the forgery? Was he killed for spreading the rumor?

Raphael turned his gaze heavenward, an abject darkness growing inside of him. Not since Lucifer's fall had there been any real discord amongst the angels, but now, with God's absence stretching further than any of them had ever dreamt He'd be gone, Raphael wondered if their gift to humanity was about to turn into a curse to the angels.

Guilt and joy were strange bedfellows.

Austin McNamara sat behind the wheel of a BMW Z3 roadster cruising down Route 4, an empty road in front of him and a caravan of stolen vehicles behind him. He was a pirate, driving somebody else's BMW, on the way to rob something called Potato Tower, which was located somewhere in the woods of Durham. There was a part of him, though smaller than he would've anticipated, feeling guilty over the theft of the vehicles that trailed behind him. Most of the vehicles they'd stolen were SUVs, though they'd also found two RVs to help cart away whatever gold or valuables they could steal.

From Potato Tower.

What a world ...

Austin couldn't deny the sheer joy of stomping down on the accelerator and shifting back up into third gear as he shot off a bend in the road. Sure, this was someone else's car, and yes, he stole it, but this was the New World, wasn't it? They'd been given the freedom by God-

By. God.

- to do this, so why shouldn't he accept his fate? Pirates stole. That was a fact. That's what he now was. It wasn't like he'd stolen this car from anyone, either, really. The Roadster had been abandoned when the Reorganization hit, so the owner of the Beamer was probably a cowboy or astronaut or superhero right now and not missing the car at all. Austin didn't miss his car, after all.

"Yeah, but you drove a busted '93 Ford pick-up," he heard Kelly's voice taunt him.

Kelly.

The smallest of knots began to tighten in his stomach. The hurt was starting. The dull ache he felt whenever they'd been separated too long. Because of their jobs, they were often separated for a weekend or a week or even, once, due to overlapping commitments, almost a whole month. He wondered what-

"Are you there, Mr. McNamara?"

Austin reached down to grab his new walkie-talkie cell phone, which they'd stopped at a Nextel store in a strip mall to steal. Luckily, one of their fellow pirates was a hacker and knew how to activate the phones through the company's still active network. At some point we should figure out just what everyone used to do in the Old World, he thought absent-mindedly. "Right here, Ms. Mathers, but I gathered you knew that," he said, glancing in the rearview mirror to see Mathers' stolen silver Mercedes-Benz CLK.

"Are we there, yet?" she asked playfully.

"Almost," Austin replied, looking down to the treasure map in the driver's seat. "What's the plan?"

"Find us a spot a mile outside of the Tower for us to park," she answered. "We'll send scouts ahead on foot, then attack the Tower when they get back."

Austin scowled. "Expecting trouble?"

"You can never be too careful, Mr. McNamara," Mathers replied, her tone more serious than Austin had heard before. "I don't want to die our first trip out."

Austin clicked off the phone and tossed it onto the passenger seat, hating Mathers for reminding him that, among other things, pirates were killed in action, too. He wished he could contact Kelly. If only he knew where she was, right now. Shaking his head, he glanced down at the treasure map to get his bearings. The cell phone had fallen on the map and he needed to brush it aside to-

He stopped. Blinked. Looked at the cell phone as if it were a magical device he'd never seen before.

"Why can't I call her?" he asked aloud.

When he didn't get a response, he picked up the cell and dialed Kelly's number.

Her adrenaline was almost gone, matching the condition of the mostly silent prince behind and below her in the carriage. "This was such a bad idea," Kelly sighed to herself as the two horses pulling the carriage came to an exhausted halt to drink out of a public fountain. Knowing the horses needed the break, Kelly stood up to stretch out her aching muscles. The whole incident last night with her abductor had left her muscles aching and, unlike Austin, she was in better than average shape.

Austin.

She wondered how her boyfriend was faring as a pirate.

"Are we at a hospital?"

Kelly turned to lean around the edge of the carriage to see the Young Prince (she'd learned that his name was Saul Stein) leaning back against the oversized red seats. His damaged legs were propped up on the opposite bench seat. Kelly was worried he wouldn't live to see the morning, then worried he wouldn't live to see noon, and was now worried he wouldn't live to see nightfall. Saul had surprised her twice already and she was hoping for a third. He was talking, at least, which must be a good sign on some level.

"How are you feeling?" she asked.

"I got run over by a car," he wheezed, forcing a smile. "How do you think I feel?"

Kelly checked the horses, who were still drinking from the fountain in the middle of this small town square, and jumped down. She opened the door to the carriage and climbed inside. "Thirsty?" she asked, reaching for a can of Sprite that was on the floor.

"Yes, please," he grunted, taking the can from her after she opened it. She watched him drink, noting that his face was pale and covered in sweat. It was imperative they find a doctor. "Warm," he said, making a face as the liquid ran down his throat.

"Sorry."

He shrugged. "S'okay. Where'd we get it?"

Kelly looked out the window, feeling a bit ashamed. "Stole it from the hotel's Coke machine. There's six or seven cans left down here on the floor," she explained, reaching down to grab a couple to hand to him.

"Thanks," he said, then leaned his head back against the seat. "I can't even feel my legs anymore. Haven't for a few hours. I'm scared."

Kelly set her jaw. "I'm trying to find you a hospital."

"I know," he said, dragging his head forward to look at her. "I appreciate it, but you don't have any idea where you're going, do you?"

The directness of the question caught Kelly off-guard, but she didn't argue the point. "No clue. Just figured it was better to do something than nothing. Hate sitting around."

Saul nodded. "Might be a good idea to find a car."

Kelly shook her head. "I've looked, but I haven't found one with the keys left in it."

"Next hospital we stop at, steal an ambulance," Saul suggested, tilting his head back. "You should be able to find the keys."

Kelly watched Saul close his eyes, then exited the carriage. If she didn't find a doctor soon ...

Captain of the King's Guard Wallace O'Malley sat in his office of the King's Castle, a large grey building built overnight by the angels on the waterfront. The desk before him was empty except for a cell phone. King Regent was next door at the Aquarium, giving a group of girl-band, mystery-solving rock-stars a tour of the facility. "What the fuck are they supposed to be?" he'd asked one of his guards as the King led a group of twelve of them out of the castle.

"Some odd mix of Jem and the Holograms and Josie and the Pussycats and ... shit, that cartoon with the shark who was a big pussy. What was the name of that cartoon?"

The guard could've been speaking Arabic to O'Malley. "I have no fucking clue what you're talking about," he'd replied. "Is that chick wearing a furry tail?" he asked, dumbfounded, staring at the backs of the women.

"No idea," the guard grinned. "We were trying to figure out if it's part of the costume or, you know, real. God knows I'd sure as fuck like to find out."

O'Malley crossed his arms and turned his attention to the guard. "Have the bugs been planted in the guest rooms, yet?"

The guard, realizing he'd crossed a line, coughed once and straightened his posture. "I'll get right on it, sir."

"Do that," O'Malley had replied.

That was an hour ago. The cell phone started beeping the theme to the *Jeffersons*. "What the fuck is wrong with people?" O'Malley groused, reaching for the phone, expecting it to be Jim Catlin. Eyeing the Caller ID, wanting to see an unidentified string of numbers for the phone he'd given Catlin, O'Malley instead a different string of numbers. Should he answer it? It could be Catlin, but if the abductor was calling from a different phone, that likely meant trouble. O'Malley took less than a second to make up his mind.

He set the phone down, and went back to waiting.

What kind of sick fuck would want to know if a furry tail sticking out of a woman's ass was real?

Austin clicked the cell phone off and tossed it onto the seat. He didn't want to leave a message, figuring Kelly'd see his number and-

"Shit," he swore, realizing he'd used a different cell phone. Kelly would see the numbers but not realize who it was who called. He reached down for the phone to call her again when he heard the rapping of knuckles on the driver side window. Knowing it had to be Mathers, Austin let his hand move past the phone to collect the treasure map.

"What's taking so long?" Mathers asked as Austin opened the Z3's door.

"Just checking the map," Austin replied.

"To hell with the map," Mathers smiled, punching Austin lightly on the shoulder.

Austin ignored Mathers' playfulness and nodded to the building they'd parked beside. A handful of pirates were approaching the door with a tire iron they'd taken from inside one of the RVs. "Figured we'd make more money robbing a Dunkin Donuts?"

Mathers grinned. "Nah. Just felt like a muffin. Bet you can't guess my favorite kind of muffin." She let the light moment sit between them just long enough for Austin to get uncomfortable with the two of them looking at one another. When Austin finally turned away, Mathers pointed in the opposite direction. "I believe we've found Potato Tower."

Austin looked across the small highway. Sure enough, what looked to be a mile or two into the woods, Austin could see the top of a white tower rising above the tree line. "We're really going to do this, aren't we?"

"We are. Excited?" Mathers asked, dropping her voice and letting her hand reach out to massage Austin's upper arm.

Austin brushed the hand aside. "Corn, right?" he asked.

"Hmm?"

"Favorite muffin."

Mathers smiled, shrugged. "Maybe I'll let you buy me breakfast sometime and you can find out."

Austin rolled his eyes. "Seriously, stop."

"Stop what?"

"I have a girlfriend."

"And she's against playful repartee?" Mathers smiled. "I thought you said you could handle the freedom of being a pirate."

Austin shook his head. "Let's just send some scouts to check Potato Tower out, okay?"

Mathers folded her arms under her breasts. "Already done, *Mister* McNamara," she replied. "I sent Hector and a few others off as soon as we arrived."

Austin nodded. "Any word from Carl?"

"The nerd we left at the beach?"

"The biochemist? Yeah."

"Not a peep. Nothing for us to do except wait." For the second time in under a minute, she playfully punched Austin's arm. "Come on, Mr. Serious, if you refuse to buy me breakfast, I'll steal you a doughnut. What's your favorite kind? Oh wait, let me guess? Plain, right?"

"That doesn't mean anything," Austin snapped back, but followed after her, anyway. He *was* kinda hungry.

A double-birthed scowl had settled across the silvery skin of Berathon, the angel in charge of pirates. The angel hovered between the sun that was nearing its zenith in the sky above and the *Puritan,* which was reaching its nadir in the ocean below. Enimon was late; the angel who'd shared with him the rumor of the forgery of God's word was supposed to meet with him here, thirty human minutes ago, with new information. thirty minutes, to an angel, was but a blink of an eye, and Berathon tried to convince himself that Enimon was, most likely, tied up with his astronauts and had simply lost track of a half-human-hour.

The angel was having only limited success, and that success was born, not out of comfort, but by the drama that was playing out on the Puritan below him. Scanning the skies once more for Enimon and not finding him, Berathon decided it was time to involve himself aboard the ship below.

"She stole the carriage?"

"For the tenth time, yes," Frederic Kornell snapped at the New World Royalty around him: Princesses Samantha Dixon and Georgia Mulrooney, and Princes Chad Lasorta (the Blond Prince) and Reece Knobe (the Norman Osborn Haired Prince). "Kelly took the Young Prince to seek medical attention."

"Well," Prince Chad asked, "what did she think we were supposed to do with one horse for the four of us?"

"I'm certain," Frederic snapped angrily, "she figured five healthy people could fend for themselves while a guy whose horse had been hit by a Hummer was taken to the hospital."

"Well," Prince Chad said in exasperation, "what are we supposed to do about it? Wait for her?"

"I'm not waiting," Georgia insisted. "She's very selfish for doing what she did, and I have no patience to sit here and wait to see if she comes back. Ranger," she said haughtily to Frederic, "find us a ride and lead us to Kent Harbor."

Frederic shot her a look to let her know he wasn't about to be bossed around. "Find your own damn ride. I'm going to look for Kelly." Pause. "And Saul," he said quickly, stealing a glance at Samantha.

Samantha wasn't paying him any attention, however. She stood by silently, stroking the quilt she'd stolen from their room and folded into a square.

"Don't expect us to follow you," Prince Chad replied with a wave of his hand.

"I wasn't," Frederic shot back.

"So what are we supposed to do?" the Prince asked for the third time.

Frederic gave him a final look before walking away. He'd had it with this group. "Like I give a crap."

Prince Chad snorted in disgust. "Have fun chasing her down," he called after him, his eyes already dancing towards Samantha. "Though if I had one as beautiful as Princess Samantha in my company, a hundred thousand other women couldn't tear me away."

The Prince's words brought Samantha out of her daze. Hugging the quilt (and the angel's harp that was hidden away inside the folds) tight to her chest, Samantha gave Prince Chad an elegant smile. "Prince Chad … your words …"

"Yes, Princess," Chad replied, running his hand through his gelled blond hair as he stepped towards her. "What service may I provide you?"

Samantha waited until the Prince stood before her, then dropped her smile and flipped him her middle finger. "If you can't read sign language, get one of the other two to translate. I'm with Frederic."

It would come as a surprise to Potato Johnson that his glistening Ivory Tower was being called "Potato Tower." Perhaps not as much of a surprise that there were, at this moment, fifty pirates in a Dunkin Donuts parking lot a mile away waiting to raid his wealth, but less of a surprise than that there were people desiring to steal his gold. Growing up with hippie parents in a less-than-stellar house, where freeloaders were always stopping to sleep on the couch or on the floor or in the even-worse-condition barn out behind their house, Potato was acutely aware of the want that went with seeing others with things he didn't have.

Standing in a room halfway to the top of his tower, Potato looked out at the transients that had come into his employ. These were the people who'd rejected the aliens' gift and taken to the woods. Scanning the nearby hills, Potato couldn't make out their encampments, but when the sun fell each night the fires would alight. The numbers had been halved when the transients building a stone wall around the tower had joined with Potato.

At last count, there were thirty-two transients in all, though six of them were children. In time, he'd send them into town to get weapons, but for now he alternated his tasks between the ridiculous (going into town and bringing back all the Twinkies or one copy of every DVD they could find) and the exhausting (building the stone wall or cleaning the Ivory Tower). He wanted them tired and beholden to him.

No sleeping on the couch without doing some work around the yard. Wasn't that what his parents always said?

Potato grinned to himself; apparently he had learned something of value from them.

Outside the Ivory Tower, Hector and a second pirate, Ken Jakarski, stood behind a cluster of trees and watched the activity, gathering information. "I count twenty-five adults," Hector whispered to the pirate next to him. "One main entrance at the base of the tower. Gold's supposed to be inside, spread out over several floors if Berathon can be trusted," he grunted. He was in a bad mood and wanted to take it out on someone, anyone. Why was Austin put in charge of the raiding party? It was Hector that had stood up to Samuel at the First Night Feast. Austin spent most of the fight on the floor. And the whole *Cottonmather* stunt was a big failure, unless getting the *Plymouth Rock* sunk and the *Puritan* flagged as the next *Cottonmather* target was considered a success.

"Who are those people?" Jakarski asked.

"Dunno, but by the looks of it they're not part of the angel's plan," Hector replied, letting his agitation grow. "Unless they're dream was to be some rich guy's gardening staff. Come on, let's get back to base. Quicker we get back, quicker we can return and do some pirating."

Inside a stolen Cadillac Escalade, Teddy Levenson stewed silently as Carl Yesek yapped away in the seat next to him. Teddy was less than thrilled when he discovered that Austin and Mathers had left Carl behind to see who it was coming on the last boat from the *Puritan*, but took comfort from the fact that no one had seen what he'd done to Captain Crumb.

And he wasn't telling.

Teddy had no idea how Carl, Austin, Mathers, Hector, or any of the other pirates would react. Hell, he didn't even know if the old bastard was actually dead or just severely injured. Either way, Teddy had no intention of ever heading back to that ship to find out.

Austin and Mary Mathers stood on the counter inside Dunkin Donuts with their fifty pirates spread before them in the shop and out in the parking lot. The store wasn't big enough to hold all fifty pirates, so they had smashed out the front windows to accommodate the overflow crowd.

The doughnuts and muffins were stale, but there were still enough beverages and coffee to satisfy them.

Mathers outlined their plan. She tried her best to give them a speech they'd expect from a pirate. "Listen well, ya bastards! The Potato Tower is just over a mile into these woods. Hector and Ken tell me it's guarded by a bunch of woodspeople, so expect some resistance. Here's the plan. My crew will cut to the south, and McNamara's to the north. We'll form a half-circle around the Tower and when we're all in position, we'll rush the Tower and scatter the woodsmen. Let them go – we're here for gold and the Jolly Roger. The pirate who finds the flag," she grinned as she issued the challenge, "will lead the next raid! And the pirates who lead the raid always get a double-share of the bounty! Huzzah!"

"Huzzah!" the pirates shouted back.

"Mr. McNamara, any words of wisdom?" Mathers asked, turning to her co-leader.

Austin had been milling this moment since Mathers had started talking. He wanted no part of a raid that would result in the death of the woodspeople, and given the nervous energy running through the crowd, he knew that was a distinct possibility. But could he say that? Surely once they attacked the woodspeople would defend their castle, wouldn't they? It had been his idea to only half-encircle the Tower, giving the woodsfolk an escape route he hoped they'd take.

"Well?" Mathers prompted. "Are you going to say something, or did you shove so many stale doughnuts down your throat you can't talk? Get this man some milk, pirates!"

The crew roared in laughter and one of the pirates near the beverage cooler grabbed a plastic bottle of strawberry milk and hurled it towards the counter. The bottle missed Austin and Mathers and crashed into the mostly-empty doughnut trays behind them.

Austin looked out at the crowd, trying to think of something. "Well," he said, settling for the quickest out, "I could say something, or we could be going to get our gold! Would you rather listen to me, or steal some gold?"

"Gold!" the pirates shouted.

"Alright, then!" Austin whooped. "Let's get the ATVs out of the RVs and go steal us some booty!" Pause. *Go ahead*, his brain suggested. *Say it.* "Huzzah!" Austin shouted, giving in.

"Huzzah!" the crew shouted back.

Kelly pulled the carriage into her third hospital of the day and raced inside, wishing she had something to change into besides this increasingly-ridiculous dress. She burst into the emergency exit, thankful the automatic doors were still working. *How long until the electricity gives out?* she wondered, then pushed the thought aside.

There was no one at the desk.

Shit.

Shit shit shit.

Breathing hard, Kelly tried to calm herself. She knew something about setting broken bones, having rigged a splint or two for animals caught in bear traps over the past few years, but Saul needed serious attention. He'd lost a lot of blood. Could she rig up a blood transfusion?

She didn't want to find out.

In the distance, something crashed onto the floor.

Kelly jerked her head towards the long hallway before her. A set of double doors, roughly twenty feet down the hall, she guessed, blocked most of her view, but she was certain the crash had come from that direction.

Someone was in the hospital.

A doctor? She hoped it was a doctor, or at least a nurse, but knew that doctors and nurses were usually pretty good about not knocking things over.

Especially in hospitals.

Before she realized what she was doing, her feet were taking her towards the door. She had to risk it; Saul wasn't going to last the night and he was her responsibility. The nutbag who'd injured Saul was the same guy who abducted her, after all. She was responsible.

Figuring a brave front was better than a timid mouse, Kelly slammed through the double doors and into the hallway beyond. Not ten feet from the doors was a knocked over medical cart. Between her and the cart there were two doors – one on each side - leading into what she guessed were operating rooms. *Was the person who knocked over the cart coming or going?*

"I'm looking for a doctor!" she yelled, not wanting to walk into a trap. "Please, I have a friend outside who's been badly hurt! He needs medical attention!"

She paused, waiting, straining her ears for a sound, any sound. At first, there was nothing, but then …

Hushed whispers coming from down the hallway.

Kelly couldn't make out any of the words, but there were definitely several voices arguing with one another. Should she push the issue? Wait? While she was pondering, the decision was made for her.

Down the hallway and to her left, a woman exited an operating room. Then another. Then several men. All dressed in bright orange, oversized suits. Ten, in all, exited out of the operating room and into the hallway.

Astronauts.

None of them looked pleased to see her.

"My name is Vanessa Yvgenilenko," the first woman announced in a reasonably calm voice. "I used to be a doctor. Now I'm an astronaut. The men," she motioned to four of the men who started to walk towards Kelly, "will bring your friend inside. Please, come and join us. Stay away from the doors. It is not safe."

A puzzled look fell on Kelly's face. "Why?"

"How was your friend injured?" Vanessa asked.

"Hit and run," Kelly answered, seeing a small wave of relief wash over the astronauts. She stepped to the side to let the four men who would bring Saul in pass.

"Then there is hope he can be saved," Vanessa announced, relief evident in her voice.

"Why?" Kelly asked again. "What's going on? What are you people doing hiding here?"

Vanessa shook her head. "In time, we will tell you everything we have seen." The doctor-turned-astronaut glanced at the nervous expressions behind her. "Though I doubt you will believe a word of it."

Kelly stood there, feeling numb. Whatever it was these people had experienced, it had definitely scared them.

Vanessa looked hard at Kelly for a few moments, then slumped forward, clearly struggling. "I guess you have a right to know, since we all consider ourselves very much in danger for what we witnessed." Vanessa wiped her hands across her face several times, looking extremely tired. "Haven't slept since the night before."

"What did you see?" Kelly pressed. She needed to know.

Vanessa removed her hands and looked to Kelly with hollow eyes. "We saw … we saw an angel die. Enimon, the angel in charge of Astronauts, has been murdered."

"By who?" Kelly gasped, but there was no reply as the four men returned with Saul carried on a stretcher.

"Bring him in here," Vanessa nodded to a room, leaving Kelly's last question unanswered.

The pirates charged out of the woods.

Austin was caught by surprise, as Mathers had trumped the allotted starting time by five minutes. "She must want to be the one to find the Jolly Roger," Hector said beside Austin as the former mechanic started his own charge.

"Yeah," Austin grunted, his feet rooted to the ground. The presence of the woodspeople unnerved him; they weren't supposed to be here and Austin didn't want anything to do with them. This was supposed to be a simple robbery against an unguarded tower. Had Berathon set them up?

Probably, Austin frowned.

What was it Crumb had said? The angels didn't want them *acting* like pirates, they wanted them to *be* pirates, with all that entailed.

Austin watched as the pirates attacked the woodspeople. His planned "out" for them worked, to an extent. Some of the woodspeople fled into the woods opposite the pirate attack but others, too panicked by the sudden oncoming rush, ran towards them, or in circles.

One of the woodspeople stood his ground. A pirate ran towards him, sword held high, screaming and whooping. The woodsman grabbed the pirate's arm and twisted it back, then slugged the pirate in his face.

"Ow! That hurt!" the pirate screamed from his knees.

The woodsman raised his hand to strike again, but a second pirate, seeing what was happening, came up from behind him and stabbed him in the shoulder with a hunting knife. The woodsman grunted and turned on the second pirate, who let the knife stay lodged in the woodsman's shoulder.

"Holy shit," the pirate said, astonished at what he'd done. "I just stabbed a guy."

"Wrong," the woodsman replied. "You stabbed me."

"I guess I did," the pirate said, right before the woodsman slammed his fist into his face, breaking his nose.

Austin tried to tell himself this was expected, but the brutality of what was going on was hard to stomach. All around them pirates and woodspeople attacked each other, but they were still mostly people in costumes playing a part. To Austin, the scene looked more like a bad Halloween brawl than a real fight, except …

Except with each punch thrown, with each wound incurred, the brawl was gaining in intensity. The woodspeople that stayed and fought gained it first, a real urge to protect this tower – or rather, Austin realized, seeing the women and children, the woodsmen were protecting each other. They couldn't care less about the tower, which was why their punches held purpose. The woodsman who'd been stabbed was enraged, lashing out at any pirate that came across his path.

The next pirate in his path was Hector.

The woodsman raised his fist, but Hector was ready. When the punch came swinging down at his face, he casually stepped aside and slammed his left fist into the larger man's kidney. Already weakened from the stabbing, the woodsman was dropped to his knee.

Austin held his breath as Hector reached for the hunter's knife at his belt.

He was going to kill him.

Austin rushed forward. "Hector, no!" he yelled, and Hector held the knife in place, turning to face him.

"Why not?"

Austin thought quick. "You want to be the one to find the Jolly Roger, right?" A flicker in Hector's eye and the knife dropped ever-so-slightly. "Look to the Tower, Mathers and that Jakarski guy are heading inside."

Hector turned and saw across the short distance that what Austin said was true. Sheathing the knife, he nodded and broke into a run.

Austin looked down to the woodsman. "Here," he said, extending a hand, "let me help you- ooof!" The woodsman's fist buried itself in Austin's stomach, doubling Austin over. The woodsman forced himself to his feet, then reached behind him to remove the pirate's knife as Austin, gasping for breath, fell to his knees. With one hand holding his stomach, Austin held the other aloft. "No," he gasped, "wait … I … saved …"

The woodsman's response was a boot to Austin's face. "Thieves!" he grunted. "Why do you do what the angels tell you?" Another boot, this time to Austin's rib cage. "They've turned you into killers!" Kick. "They tried to rip my family apart! And why?" Kick. "Because when I was a kid I dreamt of being President and my wife dreamt of being Santa Claus?" Kick. Kick. "For that they tried to take my kids! My kids! What kind of gift from God demands that children be ripped away from their parents?"

Austin had no answer, meekly trying to cover himself from the man's attacks.

The woodsman wasn't done. He stomped a boot down hard on Austin's ribs, pinning the Old World Lit professor to the ground. The woodsman then dropped down on top of Austin, straddling his chest and pinning Austin's arms to his side. The woodsman raised the knife above his head, "Well, Mr. Pirate, I've got a message you can take back to the angels when you see them in heaven. That message is this: Fuck you and Fuck God."

The woodsman swung the knife down for the killshot and Austin lurched hard to the side, trying to knock the woodsman off balance. Desperately, Austin reached for the pistol at his side. His fingers grasped the handle-

A gunshot cracked through the late afternoon.

Austin blinked. Had he pulled the trigger? He looked up to see the woodsman look down at his own chest and the gunshot wound that had opened him up. "Whu .... whu ...?" The woodsman choked up blood.

Austin was still trapped beneath the man's weight. He hadn't been the one to shoot the woodsman. Who-?

He should've known.

Mary Mathers placed her feet on either side of his head and grinned down at him. "I think it's fair to say you owe me one, Mr. McNamara." Her eyes locked on Austin's, she raised her pistol to the woodsman's coughing, sputtering face, and pulled the trigger.

Berathon floated to the deck of the *Puritan*, and the remaining crewmen spread outwards, giving the angel room. Berathon ignored them, his eyes focused on the wheezing form lying still on the deck – Captain Crumb.

"Teddy jumped on him," one of the pirates explained.

Berathon dropped to one knee and placed his hand on the back of the Captain's neck; it was clearly broken. "You're going to die," he said.

Crumb spit up blood in response, then coughed out two words. "End ... it."

Berathon nodded. Holding his arm out straight, the angel said a silent prayer and a flaming sword burst into existence before him. "May your soul find peace at the end of my sword," Berathon said softly, then drove the flaming tip into Crumb's back, piercing his heart.

Crumb was dead in seconds.

Berathon said another prayer and the flaming sword vanished. With sad eyes, he turned to the crew. "Wrap him in chains, then commit his body to the waters," he ordered. The crew obeyed, half moving to Crumb and the other half moving below deck to search for a chain.

'They're starting to understand,' Berathon thought to himself. 'God's gift does not excuse one from consequence.'

The angel was watching the crew move somberly about their task when his eyes came to rest on the door to Crumb's cabin. Mollug. A tight thrill ran up the angel's spine at the thought of the unguarded cabin. Crumb was dead and Mathers and McNamara gone. The parrot who'd overheard his conversation with Enimon about the possibility of God's word being forged was now within his grasp. The angels could not risk the humans discovering the rumor the angels feared. Tragedy though Crumb's death was, it was also an opportunity for Berathon to protect the angels' secrect.

Knowing he needn't explain anything to the crew that was left, Berathon started to walk across the deck, but found that an opportunity fortuitously gained was not his for long.

"Berathon."

The angel ceased his march, and turned his head skyward where an angel hovered in the setting sunlight. "Yes, Ocilael?"

"There has been a murder."

Berathon nodded, pointing back to Crumb. "The Captain of this ship, Ezekiel Crumb. Murdered by one of his crew, Theodore Levenson." Berathon folded his arms across his chest, more upset at the intrusion of Ocilael than the murder. "It's pirate business. There is no need for you to be present."

The angels had attracted the attention of the crew, who stopped their activities to watch Ocilael drop to the deck. "There is every need for my presence wherever yours finds itself, Berathon."

"Speak your mind, Ocilael," Berathon countered. "I have no time for your games."

"The murder of which I speak is not that of your pirate," Ocilael seethed through clenched teeth, "but the murder of an angel."

"What?" Berathon asked, shocked. An uneasy murmur made its way through the crew around them.

"The angel Enimon has been murdered."

Berathon felt something lurch inside him – *That is why he was late for our meeting.*

Ocilael wasn't finished. "I have decreed that you, Berathon, are the prime suspect. You will come with me to face the questions of your brothers."

Mathers and Austin made their way inside the Tower, blinded instantly by the sheer brilliance of the gold that surrounded them. "My God," Austin blurted. "I've never seen so much gold in my life. There wasn't this much gold in Smaug's cave."

"Who's Smaug?" Mathers asked, her eyes dancing over the coins and trinkets.

"Nevermind," Austin said, doubting Mathers had ever seen, or read, *The Hobbit*. "Not important. Although, come to think of it, he seems like your kind of guy."

"Why?" Mathers asked. "Because he's rich?"

"No," Austin said, stepping forward, "because he's territorial, breathes fire, and enjoys scaring the crap out of people."

Mathers nodded, letting a grin spread over her face. "You're right. Sounds like my kind of man." There was one main staircase and two smaller staircases leading from the chamber. "You take the left," she said, "and I'll take the right."

Austin nodded, glad to be out of her presence. *Or am I?* he wondered. *Stop it. You almost died and you're flirting with a gorgeous psycho. Get focused.*

Pushing the thought aside, Austin moved up the narrow, curved staircase. The sounds of battle and pillaging echoed through the hallway, hiding his footsteps. The staircase curved with the building, meaning Austin was constantly rounding a corner. Thirty or forty steps up, he saw a pirate standing at an opening above him.

Hector.

Austin started to call out to his friend, when Hector suddenly rushed forward into the room. Concerned, Austin hurried to the doorway when the sight before him knocked him still.

A man in a track suit was slumped against the far wall, near a fireplace. He wasn't dead, but he wasn't ready to get to his feet, either. "Must be the man called Potato," Austin's mind reasoned on its own. It was the other two people in the room that had his attention: Ken Jakarski and Hector Ladronne.

Jakarski had the Jolly Roger in his hand and his gun out, pointing it at Hector. "Fuck off, Paco," Jakarski grinned. "Flag's mine. Got it fair and square."

"You did," Hector replied. "And now I'm going to take it from you. Unfair and unsquare."

Jakarski laughed. "No chance. I'm the one with the gun."

"But I'm the one with the gold," Hector smiled, holding out his hand to show Jakarski a handful of gold coins.

"A handful of coins?" Jakarski laughed. "You've got to be kidding. This place is loaded with all the gold I can carry. What the fuck do I want with your handful of coins? Besides," Jakarski grinned, "you heard Mathers' deal. Whoever gets the Roger gets a double share next time out. So take your gold coins and choke on 'em."

Hector grinned. "You've got it all wrong, Jakarski. I wasn't offering them as a bribe."

"Then what?"

Hector tossed the coins at Jakarski's face. Raising his hands to protect himself, Jakarski's hand slipped on the pistol and he fired.

Hector fell to his knees.

Austin started into the room, when Hector jumped back up, freezing Austin in place once again. Hector charged Jakarski, knocking him backwards and causing the pirate to drop both the pistol and the flag.

"Son of a bitch!" Jakarski roared, regaining his balance. "I'm going to fucking kill you!" He rushed towards Hector. As he had with the woodsman, Hector waited for the punch to come, then sidestepped, but this time instead of nailing his opponent with a punch, Hector pushed Jakarski away. Jakarski spat in anger, then charged again. Hector repeated the move, but this time shoved Jakarski harder.

Into the fireplace.

Jakarski screamed and Potato recoiled in horror as the fire took hold of Jakarski's costume and flesh. Austin's eyes went wide. Had Hector meant to do that? Did his friend just shove a guy into a fire just so he could claim the pirate's flag and a larger share of gold? He looked to his friend but couldn't see his face. Quietly, purposefully, Hector bent down to grab the Jolly Roger and turned to look at the spot where Austin had stood.

There was no one there.

Down the staircase Austin ran, taking several steps at a time.

What the hell was going on? Was this all really God's plan?

Hours later, when the pirates were done hauling out all the gold they could carry to the SUVs and RVs and had left the Potato Tower behind, Teddy Levenson strolled out of the woods and into the Tower. He found Potato Johnson standing in the doorway, his body beaten and bloodied.

"What do you want?" Potato asked. "I thought you fucking pirates were done robbing me."

Teddy smiled. "I'm not with them. Not anymore, at least. Tell me something, Potato," Teddy asked, "for all the gold they carried out of here, did it really set you back financially?"

Potato looked sideways at the fat pirate. "What? N-no, I don't think so. I am – was – the richest man in the world, after all."

Teddy slapped Potato on the back. "Wanna get even richer? And in the process lay a trap for those fucking bastards?"

Potato didn't know where this was going, but found himself nodding. "Yeah."

"Great," Teddy said, hugging Potato to him. "Have I got a plan that will get us both what we want."

"What's that?" Potato asked.

Teddy looked out at the woods around them. "You're going to build a casino, and I'm going to run it for you."

"What?"

"In a year or so, when we're rolling in more money than we've ever dreamt of, those pirate bastards will be drawn back to this place, and you and me will be waiting for them with an army of mercs that will rip them to shreds. Sound like a good plan?" he asked, turning to Potato.

Potato thought for a moment, then smiled. "Yeah, it does."

Father Thomas Otten knelt in the first row of pews inside the church he'd spent the last thirty-two years leading. Something was wrong with the world – that much was obvious. He needed answers. The angels had told him he was one of the few priests left in the world and that bore with it, Otten believed, an even greater responsibility here in the New World than it had in the Old World.

Something is wrong.

Otten had felt a restlessness inside of him since the Reorganization that was as uncommon to him as anything he'd ever experienced. He believed his place was here, with his church, but with every passing day it became harder and harder to stay. What kept him was no longer the sense of duty but the simple reality that he didn't know where he would go if he did leave.

He spent most of his time here, in prayer. Sometimes the prayer was silent, and sometimes it was aloud to the emptiness. The emptiness bothered him more than anything else. He'd never, in all his left, felt an emptiness inside a church. God's presence had always been tangible to him, but now …?

The angels said God was missing. How was that possible?

Thomas Otten suddenly knew why he could no longer stay in his church. God was not present here. He was present in his heart, but not in the church.

Father Otten rose to his feet, his knees stiff from the long session of prayer.

His mind had been given a purpose and he would leave at once.

Father Thomas Otten was going to go looking for God.

Chapter Ten
Off Balance

In the moonlight, Austin McNamara stood on cooling sand and looked out on the waters of the Atlantic Ocean. He'd stood on this beach - Long Sands, the locals called it - probably a hundred times in his life. Vacations, mostly with his parents, though for one glorious week with his then-girlfriend Jessica Jenkins after their freshman year at BC. He'd seen countless ships from this beach, but none like the sole ship that claimed the waters this night - the *Puritan*. A pirate ship. *His* pirate ship.

Around him, the activity of pirates. Joy still dominated their mood, but the shimmering gold they loaded onto the landing boats and out of the SUVs and RVs that had carried their bounty from Potato Tower in Durham was starting to feel a bit too reminiscent of work. They'd found Carl Yesek nearly unconscious in the woods near the Dunkin Donuts they used as a base of operations. Last thing he remembered was Teddy Levenson yelling, "Look out!" and then getting hit on the back of the head. Teddy hadn't come back; their search party found no signs of him.

Mary Mathers and Hector Ladrone were keeping the spirits of the crew high. As the first load had left the beach ninety minutes ago, bound for the *Puritan*, the crew had sagged. They were tired, aching, and needed to wait for the landing boats to return before they could do anything more. Mathers had suggested they raid a local restaurant for food, and her words were like magic, as the entire crew seemed to instantly remember they hadn't eaten for nearly twelve hours.

"You recommended the beach," Mathers had said to Austin with an unmovable smile on her beautiful face. "Any good restaurants we can steal from?"

Half-heartedly, Austin had pointed to their far right. "Joint over there called the Goldenrod. Good food. Better taffy."

"Sounds yummy," Mathers beamed. "Come," she said dramatically, "let us lead our victorious crew to—"

"I'll pass," Austin mumbled, turning his back to the vacation town. "Not hungry."

Mathers wrapped her arm in his and pressed herself to his side. "I like your style, Mr. McNamara. Send the crew away so that we may have the beach to ourselves."

Austin tugged his arm free, feeling foolish in his pirate's uniform. "Quit it. I'm not interested."

Mathers had placed her hands seductively on her hips. "Bullshit. I've seen the way you look at me. Not with the open lust of some of them," she jerked her finger towards the crew, "but with a mixed desire." Casually, she unbuttoned the next closed button down on her blouse, revealing just a hint of the round breasts beneath. "You may have a girlfriend, Mr. McNamara. You may not approve of the games I play." Mathers opened the next button, revealing a silky black bra that seemed, to Austin's muddled mind, very content with its job. "You may not even like me, but don't pretend you're not interested. I am very familiar with your type of manhood."

"And what type is that?" Austin snapped, but unquestionably curious. *Something about this woman ...*

Mathers' eyes bored into his. "You're the kind of guy that likes to play it cool, that likes to pretend nothing gets to him. But inside, you're dying with jealousy and suspicion. You're the kind of guy that obsesses over your girlfriend's ex-boyfriends, who squeezes his eyes tightly to try and remove the image of your girlfriend getting hot with another guy. You always try to measure up to what she had before, listening for every comment she makes about her past loves. You hate it when—"

"Christ," Austin mumbled, throwing up his hands. "Were you a shrink in the Old World?"

"No," Mathers shrugged. "I was a model for a shopping channel."

"What?"

Mathers pushed on. "The way you are, Mr. McNamara, I'm fairly confident you're dating a woman you don't feel you deserve. You feel, deep inside, that she's biding her time with you between her last studly boyfriend and her next princely boyfriend. She's the kind of girl that should be dating the movie-star quarterback, but she's taken pity on the geek."

Austin looked at Mathers blankly, mentally trying to decide how correct she was, and if it made any difference to anything. There was no denying—he didn't even try—that the person Mathers described sounded like the Austin McNamara of a year ago, but that wasn't the Austin of today. Right?

Right?

"She runs the relationship," Mathers stated flatly, as if she had watched the entire relationship of Kelly and Austin from start to present. "Perhaps she's not the domineering type—most likely, she's not—but she's the one who ends up deciding where you go out to eat, what movies you rent, when you make love. Far from being abhorrent, that's the kind of woman you like, Mr. McNamara. The kind of woman who, though subtly and without malice, is in complete control. That arrangement makes you feel safe. Secure. You can be a passenger, making suggestions, keeping her happy, but you don't have to be the lead dog." Mathers took a step towards Austin, who tried to take a step backwards but found himself rooted to the spot. "Mark my words, well, McNamara. Crumb has seen something in you and, right or wrong, he's placed his trust in you— protecting your stupid parrot, giving you the co-lead on this mission, taking you into his confidence. The time is going to come when you're going to need to be the lead dog you've spent your life trying not to be. There's two ways you can accomplish this. One, you can grow a pair." Mathers let out a small chuckle, the sparkle in her eyes telling him she didn't think that was possible. "Two, you can find yourself another security blanket." Her voice dropped seductively lower. "Me. Follow my lead, and I'll get you through." Mathers began to slowly back away. "Or don't, and you'll lose in the New World the way you would've eventually lost your woman in the Old World. Because you're a passenger. Now go ahead, I've seen you fumbling with your cell phone all day. Call her. I can guarantee she isn't sitting around waiting for the New World to reveal itself to her. Wherever she is, whatever she's doing, she sure as shit isn't sitting around and letting someone else drive her." Mathers stopped, grinned, and brought her fingers to her lips, giving Austin a coy look. "Or was that too strong a sexual metaphor for you, baby?"

Austin shivered. That was ninety minutes ago, but the conversation was playing over and over in Austin's head on a continuous loop. The only break from Mathers' rant was when he picked up the stolen cell phone in his hand and dialed Kelly's number. No answer. Time and again, no answer. From her, at least. Her voice mail answered him every time, but Austin didn't want to leave a message. He wanted to *talk* to her, not pass along a Hello. As his fingers hit the keys to redial her number, Austin picked up the voices of Hector and Mathers in the returning crowd behind him calling to the returning landing boats. Cursing them because they were available to be cursed at, Austin slid down the beach, listening, once again, to the never-ending ringing of Kelly's phone.

The familiar click came, signaling the voice mail message, when Austin's mind made the point that the phone had only wrung four times, not the five it took for the voice mail to activate. *She's picking up her phone!*

"Who the fuck is this?"

Had the Little Mermaid chosen that moment to walk out of the Atlantic Ocean and fire a whale's harpoon through his chest, Austin wouldn't have been more surprised to hear a rough male voice on the other end.

"Well?" the voice asked again in response to Austin's silence. "You've been dialing this number all fucking day, so I'm guessing you ain't got the wrong number. Who, the, fuck, is, this?"

Austin's throat had gone dry, but he forced out a response. "Where's Kelly? Who are you?"

"Kelly?" the gruff voice asked, letting out a menacing chuckle. "Kelly Reed? The bitch who owns this phone? What do you fucking care?"

"I'm ... I'm—"

The voice on the other end let his chuckle turn into a full-blown laugh. "Is this the one and only Austin Fucking McNamara?"

"Where's Kelly?" Austin asked again, failing to suppress the growing panic inside of him.

"This is too fucking rich," the gruff voice laughed. "Kelly Reed. You want to know where that uptight bitch is?" the voice challenged. "I'll tell you where she is. She's dead."

"No!"

"Yes," the voice admonished. "She went to the First Night Feast, got drunk out of her mind, got abducted, passed out then around by five princes like a porn queen, then rescued by the King."

"Regent?"

"You know of another King of New England? Regent saved her used ass, but before he could bring her to safety, he was betrayed by a friend." The voice on the other end dropped low, as if letting

Austin in on a secret. "This prince, some creep named Jim Catlin, the King's supposed friend, called her more trouble than she was worth and ran her through with his sword, killing her."

Austin dropped to his knees in the sand. "This ... this can't be ..."

"Keep telling yourself that, sport," the rough voice chided. "But ask yourself how your girlfriend's phone came into the possession of the King's guard. I'll tell you how—because I lifted it from Catlin right before the King let him go."

Austin's voice was working on autopilot. "Regent let him free?"

"Of course. Catlin was his buddy. Kelly Reed was just some ass he used to fuck. Bye-bye now, Austin. I don't suspect you're man enough to come get confirmation from King Regent, so I doubt we'll ever talk again."

"No! Wait!" Austin was completely numb. "How do I know you're telling the truth?"

"That's what makes this so rich, you little shit. You don't."

Captain of the King's Guard Wallace O'Malley hit the end button and tossed Kelly Reed's cell phone onto the empty tabletop of his desk. He let out a long sigh and rubbed his eyes with his thick fingers. The day had been too long. Catlin still hadn't reported in, which meant, in all likelihood, that either Catlin was dead or that he'd failed. Which meant, in an even greater likelihood, that Frederic Kornell was still alive.

O'Malley hated loose ends.

Turning in his swivel chair, O'Malley looked out across from his window on the castle's third floor towards the New England Aquarium. The King had taken a group of giggling New World— what was the phrase his subordinate had used?—hot female mystery-solving rock-stars into the building earlier in the day. He hadn't yet returned. The last update O'Malley had received reported the King had ordered the women to play a concert for him, which they were all-too-happy to do. During the third act's performance, someone had apparently stolen a penguin who, for some reason, was wearing a valuable diamond around its neck, and now all of the "hot sexy female mystery-solving rock-stars" were trying to solve what they were actually calling a kidnapping while the King looked on with a long, dour face.

The King was turning into something of a joke. O'Malley couldn't have that.

Which is why, after taking it as a sign of good fortune that the incessant caller was Austin, he'd told the lie he did. A bit too over-the-top, he realized, but the shock of the news of Kelly's "death" would probably mask the over-dramatization to Austin's muddled brain.

A pirate attack should bring the King around. And if it didn't … O'Malley shrugged to himself.

Kings were easily replaced.

O'Malley had said it so many times now, it was becoming something of a mantra: No one, not even the King, was going to fuck up the New World for Wallace O'Malley.

"Austin. Austin!"

Crumpled down onto his knees, staring out at the ocean because it was in front of him, Austin waved Mathers' incessant calling away.

Mathers wasn't easily dismissed. "God-damnit, Austin!" she shouted through clenched teeth. "We've got major problems."

Austin shook his head, turning his gaze to the cell phone from which he'd heard the news. "My girlfriend's dead."

"What?" The news caught Mathers by surprise, trumping her own bad news.

Austin, consumed by the news, turned half-heartedly to Mathers and showed her the cell phone. "I just called her number. Some … some guy, one of the King's guardsmen, I think … said she was dead." Talking about it brought Austin one step out of his daze. "She … Kelly was at a party … First Night Feast … she got drunk and … and kidnapped and ra…" Austin couldn't bring himself to say the word. "She was killed and the King, fucking King Brad Regent, let her killer go because he was buddies with the guy."

"Austin," Mathers said, putting a hand on the troubled young man's shoulder, "I'm sorry, but …"

"But what?" Austin fumed, taking another step out of the daze.

"Shit," Mathers said, shaking her head, feeling half-foolish for the game she'd been playing with Austin not an hour earlier. "I don't know what. Maybe the guy's pulling your chain. I mean, there's no way to know, right?"

Austin's face instantly brightened, clarity coming back to him. "I can go to Boston and confront Regent."

"Confront the King?" Mathers didn't know whether she should be impressed or dismayed at the decision.

"Yeah," Austin said, clarity turning into obsession. "That's the only way to know, right? Confront the King and find out if the story is bullshit or not." His eyes locked onto Mathers and she saw in them a purposeful desperation. "Kelly is not dead. I don't believe it. But the guy on the phone knew my name. Why would he know my name? Something's happened to Kelly and my guess is that Regent is at the bottom of it. If that fucking bastard has done anything to her, I'll kill him."

The final three words hit Austin with a newfound depth. How many times, he wondered, had he uttered those words over the course of his twenty-eight years? How many times had he heard them come from his friends? How many of those hundreds of times ever had any real meaning? None, he guessed. "I'll kill him." "I'll kill the bitch." "I'll kill that fucking asshole." "I'll kill you." Mostly meaningless hyperbole in the Old World. But in the New World ...

Crumb's words: *The angels don't want you to act like pirates, Austin, they want you to be pirates.*

"I'll kill him," he whispered, finding strength in the words. He was acutely aware that he didn't know if he really could kill someone, but if Regent had something to do with Kelly's death ...? "Time will tell," he muttered, rising to his feet.

"Austin," Mathers started, but Austin cut her off.

"I'm leaving."

"What?"

"I'm going to Boston. To see the King. To see-"

"Austin." It was Hector's voice that called to him now. Austin looked passed Mathers and saw that most of the crew of the *Puritan* was standing around him, watching with rapt attention. "Austin, if the King of New England killed your girlfriend," Hector said with an icy boldness, "then revenge is yours. But if it was the King ... you ain't gonna be able to do it alone."

"I don't-"

"We're pirates now, Austin," Hector repeated, raising up the Jolly Roger he'd taken from Potato Tower. "You want revenge on the King?" Hector turned to the pirates around them, "Hell, I'm sure the rest of us could find something of value in Boston we wouldn't mind stealing. What say you?" he called to the pirates around them. "Are you ready for your next plunder?"

"Huzzah!" Mathers shouted, rising to the moment.

"Huzzah!" the crew answered.

Austin shook his head. "Guys, no offense, but I can't see Captain Crumb okaying an assault on Boston. We're not ready yet."

Austin's words brought the momentary cheer in the crew to a dead silence. Confused, Austin turned to Mathers for an explanation.

"Austin," she explained slowly, "I don't think we have to worry about getting Captain Crumb's permission."

"Why?"

"Crumb is dead, Austin," Mathers said pointedly. "Teddy Levenson killed him."

Kelly Reed awoke with a start, not knowing where she was. For an instant, she thought she was back in the apartment she'd shared with Austin. Her waking thought was that it was Saturday, the Red Sox had an afternoon game, and she and Austin were supposed to spend the day shopping for a wedding present for a mutual friend. She wanted Austin to go with her, but with the afternoon Sox game, he'd spend the day bitching and moaning in that cute, pathetic way he had.

The thought lasted only a moment, replaced with the reality of where she was and what had happened.

"Awake?"

Kelly turned to the door to see a silhouette of a woman with her arms folded across her chest and her side leaning against the frame of the door. "Kind of," Kelly replied, rubbing her eyes. "Valerie, right?"

"Vanessa, actually," the woman replied kindly, stepping into the room and flicking on the light switch.

"How's Saul?" Kelly asked, thinking of the Young Prince who'd been nearly killed when they were attacked the previous night.

"He'll live," Vanessa replied, running a tired hand through her thick, black hair. "Extensive damage to his lower regions, and there's no guarantee he'll keep his right leg below the knee, but he should pull through."

Kelly nodded, feeling numb.

"You were lucky to find us here," Vanessa added, sitting on the edge of the hospital bed.

Kelly gave a half-hearted shrug and smile. "Actually, I think we were more lucky to find a doctor."

Vanessa returned the smile. "True." The two women sat in silence for a few moments, trying to absorb all that had happened, both wanting to ask the other questions about their New World experiences but unsure how willing the other would be to discuss their respective tragedies. "Would you like some coffee?" Vanessa asked, breaking the silence.

"No," Kelly shook her head. "Water would be nice, though."

Vanessa nodded, then walked to the room's sink. "Princess, huh?" she asked, and Kelly caught a slight trace of an Eastern European accent. "What did you do in the Old World?"

Kelly looked down at her Princess outfit and wanted, more than anything, to be out of it and into a pair of jeans and one of Austin's sweatshirts. She always took one of his sweatshirts when she was away from him for more than a week as a way of having him physically with her. "I was a painter-slash-photojournalist," Kelly replied, nodding her thanks as Vanessa handed her a Dixie cup of lukewarm water. "A naturalist," she added. "The photos paid the bills, and the painting filled my passion."

Vanessa smiled. "Far cry from being a Princess."

Kelly sighed. "No kidding. Christ, I can't even remember what I was thinking when I was ten. I don't remember ever really wanting to be a Princess, except for maybe that month after I saw *The Princess Bride*." Kelly shook her head, letting out a small chuckle as she drained the last of the water from the Dixie cup. "Guess I should be glad the angels turned me into this as opposed to a Care Bear or Cabbage Patch Kid or whatever else I dreamt of being that year." Vanessa took Kelly's cup and moved to the sink to refill it. "What about you?" Kelly asked. "Do you remember wanting to be an astronaut?"

Vanessa nodded without turning back to Kelly as the water poured from the faucet. "It was all I ever wanted to be. My family lived a few miles outside of Star City, the Soviet version of your NASA. From my earliest memory, all I wanted was to be an astronaut and travel on a rocket ship." She returned with the cup. "But the Soviets were not so keen on women astronauts. After the Soviet system collapsed, my father moved us to America, where I enrolled in medical school." Vanessa reached out to touch Kelly's hand gently. "When the Reorganization came, and the New World replaced the Old, were you happy?"

Kelly frowned. "Not really, no. I was - still am, I guess - angry."

"Why?"

"Angry at being taken away from a job I loved. Angry at getting separated from my boyfriend." Kelly took a sip, thinking back. "Most of all, I guess I was - am - angry at being told what to do. I always hated that, whether it was my parents, my school teachers, my boyfriends." A devilish grin appeared on her face. "Or even God and the angels, I suppose. Pretty insubordinate of me, huh?"

Vanessa returned the grin. "I'm sure God will understand."

Kelly finished off the second cup of water. "What about you? How did you feel about the New World?"

Vanessa rose from the bed and motioned with her hands to her bright orange space suit. "I loved it. Over the past few years, the idea of going to space came back to me all over again. Not six months ago, I applied for a medical position with NASA. I didn't dare allow for the possibility of actually going to space, but to work for a space program ... let me say that when the angels made that impossible dream come to reality, I was more than thrilled." Vanessa's mood turned dark. "But now ... now it appears that my dream has been denied me yet again."

Kelly nodded, wondering if she should ask the obvious question. She decided there was no time like the present. "Vanessa ... what happened? You said you saw ... an angel die?"

Vanessa's shoulders sagged. "Enimon, the Angel in Charge of Astronauts, was taking us south. There were more New World astronauts than the Old World infrastructure could handle, and there was a delay in completing all the requisite new facilities. Castles took precedence," she said, forcing a smile as she looked to Kelly's Princess outfit, "and the angels aren't unlimited in their power. We were being led to Virginia, where a new facility was being prepared. There was about forty of us in the group; we were aboard two buses. Not yellow school buses, either, but fancy coaches - large seats, bathroom, kitchen, bar. It was a great experience," she said, her voice showing real emotion. "I will tell you this, Kelly. You do not find too many unhappy astronauts. There's something about a love of space that makes one see the brighter side of life. Most of us, too, were middle-aged, having been children during the so-called space race or even, like myself, during the 1970s, when the Apollo missions were active. We have grown up - despite our being doctors, accountants, engineers, schoolteachers, factory workers - with a deep love for space and space exploration. We were - there is no other word for it - giddy. Simply giddy. The whole of the world, it seemed, had been changed just for us."

She paused to let out a soulful sigh. Kelly said nothing, letting Vanessa tell the story at her own pace. When the doctor-turned-astronaut spoke again, her voice was the low, painful tone of one who'd lived through a nightmare. "Enimon was with us on our bus when it happened. He'd been ... troubled, I think, is a fair way to describe his mood. We asked him what could possibly be wrong, and he wouldn't answer. He put up a brave front, after that, but you could see storm clouds behind those silvery eyes." Vanessa shook her head and wrapped her arms around herself, as if she were suddenly cold. "We were the second bus in the convoy. We heard an explosion and then, before anyone could even ask what had happened, we were driving through fire and ... and we hit something. The first bus. Or, rather, what was left of it."

Curiosity had Kelly firmly in its grasp. "What happened?"

Vanessa hadn't heard the question, lost as she was in the memory. "Enimon took off immediately, crashing through the side of our bus as we came out the other side of the fire. Our bus screeched to a halt and we all rushed to the windows to try to see what had happened. What we saw ..." she shook her head, "... it was ... monstrous. Twice the size of Enimon, it looked like ... like ..." she turned her eyes to Kelly to show that her words were inadequate to describe just what she'd seen. "It looked like an angel on fire," she whispered. "Red and burning, its wings sent fire to the ground with every beat. Its face was ... human but ... not human. It's hands were ... were like the talons of a hawk or eagle. Big. Vicious. They raked at Enimon's face and tore at his wings. For ... I don't know ... ten seconds ... ten minutes ... Enimon fought this ... this nightmare. And then you could almost see it in his eyes, the moment he knew he couldn't defeat this creature. He called out for help, but no angels came to his aid. He tried a desperate gamble, swooping under the creature, but ..." Vanessa's body shook. "The fire creature caught hold of one of Enimon's wings and snapped it like a twig, then tossed Enimon to the ground, near the bus. He ordered us to leave, and, somehow, the driver was able to obey. As we pulled on down the highway, I saw Enimon move to his knees. It was clear," she said, staring at Kelly to reinforce that she was telling the truth, "he was praying, but ..." doubt crept into her eyes, "it looked like he was praying into his harp." Vanessa shook her head. "It also looked like he was playing it, but ... you must think me crazy."

"No," Kelly said, enraptured by the story. Whether she believed or disbelieved what she was hearing hadn't been decided, but she did not think Vanessa crazy.

Vanessa wiped a single tear from her face. "I would have thought myself mad, except ... while Enimon was praying, the fire creature drove a flaming sword through Enimon's chest." Vanessa looked to the ceiling, as if it were heaven itself. "Enimon let out the most awful scream I'd ever heard. We were all filled with an incredible sadness, and then ... as the fire creature pulled Enimon's body up into the sky, we all heard his voice, one last time. 'Find the harp!' he screamed into our ... our what? Our brain? Our soul? We were all knocked instantly unconscious." Tears began to flow down Vanessa's cheeks. "Praise be to God, Kelly," she said, "we saw an angel die and I'm so scared I don't know what to do. What the hell was that thing that killed Enimon? Did someone dream of being a ... being a ... fire angel? Demon? How far did the angels go in granting dreams?"

Kelly didn't know, and told that to Vanessa.

"Do you know what scares me the most, though?" Vanessa asked, coming quickly to sit on the bed. "We haven't seen an angel since then. All day we kept waiting for an angel to show up and tell us what to do, but ... nothing. It's like all the angels have suddenly disappeared."

Berathon stood alone on a cloud, his arms chained together behind his back. The brightness of Heaven had never seemed so harsh to him, but then, he'd never been the center of all heavenly attention, either. Around him - though none stood within twenty feet - all of the angels of Heaven gathered to hear the words of Gabriel, Ocilael, and see what most had only seen in nightmares - one angel dead and another in chains.

At the feet of Berathon, Enimon's body laid in a state of semi-decay. Sunlight caused an angel's body to diminish, but the light of Heaven was not that of the sun, and so Enimon's body lay there, dead but not disintegrating anymore than it already had. It was, all angels readily admitted, a horrific sight. Half of Enimon's stomach was gone, as were various spots over his legs and arms. His face was largely untouched, though the left half of his nose was gone, and his lower lip had burnt away, leaving the sickly sight of his teeth and gums open to the world's eyes.

From out of the host of angels, Gabriel, Ocilael, Raphael, and Azrael came to stand before him. Berathon tried to read their faces and found it was not hard. Angels were not good at hiding emotions. For centuries, the only two emotions angels had ever needed to show were joy and reverence. Occasionally, confusion, such as the time God lifted the boulder that then fell on top of him, setting this entire drama in motion. Gabriel's face showed a troubled concern, mirrored closely by that of Raphael. It was the other two faces that drew Berathon's attention. Ocilael's jaw was set firm and his eyes were cold and harsh. As the Angel in charge of Law Enforcement, they had turned to Ocilael to preside over Enimon's murder. As for Azrael ... Berathon stared long into the eyes of the usually cheerful angel and saw ... joy and happiness. Azrael appeared as he had days ago, as if there was no dead angel laying on the floor of Heaven before him.

"Berathon," Gabriel started to say, then noticed the chains that bound his arms. "Ocilael, what is the meaning of that?" he asked, pointing. "Free him."

"With all due respect, Gabriel, Berathon is a suspect."

Gabriel didn't try to hide the agitation that came to his face. "Remove those chains at once. A suspect is not the same as a criminal."

Reluctantly, Ocilael did as he was ordered, and within moments Berathon's hands were free once again. "Gabriel," he said quickly and with great force in his voice, "I am willing to forgive the actions of Ocilael due to the tragedy that has befallen our brother Enimon. But there are questions - dangerous questions - circulating through the Host. We are all in need of answers."

Gabriel brought his hands to his temple; as the Angel in charge of the Reorganization his life had been a non-stop blur of activity since they'd received God's Word. "I know, Berathon. Juramel and Raphael have brought these concerns to my attention." Gabriel gathered himself and looked out around him at the gathered angels. "There are two mysteries that plague us, my fellow angels. The first," he motioned to Enimon's body, "is the death of our brother. Ocilael believes, and there is no reason, as I see it, for us to doubt his word, that Enimon was murdered."

A knowing murmur went through the Host. Murder was what they had all surmised, but to hear it aloud gave it a weight they had all inwardly hoped to deny.

"The second mystery," Gabriel continued, and this time there was no stopping the shaking that touched his voice, "that I was unaware was circulating until this past hour, is that some of you believe God's Word has been forged."

A massive outbreak of protests and accusations erupted from the Host at Gabriel's words. Far less than half of all angels had heard the rumor, and their confusion and desperation drowned out those who demanded answers from Gabriel. Amidst it all, Berathon stood silently, watching for any sign from any angel that they knew more than they were sharing. So far … nothing, but then, he was not, nor did he pretend to be, an expert in such matters.

"Silence, silence," Gabriel pleaded and the angels, desperate for knowledge, quieted down within moments. "It is with a heavy soul that I must admit to you all that we believe the two incidents to be connected." Gabriel rested his eyes on Berathon.

"How so?" Berathon asked, feeling it was up to him to draw more information out of Gabriel.

"Because," Gabriel sighed, "Enimon was to meet with you this afternoon, to continue a discussion that had started days ago. A conversation about the veracity of God's Word."

The murmuring of angels began again; Berathon discovered in its rolling hum that there was, after all, something about angels he hated.

"Don't deny it," Ocilael said from Berathon's left, though Berathon had made no effort to deny Gabriel's accusations. "Juramel," he pointed to the angel at the front of the crowd, "told us this. Have you any reason to deny Juramel's words?"

Berathon shook his head once, slowly. "Of course not. I was to meet with Enimon today to discuss-"

"Your words could be considered blasphemy!" Ocilael charged, pointing a finger at Berathon. "What is even worse, my brothers," Ocilael said, raising his voice to the crowd, "is that Berathon's blaspheming threatened everything. His words ran the danger of falling into the hands of the humans. So willing was Berathon to spread his lies that he allowed his conversation to be overheard by one of his pirate's parrots!"

A gasp went through the crowd, causing Berathon to frown. Were angels so easily persuaded?

"Luckily," Ocilael announced proudly, "that is no longer a problem." Reaching into his robe, the angel retrieved the hooded and restrained form of Mollug. "Listen well, to the madness of the creature at Berathon's blasphemy!" With a grand show, Ocilael ripped the hood from the bird. Mollug, whose body had been still, suddenly screeched to life.

"GABRIEL HAS FORGED GOD'S WORD! <squawk> LUCIFER IS OUR ONLY HOPE! <squawk> GABRIEL HAS FORGED GOD'S WORD! <squawk> LUCIFER IS OUR ONLY HOPE!"

"What?" Berathon asked, stunned. Those were not his words, nor the words of Enimon. "The parrot lies!"

His words were drowned out by the outrage of the crowd. Ocilael let Mollug's madness screech for several minutes before replacing the hood over the bird and instantly silencing him. The crowed mimicked the mimicker, falling deadly silent. All eyes were on Berathon.

"Do you deny that those are your words?" Ocilael asked.

Berathon grit his teeth; that such treachery ran rampant in Heaven was a sign that something was definitively wrong with the world. "Of course. Those are not my words."

"Oh?" Ocilael challenged. "Then are they the words of Enimon?"

"No," Berathon admitted. "Those words were never spoken by either of us, as far as my knowledge permits me to reveal. The parrot repeats the words of another."

"And who would that be?" Ocilael asked. "Me, I suppose?"

"Were you the one who removed the bird from the *Puritan*?"

Ocilael nodded. "It was I, though I turned the bird over to Gabriel at once. And Gabriel, I will add, was informed of my visit to Earth to take the bird, and watched me the entire time. Do you want to accuse Gabriel, God's appointed leader of the Reorganization, of blasphemy?"

Berathon looked to Gabriel, who could only hold the smoldering gaze for an instant before turning away. Berathon nodded inwardly. Something, indeed, was rotten in Heaven. He turned his gaze back to Ocilael. "I would accuse no angel of blasphemy without direct proof, Ocilael. It is a pity you do not share my belief in the goodness of the Host."

"Bah!" Ocilael said disgustedly. "You admit to spreading blasphemous rumors and yet you challenge the word of others? You should be stripped of your wings simply for-"

"Let us see the Word of God," Berathon challenged, his eyes moving from Ocilael's, to Gabriel's turned face, and finally to that of the Host itself. "My words can only be blasphemous if the Word of God is, indeed, the Word of God. Let us see God's letter, Gabriel, so that we may all examine the document."

Berathon expected Ocilael to challenge his request, but the angel did nothing more than increase the agitated look that had seemed to become permanently etched to his face. Berathon decided to press his case, feeling as if an opening had been given to him, but feeling an even greater need for the truth to come out. Ocilael was right about that, at least; rumor mongering had no place in the words of angels.

Gabriel's body shook, then the head of the Reorganization raised his head sadly. "No, Berathon, I will not show you the Word of God."

"Why not?" Berathon challenged.

"Because," Gabriel let out a deep sigh, "because I cannot. There is a third mystery that I had hoped to keep from the Host."

"And that would be what, exactly?"

"God's letter ... the Word of God itself ... has been stolen."

The crew of the *Puritan* stood on deck, looking down at the dead body of Captain Ezekiel Crumb. "Commit his body to the sea," Mary Mathers ordered somberly, and a group of pirates moved to obey. Crumb's body had been placed on a large piece of canvas; the pirates grabbed the sides of the canvas and lifted Crumb into the air. They walked to the port railing and waited. Someone needed to say something. Mathers, sensing this, spoke before another could claim the moment. She was saddened to see Crumb dead, but his death had caused a void that she had no intention of letting anyone but herself fill.

"This has been a day of great triumph and great tragedy. While half of us stole a King's ransom in gold from Potato Tower, the other half watched in horror as our Captain was murdered by one of our own." Mathers eyes found Austin's in the crowd. "Another of our number learned today that his Old World love was murdered ... murdered, it appears, with the approval of the King of New England. We do not know if what we have learned is true or false, but I swear we will solve this mystery before the first snowfall. We all know the King will eventually raise a Navy to come after us, so I say that we hit them before the King can come after us." Mathers walked to Crumb's body and placed a gentle hand on the old man's chest. "We also have the murder of our Captain to avenge." Mathers looked back to the crew. "What I have suggested is dangerous. We are not killers, but we must all recognize that the law of this land offers us no justice. What does the King care of the death of a pirate captain? We already suspect he has murdered a loved one." Mathers shook her head. "We must find our own justice."

Before her, the crew began to nod solemnly.

Mathers turned back to Crumb. "We commit our Captain to the sea and pray that his soul finds Heaven. God ordered the New World, and so we pray that He find Captain Crumb and calls him home." Though she believed in aliens and not angels, Mathers knew that the majority of the crew did not share her view, and it was the crew she needed. "Amen," she said, speaking a word she didn't believe.

"Amen," the crew replied.

Mathers nodded to the pirates that held Crumb's body, and those at his feet pushed the canvas higher. Crumb's body slid off the canvas and splashed into the waters of the Atlantic Ocean.

The eyes of the crew, one at a time, turned back to Mathers. All seemed to recognize her, without question, as the only one with a right to speak. "Hector!" she called, raising her voice. "You have captured the Jolly Roger. Raise it to the sky!"

"Aye-aye, Captain!" Hector shouted, and with his unchallenged words the crew of the Puritan recognized the Old World shopping channel model as their new captain.

"Tonight," Mathers shouted, "we drink!" She stalked across the deck, the crew parting for her, until she came to a stack of alcohol. "It was not just gold coin we stole, but liquid gold as well!" Mathers reached down and pulled out a bottle of Crown Royal. Removing it from its protective purple bag, Mathers removed the top and took a big gulp of the drink. "Huzzah!"

"Huzzah!" the crew roared.

"Tonight we drink! Whether in joy or sorrow, we drink to the day gone past! And tomorrow," she smiled, "or the next day if we are too hung-over, the *Puritan* sets its sights on the King of New England! If the angels want pirates, pirates we shall give them! By the end of the year there shall be no pirate ship more accursed on the shores of New England than the *Puritan*! Huzzah!"

"Huzzah!"

As the crew crowded towards the liquor, Austin slid away from them, towards the elevated forward deck. In his heart, he believed Kelly to be alive, but he couldn't let go of the troubling thought that something was very, very wrong. Even more, he believed completely and fully that King of New England Brad Regent, her ex-boyfriend, was right in the middle of it.

Glancing down at the pistol and sword strapped to his waist, Austin wondered just how far he was willing to take this whole pirate business.

Chapter 11
Becoming

Jim Catlin had never been to Newport, but a groupie in Springfield he used to hook up with would talk about Newport like it was the greatest spot on Earth. It was all "Mansion this" and "Breakers that." Catlin would only marginally pay attention, knowing that was part of the unspoken deal between them. He'd get sex, she'd get to feel like someone cared what she thought for a few hours. Around the league, she was known as the "Newport Girl." Jim had long forgotten what her real name was.

After Kelly and Kornell had driven him off the other night, he had panicked and fled. There was no reason to lie. Catlin had always had the ability to be brutally honest with himself, and the New World hadn't changed that. He would've killed Kornell if it wasn't for Kelly's involvement. Truth was, he hadn't suspected she'd jump in. The deeper truth was that his back was still hurting like a bastard from the whipping he'd taken at the behest of his buddy the King.

Catlin needed to get out, get away, regroup. He needed time to think, which had never been his strongest asset. Fleeing south, Catlin had no idea where he was going until he saw Newport on a highway sign. He'd read the sign, thought of the groupie, and figured it was as good a place as any.

The Mansions were impressive, he supposed. Just looked like big buildings. though, to be honest. Still, they'd do.

He pulled his Hummer off the road and hid it behind a group of shrubs. He didn't think anyone would care if he pulled the vehicle up to the front gates, but there was no reason to be rash, wanting to disappear for a few days. Exiting the Hummer, Catlin grabbed the cell phone Captain O'Malley had given him with a hint of hesitation. He'd yet to call O'Malley; Catlin had no trouble admitting his faults to himself, but he hated admitting them to others. Better to just not call O'Malley than call and have to admit he failed.

Moving around to the back of the mansion, Catlin looked for an open window or cracked door. He wasn't expecting one, but if a gift presented itself to him he wasn't going to turn it down. Catlin was so intent on the building that he almost ran into a man standing at the base of the back steps.

"Hello, Jim," the man said quietly, confidently.

"Who the fuck are you?" Jim asked. The man was hidden in the pre-dawn dark, keeping Catlin from seeing his face. The shadows couldn't hide the man's bright orange suit, however. "What the fuck are you supposed to be?"

The man glanced absently down at his suit, as if he'd forgotten the clothes he wore. "I'm supposed to be an astronaut," he replied, his voice rich and welcoming.

"Astronauts live in mansions now?"

The man glanced behind him. "Anything is possible in the New World, Jim."

Catlin frowned. "That's the second time you called me by name. Do I know you, sport?"

The man shrugged. "I was told you would arrive here this morning by the angel Raphael. He is the angel in charge of Royalty, is he not?" The man looked at Catlin's black clothes. "Forgive me, Jim, but you do not look like a prince." The man raised a hand to silence Jim before Catlin could let loose his agitated reply. "I was hiding here when Raphael came. He told me to tell you that he'd left a gift for you, in the master bedroom."

"What kind of gift?"

"Your true New World identity."

"My what?"

"I only deliver the message, *sport*," the man replied, turning his back on Catlin. "You can go inside and claim your destiny, or you can not. It is your choice."

"Where the fuck are you going?" Catlin had a bad feeling about this man and the mysterious gift supposedly awaiting him inside. It felt like a trap, but then, to Catlin everything felt like a trap.

"If you have seen what I have seen," the astronaut replied, "you would want to keep on the move, as well."

"Oh yeah? What did you see?"

The astronaut turned back, his eyes seemingly glowing through the dark. "I saw an angel die, Jim Catlin," he said darkly, then turned and left Kelly Reed's abductor to his thoughts.

The *Puritan* began the New World with one captain and 107 crewmen; not a week into the New World, they'd already lost their captain and ten crewmen. Captain Ezekiel Crumb had been killed by one of the departed crewmen, Teddy Levenson, the day before. The fate of the other nine missing crewmen was currently known to only one member of the pirate ship – Austin McNamara. Not coincidentally, Austin was the only member of the crew not hung-over this morning.

The crew had celebrated long through the night, drinking to their success at their plundering of Potato Tower. Austin had never been a big drinker, but even if he had, the news he'd received last night of Kelly's death brought with it a numbness that no amount of alcohol could match. While the crew drank and sang and partied, Austin had grabbed a six-pack of Budweiser and climbed up to the crow's nest to think, sulk, and plot.

Kelly was not dead. She couldn't be, he reasoned, because, to him, she still felt alive. There was no loss inside of him that he somehow knew he'd feel if she were truly gone. All through the night, nursing all six of the beers, Austin stood and looked out across the ocean and back to the shore. A few hours before dawn, while he was deep in thought about why someone would tell him Kelly was dead and the rest of the crew had passed out, he'd noticed a small group of pirates steal quietly towards the landing boats, drop one into the water, and put off for the beach.

Not everyone, it seemed, was cut out for the life they dreamt about as children.

Austin couldn't blame them. He'd spent a good part of the night wondering if he was cut out for this life. He'd thought of Father Otten once during the night, wondering what his old priest was doing. Otten was the only person he'd met (though, admittedly, most of the people he'd met in the New World were aboard this ship) that had the same profession in the New World that they had in the Old World. Austin wondered how his thoughts differed from Otten's about the New World, but the thread was quickly dropped. Though raised Catholic, Austin was not an overly religious man anymore, and the religious significance of the New World, while intriguing, paled before the practical problem of Kelly's alleged death.

His mind replayed his conversations with Mary Mathers the previous night, wondering if he could trust her to help him go after the King. He knew the crew couldn't care less about his problem – everyone aboard the *Puritan* had lost touch with loved ones, after all, so why should his own problems take precedence over theirs? – but perhaps Mathers would allow him to get the information he needed while they robbed the King of New England.

He shook his head, trying to stay awake. The sun was on the rise; Austin guessed it was about 10 AM and the crew was finally starting to awaken. The morning would no doubt bring some kind of clarity. They weren't ready to attack the King of New England, Navy or no Navy. If he were captain, he'd argue for more practice. Looking down to the captain's quarters, he watched Mathers emerge from behind the closed door. She'd put on a good show the night previous, but Austin's eyes had been locked on her most of the night and he knew she'd drank less than any of them, including himself. She was their captain now, and he felt a confidence in her that he hadn't felt with Crumb, though he realized that made little logical sense.

Still, he was fine with her ascendance, as he was with her naming Hector second-in-command.

So long as they quickly made their way to Boston. Austin wanted answers and the only place to get them was with the King.

Father Thomas Otten awoke to watch the sun rise, as he had for as long as he could remember. He couldn't remember the exact morning when he'd started rising early to see the sun's light break the horizon, but then many of his pre-crash memories were lost. Otten was one of two men who had survived a train crash back in 1966; he'd just graduated high school and was on his way to seminary school when the commuter train he was on came off its tracks. There were only two survivors of the crash: himself and a man from Nevada.

What was his name? Otten scratched his head, frowning, then let the question drop as the day's first rays shot across the still waters of the Atlantic Ocean. Beautiful. The kind of natural moment that had always reinforced Otten's faith in God. Surely any sight as beautiful as this had the Creator's hands behind it.

For the next fifteen minutes, Otten prayed. His morning prayers were always a mix of established prayer and personal thoughts. Father Otten addressed the Lord directly. Since the Reorganization, Otten's prayers had taken a more inquisitory tone. He'd attempted to check himself; Otten had always found questioning God about the events of the world to be unfair. God was not a puppeteer pulling the world's strings. He was not sitting in Heaven, orchestrating the world as if it were a story. The world needed to make its own decisions, live with its own consequences. Blaming God for the negative robbed Life of its wonderment.

There was something different about the Reorganization, however. The change from Old World to New was, according to the angels, orchestrated on the Word of God. If this was God's design ...

Who am I to question God?

Was it blasphemous to question God? Of course not, Otten reasoned. The blasphemy didn't come from the question itself, but from the intent of the speaker. Otten's questions about the New World were not made to criticize God, but merely to help himself understand what God's purpose for humanity was in the act rendered. That was the question that had nagged at him since the angels had come to Earth to tell the world about the Reorganization – what did God want humanity to learn from this experience? What was humanity supposed to-

Michael Scranton.

The name of the train wreck's other survivor came back to Otten like an unexpected thunderclap. A small wave of dizziness rolled through Otten, and he leaned forward to steady himself against a wooden railing. That's what he got for not having his morning coffee, he thought, shaking his head clear, then pushed thoughts of Scranton aside to finish his prayers. Otten had decided that he was going to find God. How he would accomplish this was an unknown that he intended to solve on the road. His prayers would lead him forward, would let him know where he needed to be.

Had the Reorganization never occurred, Otten knew he would never have been so audacious as to assume he could physically find God. But the angels had said that God was lost somewhere on Earth, and Otten intended to find him. God, he believed, would not come to him in person as He had in spirit all those years ago. For long hours Otten had prayed, seeking an answer to where he should begin his search. With the clarity of the morning sun, the answer had come to him.

New York.

Otten pushed back from the railing, took a final glance at the waters he'd prayed over for over three decades, and turned to start

his quest. On the other side of the quest, he hoped, was God and the answers to all the questions the New World had raised.

"You can cook?" Frederic Kornell asked, amazed as he watched Samantha arrange chicken, vegetables, a baked potato, and sauce onto two plates.

"Surprised?" Samantha asked, wrinkling her nose at the ranger.

"Yeah," he nodded, taking a plate from the gorgeous redhead.

"Why?" she asked as they moved out into the empty diner. Looking out the front window she saw Frederic's horse, Alfred, tied to an abandoned pick-up truck.

Frederic didn't bother lying. "Because you're gorgeous," he blurted, following her to a table. As he passed the counter, he noted the wrapped package she'd been carrying with her since they left the hotel.

"That's so sexist," she shot at him through a smile, loving the compliment.

Frederic didn't argue, taking a seat in the booth opposite to her, the package momentarily forgotten. He supposed it was sexist, but he'd noticed over the past few days how much she loved it when he told her how beautiful she was so he didn't think she really cared. The grumbling in his stomach told him to quit thinking and eat, and Frederic dove into the food, not having eaten anything in over a day. "Ish delishish," he mumbled through a mouthful of food, confident that it would have been even if he wasn't famished. "Mom always said southern women make the best cooks," he grinned after swallowing his bite.

Samantha stuck her tongue out. "Is that why you're with me? Because you were hoping I was a good cook?" Under the table, she rubbed her leg up and down his leg.

Frederic grinned. "Something like that. Ow!" he gasped as she kicked him playfully.

"When we finish eating," she said, dropping her voice, "how about we find ourselves a house with a water bed. I've always wanted to make love on a water bed."

Frederic coughed with a mouthful of vegetables, his eyes glancing around the empty diner.

Leaning back in her seat, Samantha smiled. "Freddy, Freddy, what am I going to do with you?"

"What?"

"That look of nervousness you get on your face every time I say anything remotely sexual out loud," she explained, drumming her fingers on the table. "Look around, there's no one here. It's just you and me – a ranger and a princess – sitting in a diner that we broke into, eating food that we aren't paying for as your horse stands outside, tied to a busted up Chevy. I mean, look at that," she pointed to a man walking down the street, "there's an astronaut walking down the middle of the road. An astronaut. The whole world's gone insane and you're worried because I said, to an empty room, that I've never had sex on a water bed."

"Sorry," Frederic mumbled, dropping his gaze to his plate.

Samantha laughed lightly and the two settled into a comfortable silence, eating the food Samantha had cooked. Frederic was glad for the break. He'd always been a loner, though, truthfully, that was less the result of a personal desire and more because he'd never had that many friends. There wasn't a plethora of teachers at his old job wanting to have lunch with a janitor, just like there'd never been many kids in school who wanted to eat lunch with him. Humans adapt, he believed. The words were his mother's, and he felt a sudden stab at her absence. He wondered what his dad was doing in the New World, wondered if he was-

"What's wrong?" Samantha asked, slightly concerned. "Your face just got all storm-cloudy."

Frederic slowed his chewing, delaying the answer. "Nothing," he grunted when the moment to reply couldn't be ignored any longer.

"Come on," she said, reaching across the table to lightly touch his hand. "What is it?"

Frederic took a sip of his milk, avoiding eye-contact with her by looking out at his horse.

"It's Kelly, isn't it?" Samantha said suddenly, pulling her hand away with a jerk.

"It's not," he said, turning back.

"What is it about girls like her?" Samantha asked disgustedly. "I've never been able to figure it out."

"What do you mean?" Frederic asked, realizing this was a potentially dangerous road given Samantha's penchant for sudden mood shifts, but glad for the diversion.

"I mean, really, I never got jealous when my boyfriends would ogle Pam Anderson or Britney Spears. They're hot. I understand. I could even stomach when guys would lose themselves over Buffy or Jennifer Garner," Samantha explained, exasperation evident in her voice. "Some guys are just into girls who can kick their ass. Fine."

She pointed a finger at Frederic. "But when guys fall for those ... those ... Katie Holmes types." Samantha shook her head. "I hate cute girls. I hate them."

Frederic didn't know if he should be amused or silent. "I wouldn't call Kelly a Katie Holmes-type," he said, settling on trying to reason Samantha out of her sudden ill mood. "She's more like a ..." he struggled to find the best example and failed. "I don't know exactly. But she's not what I'd call cute. Definitely not a Katie Holmes, but not an ass-kicker or bimbo, either. She's like ... independent. Self-confident."

"Is that why you've got a thing for her?" Samantha asked point blank.

"What?" Frederic asked, shaking his head. "I don't have a thing for her."

"I've seen the way you look at her. I've seen how driven you are to find her."

"She's my responsibility," Frederic tried to reason, knowing it was only a part-truth.

"Why?"

"I ran into her right at the start of the New World," he explained. "The angel Raphael asked me to take her to Providence. Her boyfriend was there-"

"She's got a boyfriend?" Samantha asked, finding a ray of light and clinging to it with everything she had.

"Yeah," Frederic said quickly, seeing a way out. "Austin. His name's Austin. He's a pirate. Look, Sam," he said, reaching across the table to take her smaller hand in his, "I have to find her. She's supposed to be under my protection."

"What does that mean?" she asked.

Frederic gave her a small smile. "It means she's the ex-girlfriend of the King and if something happens to her he's going to send his goon squad out to kick my ass."

Tilting her head slightly to the side, Samantha asked, "She used to date the King? King Regent?"

"Yep."

"But why did Regent put you in charge of protecting her?"

Frederic had to stop a frown from appearing on his face. He didn't want to get into all of the details. "Just 'cause I was there, I guess," he said quickly.

Across the table, Samantha eyed him carefully, feeling a sudden cloud come between them. She knew it was her own fault, to some degree. When Captain of the Guard Wallace O'Malley had come to her at the end of the First Night Feast to see if she was interested in spending the night with the handsome ranger, Samantha didn't think it would be anything more than a one-night fling. That's why she stole his money before he woke up the next morning. She'd been shocked when she found out he was accompanying her, Kelly, Georgia, and the three princes to Kent Harbor, Maine and had mistakenly assumed it was because of her. When she realized her error and that the real reason was Kelly …

Jealousy was not an unknown commodity to her in the Old World, and she found it wouldn't leave her alone in the New World, either.

His eyes avoided hers, and she took the opportunity to glance over at the wrapped package on the counter-top. She'd come with Frederic because she thought he was better protection for what was inside those hotel bed sheets than the other two princes. She still felt that way.

"Do you trust me?" Frederic asked suddenly.

"Of course," Sam replied without thinking.

"Then tell me what's in those sheets that you've been carrying."

Samantha looked to the sheets, weighing her options. At last, she shook her head. "No. I can't."

"Then you don't trust me," he said flatly.

"It's not that," she said quickly, turning back to him. "It's just …"

"Just what?"

She answered his question with one of her own. "Do you trust me?"

"Of course I do," he said, hurt. "How can you even ask me that question? Of course I trust you."

Putting aside the fact that he'd never asked her if she knew what happened to the money that was in his pockets the night they'd slept together, Samantha blurted, "But you don't know anything about me." She felt herself blush. "Not about the Old World me, at least."

Frederic threw up his hands. "I don't need to know anything about the Old World you. This," he motioned to his ranger outfit, then to her princess gown, "is just window dressing. We're still the same person inside." Frederic felt something catch inside him – did he really believe what he was saying? Did he really think if Samantha could see the Old World Frederic – a fat janitor living in a crummy apartment who still spent most Friday nights either crying over his mother's death or downloading internet porn – that this gorgeous woman would have anything to do with him?

Samantha shook her head. "It's not that easy. We can't just forget who we are."

"Are you going to tell me what's inside those sheets or not?"

"What did you do in the Old World?" she blurted, the words coming from out of nowhere. She hated what was happening, both of them trying to keep the other from getting to answers they didn't want to share.

Across the table, Frederic swallowed hard, wondering what she'd do if he told her he was a janitor. "Do I lie to her?" he asked himself. "Do you want to keep fucking her?" his father's voice replied sarcastically.

"Well?" she asked.

"I was a teacher," he lied.

"What did you teach?" she pressed.

"High school," he continued, almost to spite himself.

"Subject?"

"History."

"Who won the Presidential election of 1862?"

Frederic climbed out of the booth. "What is this? A test?"

Samantha begged herself to stop but, like Frederic, she was adamant at heading down a path she knew she should avoid. "If you were a history teacher, you should know."

"Do you?" he countered, then thought better of it. *Fuck.* "There was no presidential election in 1862," he answered, meeting her challenge, thanking God for the History Channel. "Lincoln was elected in 1860 and re-elected in '64." He paused, letting the moment sit, and then turned to her package on the counter top. "What's in it?" he asked, acutely aware that he was between her and it. Turning back to her, he took a slow step towards the package.

"It's mine!" she yelled, rising to her feet.

"What is it?" he asked again, taking another step. One more step and it would be in his hands.

"Don't touch it!" she yelled, standing in place. "Don't you dare touch it!"

"Then tell me what it is!"

"No!"

"Fine!" Frederic threw up his hands and headed for the door. "You can find you own way to Kent Harbor! I'm going to find Kelly!"

Samantha froze, caught between wanting to keep it a secret and wanting protection. Really, what did she care if he knew what it was? Wouldn't he eventually find out? Sure, she reasoned, but when he did, she felt like everything would change, that the New World would turn inexplicably dark for her. She felt ashamed, too, that she'd stolen it. That was the truth of it. She'd stolen from a dead angel and knew that telling anyone would-

He's really leaving.

"It's a harp," she whispered, hanging her head.

"What?" Frederic said from the door, his hand resting an inch from the handle.

"It's a harp," Samantha repeated, louder. Walking slowly to the counter, she unwrapped the object and held it out before her. "It's a harp," she said for the third time, not knowing what else to say.

Frederic shot across the room, taking the instrument from her. "It's beautiful," he said, examining the white and silver object. "Where'd you get it?" he asked.

"I stole it."

"Where? You sure as heck didn't steal this from a Target."

Samantha touched his arm gently so that he was looking at her when she told him. "I stole it from an angel."

Frederic looked at her, blinked, was certain he'd heard her wrong. "I've never heard of that store," he said flatly, trying – and failing – at humor.

"It gets worse."

"Can it?"

"The angel … I think he was murdered." She grabbed his arm tightly, slightly surprised at how panicked she felt now that she'd admitted it to someone. "What do we do?"

"I don't know." Frederic shook his head, wondering how two people could grow closer together and further apart at the same time. "This is bad, Samantha. Very, very bad."

"Dreaming of me?"

Austin was startled out of his sleep by Mary Mathers. It took a few moments for him to remember where he was – crows nest of the *Puritan* – and another few to realize they were moving. Rubbing his eyes to clear them, Austin focused in on Mathers. All he could see was her head; she'd climbed up to him.

"Rise and shine," Mathers smiled at him. "You can't sleep the entire day away."

"What time is it?" Austin asked, rubbing his neck.

"A little after three," she replied, running a hand through her wind-blown blonde hair. "We need to talk."

"I know," Austin nodded, wishing he had a glass of water to rinse the dry out of his mouth. "We can't hit Boston. Not right away. It's too big for us."

A look of slight surprise came over Mathers's face; this wasn't the direction she was headed, but she decided to let Austin ride this wave out to see where he was going. "Go on."

Austin twisted his neck to the left, letting his bones crack to relieve the stiffness. "Even if Regent doesn't have a Navy up and running yet, he must have some kind of protection around him. Plus, the *Cottonmather's* out there somewhere. We handled ourselves against the transients around Potato Tower, but they weren't a real security force." Stretching, he stifled a yawn. "Make no mistake, Mathers," he said as he rose to his feet, "I'm headed for the King, but I've got no idea what's waiting for me."

Mathers nodded up at him. She'd come to all of these conclusions over night as well. "Maybe I made a mistake naming Hector my Commanding Officer."

Austin shook his head, thinking of what Hector did to get the Jolly Roger. An involuntary chill shot up his spine as he wondered if the New World was changing Hector or if he would've killed someone in the Old World to gain possession of something he wanted. "No, you made the right decision. If we're not making steady progress to Boston, I'm bailing anyway."

"And take on the King's security forces all by yourself?"

Austin nodded. "I've gotta know if Kelly's in danger. The only reason I didn't bail out last night with the others who left is because my gut tells me she's alive and because I'm going to need help getting to Regent."

Mathers eyed the younger man carefully; Crumb was right, she believed, to single him out, but Crumb was concerned only with the angels/aliens problem. She wondered what Crumb would do to keep him here. "Austin," she said, remembering why she'd climbed up to see him, "there's something I need to tell you."

"What's that?"

"It's your parrot, Mollug. He's missing, and the crew claims it was the angels who took him. Why would the angels want your parrot?"

Austin had completely forgotten about Mollug. "Damn," he swore, shaking his head. He thought of what the bird had squawked, and remembered that Crumb had told him to tell no one as he glanced down at Mathers. "You don't know?" he asked.

Mathers shook her head. "Crumb never told me."

Austin saw no reason not to tell Mathers now that Crumb was dead. "Mollug kept repeating the same phrase over and over. He said, 'Bad words float through the clouds of Heaven' over and over again. Crumb thought Mollug must've overheard someone – the angels, most likely – talking about something humans weren't supposed to know."

"If the angels kidnapped him," Mathers said, wheels spinning, wondering about the 'bad words,' "that would give credence to what Crumb thought."

Austin frowned as he looked to the sky. "Makes you wonder what's going on in Heaven, doesn't it?"

Mathers, who'd been seeing aliens and not angels, nodded despite herself.

Berathon had allowed himself to be forced to the side as the Host crowded around Gabriel and Ocilael. Three mysteries consumed the angels: who had killed Enimon and stolen his harp, was God's Word forged, and finally, who had stolen the letter that was God's Word? Ocilael, the Angel in charge of Law Enforcement, had accused Berathon of being a suspect in Enimon's death, because the two angels were due to rendezvous when Enimon was murdered.

Berathon knew it had been an easy charge to make; the angels, shaken by the arrival of God's Word and worn down from the exertions reorganizing the world, were caught completely off-guard by the murder of Enimon. Angels hated controversy, and the quicker these mysteries were solved, the better the Host would feel.

"Are you trying to escape?"

The voice was Azrael's. "Am I being kept here?" Berathon asked.

Azrael smiled. "Of course not, my brother. Though you must admit it would look … strange … if you were to flee- that is, to leave while we decided on a course of action."

Berathon eyed Azrael carefully; the angel had been given no direct duties in the Reorganization. His job was simply to assist Gabriel in the running of the New World. "Tell me, Azrael, what happened to the parrot Mollug? The words he repeats are not words spoken by either Enimon or myself."

"What are you suggesting? That someone – Ocilael, perhaps – has tinkered with the bird?"

"I'm suggesting nothing," Berathon snapped, his mood growing darker by the minute.

"You should be careful about the words you speak," Azrael confided. "You have never been among the more popular of angels. Have you not noticed that the assignments we have all been given seem oddly appropriate?"

"What do you mean?"

"Our personalities, what little individual personalities we have, seem ideal to our new assignments, don't they? You have always been a bit of a brooding angel. Do you remember the day God tried lifting the unliftable rock? Where were you that day? Off by yourself, mumbling about how stupid it all was. Do you remember how aghast the Host was when God flooded the Earth? Where did you stand on that act, hmm? You were one of the few who openly supported the destruction of nearly all life on the planet."

"Do you have a point?" Berathon asked.

"Gabriel has always stuck his nose in everyone's business. Who better to run the Reorganization than-"

"Again, Azrael," Berathon said, stepping into Azrael's chest, "do you have a point?"

"We are what we are, Berathon," Azrael challenged, "but the New World has exaggerated our shades of difference. It makes one wonder, if they were so inclined, at whether God's purpose in ordering the Reorganization was to change humanity, or the angels?"

Berathon opened his mouth to disagree, then snapped it shut. "Your point is nothing more than another question," he scoffed, though there was no force behind it.

Azrael pressed his point. "That is, if it truly is God's Word that has ordered the reorganization. Would God really want angels, after all this time, to become wholly individual? Wasn't individuality to blame for Lucifer's fall?"

"More questions and no answers," Berathon groused. "You haven't changed in the New World, Azrael."

"Haven't I?" Azrael asked, reaching into his robe. "Whether it is God's Word or a forgery," he whispered, "the effect has been the same. The real question is who stole the Word, and for what purpose? To try to stop suspicion from rising in the Host, or to foster it? Whatever the reason," Azrael stepped in close as he pulled an object from his robe and handed it to Berathon, "there is no denying there is a split amongst the Host. There are factions rising within our ranks."

Looking down at the object in his hand, Berathon was shocked to find it was the bound Mollug.

"The greatest secret of the angels," Azrael said in a low voice that was so unlike anything Berathon had heard from the typically frivolous angel that it sent a cold wave through him, "is that, for all our power, for all our accomplishments, we are, without question, outstripped by humanity as God's greatest creation. They had better be. If we cannot trust the Host and we cannot find God, humanity is all we have left."

"Does anyone else feel ridiculous in these clothes?"

Morning had brought a renewed sense of purpose to Kelly Reed. Vanessa Yvgenilenko's story about the fire creature that had killed the angel Enimon, combined with the sense of relief at having found the Young Prince medical attention, the realization that her caravan had been attacked by the same person that had kidnapped her, the cold fact that she was separated from not only Austin but Frederic Kornell, the ranger that had been assigned by Brad Regent to protect her, and the unmistakable benefit of her first good night's sleep in days had combined to focus and clarify the New World for Kelly.

What she recognized was that all the sense of silly joy that she'd felt from the angel Raphael and her magical ride to Providence with Frederic was gone, replaced by a very tangible sense of danger. Kelly had never been the kind of person who sat back and let life happen, and the imbalance caused by waking up as a princess was now gone. She wanted answers, yes, but more than that she wanted control back. The world could do whatever it wanted, but she wasn't going to be someone's pawn, nor beholden to the silly dreams of her childhood.

"What was that?" one of the astronauts asked, turning around from the small table in the hospital's first floor break room. The older man offered Kelly a small smile.

"I asked if anyone else felt ridiculous in these clothes?" Kelly repeated, pulling her silky, poofy gown outwards. She'd come to the break room, hearing conversation, to find five astronauts sitting around a small table sipping coffee.

"Not really, no," the astronaut repeated with a small smile on his face. "Feels right somehow. Besides," the elderly man shrugged, "we don't exactly have any clothing options." He offered Kelly his hand and introduced himself as "Ronald Rollins."

Kelly smiled and shook the man's hand. "Kelly Reed. Pleased to meet you, Ronald. I figured we could just go down to the nearest mall and borrow some-"

A commotion outside in the hallway caused Kelly to stop in mid-sentence and glance toward the door to ascertain what the shouting was about. Her eyes caught Vanessa's as the doctor-turned-astronaut burst into the room. "What is it?" Kelly asked, trying to gauge the expression on Vanessa's face.

"Great news!" she exalted. "One of the astronauts from the first bus survived!"

The five astronauts in the break room broke out in excited whoops and with astonished expressions. "Someone survived?" Ronald asked, thinking of the massive explosion that had resulted, they thought, in the death of everyone in the bus that had been ahead of them when Enimon was attacked. "Who?"

Movement in the doorway turned all eyes in that direction to see a tall, late-thirty-something astronaut round the corner with a confident smile on his face. Blue eyes sparkled under a head of tousled, short, light-brown hair. Kelly felt a butterfly flutter somewhere inside of her; in her instant assessment of the newly arrived astronaut, she was more confident that he had emerged in the New World not from the Old World like everyone else, but rather from a movie in which he played a fighter pilot or cowboy.

"Mike!" Ron exclaimed, slapping the man on the shoulder. "How did you survive?"

Mike shook his head, his eyes taking in the gaze of everyone in the room, but lingering, Kelly noted, on Vanessa's for just a half-second longer than everyone else's. "Don't know. The bus exploded … I woke up on the side of the highway much later on."

"How the hell did you find us?" one of the other astronauts asked, but the newest arrival shook his head.

"I just … started walking," Mike said, looking out beyond the walls of the hospital. "Saw the lights were on in this hospital from a hill and figured … hell, I figured it had to be someone. When I got a little closer I noticed a few of you walking around outside with your orange suits. Dumb luck, I guess."

Mike smiled. Everyone in the room smiled with him. It was that kind of smile, a boyish grin shining through a life of experience that made people want to smile if he smiled, or frown if he frowned. Kelly felt the pull of his smile, sensed that something was off. *Dumb luck?* What was that? It was completely illogical, almost utter nonsense and yet … those eyes, that smile, that confident shrug of the shoulders …

Kelly felt the corners of her mouth pull into a small grin as those blue eyes made contact with hers almost against her will.

"My, my," she sighed inwardly, despite herself.

Mike seemed to hear her silent plea, nodding ever-so-slightly before turning back to the other astronauts.

Catlin had stood outside the mansion for several hours, mulling over the stranger's words, then moved inside. The day had been spent walking through the first floor of the mansion. The refrigerator, he found much to his delight, was stocked with beer and the pantry with food. There had been nothing on TV, but there was a large screen plasma TV and a fully stocked DVD collection. Catlin was surprised to find that a mansion like this (which he thought he remembered the groupie telling him was used only for tours and that no one actually lived here) had not only *Scarface*, *Slap Shot* and *Major League* (without doubt the three greatest movies ever made) but a rather extensive collection of porn.

After the three full-length movies, though, Catlin wasn't interested in watching anything else. The lure of the alleged gift waiting for him upstairs was too much.

Catlin let the credits at the end of Major League roll as he walked up the large marble steps. Truth was, he never wanted to be a prince and he didn't know why the angels had made him one. When he was ten … if he dreamt of anything at ten it was burning ants with a magnifying glass or destroying a city Godzilla-style or being Hulk Hogan.

"Now that would be cool," he thought, coming to a landing halfway up the staircase. "There's gotta be tons of wrestlers out there, right?" he said aloud. "Too bad the cable don't work for shit."

Moving upstairs, Catlin searched for the master bedroom. The wide staircase led him to an open area in the middle of the second floor. Like the staircase, the floor was a speckled green marble. Behind him, an open den sat before a set of bay windows. The setting sun sent shadows spiking across the floor. In front of Catlin a set of open double doors led into a library. To his right a hallway led down to a small statue of a deer. "Rich people," Catlin mumbled. Turning left, a short hallway ended in a set of wooden double-doors. Catlin guessed that was the bedroom.

Approaching the doors, Catlin had an image flash through his mind of a wrestling ring, three Carmen Electras, a large magnifying glass, and a backyard full of giant ants. "Must be why the angels picked kiddie dreams," he mumbled, chuckling to himself.

Not only was Catlin never afraid to be baseline honest with himself, he also found himself to be one extremely funny motherfucker.

Catlin pulled the doors open, feeling his pulse begin to quicken. The doors opened wide and Catlin stood there, stunned to his core. "What the hell?"

Standing before him was a wrestling ring, three Carmen Electras, and a large magnifying glass pointing out the back window towards the backyard. "No fucking way."

"Not yet, anyway."

Fingers snapped and in a bright white flash the ring, the women, and the magnifying glass were gone.

"What the fuck?" Catlin blinked his eyes as a normal bedroom replaced his fantasy image. Standing off to the side, his face covered by the shadows, was an angel. "Who the fuck are you?" Catlin asked.

"Really, you should try and swear less."

"Fuck you."

Snap. "Wouldn't you rather procreate with Ms. Electra?"

"Whoa," Catlin gasped as a short burst of white light on the middle of the bed popped. In its wake, Carmen Electra appeared on the bed.

Snap. Carmen vanished.

"Bring her back."

The angel shook his head. "That was merely a demonstration, Jim Catlin. A sign that we have the power to give, and to take away. You were recreated into the New World as a prince, but you know that to be a lie."

"No shit. I looked like a fag in that outfit."

"Would you like to be what your childhood dreams wished you to be?"

Catlin shrugged. "Can't remember what that was."

"So you're afraid."

"I ain't afraid of shit."

"Then lie on this bed and sleep," the angel stated plainly. "When you awaken, you will be what the ten year old James Catlin dreamt of being."

"You gonna tell me what that would be?" Catlin asked.

The angel smiled. "What would be the fun in that? But if you do take the offer ... well, I am certain we could construct a few Carmen Electras for you to play with."

Catlin thought for a few moments, then smiled broadly. "What the fuck. I like gambling. Let's roll the dice."

"Hello."

Kelly looked up from the sketch she'd been penciling to see Mike the Handsome Stranger enter the hospital's reception area. "Hey," she said, ignoring the man's smile.

"They tell me you're an artist."

Kelly nodded.

"What are you drawing?" he asked, coming to stand beside her.

"You tell me," Kelly replied, stepping aside so Mike could see the paper.

"It's … horrendous," he said, frowning. "What is it?"

"It's what attacked you," Kelly explained, looking down at the image of an giant angel, its entire body radiating flame.

"That attacked us?" Mike asked, surprised. "I thought the engine exploded."

Kelly shook her head. "According to the others, this is what attacked you and killed Enimon."

Mike backed away from the image. "What was it?"

"No one knows. And since no one's seen it since…"

"Is that why everyone's on edge?" he asked. "They think it might still be out there?"

Kelly's reply was stilled as Mike's cell-phone rang. "Excuse me," he said, flashing his smile, as he answered the phone. "Yes?"

Kelly turned back to her drawing, studying the image, wondering if such a creature as this … this fire angel was the result of a New World transformation and, if so, why the angels would create such a being? Beside her, she heard a light voice come across Mike's cell phone. The voice said only two words: "Catlin's in." Catlin? Why was that name familiar? Why did her head feel suddenly as if was trapped inside a bowl of pea soup? Mike's only response was to end the call. Kelly felt him turn back to her and lock his eyes onto her face. Like a stupid school girl, she felt blood rush to her cheeks.

"You're very beautiful," he said, reaching out to touch her arm.

Kelly turned, feeling her cheeks burn as his sparkling blues locked onto her. Her mind flashed a hundred possible responses. Her mouth chose, "I'm taken."

"I don't see a ring," Mike smiled.

"Boyfriend."

"Pity. What does he do?"

"He's a pirate now, but he was a Lit professor in the Old World," Kelly answered, glancing towards Mike's cell phone. She'd lost hers somewhere along the way. Her eyes came back up to meet Mike's and she saw that he'd seen the glance. "What did you do in the Old World?"

Mike shook his head. "A little of this, a little of that. I traveled a lot."

"Salesman?"

"Independently wealthy."

"Lucky you."

"Lucky me."

Kelly couldn't think of anything to say and Mike apparently wanted nothing but to stand there and smile at her. It made Kelly feel uncomfortable, but also ... warm. She'd never really had a thing for older guys, but Mike radiated an easy, all-American charm. He had a face that seemed almost ageless ... a mix between Brad Pitt, Dennis Quaid, and George Clooney. ("I'm turning into my mom," her mind mumbled.) The longer the moment went on, the more Kelly wished he'd stop looking at her as she simultaneously wished the moment would last. Feeling stupid at her own feelings, she tried to think of something, anything to say. "So, um, what's your name again?" *Stupid. What the hell's wrong with me?*

"It's Mike," he replied. "Michael, actually."

"Michael what?"

"Michael Scranton."

"Well, Michael Scranton," Kelly said, regaining her balance as she scooped up her drawing, "if you don't know what this is," she flashed the fire angel, "then I'm going to go see if anyone else does."

Father Otten said a quick blessing for the town that had become his home as his 1996 Ford pick-up passed the "Exiting Port Gloucester" sign the town's council had erected several years back.

"Come Back and See Us Again," read the words at the bottom of the sign.

"With God's blessing," Otten remarked, glancing down to the road atlas beside him on the seat.

A sudden sharp mental pain caused his body to convulse and his world turn white. His left foot shot out to tap the brakes, slowing the truck, as the white flash slowly rolled away from the Catholic priest. Otten inhaled sharply as the white receded to leave a single image in his mind:

Michael Scranton, his fellow train wreck survivor.

Why had he thought of Scranton for the second time today? Why was the image of the man so vivid in his mind? The man must surely be dead by now, he reasoned, blinking his eyes as he regained full composure, or pushing ninety. "It must be the journey," Otten reasoned aloud, that fateful train trip the last time Otten had undertaken a travel of long-distance.

And yet … Otten pushed the thought aside, and brought his destination back to the fore. New York. There were answers in New York.

With God's blessing …

Jessica Jenkins sat on a cliff, overlooking her entire world. There was nothing but water. The island she'd been placed on by the angels was no bigger than five or six city blocks. She was starving. The last angel that had come to visit her promised to bring her some food, but that had been two days ago now. There were plenty of berries in the island's shrubbery and she'd eaten some of them, but she craved something real, something substantial.

Partly out of boredom and partly to get out of the sun, she'd entered the small forest on the island and climbed to the top of the small hill at the island's far beach right. In front of her was a cliff, maybe fifty feet high. Down and to her left was the island's beach. Further to the left, the beach wrapped around the forest.

She couldn't believe she'd dreamt of such a life, nor could she believe the angels would really put her out here in the middle of nowhere. Why would they do such a horrible thing?

Biting her lip, Jess turned to face the back of the island, looking out across the waters to take in what she'd been calling the other half of the Pacific Ocean. She'd reasoned she was somewhere between California and Hawaii by comparing the time on her watch (which she assumed was still on East Coast time) and the passage of time here on the deserted island. The waters held nothing but an expanse of blue, so Jess glanced down at the island. She'd walked up a large grassy field that sloped out of the forest and up to the edge of the cliff. On the left edge of the field, an outcropping of rocks looked as if they'd been pushed out of the ground. Now that she'd gotten past her total freak out stage, she could appreciate (as much as she wanted to leave) just how beautiful it was here. Like an island version of Eden.

Her eyes were drawn back to the rocks. From this angle, it almost looked like there was an entrance to a cave down there.

Sensing a presence behind her, she took her eyes off the cave. Thinking (hoping, really) that it was a returning angel, she looked to the sky. A thrill ran through her as she saw the flapping of wings attached to what looked like a human body.

Just as joy reached its peak within her, she dropped down into the tall grass. It was as if an invisible hand had forced her down. Jessica wasn't complaining. The angel that was coming towards the island was ...

It wasn't beautiful; it was horrific.

Jess held her breath as the being came closer ... closer ... *what is that thing?*

The being was nearly upon her and the reporter in Jess wished she had a camera. What she was seeing she couldn't be seeing, and yet ... well, there it was, alive and apparently real ...

An angel. On fire. Laughing like the devil himself.

Chapter Twelve
Derailed

Berathon sat on top of the world, frowning down into his hands at a bound parrot. Sitting here, atop Mt. Olympus, the entire world unfolded before his gaze, and the angel did not like what his silvery eyes brought to him. Angels were beings of Order, and the New World was one of chaos as childhood dreams made real intermixed with one another – cowboys fought robots, pirates plundered doughnut shops, superheroes shared office space with actors, lounge singers, and the starry-eyed who dreamt simply of leaving their small towns for New York. There were now nearly a thousand professional sports teams in North America alone. New England had a King, original England had a hundred King Arthurs, and Paris had a Fuhrer.

And somewhere out there, amongst the ants called humanity, God walked unseen.

Berathon placed the bound parrot Mollug on the arm of Zeus' throne and rose to his feet, stretching his legs, arms, and wings. Olympus. Home of the so-called Greek Gods, one of God's earlier attempts at creating humanity, predating even the angels.

The angels, in fact, were God's reactionary creation to the Pantheon, a supposedly sexless, emotionless response to the debauchery of Zeus and his ilk. "We were failures, too," Berathon said to the empty throne room. It was through the angels that God realized the hedonistic urges of the Pantheon were a part of the world; free will, personality, the desire for the forbidden fruit … all of it was an intrinsic part of life that could not be denied.

Tearing his eyes away from Washington, D.C., where the 142 Presidents of the United States argued over whom would address the nation once the broadcasting infrastructure was operational, Berathon turned his attention to Mollug. The parrot was bound in leather; removing the hood would cause the bird to flail in the grips of madness, shouting a phrase repeatedly. The phrase, once upon a time, repeated words that Berathon had spoken, but now … now the bird had been tampered with and it spoke the words of someone else, words that called for the return of the angels' greatest betrayer. From "Bad words float through the clouds of heaven" to "Gabriel has forged God's Word! Lucifer is our only hope!" Who had said the new words? What did they mean?

"Too many questions," Berathon mumbled.

"Ah, an angel pondering," a seductive female voice said from the nether. "As rare a beast as a droplet of water in the ocean."

Had Berathon a heart, it would have run cold. Turning, he could not hide his surprise. "Aphrodite," he said, meeting the gaze of a toga-clad woman in the doorway. "Who let the dogs out of their cage?"

Aphrodite smiled, stepping deeper into the room. "Tsk-tsk, Berathon," she pretended to scold. "God would not approve of that language. He does not like his children referred to as dogs." She stopped ten feet from him; Mollug and Zeus' throne were five feet to her left. "Unless, of course, you are a dog."

"Where are your brothers and sisters?" Berathon asked, feeling his feathers stand rigid on his back.

Aphrodite's eyes flashed anger; the emotion lasted for less than a second, but Berathon's attentive gaze caught it. "They remain in their cage," Aphrodite explained, using the angel's derogative term for Purgatory.

The angel let his contempt flow freely. "No doubt engaged in an incestuous orgy. Tell me, goddess of love, how recently have you honored thy father and mother?"

"You should retract your lies, Berathon, before I forcibly push them back down your throat. It has always amazed me the level to which Christians spread their lies to grow their own power. Such as the primacy of your own creation."

The angel and goddess glared hate at each other until Berathon broke the silence. "What are you doing here, Aphrodite? Who freed you?"

The goddess choked back words of hate, letting the rising anger play out in a smile beneath her golden mane. "First you must answer a question."

"Bah!" Berathon snorted. "Always a game with an Olympian. One of the many reasons God locked you away. Twice."

Aphrodite let the retort wash by as her delicate fingers moved to her bosom. Waiting until Berathon's silver eyes were locked onto her icy blues, the goddess pulled her toga open several inches, revealing an ample portion of her breasts. "Tell me, Berathon, what do you see when you look at me? Save the insults," she said quickly, "and concentrate on the physical."

Berathon knew he would receive none of the answers he wanted until the Olympian's game was over. There had not been much contact between the angels and Olympians, but Berathon knew enough of them to know honey worked better than poison. "I see a woman with blonde hair, blue eyes, and fair skin."

Aphrodite smiled, rising to her feet. Reflexively, Berathon steeled himself for an attack, but the goddess made no move towards him. Instead, she let her toga fall to the ground, leaving herself naked before him. "Do you find me a beautiful woman?"

Berathon frowned. "All of God's creations are beautiful."

Aphrodite's eyes sparkled with laughter. "Typical answer from an angel. I am going to bathe in the pools, Berathon. Bring my toga to me and I will tell you everything I know."

"What makes you think I will play your game, Olympian? If you are not aware, there are three mysteries now plaguing the Host. Mysteries that hold my attention more than you ever could."

Without turning, Aphrodite taunted him as she made her way to the far exit. "Bring the bird. I want there to be at least one male in the room."

All but fifteen members of the pirate crew of the *Puritan* ran off the beach, screaming like madmen, raiding the small beach town for anything and everything they desired. Three pirates walked after them – the ship's new Captain, Mary Mathers; the ship's new Commanding Officer, Hector Ladronne; and Austin McNamara. The twelve remaining pirates were left aboard the *Puritan*.

"You should have left me on the *Puritan*," Austin groused. "Goddamn, how did pirates ever walk across soft sand in these ridiculous boots?"

"The plundering will do you good," Mathers chided. "You need to focus."

"I need to find out if Kelly's alive," Austin corrected.

Mathers shook her head, her blonde hair tied back in a tight ponytail. "You need to prepare yourself to ask the question."

Austin stopped in the hot sand. "What are you, fucking Yoda all of a sudden?"

Hector stopped, too, turning back. "She's right, Austin. Remember the bar fight during the First Night Feast? You didn't do much brawling. If we're going to sail on Boston, if we're going after the King, then you need to be a little less professor and lot more pirate. You need to let that part of you out that surfaced after the Feast, when you robbed the hardware store and came up with the plan to paint the side of the *Cottonmather*."

"Oh, yeah," Austin snapped, "that worked out great. Let me ask the crew of the *Plymouth Rock* how funny that was. Oh, wait, they're all dead."

Now ten feet ahead of them, Mathers stopped. "If you stop complaining and start thinking, Austin, you can look for a shoe store and steal a pair of Nikes. That'll take care of your precious little feet."

Austin kicked the sand at his feet and pushed forward, stomping past Hector and Mathers without a word.

They let him go and Hector walked to Mathers. He sighed, shook his head, "Why do you have to push him like that?"

"What do you care?" Mathers asked, glaring at her C.O.

"He's my friend," Hector replied defensively.

"Oh, please," Mathers groused. "You don't know anything about him. How can you say he's a friend?"

"I know you play favorites with him."

"Jealous?"

"Concerned," Hector shot back. "What benefit is it to the ship if you play favorites with the least likely pirate aboard the ship?"

"Least likely?"

"Except for Carl," Hector said, shooting his thumb back at the ship where they'd left Carl in charge.

Mathers narrowed her gaze, choosing her words carefully. "Captain Crumb saw potential in him."

"Yeah, well, Captain Crumb is dead. Turns out he wasn't so hot at reading people. Unless you think he was riding Teddy in order to get squished to death."

Mathers set her jaw. "Are you questioning your Captain, Hector? Do you know what the penalty is for mutiny?"

Hector laughed. "Suddenly you're a character in *Treasure Island*?" Hector pointed to his head. "Don't take yourself so seriously you lose the crew, Mathers. We ain't raiding this town for gold and we ain't going to bury whatever we take on some deserted island. You're right, though, that I don't know Austin all that well. But after what I've seen, my guess is that, for as soft as he looks on the outside, there's a bad dude inside of him just waiting to get out. You push him too much, my guess is he'll crack. You don't want that."

Mathers, thinking of Crumb's belief in Austin's hidden potential, shot back, "Maybe that's exactly what I want, Hector."

Mollug in one hand, Aphrodite's toga in the other, Berathon entered an ornate, underground room containing a large pool and a naked goddess. Aphrodite floated in the middle of the pool, making a concerted effort, it appeared to Berathon, to keep her breasts partly above the water's smooth surface.

"Legends often cite the sea as the origin of my birth," Aphrodite said, staring at the ceiling.

Berathon dropped the toga onto a sofa along the wall, and placed Mollug gently beside it. "More Christian lies?" the angel asked, trying and failing to act with the same detached arrogance as the Olympian.

"Do you know why I find it interesting you see me as a beautiful woman?" Aphrodite asked, staying in control of the conversation. When Berathon refused to answer, she continued on her own. "Not all see me as woman," she explained, now turning to the angel and floating towards the edge of the pool at which he stood. "I have been rendered as woman because the societies and cultures that have worshipped and studied me have been overwhelmingly patriarchal. It is much the same reason why, in the images of me today, I have been rendered, in their eyes, as white and not with a darker skin tone. But, in truth, I have none and all of these attributes. I am whatever you see me as – male or female, pale or dark, blonde or red. Aphrodite has become my name, but once it was Hermaphrodite."

"I see your time in Purgatory has failed to cure you of-"

Aphrodite reached the edge and pulled herself partly out of the water to lean against the marble, fully exposing her breasts. "Why does a sexless creation such as an angel see me as female? And,"

Aphrodite looked down at her breasts, "one with such large endowments?"

Her words gave Berathon pause, but he answered with reason as best he could. "I have always thought of you as female," he answered slowly. "I have never heard of you as anything but the most beautiful woman in all existence, so it is only natural that I perceive of you in this way."

"Hmm," Aphrodite shrugged, dropping back into the water. "There are no pools in Purgatory."

"Purgatory was not created for comfort."

Aphrodite dropped fully beneath the surface then reemerged. "The stench of that place shall never leave me, I fear."

"Then you must owe a significant debt to whomever it was that freed you."

"I do," she admitted. "And when I discover whom it was, I shall repay them."

Berathon frowned. "Are you telling me you have no idea who freed you?"

"I am," she admitted, her air of indifference leaving her for a moment. "But whomever it was left at the gateway a note. At least, I thought it a note, but it was not addressed to me."

"To whom was it addressed?" Berathon asked, his anger at a controlled boil. "Artemis, perhaps? 'Tis a pity it's not your half-sister; the world could use her abilities more than yours."

Aphrodite stilled herself in the water and dropped all pretense of detachment. "It was addressed to the Host."

Berathon frowned. "Where is this letter?"

"Tucked inside my toga," the goddess explained.

Berathon spun on his heels, tearing into Aphrodite's dress. His hand gripped a scroll and before he had removed it, he knew that it was the letter that had been stolen from Heaven. A deep frown descended on Berathon as his fingers unrolled the scroll, his eyes needing a physical proof his soul did not.

"Tell me, angel," Aprhodite said, suddenly beside him on the deck, "why an Olympian was left the Word of God?"

In the western half of Massachusetts, in a faceless service area, Father Thomas Otten filled the tank of his black Ford pickup truck, wondering if he should leave money for the fuel. The fifty-seven year old priest's eyes looked around him at the emptiness of the parking lot and the apparent emptiness of the building behind him.

When his eyes rolled over the large, yellow McDonald's "M" logo, his stomach growled.

When would stores run out of food? When would gas stations run out of fuel? Would they? Or would the angels continuously replenish all that humanity had come to take for granted?

The fuel line clicked off, signaling a full tank. Otten moved to the small booth where an attendant would have normally sat, prepared to pay the $25 for the gas, but found the register smashed and the booth ransacked. The money he would leave would not find its way to the station's owner. Otten wondered what had become of the men and women who worked here, or inside at the fast food restaurant? So-called menial jobs that were underappreciated by the populace at large... but now that they were gone, how long would it be until they were missed?

The priest's stomach growled a second time, and his eyes again fell upon the golden arches. After a moment's pause for reflection, Otten found his feet walking in the direction of the service building. He wondered if it was curiosity or hunger that fueled his walk, but as he reached the edge of his truck, a wave of dizziness struck him and he fell against the rear quarter panel.

Otten regained his composure after several moments; it was the second attack of dizziness today, but worse than the episode at the beach this morning. Forgetting the service area, and driven by a renewed urge to get to New York City, Father Otten moved back to the attendant's booth and grabbed several candy bars and bottles of water.

Unseen to the Catholic priest and standing atop the service building, two angels watched with stern faces. "Interesting," Ocilael remarked. "I wonder if I should arrest him for stealing?"

"You make a mockery of a man of God," Raphael replied, the tone of his voice mixing a disgust for Ocilael and a reverence for Otten.

Ocilael did not respond until the two angels watched Otten's truck pull away, continuing west. "Why did you ask me to observe this event?" Ocilael asked.

"It is my belief that this human has the right idea," Raphael answered. "He searches for God, while we, the Host, solve other mysteries."

"Enimon's murderer is not a concern to you?"

"Of course it is," Raphael replied, "as is the question of God's Word being forged." Pause. "But it is my deeper belief that finding

God would bring answers faster that attempting to solve the mysteries individually."

Ocilael let Raphael's words sink, then replied, in a softer voice, "Perhaps you are right, but it is not our decision. On either account. It is the decision of God to hide himself away from our eyes. It is the decision of Gabriel to prioritize the mysteries. Or am I to gather that you are questioning Gabriel's judgment?"

Raphael turned away, his eyes searching for Otten's truck. "I would not wish Gabriel's burden on anyone ..."

"But ..."

"But I would rather our efforts were to find God first, and solve the mysteries second."

Ocilael nodded. "In the coming days and weeks, Raphael, you and I will find ourselves on opposite sides more often than not." He placed a hand on Raphael's shoulder. "Know well in your heart that I do not act for any reason but the good of the Host."

"As do I," Raphael answered.

"As do you," Ocilael acknowledged, then spread his wings and took flight, leaving Raphael to wonder if Ocilael would have the same attitude if it were Raphael's words and not his own that were in favor with Gabriel.

The angel fell into a deep, meditative trance, his mind desperate in its search for answers. So deep was his pondering that he missed the sight, five miles to the west, of a third wave of dizziness seizing Father Otten. It was the worst of his spells, knocking him momentarily unconscious.

Its driver unconscious at the wheel, the 1996 Ford pickup failed to turn at the next bend in the highway, hit the guardrail hard, and flipped.

Berathon's body shook as he unrolled the scroll that contained the Word of God. "Unbelievable," he gasped.

Beside him, Aphrodite pulled on her toga, Berathon's initial sense of dread enveloping her. "If this scroll contains the Word of God, why was it delivered to me?"

Berathon shook his head. "Too many mysteries plague us," he said quickly, his eyes scanning the document. "It appears to be authentic ... I must return with this document to the Host at once." His mind raced at the news – if the document was authentic, then the rumors circulating about its forgery (gossip that he and Enimon had engaged in) were false, as well.

"What about the bird?" Aphrodite asked.

Berathon frowned. Azrael had stolen the parrot from Ocilael and Gabriel and given it to him. He couldn't walk back into Heaven with Mollug without heightening Ocilael's already raised suspicions. His eyes turned to the Olympian, a plan formulating in a heartbeat. "Aphrodite," he said sternly, "the Host requires a favor."

"The Host can copulate with the clouds," Aphrodite snapped, folding her arms under her breasts. "Of course," she glanced below Berathon's waist, "the Host can't actually copulate with anyone, can they?"

Berathon checked his anger, speaking through clenched teeth. "Then think of it as a favor to God, your Creator."

"God locked us away," Aphrodite answered angrily. "Twice, as you well know. I will do no favor for Him, Creator or not."

"Then name your price," Berathon said flatly. "I am in need of assistance and there is no one else to whom I can turn." As the words left his mouth, Berathon realized just how true they were. Always a loner, he'd lost one of the few angels he called friend with Enimon's demise. Where else was their support? The Host was dividing into two camps – either with Ocilael or Raphael. If he brought Mollug back into Heaven, Ocilael would frame it in the worst light, Raphael would argue on principle, and Gabriel (the Great Facilitator) would waffle somewhere in the middle, seeking the most peaceful resolution instead of one based on the wisdom of rule. And what of Azrael? Azrael had delivered Mollug to him, but that was no reason to trust him. Azrael was widely recognized as the most inconsistent of all angels. Humans had a saying they applied to one who was unique: "They broke the mold when they made you." With the angels, the joke about Azrael had always been that God had broken the Azrael's mold early in the process ...

A seductive smile came to Aphrodite's ever-youthful face. "Then it isn't the Host who needs me, but you."

"I act for the Host."

"Do you?" She glanced to Mollug.

"Damnable Olympian," Berathon muttered. "If you insist, then yes, it is I who need your help. If you will not give it freely, then name your price."

Aphrodite gave Berathon the appearance of thinking it over, but she knew it was too rich an offer to let pass. The only question was how far to push her request ...

"My price is three favors," she said, delighting in the discomfort of angels. "One, I want you to find out who released me."

"Done."

"Two, I want you to assure me that I will not be returned to Purgatory."

"I cannot speak for the Host-"

"I want your word that you will fight for it," she pressed, taking a step to him and jabbing her finger into his chest.

Berathon grunted, "Fine. And the third favor?"

Aphrodite let loose a wild smile. "I want you to have sex with me."

The words stunned Berathon. "Don't be absurd, Olympian. As you know, thanks largely to the hedonism of Olympians, angels were created sexless."

"Yet you have gendered yourselves male, have you not? Referring to one another as 'brother' or 'he.' Even your names – at least those that have been adopted by the masses – are gendered male: Raphael, Gabriel ..." Aphrodite placed her hands on Berathon's smooth, bare chest. "You intrigue me, Berathon," she whispered, sliding her body to his and kissing him deeply.

Berathon was too stunned to react, yet as the Olympian's hands ran over his skin, as her mouth pressed against his, a spike of desire rose from someplace deep, hidden, primal. His hands wrapped around her waist and pulled her to him, pressing their bodies tightly together ... coherent thought drowned out by emotion.

Across the pool, hidden in the shadows of a doorway, Azrael watched, a look of joyful wildness in his eyes conflicting with the look of deep concern upon his face. With Azrael, there was no telling which of the two conflicting emotions was dominant, or whether their outward appearance hid a deeper truth inside.

Kelly Reed sat at the bed of Saul Stein, trying to wish him out of his coma to no avail. She needed a plan. All her life she had needed a plan and the Reorganization hadn't changed that. Goal oriented, her high school guidance counselor had said. Driven, her college advisor had said. Obsessed, Brad had said. And Austin ...

Kelly rubbed dirty hands over her tired face. She needed sleep. *And Austin?* her mind asked, making her complete the thought. Truth was, Austin had never expressed an opinion on the matter. He was happy for her, supportive to a fault. Was that better, or just an absence of opinion?

"Penny for your thoughts?"

Startled, Kelly turned in her seat to the door where Michael Scranton stood in silhouette, his hands tucked behind his back. She was glad to see him and disheartened to see him all at once. "Just tired," she said weakly.

"How is the boy?" he asked, staying where he was.

"Unchanged," she said, motioning to the machines that monitored and cared for him.

Michael looked at the machines and nodded. "A shame, isn't it? That we leave the minute-to-minute care to machines?"

Kelly nodded, unsure of what the proper response should be.

"I have a present for you," Michael said, stepping into the room. He handed her a gift-wrapped box, large enough to fill her lap. "Vanessa assisted me. I hope we have chosen well."

Kelly eyed him suspiciously, but opened the gift. Looking inside, she couldn't help but smile.

"The other astronauts told me you were unhappy with your costume," he said warmly, stepping closer and running a hand over her Princess gown. "While it is striking, I can see how you would find it impractical."

Kelly nodded, her hands running over the black sweater and dark blue jeans as a pirate would run his hands through gold coins discovered in a hidden treasure chest. "Thank you."

Michael let his hand rest on her upper back. "You're welcome. As I said, Vanessa assisted me; it was, to be honest, her idea. She would've brought it herself, but she also needs rest." Michael's eyes caught sight of a drawing on the bed and worry came to his face. "Are you still concerning yourself with this … this monstrosity?" he asked, reaching for Kelly's drawing of the "fire angel" that had murdered Enimon. "Why would you continue to concern yourself with this?"

"Aren't you curious?" Kelly asked. "All of your fellow astronauts aboard your bus were killed by that creature."

Michael shook his head. "It seems so hard to believe that such a creature could even exist."

"Said the astronaut to the Princess."

Michael's eyes left the picture and centered on Kelly. "But why would the angels create such a monster?"

Kelly shook her head. "Good question. Next time Raphael – or any angel for that matter - shows up, I intend to ask him."

Michael said nothing, holding her gaze. For the second time Kelly felt herself unable to pull away from that gaze. She was unable to tell if she was floating or drowning, or even if she wanted to pull her eyes away. Michael smiled. Kelly smiled. The weight of Saul and the fire angel seemed to lift from her shoulders.

A voice from the doorway: "Michael, are you in here? Our reservation was for- oh."

Michael and Kelly turned to the door to see Vanessa standing there. Unlike Michael, who remained in his orange astronaut's uniform, Vanessa had changed into an evening gown. Kelly felt blood rush to her face, suddenly feeling the weight of Michael's hand on her back. "Vanessa, you look wonderful," Michael beamed. "I was delivering to Kelly her gift."

"I thought we were going to do that in the morning?" Vanessa asked, stealing a catty glance at Kelly.

"I know, I know," Michael said, gently touching her face to bring Vanessa's attention back squarely on him, "but I just couldn't wait. It was her complaint, after all, that sent us on our afternoon trip. Now come, as you said, our reservation awaits."

"Reservation?" The word hadn't fully left Kelly's mouth when she regretted saying it. The icy look on Vanessa's face told Kelly the astronaut wished she hadn't said anything either.

Michael half-turned to Kelly, blocking Vanessa's vision. "A joke, of course. We noticed a wonderful restaurant several blocks from the hospital. We've decided we could use a nice meal. If you'd like to join us ..."

"No," Kelly said quickly, shaking her head a bit too vigorously. "I need to watch Saul."

"What you need," Michael said gently but firmly, "is a good night's sleep. Find a bed and free yourself of your burden for a few hours."

Kelly nodded as Michael took Vanessa's arm in his and led her from the room. She ignored Vanessa's last glare, but as Michael left the room all the weight of the world came crashing back down onto her. Sleep was what she needed. *More than a plan?*

More than a plan.

And this has how much to do with Michael Scranton?

"Nothing," she mumbled. "Nothing at all."

It wouldn't be until later, just before sleep finally descended, that Kelly would realize Michael had taken her drawing of the fire angel. Her mind tried to tell her that meant something, but her body was too far gone to let the thought coalesce.

Kelly slept, and dreamt of Austin and Michael fighting over her. She would awake before a winner claimed victory.

Berathon watched Aphrodite walk down the mountain away from him, knowing that when the clouds of Olympus enveloped her, she would exit them at her destination. He didn't know if he could trust her, but what he most wanted was her to be gone, away from him. While walking back into Heaven with Mollug in hand would have raised questions, returning with Aphrodite would have sent shockwaves through the Host. God had forbidden the Host from ever seeking out the Olympians, which made her appearance all the more troubling.

"Mystery upon mystery," he said aloud, his eyes losing Aphrodite's form in the clouds below. He formulated a plan – return to the Host with the Word of God, then solve Enimon's murder. He would start with Enimon's Harp, then-

"A strange location for an angel is Olympus."

Berathon raised his eyes to the Heavens. It was, apparently, the day for surprise visitations. "So I have heard," he answered, turning to face his guest and finding there were two. "Hello, Ocilael. Azrael."

"It is against God's Word to visit Olympus."

Berathon shook his head. "It is not. It is against God's Word to contact Olympians; His Word says nothing of visiting Olympus."

Ocilael gritted his teeth. "You make a mockery of God's intent."

Shrugging, Berathon explained, "When you are suspected of murder, you find yourself caring less about intent, and more about actuality."

"You speak of details," Ocilael fumed. "The residence of the Devil."

"Spare me your clichés, Ocilael," Berathon said disgustedly. "I have found something-"

"So I have heard. An Olympian, according to Azrael. It appears you did break God's Word." Ocilael grinned as Berathon frowned.

"Did you send Azrael to spy on me?"

"Azrael comes and goes where he pleases."

Berathon held Ocilael's gaze, a building hatred growing within him. "You are making an enemy where you have no need of one," he challenged. "I came here to reflect-"

"Because Heaven is not large enough for privacy?"

"Because from here I can see the world from a different point of view."

"And Aphrodite just happened to be here?"

Berathon nodded.

"Why should I believe you?" Ocilael asked. "You are acting more and more recklessly."

"Recklessness does not equal guilt."

"Doesn't it?"

Angrily, Berathon tossed the discovered scroll to Ocilael. "Someone freed Aphrodite. Someone left her that scroll, the stolen Word of God."

Ocilael's eyes bulged in surprise as he caught the document. "Who?"

Berathon shook his head, but his eyes went to Azrael's. "Perhaps Azrael can tell us. What else have your eyes seen this day?"

Azrael frowned, but his voice was airy and light, almost joyful. "Mine eyes hath seen the glory of the coming of the Lord."

"This is no time for games, Azrael," Ocilael said disgustedly.

Azrael looked out from Olympus and onto the Earth, his eyes focusing on a scene in southeastern Massachusetts. "No," he said slowly, "it isn't. Look, there, in the kingdom of New England ... we have either found an answer or a very large clue ..."

Frederic Kornell rolled off of Samantha Dixon, breathing hard. They'd spent the day arguing – over what to do with the angel's harp, over where to go, over where to turn for help. Samantha argued they should go west, get as far away from New England as possible. She had said it, in part, because she knew Frederic wouldn't agree. His "duty" required him to find Kelly. Frederic argued they should ditch the harp and concentrate on finding Kelly, then head north, to Kent Harbor, their original destination. He had said it, in part, because he knew Samantha wouldn't agree.

Long hours were spent trying to make the other feel worse, to be "right" solely to win an argument. At one point, while they were riding Alfred, Frederic's horse, through the center of some small town, Samantha had argued they should find the wandering astronaut they'd seen earlier from the diner. When Frederic asked why they should try and find a total stranger, Samantha had replied, "Because he was hot."

That exchange had led to an hour's silence. Frederic stopped paying attention to where his horse was leading them. In the silence, each came to regret the harsh words, seeing them for what they were – born from the fear of the angel's harp. Frederic came to the realization first, but he adamantly refused to speak them, figuring

Samantha would throw them back in his face. Not five minutes after his own wall had crumbled, he felt Samantha's body slump into his back and her hands wrap themselves around his waist. She began to sob, apologizing through a shaking voice and a running nose. Frederic replied in kind, minus the snot.

They stopped the horse, dropped to the ground, and held each other, apologizing and crying until the afternoon's hate gave way to the early evening's care, which slid quickly to dusk's passion.

Alfred paid them little mind, meandering to a nearby flower box. Samantha muttered, "Let's get a room." She giggled and once again Frederic found the giggle to be about the greatest thing in the universe.

"Forget a room," he replied. "Let's duck in here."

It was an Italian restaurant, expensive, but Frederic hadn't noticed until after he'd exposed Samantha's breasts and she teased him by refusing to "fuck on a table." Instead of cringing at her public language as he had earlier, Frederic's eyes searched for a more proper place. In truth, Samantha didn't care at all, in that moment, where they fucked. She was hoping he'd see one of the oversized booths and take her there, but the ranger's eyes had spied another location. Taking her hand, he pulled her to the side of the open dining room, where stairs led up to a walkway on the second floor. Here, a ring of tables and booths alternated along the circular wall – the middle of the floor was open, allowing them to see the dining room below.

"Where are you leading me?" Samantha asked, enthralled, as Frederic passed table after table.

"There," he pointed, grinning wildly at a set of large, black curtains. "The VIP lounge."

That had been a half-hour ago.

Now, as Frederic redressed himself and Samantha watched, they both felt the barest twinge of regret, and both pushed it aside. "Stay in bed," Samantha said, running her hand along Frederic's sweaty back.

Frederic turned, smiling, and pointed to the silver pole by her head. "This isn't a bed; it's a stripper's mini-stage."

Samantha punched him playfully. "Geez, really?" She heightened her southern accent, "Ah've never seen a stripper's stage before. And ah thought all beds had a metal pole in the middle."

"Sorry," Frederic mumbled, wondering absently why an upscale restaurant like this place had a room like this. "You hungry?" he asked.

"Starving."

"Let's raid the kitchen."

"You raid the kitchen," Samantha smiled. "I cooked lunch. You cook dinner."

Frederic nodded, rising to his feet to pull on his tunic when Samantha's hand shot out to grab him. "Did you hear that?" she whispered.

The ranger's body tensed as he strained his ears.

"Someone's downstairs," she replied, her eyes snapping to the angel's harp that lay covered in bed sheets on the table beside them.

Frederic nodded. He could hear conversation and as he moved quietly to the black curtains that cordoned off the VIP room, he detected the unmistakable smell of roasting duck. Pushing the curtain aside just enough to peer out, he saw a man and a woman – the man dressed as an astronaut (was it the same astronaut from earlier?) and the woman in an expensive evening gown – standing behind the bar and helping themselves to the restaurant's alcohol.

Stifling a chuckle, Frederic returned to the bed to a pale Samantha. "No need to worry," he smiled, whispering as he lay beside her, his hands roaming freely over her lightly freckled flesh, "just two people looking to have a romantic evening alone in a fine restaurant."

Samantha's right hand cupped his face. "What do we do? We should get out of here, right? Right?"

Frederic shook his head. "We stay here. Wait it out." Rising from the stage, he moved behind the small mini-bar along the left wall. Smiling at what his eyes discovered, he raised a gigantic bag of pretzels in one hand and bag of popcorn in the other. "Dinner," he whispered gleefully, "is served."

Samantha rolled her eyes and forced a smile, but all she could think about was the angel's harp, and all thinking about the angel's harp did was to fill her with a sense of dread. Rising quickly, she grabbed the large bundle and walked to Frederic. "Hide it behind the bar," she whispered.

Frederic nodded, seeing the panic in her face, and took the bundle. As he moved to place it at his feet, the harp shifted in his hands and he clasped them together quickly to prevent it from crashing. His hands had come together in the center of the harp, and beneath his hands, and beneath the bundle of sheets, a muffled, solitary hum emanated.

Frederic's eyes flashed, "Don't worry," to Samantha, but her eyes were now glued to the curtain. Together but separately, their ears strained to hear anything from the couple below and as the muted conversation kept on keeping on, they relaxed, if only slightly.

They had, they felt, avoided detection.

Downstairs, at the bar, in the moments just before the harp slipped in Frederic's grasp, Vanessa had said to Michael the following words: "Should we check on the duck?"

Michael's face betrayed a momentary distraction as a sensation of beatific humming touched the base of his neck. "Yes," he replied, smiling broadly and charmingly as he took Vanessa's elbow in his hand, "let us check on our meal."

As they moved towards the kitchen, Michael's eyes looked to the mirror behind the bar, noting the presence of a VIP room on the second floor.

He smiled, thanking the Fates.

Berathon, Ocilael, and Azrael flew hard across the Atlantic Ocean and towards the northeastern seaboard of the United States. Dread hung heavy in all of them at the sight in the near distance, increasing every two seconds, when a deep BOOM rumbled up from the earth towards them.

"Did you hear that?" Azrael asked, freezing in mid-flight.

"Hear what?" Berathon asked, pulling up.

"Ignore him," Ocilael grunted, staying on course.

Azrael's wild eyes connected with Berathon. "I thought … I thought I heard a harp," he said, his eyes searching the landscape beneath them.

Berathon frantically searched below them, his senses straining, but the BOOM – BOOM – BOOMing caused by the creature that had brought them here didn't allow lighter sounds to come through. "We'll have to check later," Berathon said to Azrael, who now looked on nonchalantly.

Berathon ignored Azrael, and flapped his wings hard, moving towards the now floating Ocilael a mile away. Berathon altered his approach angle slightly, wanting a look at Ocilael's face, wanting the chance to read his fellow angel without pretense. What he saw worried him; Ocilael's face showed a deep concern.

"It's horrific," Ocilael said as Berathon came to rest near him.

Berathon looked down, nodding in agreement. "Who would create such a thing?"

Ocilael shook his head. "I … I don't know. Surely, it could not have been an angel …"

Berathon didn't answer, his eyes locked onto a fifty-foot tall giant monster. Part dark green, part brown, what looked like a clay-mation monster from the early B-horror movies trudged through the center of this apparently empty town. The creature looked like a cross between a Godzilla antagonist and a Ray Harryhausen monster – humanoid, but born from a nightmare. In its wake, a sickening trail of lumpy clay and wet muck slopped off the creature's legs and back. It stomped forward, its two bulging eyes locked on some distant sight.

"What do we do?" Berathon asked.

"I can think of only one option," Ocilael declared, drawing his sword. "We must kill it."

Below, somewhere deep inside the muck and clay, the mind of Jim Catlin was driven forward by but one thought:

Kill.

Kelly.

Reed.

Kill.

Kelly.

Reed.

KILL.

KELLY.

REED.

Chapter Thirteen
The Devil You Don't Know

What a dreadful town.

The thought belonged to the Olympian goddess Aphrodite as she strolled down the center of a seemingly deserted street. She wore the traditional white tunic of her kind. Inside a pocket of the tunic, a crazed parrot, hooded and bound to keep it still and quiet, sat as still as a stone. Her sumptuous blonde hair had been hastily tied back, yet still looked as if it had taken a team of stylists a hundred years to perfect. Such was the benefits of being a goddess, Aphrodite mused.

Noise from somewhere ahead and to her left came to her in the sound of breaking glass and wild yelling. Perhaps that was where this Austin McNamara was that Berathon had asked her to seek.

The goddess did not know whether to be overjoyed at her release from Purgatory, confused at the reordered world, or angered that her fellow Olympians were still locked away. That Berathon would assume she would fall to either the first or the last caused her to take the middle position. *I will be bemused*, she reasoned, knowing that reason was not one of her strong suits.

To her right, slumped forward on a park bench, sat a young man dressed as a pirate.

"Mortal," she commanded as she approached, "tell me where to find Austin-"

Aphrodite's voice was caught in her throat as the young man sat back to look at her. "Austin McNamara?" Austin asked. "You're looking at him." Austin looked her up and down – *Are there any unattractive women in the New World?* "Who are you supposed to be?" he asked.

Blinking, her heart caught somewhere between her stomach and throat, the goddess choked out, "Do you not recognize me, my love?"

"Nope," Austin shrugged.

Aphrodite stepped close enough that Austin could've reached out and grabbed her around the waist. "I admit," she said, the hint of a frown creeping onto her face, "that your dress leaves a good deal to be desired and that, truthfully, this form you have chosen is far from ideal—"

"What?"

"—but as surely as I can see your soul, I know it is you who sits before me."

Austin glanced around to see if any other pirates were around. None were. "Right, then," he said slowly. "You're right that I'm sitting before you, but I'm telling you, lady, I have no idea who you are."

"Nor does it appear you know your true self."

"And that would be?" Austin asked, then repeated his earlier question. "And you are?"

The goddess reached down and drew Austin to his feet. "I am Aphrodite, of course—"

"Of course."

"—and you are Adonis."

"Who the hell is mmmfff-?" Austin started to ask, but was stopped short as the goddess kissed him passionately. Later, he would try to convince himself that he had tried to resist, but as soon as Aphrodite's lips touched his, he was transformed into nothing but raw desire.

Happenings in Massachusetts attracted the attention of the Host in Heaven at a level unseen since the early 1620s, when the *Mayflower* struck (figuratively) Plymouth Rock. Not even the Witch trials of Salem seven decades later drew the attention from the angels that the current situation enjoyed. The situation was best understood by the angel Raphael, who alone among the Host understood the triangulation of events conspiring to crash into one another. The three events were as follows:

The first event was the most obvious: the angels Ocilael, Berathon, and Azrael hovered above a fifty-foot tall giant monster. The monster, its skin a blotchy mass of green mulch and brown clay, stomped forward, each step sending a resounding BOOM through the nearby populace. The creature was horrific, and Raphael knew that the muck and clay was a human transformed. The human was Jim Catlin and Raphael knew this because Raphael was the Angel in Charge of Royalty and Jim Catlin was placed into his care when it came to the attention of the angels that what Jim Catlin dreamt of being was evil. At that moment, the angels had two options – to lock him away with the other Nightmares, or to take the intent of God's Word above its literal meaning. They chose the latter - or rather, Raphael admitted, Gabriel chose the latter because Gabriel read the heart of the modern Jim Catlin to be free of the evil of the ten year old Jimmy Catlin.

Someone, it seemed to Raphael, had now undone Gabriel's act of kindness and unleashed whatever darkness still lay in Catlin's heart.

The second event, which Raphael had come across on accident, was the ranger Frederic Kornell, the man that Raphael had asked to bring Kelly Reed to Providence, Rhode Island, on the day the Old World became the New. Frederic was with a red-haired woman, exiting onto the roof of a building, in order to view the Catlin monster. The woman (he concentrated on her for a combination of moments, first to get a clear view of her face and soul, and then to remember her name, Samantha Dixon) carried with her an awkward package.

Since they played no direct role (or so Raphael thought) in the unfolding drama, he let his eyes leave them (and the couple that exited the building on ground level, an astronaut and a woman in an evening gown) for more pressing matters. Had he known, of course, that the package Samantha carried was the harp of the murdered angel Enimon, Raphael would have left Heaven at once to relieve her of the piece of evidence.

The third event that caught Raphael's eyes was that of Kelly Reed, sitting by the comatose body of Saul Stein. Raphael cursed himself at the sight – both Kelly and Saul were Royalty, meaning they were under his care, but in all the hustle of activity since Enimon's body was discovered, he hadn't paid close enough attention to the happenings of humanity. How had Saul been injured, he wondered? And was the ranger Kornell still with Kelly, or had he abandoned her? An unnerving tickle of doubt crept inside of Raphael at that moment and he wondered if distraction was the goal of whomever it was behind Enimon's murder, the (alleged) forgery of God's Word, and the theft of God's Word.

The eyes of the Host concentrated on the Catlin monster …

"We are agreed?" Ocilael, the Angel in Charge of Law Enforcement, asked, floating high above the muck and clay monstrosity.

"We are," Berathon, the Angel in Charge of Pirates, replied, drawing his flaming sword.

Behind them, Azrael, an Angel with no specific duty, watched silently, his eyes laughing and his face frowning.

Ocilael dove hard at the giant creature, slicing his sword into the giant's right shoulder. The blade cut deep, leaving a five-foot slash in the giant's shoulder. Catlin roared in pain, turning his neck-less head to view his attacker, but Ocilael's flight path had carried him behind the creature, and instead of his attacker, the giant saw Berathon. "AN-GEL!" he roared, each syllable its own word. Catlin stopped his forward march to square his body to the angel above him, crushing a car underneath its left foot. "KILL!" he roared, reaching for Berathon, who floated out of reach. The giant turned, confused, towards his shoulder when his right hand failed to rise towards the sky, its bulbous, pupil-less eyes, one yellow and one white, noting the gash.

The giant's contemplation created an opening. Ocilael arced back around, diving first for the street then shooting straight up on the giant's right flank, where the damaged right arm hung limply. The angel drove his sword just above the giant's elbow, and as Ocilael shot towards the sky, the sword cut deep through swamp muck and soft clay, shredding the giant's tricep.

The Catlin monster was ready for him this time, and as Ocilael's sword burst through the top of the giant's shoulder, Catlin's still upraised left arm swung towards the right, crashing into Ocilael and sending the angel hurtling towards the roof of a residential house three blocks away.

Berathon watched Ocilael's body smash through the top of the triangular roof, the impact sending his body flailing, spinning violently and crashing into the garage of a nearby house. Gripping his sword, Berathon turned back towards the giant. His plan was to continue Ocilael's assault, and attack the right arm, but as his eyes refocused on the creature his plan evaporated as the two wounds healed themselves in a matter of seconds, as clay and muck from the creature's arms rewove themselves over Ocilael's handiwork.

"God damn him," Berathon whispered as the giant began to laugh. Deep inside the muck and clay, the creature's primitive mind shouted its one mission in life:

KILL.

KELLY.
REED.

Exiting out the side of the restaurant, Michael Scranton and Vanessa Yvgenilenko looked down the street, through three blocks of a small town residential neighborhood, to see the image of the giant and the angels. Michael frowned and Vanessa screamed. "Keep your voice down," he hissed and Vanessa instantly obeyed.

"What ... what is it?" Vanessa asked.

Michael didn't reply. In truth, the appearance of the muck and clay giant did not disturb him.

The appearance of the angels, on the other hand, threatened his plans greatly. He turned to look up at the roof, hoping the ranger was smart enough to stay inside. "The last thing we need is for the harp to fall into the hands of angels," he muttered.

"What?" Vanessa whispered. "Harp? What harp?"

Michael turned to her, frowning. "Did I say that aloud?" Grabbing her by the shoulders roughly and ignoring her yelp of protestation, Michael slammed her back against the wall of the restaurant. From out of nowhere, a gilded dagger appeared in his hand a split moment before he drove it deep into her stomach.

Vanessa's eyes went wide with shock mixed in equal parts surprise and pain and her body went limp. "Why?" she choked, droplets of blood sputtering up and out of her mouth.

Michael shrugged. "I think what it comes down to, really, is that I just like to watch people suffer. We all have our faults."

Atop the roof of the Strada Trasversale Restaurante, Samantha and Frederic looked out across the small town at the muck and clay giant, fear descending on both of them. "What ... what is it?" Samantha asked, clutching the harp of Enimon tighter to her chest.

Frederic shook his head, more concerned with the three angels fighting the creature than the creature itself. The ranger was reasonably certain they could outrun the giant aboard Alfred, or, if the horse had to be abandoned, in a stolen car. But the angels were another matter. The angels were faster and in greater numbers. "We should go back inside," he whispered.

Samantha nodded.

Their feet didn't move.

Frederic's hands began to sweat and the panic that had crept into his heart before gnawed at him. He heard the voice of his father: *You thought it was going away just because that assassin was run off? Hell, no. Kelly ran him off more than you did, mama's boy.* "No!"

"What?" Samantha asked, the ranger's shout pulling her eyes away from the battle. The angel that had been sent crashing across the rooftops had returned, driving his flaming sword into the heart of the creature to no effect.

Frederic's eyes glanced towards the angels. The two that were engaged with the giant were too pre-occupied to notice them by anything more than dumb luck. The third angel, however-

"Shit."

The third angel had spotted them.

"What?" Samantha asked, grabbing the sleeves of his tunic.

"Get inside," he said, backing up, and quickly shooting his eyes away from the third angel. He wanted the third angel to think he was backing up because of the battle, not because he knew that the angel had seen them. "Get inside," he repeated, his heart hammering so badly in his ears that he didn't even know if the words were coming out.

Samantha saw no reason to argue, turning and running towards the door. She had taken four steps away from Frederic, and had five more to go before she reached the door, when her heel snagged onto her flowing, light-blue dress and sent her flying forwards.

The package in her arms shot free, and Samantha grasped onto the sheets that held the harp inside. It was the worst thing she could've done. Her left hand grasping the sheet did nothing to slow the harp's momentum, and worse, by holding onto just one end, the harp's forward motion caused the sheets to unravel. Projecting outward, almost as if the sheets had vomited beauty, the golden harp slammed into the door, then crashed to the concrete surface of the roof.

Frederic and Samantha winced as the harp thudded against the door, then bounced, then skidded across the roof. Frederic was certain the angels would have heard that sound even with the battle raging; it reminded him of when he watched scrambled porn as a teenager in the living room of the small apartment his family lived in. He was always far too scared to turn up the volume, but every sound, no matter how tiny, that he did manage to generate seemed to him like the tolling of the church's massive bells.

The harp's journey had not damaged the golden frame, but it had jostled the strings, and when the instrument had finally stopped its slide, the strings kept vibrating.

Quietly at first, but then in a quick rise in pitch, the most beautiful sound Frederic and Kelly had ever heard came wafting up off those vibrating strings. Beautiful, tragic, sorrowful, uplifting, enlightening ... the sounds of the harp were simultaneously all of these things. The music seemed to reach inside of Frederic and Samantha's souls and gently squeeze, pushing tears to the surface.

On the ground below, where Michael stood and Vanessa sat against the wall of the restaurant, running tears came instantly to Vanessa's cheeks as the sound of the harp's music reached them. Her hands clutched her stomach, trying and failing to staunch the flow of blood. She understood none of what had happened, but through the pain and confusion she found a way to lay the blame at the feet of Kelly Reed. She wasn't sure how, or why, but as her vision began to blacken, it was the only coherent thought upon which her mind could cling.

Tears did not find their way to the surface of Michael's face. Indeed, the music sent a deep frown to the handsome man's face, and his eyes went directly to the angels. "Damn them," he growled, as all three angels turned towards the roof of the building.

The distraction allowed the Catlin monster an opening. As Ocilael and Berathon paused in their attacks and floated in mid-air, their heads turned, drawn to the music that they instantly recognized as belonging to their fallen brother Enimon. Angels understood music easier than they understood words; music was God's second language, the language of the angel's.

Berathon and Ocilael had each begun to translate the music of Enimon:

An angel afire,
An angel ablaze,
My body a pyre,
His presence a maze.

From whence did he come,
From where was he born,
My mind is undone,
His body, God's scorn.

The words transitioned into a series of images, but neither Berathon nor Ocilael would view them as the hands of the Catlin monster closed suddenly around them, squeezing hard. The two angels struggled to free themselves, stabbing their flaming swords into the muck and clay, and each thought they had secured their freedom as the giant's hands opened their fingers, leaving the two angels resting only against the giant's palms.

Thoughts of freedom lasted less than a second, as the giant slammed his hands together above his head, slamming the bodies of the two angels into one another. Pain came to both of them, but when Catlin pulled his hands free, only one of the angels remained in the sky.

The other angel fell, its wings ablaze from the other's sword.

And as he fell Ocilael's face asked the question his throat could not: "What have you done to me, brother?"

Austin kissed and kissed and kissed the goddess Aphrodite. He had believed that she was not a real goddess, that she was merely the personification of someone's childhood dream, but somewhere around three minutes into the face-sucking he began to believe that this woman really was who she claimed to be. He knew that the other pirates were around, but he didn't care. He knew there was the whole business of the bird's kidnapping, but he didn't care. He even knew that somewhere out there he had a girlfriend, Kathy or Kelly or something like that, but he just did not care.

At least until Aphrodite pulled away. Austin stepped back and banged the back of his knee onto the bench. He fell back with a thump, and his world came rushing back to him.

"Hmmm," Aphrodite frowned. "That was ..."

"Amazing," Austin said despite himself.

"Disappointing, actually," the goddess said, looking down at the flushed face she had thought was that of Adonis. "Oh, there it is," she said, nodding.

"There what is?"

"The flaw," she explained. "Flaws, really."

"Flaws? What flaws?"

Aphrodite gave him a small, pleasant smile and stroked his cheek. "Let's not go through the list," she explained, as if he were a child. "The major flaw, however, is your utter lack of devotion to me."

"Well, I do have a girlfriend," he said, wincing as the physical impact of the guilt over what he'd just done hit him hard.

"Yes," Aphrodite nodded. "Kathy or Kelly or something."

"Kelly!" Austin said quickly. "Her name is Kelly."

"Kelly, Kathy … so long as it's not Persephone, I haven't any quarrel with her." The Olympian studied Austin for a second, then remembered why she was here. "You are Austin McNamara?" Austin nodded. "Then this is for you," she said, reaching into her toga. For a second, Austin thought she was going to pull aside her clothing and reveal her nakedness, but instead she simply removed-

"Mollug!" Austin yelled, jumping up and taking the parrot from her hands. "Where … how?"

"Berathon," she explained. "He desired for me to bring this bird to you, and entrusted me with helping you solve its riddle."

"Riddle? What riddle? Oh," he said, shaking his head to clear the cobwebs. "You mean what he says when you take the hood off. 'Bad words float through the clouds of Heaven'."

Aphrodite shook her head. "That's not what he says. He screams, 'Gabriel has forged God's Word. Lucifer is our only hope'."

"No."

"Yes."

"No." In the distance, he could hear the other pirates calling for him, but paid them no attention. There were only so many times a man could get excited about knocking over a doughnut shop.

"I can assure you he says nothing about 'bad words' or 'clouds of heaven'," she explained patiently. In Purgatory, it was easy to forget just how stupid mortals were. "I listened to him on the way here from Olympus."

Austin looked down at the still parrot and moved his hand to remove the hood when Mary Mathers and Hector grabbed him. "Austin!" Mathers screamed. "You were supposed to be watching the *Puritan*!"

"Oh," Austin said wryly, "perhaps you didn't see the freakin' Olympian goddess standing here."

"Damn," Hector whistled, his eyes looking upon Aphrodite's face for the first time. "Name's Hector," he said, offering her his hand.

Aphrodite refused the handshake. "I'm quite certain it is not," she said icily.

"Men," Mathers grunted. "Look to the *Puritan*!" she commanded.

The eyes of Austin, Hector, and Aphrodite turned to look out across the small beach to where the *Puritan* was anchored. The

222

Puritan, however, was not the only ship in sight. Another ship, coming up from the south, was coming hard towards the *Puritan*.

"Oh hell," Austin said. "The *Cottonmather*."

Mathers nodded. "And only a skeleton crew aboard the *Puritan*."

Frederic took Enimon's harp in his hands as Samantha grabbed the bed sheets. She was only five steps away from the door while Frederic was nearly across the roof, nearer to the ledge than to safety. "Get inside!" Frederic yelled as he ran towards her, and Samantha did as she was told, yanking open the door and ducking inside.

There was no plan in the ranger's mind but escape. There was no destination other than Not Here. Get inside, get down to the street, find a car, and run away. Or would it be better to hide out?

No. Despite the giant's savage attack on the two angels, he could not risk the third angel's intervention. Get out, get away, get to Anywhere Else.

The rooftop door swung lazily on its hinges. Frederic tucked the harp under his right arm and reached for the door with his left. The dull, worn knob seemed to glisten like the most striking gold in all the world to Frederic. The knob represented safety, to him, but his hand never closed upon it.

Azrael dropped out of the sky before him, the angel's feet slamming into Frederic's left arm and knocking it instantly numb but not broken. Frederic grunted in pain, but his momentum kept him going forward and he slammed his shoulder into Azrael's stomach, knocking the angel hard into the raised box that held the door. Frederic couldn't stop (not that he tried) and his shoulder drove into Azrael's stomach for the second time in seconds, this time driving the angel hard into the door.

Frederic felt the angel's body slump and he allowed himself a moment's thought of congratulations, thinking he'd knocked the wind out of the angel.

He hadn't.

Frederic screamed in pain as the angel, bent at the stomach, reached over Frederic's head and raked his sharpened nails across the ranger's back. Azrael's hands ripped the ranger's tunic deep enough to also draw blood from beneath the flesh.

Azrael's face smiled pleasantly, as if it were a careless summer day in a field of green, but his words contained only anger. "Murderer! Thief!" Trapped against the door, Azrael could not extend his wings, and so he slashed again at Frederic's back. The assault knocked the ranger to his knees and he dropped the harp, sending it crashing onto the rooftop.

Coherent thought had left him and Frederic's mind operated on two levels – escape and defense. Through eyes ravaged with pain, Frederic could see the angel land on its feet and approach. *To hell with the harp*, he thought. *Let him have it*. "Take it," he grunted on all fours. "I'm no murderer ... no thief ..."

"The first no, the second yes," Azrael said, now looking angry and talking happy, "but what to do with you, what to do with you?" The angel slammed his foot down onto Frederic's ravaged back, knocking his torso flat against the roof. Frederic's left arm went out ahead of him, but his right was caught beneath him, twisted back awkwardly. "Enimon was murdered and the harp holds the truth. I have seen it," he said, his voice reverential and his face a deep scowl. "I have seen the truth of Enimon's murder. An angel on fire ... we are all so foolish, so very foolish."

Beneath the angel's heel, Frederic was barely paying its words any mind. He could feel the warmth of his blood running over the side of his back, pooling under him, sticky, wet, and warm. He tried to push himself up, but his arms were in the wrong place to gain any leverage. His right hand, in fact, was trapped palm up. Flexing his fingers, trying to roll the hand over, they brushed against the handle of his sword.

His father's voice. *Do it.*

"No," Frederic wheezed.

"Oh yes," Azrael continued in a professorial voice. "We are all incredibly foolish. None of us – humans, angels – have realized just how far this will take us. Only angels have the power to recreate humanity at the turning of the world from Old to New. Only humans, however, contain the dreams needed to make that recreation possible. What I have seen from this harp," he said, looking down to the harp that hummed quietly on the roof, "is the death of an angel at the hands of a human. An empowered human, yes, but a human nonetheless. None of us have even thought of this ... we have concentrated on which angels have conspired against the Host as others have blamed humanity, but none of us, none of us, have thought of this ... this blasphemy. Not angels, not humans ... but both. A true conspiracy amongst the children of God. Angels and humans working together to corrupt God's world." Azrael's foot came gently off Frederic's back, taking flesh and blood with it. Frederic's hand clasped around the handle of his sword. Was this mad angel going to let him go? Should he attack? "Angels and humans conspiring against God … the question that plagues me is whether I want this revealed or not. I could take the harp back to the Host and let them see the truth, or I could destroy it here and save them the pain. What is an angel to do?"

"Angels talk too much," a voice said from the darkness of the doorway.

Azrael turned towards the sound, but his vision could not penetrate the darkness. "What madness is this?" he asked in an annoyed voice and through a smiling face.

"The madness of genius," the voice said.

Then from the darkness, the firing of a gun.

Frederic looked up just in time to see half of Azrael's face blown away. The bullet had slammed into the angel's forehead just above the nose and burrowed halfway through the brain before the denseness of the angel's body stopped it. The damage had been done, however, and the right, front quarter of Azrael's face snapped back. The force of the shot spun Azrael to his side and Frederic looked up to see the interior of the angel's face revealed to the world, silvery and white, spurting silver blood and oozing pure white brain, the angel's body collapsed to the rooftop at Frederic's feet.

"Holy shit!" Frederic gasped, pushing himself away as the silver blood mixed with his own. His eyes watched as the angels coughed and sputtered, the half of it's face flopping, attached only to the back of its head it appeared, by the flesh of its alabaster skin. Somehow, despite the horror of what had happened, Azrael locked both eyes with those of Frederic. "Find Mol … lug," he choked, the words barely audible.

"Mollug?" the voice from the darkness said as it emerged into the light. "That's a stupid name for a harp."

Frederic looked up to see who had shot this angel, but his gaze never made it to the man's face. Behind him, hiding just inside the doorway, was a shaking and frightened Samantha.

The man reached down and picked up the harp, then offered a hand to Frederic. "Come with me," he said, glancing over at the battle between the giant and Berathon, "if you want to live."

"Who are you? How did you …?"

"Michael Scranton," the man said, pulling Frederic to his feet. "As for how I did that … " His body was still as he pointed down at the twitching body of Azrael. "The angels aren't the only ones with secrets. Come on, let's get you to the hospital."

Berathon was unaware of the activities of the roof. After Ocilael had fallen to the ground, the muck and clay giant had torn off part of its own stomach and hurled it at Ocilael, covering him as it clamped the angel to the earth. Berathon had spun, seeking Azrael, only to find his inconsistent brother flying away.

Cursing, Berathon gripped his flaming sword tightly in his hand and hovered just out of the giant's reach. The massive creature laughed at him, its bug-like eyes swirling between yellow, white, and green. "You and me," Berathon whispered to himself.

The words had an effect on him he didn't quite comprehend. They sounded right, and suddenly the situation felt right. Him against this giant. Alone. No Ocilael, no Azrael. A thought gnawed at him from the pit of his soul, but he pushed it aside. He glanced at the massive lump that covered Ocilael, then pushed that aside, too. When the giant had smashed the two angels together, Berathon's sword had accidentally sliced through Ocilael's wings, alighting the feathers with the flame from his sword. If anything, the creature's act to trap Ocilael had extinguished the flames. Angels had no need to breathe, so Ocilael should be safe.

"Kill!" the giant called, shaking its massive arms of green and beige up at Berathon.

Think, Berathon demanded of himself. The giant was not, of course, a natural being, and the angels hadn't authorized one's creation. *As far as I know.* The giant wreaked of a child's nightmares, not of dreams. And all of those who dreamt of the darkness were locked away in the Bad Lands to keep them apart from the New World.

Clearly, that had not worked.

More mysteries, he cursed. His anger was checked only at the belief that all mysteries must, inevitably, lead them back to the same source. Anger bubbled up as Berathon leveled his gaze at the giant. They needed answers. The creature could provide some.

Every attack they'd attempted had led nowhere; the creature simply regenerated itself. Berathon drew two conclusions – either they had yet to cut deep enough, or they hadn't yet hit the vital areas. If this was a human transformed, as Berathon was certain it was, then there had to be vitals. God's Word had been specific on this account; humans must still have consequences to their actions, must still know mortality.

Without mortality, there was no Heaven.

Without Heaven, there was no ultimate consequence.

The giant roared again, taunting Berathon. In response, Berathon gritted his teeth and sheathed his sword; he would test both of his theories in one sequence. Drawing his bow, Berathon brought a psychic arrow into being and drew back on the bowstring. He let the arrow solidify, making certain to sharpen the arrow point to a razor-intense hardness. Eyeing the giant's knee, he fired and the arrow stuck, sinking almost down to the notch. It was a direct hit, but only a distraction. As the giant's hands dropped to remove the arrow, Berathon drew back again on the bowstring, and fired a second arrow at the giant' face.

A sickening squishing noise belched upwards as the arrow sank itself deep into the giant's right eye. The creature screamed in a mix of pain and rage and his hands came up to claw at the arrow, giving Berathon the opening he needed. Sending his bow back to the nothingness, he drew his sword, set it afire, and dove hard toward the giant's mid-section. Like before, Berathon dove on an arc just to the giant's side. On this move, however, he employed two new tactics. The first – gripping his sword with both hands, he aimed his grip as close to the giant's hide as he could. Knowing the thickness of the muck and clay wouldn't allow for a clean slice at that length, Berathon extended his wings at the moment of impact. The result was that as his sword sank in, it served as a pivot, sending the angel's body around to the giant's back, where he stopped himself by planting his feet deep into a patch of muck.

The giant roared again and titled toward the wounded side, but it could not reach the angel that now swung wildly at the giant's back. Hacking with a drive and purpose, Berathon began to take large chunks off the giant's hide. Unable to see what Berathon was doing and unable to feel it due to the multiple areas of pain, the giant didn't realize what the angel was attempting until it was too late. Berathon had cleared away nearly a foot of muck and clay, and while his sight was impaired by dripping mud and water, Berathon had spied his prize:

The giant's heart.

Crying out in a primal rage, Berathon pulled his sword back and drove it in hard and deep, piercing the heart. The giant began to thrash, but Berathon held his grip, twisting and thrusting his blade deeper and deeper into the heart, ignoring the foul stench and the spitting and searing steam.

The giant dropped to one knee, trying but failing to reach behind itself to tear the angel away. The death throes lasted nearly five minutes, and when it was over, Berathon felt more alive than he ever had.

The thought sickened and thrilled him all at once.

In the excitement of gaining the harp and slaying an angel, Michael Scranton made a mistake. Holding the harp tightly to his side, leading Samantha and Frederic down the stairs and towards the nearest exit, he led them out the same door he had led Vanessa out of not twenty minutes earlier. Not three steps out the door, he realized what he had done.

By the fourth step, Frederic had seen the body and screamed.

Spinning around as he damned himself, Michael went with the first plan that came to him. It was how he had survived through the years and he saw no reason to attempt another path at this moment. "Vanessa?" he asked, playing at being surprised.

"You know her?" Samantha asked.

"I do," Michael nodded, trying to look shaken. "She had come here with me. I told her to return to the hospital, thinking it the safest course of action." Michael moved to the body, kneeling down. She's still breathing. Barely, but undeniably. He hid a smile; this might work out for the best. "Quick, find transportation," he ordered Samantha and Frederic. "We must bring her back to the hospital."

Nodding, Frederic grabbed Samantha by the arm. "My horse!" he shouted, running for the corner of the building. Scranton turned back to Vanessa. Samantha pulled away.

It was an act that almost cost Samantha her life.

Thinking he was alone with the unconscious Vanessa, Michael manifested the same dagger into his hand that had cut Vanessa the first time. His intent was to drive it into her heart, but before he could send it beneath her flesh, Samantha gasped. Michael froze, the blade nearly at her skin.

The gasp saved her life. Aware now that she was there, Michael swiped the knife to the side, shredding Vanessa's evening gown to reveal the wound. "It's bad," he said without turning. "Rip your dress; I need fresh cloth to staunch the flow of blood."

Nodding dumbly, Samantha looked at her silky gown and tried without success to rip it.

"Let me." Michael was suddenly standing before her, his dagger between them. Her eyes locked onto the blade and she felt her stomach turn over as it approached her. *He's going to kill me,* she thought, but the dagger simply sliced the dress around the waist, freeing the material. "Hold this," he ordered, handing her the dagger, wanting her to feel its weight in her hands.

Scranton ripped the material in long, wide strips in his hands and bent down to Vanessa, wrapping the material around the wounds at her stomach. *I like to watch people suffer*, he thought, recalling his earlier words. *Someday that will cost me. But not today.* He finished binding the wounds just as Frederic returned with the horse.

It would do no good, he knew. Vanessa would never regain consciousness. She'd either be dead by the time they reached the hospital, or shortly thereafter.

These are the four reunions that occurred as the afternoon sun started its descent:

The first reunion ...

The Catlin monster was still twitching as Berathon freed Ocilael from beneath the muck and clay mound. Coughing up mud, Ocilael was nonetheless grateful, if perturbed. "It was an accident," Berathon explained, though not with a plethora of kindness. Ocilael nodded, expanding his wings wide to view the damage. He winced at the sight more than the pain. He'd lost nearly half of his feathers on his left wing.

"Azrael?" he asked, looking around.

Berathon turned to point away from the giant's fallen body. "He flew that way; to where I don't know."

Ocilael flapped his wings, trying to find lift, but the damaged wing provided none. Berathon took to the air and manifested his bow. Holding it down towards Ocilael, his fellow angel grabbed the ends and let Berathon get him airborne. Not ten seconds later they were once again on solid ground, this time of the roof of the restaurant, standing over the prone body of Azrael.

"His soul still clings to its body," Ocilael announced. "Return him to the Host," he commanded Berathon. "I will wait here."

"No need," Berathon shot back, not liking the presumption of a higher authority in Ocilael's voice. "Reinforcements."

The angels looked skyward to see Raphael leading a small cadre of angels.

"Just in time," Berathon muttered sarcastically under his breath.

"On that, at least," Ocilael shot back, his voice a harsh whisper, "you and I are in agreement."

Though neither shared the thought with the other, both of the angels, on their own, wanted one answer above all others – which member of the Host was in charge of protecting the Bad Lands?

The second reunion ...

Vanessa Yvgenilenko was gently laid into a hospital bed at Hollis Memorial. Frederic crawled into the next bed over, laying on his stomach. Their presence had alerted the astronauts hiding at Hollis, and while no Old World medical doctor was among their number, they managed, between the whole of them to insert breathing and feeding tubes into Vanessa, and cleanse and dress Frederic's wounds.

When the excitement had passed, and Samantha had fallen asleep in one of the room's uncomfortable chairs, Kelly Reed entered. "Hello, Frederic."

The ranger opened his eyes, blinking them a few times. Of all the things he'd seen today, this was somehow the most surprising. "Kelly? Where's the Young Prince?"

"Upstairs."

She sat down beside the bed and offered a smile. "It's good to see you."

Frederic nodded, and they sat in silence, just glad to be back in the presence of the other.

Three floors beneath them, in the hospital's old fall-out shelter, Michael Scranton locked Enimon's harp away behind radioactive shielding. If he could have destroyed it, he would have, but he knew there was no power on Earth that could destroy an angel's harp.

The third reunion ...

On a supposedly deserted island in the middle of the Pacific Ocean, Jessica Jenkins lay as flat and still as she could in the tall grass of a high cliff. Below her, an angel encased in fire had descended from the sky and entered a cave. How long ago that had been, she had no idea. She was too afraid to move, fearing any movement would draw that horrific creature to her.

Stress and frayed nerves had taken their toll on her, and her eyes began to sag as sleep tried to enclose upon her.

"Hello, Jessica."

The voice came from above and behind her and caused Jessica to jump in place, spinning around to look up into the eyes of an angel. She let out a deep sigh. "Thank God," she said, apparently without any intent of irony. "Gargamel."

"Gabriel, actually," the angel corrected, softly descending. He reached down and took her hand in his, then lifted her easily to her feet.

"Right, sorry, thanks," she said quickly. "Listen, you won't believe this, but down there-"

"Hush, child," Gabriel reassured her. "It is alright. Do you know my role?"

Jessica searched her memory, trying to remember what he had told her the last time he visited. "You're the … the angel in charge of the Reorganization, correct?"

"Correct," Gabriel smiled. "It is a tremendous burden. I regret that it has taken me so long to return to you."

Jessica felt her stomach growl. "I'm just glad you're here. I'm starving. Did you bring any food?" She was talking fast, as she nearly always did.

"No," the angel replied. "Your dream was to be alone. To be as far away from your mother as possible. To never have to rely on anyone for anything."

Jessica threw up her hands. "I was ten! My mom abused me in one way or another nearly every day of my life! I want off this island! I want to get as far away as I can from … from …" she glanced back over her shoulder at the cave and shivered.

Gabriel nodded. "Of course, my child. Humanity is free to change its path." He forced a smile, but Jessica shivered at the pain that was held in check behind the words that followed: "The angels have never been free to change their path." He looked past her, down the hill towards the cave

She felt sadness in his words, and felt a sudden urge to reach out to Gabriel and help him with his pain. Before she could act, the angel spoke again. "If you have no desire to live out your primary childhood dream, you shall have the opportunity to live out your second. Do you desire that?"

Jessica's mind felt heavy as she tried to remember just what her secondary dream had been. "Um … can't you just fly me back to Boston?"

Gabriel's eyes came back to hers, and he offered a sad smile. "Why should I fly you back to Boston, when you could do it yourself by accepting your secondary dream?"

Her memory was recaptured. *Flying. That's right.* Austin, she, and their other childhood friends always used to play make believe after school. Austin was always Green Lantern. *Was that what he was now? A superhero?* A giddiness that bordered on madness filled her and without thinking, she said, "Yes!" *Supergirl! I'm going to be Superg-!*

Gabriel reached out his hand and touched her forehead.

A moment later, Jessica Jenkins had been transformed into a dove, and her human mind was lost in the liminality between existence and non-existence.

The fourth reunion ...

The majority of the crew of the *Puritan* stood on Hampton Beach and looked out to where their ship was hurriedly trying to raise anchor. It was slow work; there was only a skeleton crew, led by Carl Yesek, aboard. They simply did not have the manpower they needed to escape. To their right, having moved up from the south, another pirate ship, the *Cottonmather*, sat still in the water. The *Cottonmather* had been in a holding pattern for nearly a half hour, and the nerves of the *Puritan* crew – both aboard and ashore – were wearing thin.

"What do they want?" Hector snapped.

In the wake of that question and to the horror of Austin, Mary Mathers, Hector, and the rest of the crew, the pirate ship answered.

The *Cottonmather* opened fire on the sitting duck that was the *Puritan*. Within one minute, seven cannonballs had ripped through the *Puritan's* hull.

Aphrodite perked up. "At last," she said, "some excitement."

None of the pirates answered the Olympian.

Chapter Fourteen
Lost at Land

"This shit is bad."

Roughly eighty pirates of the ship *Puritan* stood in the hot sand of Hampton Beach, New Hampshire and watched the dark side of their childhood dreams come to life. Before them, in the warm waters of the Atlantic Ocean, the pirate ship given to them by the angel Berathon, the *Puritan*, was under assault by the pirate ship *Cottonmather*. Theirs was the second ship they had seen the *Cottonmather* destroy – the first was the *Plymouth Rock*, the third pirate ship of Port Gloucester. The *Cottonmather* had set its cannons blazing on the *Rock* while it was still docked, and all because Austin McNamara and his closest three pirate companions had painted the *Cottonmather*'s hull with obscenities, leaving evidence that pointed to the *Rock* as the guilty party.

Austin and Hector exchanged a quick, knowing glance. They'd been waiting for this attack, in one form or other, since the bar brawl during First Night Feast. That night, one of the *Cottonmather*'s crew, a short, angry man they had nicknamed Stocky Samuel, had challenged them, fought them, and probably would've beaten them if it hadn't been for the intervention of Berathon.

"Where's that angel when we need him?" Hector asked.

Austin looked down to the cloaked and bound parrot Mollug in his hands. "Good question."

"Do you mean Berathon?"

Austin and Hector turned to Aphrodite, the Olympian goddess recently freed from her supposedly eternal prison of Purgatory. "Yeah," Austin answered, trying to forget that moments ago he'd been passionately making out with this woman. *Where the hell was Kelly?*

Aphrodite refocused her eyes, looking to the east, beyond the two pirate ships. Her eyes were focused on Olympus, but when she found her ancient halls empty, a frown fell upon her face.

"I know this is wrong," Hector whispered to Austin, his eyes on the concentrating eyes before him. "I mean, our ship's getting blown to bits behind us, but … look at her. Have you ever seen a woman this beautiful?"

"You are aware she's standing right before you, correct?" Mary Mathers, the *Puritan*'s captain, asked from a few feet away.

Aphrodite began to turn slowly, working her way from east to south.

Austin forcibly pulled his gaze away from Aphrodite to look to Mathers, wondering if the grim look on the captain's face was due to the *Cottonmather*'s assault or Aphrodite's presence. What was worse for Mathers, not having a ship to captain, or not being the most attractive woman on it? Somehow, Austin felt if he could find the answer to that question, he'd have Mathers completely figured out.

Smoke from the first fired cannons began to waft over the beach. The acrid smell burned eyes and lungs, but the sound of coughing pirates was seen more than heard, the fire of the *Cottonmather*'s cannons and the splintering of the *Puritan*'s wooden hull dominating.

"Berathon is south of here," Aphrodite announced. "He is engaged in battle with a giant monster."

"Forget him," Mathers shot at them, her voice venomous and commanding. She didn't want any of them concentrating on any giant monster nonsense "We're about to lose our ship. And all that stands between us and that seeming inevitability … is Carl Yesek."

Carl Yesek's world was moving at hyperspeed. He was in a battle. A real honest to goodness naval battle between two pirate ships, and he was in command.

The problem, he was discovering, was that this New World piracy didn't match with his Old World, childhood dreams. His dreams of piracy were born from Peter Pan and Errol Flynn. He'd imagined himself as some dashing hero, swooping from ship to ship on a rope, sabre drawn, always landing on the high ground, always battling off tens of swords at a time. When *The Princess Bride* was released, Carl went to see it five times. Between Cary Elwes and

Mandy Patinkin, and the almost over-the-top (okay, completely over-the-top) sentimentality, all of the early childhood memories came flooding back to Carl by the third viewing. By the fourth, he knew what he had to do. For his fifth viewing, he took his then-girlfriend, an almost frumpy (okay, completely frumpy) psych professor with a stormy disposition. When Mandy said the immortal line, "My name is Enigo Montoya. You killed my father. Prepare to die," Carl (who had taken the aisle seat in preparation) slid out of his seat, dropped to one knee, and said, "My name is Carl Yesek. You stole my heart. Will you marry me?"

His then-girlfriend blinked at him several times, but said yes. Carl was certain he'd heard her mumble, "What the hell, I'm not getting any younger," but she swore she hadn't said anything. She was never an overly pleasant woman, but Carl loved her nonetheless, and he was certain somewhere (perhaps buried very very deeply) she loved him, too.

They were married to Mark Knopfler's theme music. Carl had gone to college with a friend of a friend of a friend who knew a guy who'd dated a girl who was currently sleeping with a PA on the then new Billy Crystal movie, who was able to get the star to tape a greeting that said, "Have fun making the babies!" The wedding reception howled with laughter when it was played, and Carl and his then-wife smiled at each other and went immediately upstairs and made a baby.

A few years before the Old World became the New, Carl and his wife got divorced. She claimed in court that he was addicted to internet porn; Carl didn't deny it. He was just thrilled she hadn't discovered he was having an affair with the parking attendant at his office's parking lot.

The truth was, neither he nor his wife had wanted anything to do with one another after their child died. He blamed it on her; she blamed it on him. When the divorce proceedings revealed that it was, in fact, the fault of neither, it was too late. Both just wanted to be rid of the other. They were both making a good wage, so there was no alimony. Carl had thought of calling her once or twice, but he always resisted. Once, he drove to the university where she worked as a psychology professor, but when he read the name on her door – Sheila Watson, Wellington Professor of Psychology – he stormed away at the thought that she'd retaken her maiden name.

He drove the fifty minutes home angry, upset, wanting to hurt someone. Somewhere along Route 9 he formulated a plan that shocked him and thrilled him at the same time. By the time he pulled his Honda Accord into his driveway, he could barely contain himself. His hands shook as he opened the door, then locked the door behind him. As if to taunt him, at that very moment his answering machine was busy recording a message. All Carl heard was, "… if that was you who was hanging around my office all afternoon, why didn't you stop in and say …"

"Shut up!" he roared at the phone on the other side of the living room as he thundered up the stairs. "How dare that bitch act nice to me?"

Storming into his bedroom, Carl went right to his walk-in closet and undid the secret latch that opened the secret door that held his most valuable possessions – stocks, bonds, antiques, a gold coin he'd stolen as a child (from an aquarium while pretending to be, of all things, a pirate), his mother's jewels, his father's stamp collection, and Lady, his life-size sex doll, currently dressed in some of Sheila's old clothes that she'd never come to pick up.

It couldn't have been more perfect for what Carl had in mind.

He grabbed the doll by the hair, called it every dirty name he could think of at the top of his voice, slapped it hard across its rubber face and dragged it to bed where he proceeded to almost rape it.

Almost, because at the last moment, as he was tearing off the doll's clothes and slapping it as hard as he could in the back of its head, his enraged fantasy decided it was all a game he and Lady had agreed to play. It was the best sex he'd ever had and Lady – who was bought as a joke gift for Carl by his friends in the laboratory to "celebrate" his divorce – didn't go back in the closet for a week.

"Get down!"

Carl was knocked to the deck of the *Puritan* as a cannonball whistled over his head, smashing into the main mast. "Thanks," he said, rolling onto his back to thank the pirate that had saved him.

His savior didn't answer except to scream in pain at the dozens of wooden splinters that were now jammed deeply into his face.

This was becoming all too real. Carl began to realize that he was not going to make it off the *Puritan* alive. He should do something, he knew, but his voice could find no words. Or perhaps it could, but the thundering of the cannonballs negated whatever miniscule storm Carl's throat could raise to match the violence.

The masts were shattered, the deck rails hanging by nails and splinters, and still the *Cottonmather* kept coming at them. "They're going to ram us," he thought, as the enemy ship grew larger through the smoke, and in that thought was born a sliver of hope. If they're going to ran us, he mused, then perhaps they will board us.

"And if they board us," he whispered as the pirate with the face full of splinters fell over the side of the ship where a cannonball had blasted away the deck rail, "then maybe they don't intend to sink us after all."

Stocky Samuel stood on a barrel, face-to-face with his Captain. "I say we board the *Puritan* and take her crew as slaves!"

Captain Lazarus couldn't believe his ears. "Are you daft, Samuel? Take their crew as slaves? For what end? We have barely enough room on this ship for our own crew, let alone another 100!"

"I just want four!"

Lazarus punched his insubordinate crewman in the face, knocking the four-foot man off the barrel and onto the deck. "You try my patience, Samuel! I am Captain of this vessel! The only gain I can fathom," he roared, moving to stand over the fallen pirate, "is that you'd get shot!"

"Keep it up, Captain," Samuel groused, "and I'll pay the chef to piss in your soup!"

Lazarus laughed. "That might actually improve the taste." Grinning, he kicked Samuel hard in the ribs, causing Sam to double-over in pain. "So long as I'm the Captain, we do what I say."

"That time is up!" Stocky Samuel roared, unfurling himself in a dash that revealed hands now holding two pistols. He fired, his eyes locked on the surprised eyes of his captain. One blast took out Lazarus' left knee, the other hit him square in the chest. Lazarus dropped to the deck, his weight crashing onto his right knee. Samuel screamed in vengeful glee, firing both pistols a second time and each finding purchase in Lazarus's chest.

Samuel tossed the pistols aside and leapt to his feet. He moved three quick steps to where he could now stand face-to-face with Lazarus. "I'm the captain now," he said wildly, plunging a dagger into Lazarus' neck. "How do you like that, Lazarus? How do you like your death?"

Lazarus grinned as blood rushed up his throat and spilled out of his mouth and down his chin. "I ... I love it," he gasped, spitting blood over Samuel's face.

"Liar!" Samuel grinned, but the grin disappeared as the fear and pain he expected to see on Lazarus' face was missing.

As life rushed to leave Lazarus, the former captain of the *Cottonmather* matched the wildness of Samuel's grin with the lunacy of his own. "Liar? You stupid shit, what's my name?"

"Lazarus," Samuel said, not understanding.

"Laz … arus," the captain gasped. "The man who came back from the dead. You'll be seeing me again, Samuel. Count on …" his eyes rolled to white, then closed, as he fell lifeless to the deck.

"Come back from the dead?" Samuel asked the corpse, pushing aside a sudden sense of unease. "I'll be waiting." The shortest man on board turned to the crew that now looked to him. "Cease firing. Ram that ship and board. I want to personally end the lives of Austin McNamara and Hector Ladrone."

"The *Cottonmather*'s stopped firing!" Hector yelled, giving an excited voice to the thought that had crept into all of their minds during the previous ninety seconds.

"That's because her crew is going to board your ship," Aphrodite mentioned casually, as if she'd seen it a thousand times before, which, of course, she had.

"But there's nothing on that ship except for a skeleton crew," Mathers remarked icily.

"Well, they are pirates," Aphrodite shot back. "Isn't that what you'd do?"

Mathers shut her mouth, stewed silently, then thought better of it. "Austin," she barked, "say something clever."

"What?" Austin asked.

Mathers repeated herself, slower and louder, "Say something clever to shut this bitch up."

"Er …"

Mathers took a fast step to get in Austin's face. "Say something clever or I swear to God the next time I see your girlfriend I will not only tell her you made out with this slut, I'll show her the picture I took with the camera on my cell phone."

Austin felt his heart, stomach, and soul all sink to the earth. "Right," he said meekly, then turned to Aphrodite. "Um …"

Aphrodite placed a hand on his cheek, "Just don't be cheap. Anyone can call me a slut. It is far too easy, in this day, age, and culture, to label a women so cheaply." Pause. Smile. Broken hearts. Daggers from the eyes of Mathers. "Go ahead, Austin. Be clever."

Austin looked at the pirates around him and shrugged in frustration. "Sure, why not, right? It's not like we're in danger of losing our ship, after all." He turned to Aphrodite, who smiled politely. "So, um, the Trojan War."

"Yes?" Aphrodite asked. "You wish to know if it happened? It did, mostly as Homer recorded it, though all religious texts are far from completely accurate. Homer understood that it is far more important to tell a great story than stay beholden to some ancient text or set of fables."

Austin waved the answer aside. "I'm trying to be clever, not find out answers to historical questions."

"Sorry."

"That's alright," he said, softening his voice despite himself. "Here's what I want to know-"

Aphrodite smiled. "I thought you were not interested in answers to historical questions."

"Not in ones that don't make me sound clever," Austin replied.

"My apologies, Austin," the goddess bowed. "Please, continue."

Austin continued. "So, during the Trojan War, which lasted ten years, which saw the Greeks encamped on the beaches of Troy, and the Trojans mostly behind their walls, you advised the Trojans, correct?"

"More or less," Aphrodite replied, finding this all very amusing. At how easily distracted were humans she would never tire. *So much like gods*, she mused. "I did not deal much with the battle plans."

"That's good," Austin replied, "because they sucked."

Aphrodite looked as if she had been slapped. "Who are you to question the gods of Olympus?"

"You had the Achaeans sitting on the beach that whole time and you never advised the Trojans to pull of the most obvious maneuver of all."

"Which would be what?"

"To send ships around behind the Achaean fleet."

Aphrodite blinked. "What?"

"The Trojans should have let the Greeks come at them, let them get in close and attack the unbreachable walls, and as that was going on they should've sent their own ships to get behind the Achaean ships and take their navy out. Sink their ships. Now, granted, the Achaean navy was significantly larger than the Trojan fleet, but still … set the Achaean ships aflame, so when the Greeks retreated from the walls of Troy they would've been even further crushed by the destruction of their ships. You could've had them trapped between the Trojan army and navy, instead of between the Trojan army and an escape route." Austin let out a deep breath. "Clever enough?"

Aphrodite frowned. "Not worthy of Odysseus, perhaps, but a fine shred of cleverness it was, I cannot deny it."

"Great," Austin remarked, turning back to Mathers. "Now, can we get back to what we're going to do to get our ship back?"

Austin glanced back to their ship just in time to see the *Cottonmather* slam into the *Puritan*.

Carl could only count three members of the *Puritan* that were alive when the first *Cottonmather* pirate jumped off of his own deck and onto his. The pirates of the *Cottonmather* hit the deck hard, pistols drawn, only to find no resistance at all. They had not expected much, but to be met by three pirates, and one of them so badly injured that he sat in a pool of his own blood, hadn't been what was anticipated.

So they stood there, dumbly, until their new captain, Stocky Samuel, came aboard. Captain Samuel looked surprised as well, but hid it better than the others. Where they saw something unexpected and froze, Samuel saw something unexpected and adapted. Scanning the deck, he strode quickly to Carl. "Where is Captain Crumb?"

"Crumb is dead," Carl replied, breathing hard, his thin strands of hair sticking out wildly across his scalp. "Teddy Levenson killed him."

"The fat one?" Samuel asked, surprised.

"One and the same."

"So is he the captain of the *Puritan*?" he asked, thinking of his own recent rise to power.

Carl shook his head. "He's gone. Left us up the coast. Mary Mathers is our captain now."

A murmuring of laughter went through the *Cottonmather* crew. "The woman?" Samuel asked. "You are led by a woman?"

Frowning, Carl noted the laughter of the crew. It was rough, hard, malicious. These were not the same kind of men that crewed the *Puritan*. He looked for their version of Teddy or himself, but found none. Perhaps they were still aboard their ship—but then, who were the *Puritan* versions of any of the men before him? True, some of Carl's crew had taken quickly to robbing and ransacking doughnut shops and hardware stores, but these men were hardened in a manner that couldn't have occurred since the Reorganization. *That had to have been done on purpose*, Carl thought to himself, glancing heavenward. Just what was it the angels were doing by putting these crews together?

"Bring Austin and Hector to me," Samuel ordered, bringing Carl's gaze back to earth.

"Can't," Carl answered, motioning to the distance and not bothering to suppress a smile. "They're on shore."

"Pity for you," Samuel answered, slamming his fist into Carl's stomach, doubling the former biochemist over at the waist and bringing him face-to-face with his attacker. Samuel grabbed Carl's thin neck and squeezed. "Bad for you, Carl. Very bad for you. I'm going to sink this stinking ship, and you with it. Pirates, strap this nerd to the … well, well, it seems there are no masts left standing." Samuel removed his pistol from his waist and pointed it at Carl's face. "Good-bye, Carl."

"Wait!"

"For what?"

"You … you're supposed to make a threat first," Carl said, figuring if he couldn't replicate the dashing heroics of Errol Flynn or the Black Pirate, he could at least try and match their wits. "Or offer me some kind of deal … in exchange for my life."

The *Cottonmather*'s crew laughed, but Samuel held his finger on the trigger. "What could you possibly offer me?"

"What all pirates want," Carl said, thinking quickly. "Treasure."

Now the other pirates stilled their laughter.

"Treasure?" Samuel asked, his interest piqued. He didn't know if Carl actually knew of treasure, but he could use even the hint of it to his advantage. There were doubtless others aboard the *Cottonmather* that aspired to its captaincy. Doubtless more who would not live well taking orders from one of Samuel's diminutive height. He needed time to root out the conspirators that would certainly appear and win over those who simply wanted leadership … and treasure. "Go on," he ordered quickly, shoving his pistol into Carl's stomach.

Carl swallowed. Time to be witty. "There's a … a … hidden treasure, just north of here."

"Hidden?" Samuel asked, sneering. He wanted to scream at Carl, *Make this convincing!* "I suppose you have a map with a big X on it?" he asked, to the cheering derision of his crew.

"No … no," Carl said quickly. "Do you know the town of Durham?"

"Maine?" Samuel asked.

"New Hampshire," Carl corrected. "It's less than a day's sail from here."

"How do you know of it?" Samuel asked.

241

"We robbed it a few days ago."

Samuel frowned as the crew jeered. "You're trying to sell me on a treasure you've already plundered?" he asked angrily. "What do you take me for, an idiot?"

"Well, you are sinking a ship full of gold," Carl said in his best Errol Flynn. The sentence was barely out of his mouth when Samuel fired his pistol, clipping Carl in the right shoulder. Carl dropped to his knee, screaming in pain. "Don't kill me! Please don't kill me!" He looked directly into Samuel's eye as the shorter pirate's pistol jammed into his cheek. "There was more gold than we could take! It's called the Ivory Tower! There's more gold than I've ever seen! I swear it!"

Samuel pulled his gun back but kicked the boot of his heel into Carl's chest, knocking the older man onto his back. Samuel leapt onto Carl's chest, landing with his ass hard on Carl's chest. He stuck one boot against Carl's neck and raised his pistol. *The moment of truth*, he thought. "You need to do better than that," he said, as loudly and roughly as he could. "Make me believe there's a treasure out there worth our time."

Carl, breathing hard, did the only thing he could think of that would save his life.

He sold out.

"I can deliver Austin McNamara and Hector Ladrone to you."

Mary Mathers looked through a pair of binoculars out across the water to the deck of the *Puritan*. A permanent frown had etched itself across her face. *This is your time,* a voice inside her head repeated to her. *Prove yourself. Or were all those men right? You're nothing but a pair of tits, a tight ass, and a talented mouth you refuse to use?*

Mary shoved the thought aside; all the years spent trying to climb the modeling ladder, watching others leap ahead. Always the wrong body type for whatever the type of the moment was, Mary had never moved out of filler status. The big designers never called. The small designers only called because they blew ninety percent of their budget on one or two of the top models and had scratch to pay the rest. She'd blamed everyone but herself over the years – it was the fashion mags' fault for favoring straw women, it was the model agencies' fault for trying to make her something she wasn't, it was the limo driver's fault for bad-mouthing her for not sleeping with him … and on and on.

"Make your own luck," one of the aging models, a hangover from the glory days of the early Nineties had told her not three days out of rehab from under a cloud of coke powder. "Pick out one of the aging actors always hanging around – don't worry if he's married or not. Find him, take him out back, and give him the thrill of his life. Or her life, if you've got the stomach for it. If you can't make the money on the runway, make it on the side."

Mary heard the words, nodded, and then slugged her fellow model in the face, breaking the bitch's nose. She was in all the gossip columns the next day, and instantly her phone started ringing. Four weeks later, it had stopped. The only gig her agent could get her (and did it right before he dumped her) was with a shopping channel. Mary wasn't disappointed. Her four weeks of mediocre success were a financial success and an empty victory. Wanting out of the biz, Mary took the opportunity, moved down south where the channel was located and spent her days modeling ordinary clothes and jewelry for ordinary people.

Fresh start, same old problems. First day she was there, some ex-baseball sleaze pushing autographed bats and balls and framed pictures dropped his hotel key into her coffee, then slapped her ass playfully, winking all the while.

Her only reply was to kick him in the balls.

She would've gotten fired except that the other girls stepped in and all told similar stories about the guy.

That had been just over a year ago, and the past year had been the happiest year of her life. For the first time, she found herself in a serious, long-term relationship.

It was her own restlessness that did her in; not two weeks before the angels came, she'd broken up with him. Not for anything really, and certainly nothing he had done. It just seemed like the thing she needed to do.

So she did it. And didn't look back.

And now here she was, the captain of a pirate ship that was about to sink into the waters of the Atlantic Ocean.

To hell with this.

She dropped the binoculars.

"To hell with this," she said, instantly drawing the attention of the mumbling pirates.

"What's going on?" Austin asked, leaving Aphrodite's side to come over to his captain.

"They've got Carl at gunpoint," Mathers explained, "and they're busy emptying our cargo hold."

MARK BOUSQUET

Hector shook his head. "I met their captain, Lazarus, during the First Night Feast. Weird guy. Spooky as shit. Stood off to the side, at the end of the bar. Just sat and watched everyone, smoking a pipe. Old guy, but when you got up close to him you could see he wasn't kind of guy to mess with. Clint Eastwood type, you know."

Captain Mathers shook her head. "Lazarus isn't on board the *Puritan*, and it looks like some other guy is calling the shots."

"Who?" Austin asked quickly, feeling a sense of dread.

Mathers shrugged her shoulder. "Some short guy, by the looks of it."

"Oh shit," Austin and Hector said in unison.

"Mary," Austin said hurriedly, "we've got to get out of here."

"The hell we do."

"Mary-"

"Captain."

"Captain," Austin corrected himself. "That short guy, Samuel … he's been after us since First Night Feast. He's the reason why we painted the hull of the *Cottonmather*, and probably the reason they took out the *Plymouth Rock*."

"You're afraid," Mathers asked, caught between surprise and disappointment, "of a midget?"

Austin made a point not to wince. "I'd think you, of all people, wouldn't be one to judge too harshly based on appearance."

Mathers held her tongue, and nodded. "Fair point, Mr. McNamara."

Continuing, Austin added, "Right after the *Rock* sank, when we were fleeing for open waters, he sent me a message, saying he was coming."

Mathers nodded her head toward the water. "Looks like he's a man of his word."

"The ship's lost," Austin said, knowing he was sounding weak. "What will staying here accomplish?"

Folding her arms, Mathers asked, "And what would you have us do, Austin? Because I know damn sure what I intend to do, which is get those fuckers back for stealing our gold and sinking our ship!"

The crew of the *Puritan*, dazed and tired from their day of interrupted pillaging, beaten down by both the sun and the events in the waters before them, began to rouse themselves with their captain's words. Austin, used to dealing with academic committees and typically on the losing end of those battles, felt momentum coalescing behind Mathers. Which was fine with him – he wasn't

244

against Mathers here, he just wanted to make sure they didn't do anything stupid.

"Look," he said, "what's our goal? I thought our goal was to get to Boston? Has that changed? That's the biggest treasure in the state, isn't it?"

Mathers' tongue shot forward in her mouth and she began to suck her front teeth, a thinking habit leftover from childhood. "We can't run from the *Cottonmather*."

"We're not," Austin said. "We're still pirates, even without our ship. Let the *Cottonmather* have the waters. We don't have a ship to combat them anyway."

Mathers acknowledged the sentiment had merit. "They get the waters, we get the land."

"We ride on Boston by land," Austin said quickly, the plan coming to him only moments before it left his mouth. "Then we steal one of the King's Royal Fleet. Think of that. We'd be the pirates that stole a royal naval vessel. Imagine hoisting the Jolly Roger on that ship."

Mathers stopped sucking her teeth and started chewing her bottom lip. She couldn't take long, she knew that. Decisions needed to be made. Decisive decisions, hard and fast and right. Definitely right. A wrong decision, right now, and she could lose the crew. Austin's idea had merit, but …

"Austin, you want to go to Boston because you want to find your girlfriend," she said, leveling her gaze. If they were going to follow Austin's plan, she at least wanted this part about his girlfriend out in the open. "And the King? You want to humiliate him because he used to date your girlfriend."

A chuckling murmur ran through the crowd.

"Damn," Hector said. "And I thought I'd miss *The O.C.* in the New World."

Mathers laughed with the crew, though her eyes stayed with Austin. "But," she continued, motioning for silence, "you are right about one thing. We need a ship. So unless anyone knows of a pirate ship just floating around, looking for a crew, I say we go to Boston and pull of the theft the entire New World will be talking about."

The crew of the *Puritan* roared in approval. Austin smiled. Mathers smiled. They had a plan and a purpose. They were in agreement.

It all lasted three seconds.

Aphrodite said two words and the crew went silent. "Kent Harbor."

"Excuse me?" Mathers asked for everyone on the beach.

Aphrodite pointed north. "That's what it says on the sign, at least. Kent Harbor. Dreadful looking village. Menacing black castle, though. Spooky in a … well, not in a Greco-Roman way, for certain."

"Lady," Mathers said, her fingers itching to grasp the pistols at her side, "what the hell are you talking about?"

Aphrodite shot a thin smile across the sand. "A ship. Empty. Waiting for a crew. That's what you wanted, correct? Well, one waits for you in Kent Harbor." Aphrodite looked out over at Austin, then to Mathers, then back to Austin. "I know battle strategy isn't my strong suit, but I do believe it'd be a lot easier to steal one from a fishing village than one of the King's fleet."

Hours passed, night fell.

Frederic Kornell slept in a hospital bed, recovering from injuries. At his side, Kelly Reed slept in a hospital chair, her head tucked into her chest. Across the room, Vanessa slept, also recovering from injuries. Upstairs, Saul Stein also slept, also recovering from injuries.

At the door, two stood, watching over Frederic, Kelly, and Vanessa.

"New World casualties," Michael Scranton said from behind Samantha Dixon. Samantha, who hadn't realized Michael was there, jumped in place, startled. "A pity," Michael continued, pressing himself just close enough to Samantha's back that the younger woman felt his presence, but not close enough for her to move away without looking strange. "Beat up by an angel," he said. "Strange days indeed."

Samantha looked nervously towards Frederic's bed, her eyes flitting back and forth between Frederic and Kelly. "Where's the harp?" she asked, the words escaping from deep inside.

"Downstairs," Scranton explained. "Hidden away where prying eyes will not find it."

"I figured you'd have destroyed it," Samantha said outwardly, while inwardly she screamed at herself to shut her mouth.

"Really?" he asked, amused. "Why?"

"You seem like the type," she said. "I know guys like you."

"I really don't think so."

"Yeah," Samantha said, nearly spitting the words out. She turned to face the taller man, noting he still wore his astronaut's uniform. "Bet you always get what you want. You reek of money and power. Probably daddy's money."

Michael grinned, reaching out to run her dress between his fingers. "And you're not from money? A sweet Georgia peach like yourself … I bet you haven't had too much trouble getting what you want." Scranton smiled, then slowly looked past Samantha to where Frederic and Kelly slept. "I'd be willing to wager quite a large sum of money that a girl like Kelly has never stolen a man from a girl like you." Scranton brought his eyes back around to Samantha, noting the welling of tears with satisfaction. His right hand disappeared behind his back, then reappeared with a picture. While his left hand stroked her pale cheek, his right brought the picture of an overweight, angry-looking young woman flipping off the camera.

Samantha's face fell. She wanted to ask, "Where did you get that?" but she had lost all strength to give voice to her thoughts.

"Then again," Michael said, his left hand holding her chin in place so that she could not escape his gaze, "I could be wrong. Do you still think that 'ruggedly-handsome' ranger in there would be interested in the Old World Samantha?"

Unable to avert her eyes, Samantha closed them. "No," she whispered.

"Tell me, my sweet Georgia peach," Michael said, his voice and face dropping closer to hers, "how many boys did you lust after in the Old World that were lost to the Kelly Reeds of the world? As many as were lost to the sorority whores that you now resemble?"

"Stop, please stop," she said, choking out the words.

"You and I are going to become allies," Michael explained, allowing his voice to become rougher. "I will hide your harp away from the angels, thus keeping you safe from their murderous intent, and in exchange, you will do something for me."

"Why?"

"Why?" Michael laughed. "Because you and I both want the same thing. Well, two sides of the same thing, actually." Michael glanced over to make certain Kelly and Frederic were still sleeping, then leaned down to whisper in Samantha's ear. "You want Frederic. I want Kelly. Hmph." Michael pressed himself even closer, moving his mouth close enough to Samantha's ear that his lips touched them as he talked. "And no one wants Vanessa. I'll provide the opportunity, you take advantage of it."

A tear forced itself from Samantha's eye and rolled down her cheek.

"Because if you don't ... well, Frederic finds the picture, the angels find the harp, and you become completely alone in the New World. Unloved. Unwanted." He grinned. "Just like you were in the Old World."

"Move!" Captain Mathers yelled as a cannonball exploded into the sand of the beach. "Wonderful idea," she groused to Austin.

"Hey," Austin yelled back, running alongside Mathers, "how the hell was I supposed to know they'd fire at the beach. Sheesh!"

Despite herself, Mathers grinned at Austin. They were the only two in danger, the rest of the *Puritan*'s crew having already retreated back to the streets, well out of the cannonball's range.

Despite himself, Austin grinned back. Thirty feet away, a cannonball hit the beach, sending sand cascading over Austin and Captain Mathers. "I still want to go to Boston!"

Mathers nodded. "I understand," she yelled back. "And I have an idea."

"Oh yeah?" Austin asked as they reached the supposed safety of the streets. They slowed their run to a walk, both of them gasping for air. Austin took the opportunity to check his inside pocket to make sure Mollug was still there. Not a hundred feet up the road, Hector and Aphrodite waited for them. "Is this an idea I'm going to like? Or hate?"

"Oh," Mathers grinned. "I think you'll like it."

"Why's that?"

"Because, if I do say so myself, it's a very, very clever plan."

Aphrodite and Hector watched Austin and Mathers come off the beach and slow to a walk. "It's interesting," Aphrodite said, motioning with her head towards the oncoming pair.

"What's that?" Hector asked, frowning.

"You're the second-in-command, correct?" Aphrodite asked. "And yet, it seems to me that Captain Mathers spends much more time cavorting and plotting and planning with Austin." She turned to the Old World mechanic. "Tell me, Hector, have you noticed that of which I speak?"

Hector turned and spat on the ground. "Yeah. Yeah, I've noticed that."

"It's very interesting."

Hector looked at the goddess. "That's one word for it."

"What word would you use?"

Hector looked away. "Fucking angels and gods. World's gone to shit since you all came along."

The crew of the *Puritan* stood along the sidewalk, looking out to their ship. Captain Mathers, Hector Ladrone, and Aphrodite stood together, near a Mercedes. The *Puritan* was on fire, and sinking fast. Beside the wreckage, the *Cottonmather* backed away, receding into the night. The flames from the *Puritan* cast an eerie dance of light across the water, across the *Cottonmather*, and across one small vessel that moved slowly towards the shore.

Captain Mathers looked through her binoculars. "It's Carl," she said, emotionless.

"I wonder how he got away," Hector said under his breath.

"Save it," Mathers shot back, then climbed up onto the hood of the car. "Crew of the *Puritan*," she said, and all eyes came to her. "Look out on that sight and remember it. Let it burn into your memory. Remember who is responsible – the *Cottonmather*. The ship that was docked beside us and the *Plymouth Rock* on the first day of the New World back in Port Gloucester. Since then we've experienced highs and lows. We've robbed one of the richest men in the world, and we've lost our captain. Now," she motioned out to the water, "we've lost our ship. Only the *Cottonmather* remains now, of the three ships." Mathers let the moment build. "But not of the pirates. We remain. We remain," she repeated. "We remain, now lost at land, stranded on the shores most of us have known our whole lives. The *Cottonmather*, I guarantee you, thinks us no longer a threat. They think they now own the waters of the New England coast. They don't. We ride to Kent Harbor. We take that empty ship Aphrodite promises us is there. And then ... then we go looking for revenge. Those are our waters. Starting right now, the *Cottonmather* sails on borrowed time."

Mathers turned around, watching silently as the *Puritan* fell beneath the surface. "Load up," she said, quietly and unchallenged. "Our revenge starts now."

Standing across the street, a dead man chuckled at Captain Mathers' words.

It was Captain Lazarus – dead, but still walking the earth as a ghost.

Austin did not stand with the other pirates, though he, too, watched the *Puritan* sink beneath the surface. Austin stood several hundred meters down the road from his crewmates, next to an Audi A6. He'd always wanted an A6, but he'd never been able to afford one. Not so long as he'd been saving every penny for a house, at least. The keys to the car had been left in the ignition. Truth was, he had no idea how to hotwire a car so he had to find one with the keys still left in it. That it happened to be an A6 he chalked up to a little New World luck for a change.

Back up the road, he heard his crewmates cheer and he wished them well. It was time for their paths to diverge. They were headed to Kent Harbor.

Austin was headed to Boston.

To Kelly.

Chapter Fifteen
Revelations and Alliances

Captain Lazarus was dead, but not gone.

While most of the rest of the world had been transformed into their childhood dreams in the blink of an overnight, the angel Berathon had asked Lazarus to wait. "You are," the angel explained, "something of a unique case."

Lazarus hadn't wanted to be a pirate or superhero or ninja.

He wanted to be a ghost.

Specifically, he wanted to be a ghost that sought vengeance for some great crime committed against him. He'd gotten the idea from *A Christmas Carol*. Ghost of Christmas Past. Or Present. Or Future. That didn't matter. It was the haunting that he was drawn to. Why be afraid of things that go bump in the night when one can be the thing that goes bump in the night? Be the one who scares, not the one who gets scared.

Berathon suggested the pirate angle; Lazarus was willing to play along because pirates always made for great ghosts.

He served as captain of the *Cottonmather* and was betrayed, murdered by a crewman he knew only as Samuel. He was killed, but in death was given a purpose.

Vengeance.

Now the only question was, how did Lazarus want to play it?

He looked north, and smiled.

Just over the border between Massachusetts and New Hampshire, Austin McNamara pulled his stolen Audi A6 off the highway and into a gas station. He checked his watch for the time only to find a bare wrist. Years of habit couldn't be erased in … how long had the World been New? Couple of days? Weeks? He'd lost all track of the passage of time.

Rubbing his eyes to try and ward off sleep, Austin caught sight of the digital readout on the dash – 3:41.

Austin groaned; somehow knowing what time it was made the heavy darkness feel like an even greater burden, sleep a more needed act. He pulled the rearview mirror down to look at himself; the New World had aged him in interesting ways. He looked both older and more alive than before. A shave would do him wonders. So would a bath.

So would Kelly.

He let out a deep sigh. Things had been going so well in the Old World – he was on tenure track, he'd just signed a deal for his first book (an academic analysis of place in the texts of William Gibson), and, *deep breath*, he'd been looking at engagement rings. Marriage – a week ago that had been the scariest event on his horizon, the only real risk in front of him. His job was reasonably secure, he was making good money, and he and Kelly were … well, they *were*. They were together, beyond all the questions and nerves. Together, they'd moved to higher ground and, yeah, sure, it was a bit more boring, a bit more safe, but that's the place relationships were supposed to go, weren't they?

A rapping on the window should have caused him to jump in his seat, but he was just too tired to show surprise. He turned toward the passenger seat and saw an unexpected visitor. *(Unexpected? Isn't every visitor at 3:45 a.m. unexpected?)*

"Berathon."

Austin reached over, unlocking the passenger door.

Berathon opened the door and started to get in, but Austin stopped him.

"We need gas," Austin said, motioning to the pump. "Use the good stuff."

Berathon looked to the pump, then to Austin, then back to the pump. "Angels do not 'pump gas.'"

"Yeah, well, before you showed up I wasn't wearing a pirate costume," he paused to reach inside his vest and remove Mollug, "or deal with talking parrots."

Berathon's eyes popped. "Aphrodite found you. That is good. We need to talk-"

"Talk later," Austin said. "Fill tank first."

Berathon rolled his eyes. "For the love of Heaven," he groused, but moved to the pump. Austin slumped back in his seat, closing his eyes. He really did not want to do this right now. He wanted to fill the tank, fill his stomach, then take a nap and hit Boston in the morning.

"Ahem."

"What is it, Berathon?"

"What does it mean, 'Pay before you pump?'"

Samantha Dixon's face was wet, but she was done with crying. The only water on her now was coming from the hot water that poured down on her from the showerhead. *I'm done with crying.* Her grandmother had a saying she used to use every time the Dixon family was hit with a tragedy great or small – "There's plenty of time for crying, but not when a decision has to be made."

It was just such a time.

Samantha had a decision to be made. Writ large, it was simple – to kill or not to kill Vanessa for Michael Scranton. *Grandmama didn't raise no murderers.* (Except for Uncle John-John. *Shut up.*) Writ small, however, the situation was more complex. There was the matter of her relationship with Frederic Kornell and what would happen to that relationship if Michael Scranton (whom everyone in the world, but her, apparently loved like he was some kind of hero) turned over to Frederic a picture of Old World Samantha.

The young woman looked down at her body, loving every inch of it. All the diets, all the self-help books, all the research into surgery, both medical and cosmetic ... all those lonely Friday nights (and Saturday nights, and Sunday nights, and Monday nights ...). In the end, she got her new body overnight, thanks to the angel's gift of the New World. This was the princess she dreamt of being back when she was a child, when she had no idea that all of that food she jammed into her mouth had a dark side.

The only soap at her disposal was the stuff they put in the hand dispensers, which she now attempted to work into a large enough lather to wash herself. Not the best soap ever, but it would do. It would have to.

Childhood dreams. *I wonder what this is doing to the world's psyche*, she wondered. Everyone running around, thinking they'd been relieved of all responsibility, but that wasn't the case. Everything seemed to be falling apart, but why? And come to think of it, where were all the kids? And why were the angels acting like bad guys?

She scrubbed her face, but Samantha knew she could scrub all night and not feel clean. The real dirt was inside, unreachable by soap and cloth.

What of those childhood dreams of hers? Beautiful princess in some kind of danger, saved by a ruggedly handsome prince, married and living happily ever after. Was she trying to recreate that fantasy as reality? Was she really in love with Frederic, or did she just want him because she'd grown ever-so-slightly attached (thanks to the First Night Threesome, as she'd come to call it) and then instantly jealous of Frederic's connection to Kelly? Or was Frederic so important to her because she wanted protection? But she didn't need protection, did she, now that Scranton had taken possession of her— of Enimon's—harp.

Maybe, she thought as she scrubbed her arms, it didn't matter. Maybe Frederic wouldn't care that she was an ugly, mean person in the Old World. The New World package was pretty good, if she could allow herself a moment of complete immodesty. Would Frederic really care that she used to be a duck when a swan stood before him?

Samantha shook her head. It was the unknown that she always hated most.

"I'll provide the opportunity, you take advantage of it."

The words were Scanton's, but the decision would be Samantha's.

Austin pulled the car out of the gas station, wondering why he wasn't more amazed about an angel sitting in the passenger seat next to him.

"These are troubled times," Berathon said dourly, looking down at the bound Mollug in his alabaster hands.

Austin shifted into second gear. "I thought this was supposed to be the start of a glorious new age. How could we have screwed things up so badly so fast?"

Berathon shook his head, his eyes staring out the side window. "It is not you, but we, who have taken erroneous steps. There … there is a traitor among the Host."

North of Austin, at the border between New Hampshire and Maine, the now ship-less crew of the *Puritan* made their way towards Kent Harbor in a procession of nearly thirty stolen vehicles. They were stripped down, traveling light, and now without their gold.

In the middle, sitting inside a silver Mercedes Benz, Hector Ladrone drove while their captain, Mary Mathers, sat in the passenger seat. Behind them, sprawled out and sleeping, was the goddess Aphrodite.

"Nearly four," Hector said, breaking the silence that had befallen them. "Crew must be hungry. God knows I am."

Mathers nodded, pulling out her wireless phone. Clicking on the walkie talkie function, she spoke to her crew. "Lead vehicle, stop at the next restaurant. Let's get a good meal in our systems." Clicking the phone shut, Mathers looked to her second-in-command. "Good call, Hector."

"Nice to know I'm appreciated," he said, his tone dripping with sarcasm.

"Excuse me?"

"Nada," he said, waving her aside. "Just nice to know my opinion still means something." Pause. "I mean, you could've called Austin to get his opinion."

"Oh, please," Mary replied, not wanting to get drawn into this conversation. "You're jealous of Austin?"

"He has your ear more than I do."

"I'm not having this conversation," Mathers said, exhaling deeply. "If I so valued Austin's opinion, why did I send him away?"

"Because you knew he wasn't going to stay anyway?"

"Stop whining, Hector," Mathers snapped. "You're much too young to be a whiner."

"Is that it?" he asked, feeling his agitation grow. "My age?"

"Respect is earned with me, Hector," Mathers said in a low growl. "You earned respect for your actions when you captured the Jolly Roger. You want respect for your brain, do something to prove your worth."

"Like what?"

"Talk to me about Carl."

Hector glanced to his captain in surprise, then nodded. "We can't trust him anymore."

Mathers had been thinking along the same lines. "Because Captain Sam let him go?"

"Why would a psychopath like Stocky Samuel let a prisoner go free, especially when it was one of the four he was brawling with at

First Night Feast?" Hector shook his head. "Carl either sold us out, or is going to sell us out."

"You think he's a spy?"

"Why not? No one would suspect that nerdy biochemist to be a spy, not when we're without a ship. What's there to spy on?"

"You tell me," Mathers pushed.

"I know guys like Samuel," Hector explained, his foot coming off the accelerator as the Puritan procession pulled into an IHOP parking lot. "They live for power, and there's only one way that power is gained – revenge. The ability to get someone back without getting caught or punished. This Samuel guy – he wants me, Austin, Carl, and Teddy to pay for making him look foolish."

Mathers sucked on her front teeth, thinking. "But he had Carl in his grasp and let him go. Maybe Carl is right – maybe Samuel just let him go to tell us that Lazarus is dead and that he was now in charge."

Hector shook his head. "I don't buy it. Keep your distance from him. As of the moment I saw him in that boat headed for shore, Carl Yesek is dead to me."

"A traitor?"

Berathon nodded to Austin's question as the two drove south towards Boston in the A6. "So we believe," he continued somberly. "We are plagued on several fronts: God's Word has been stolen and possibly forged, Enimon, the Angel in Charge of Astronauts, has been murdered, and someone has stolen his harp."

"Is that important?" Austin asked. "No offense, but if he's dead he's not going to miss his harp, is he?"

Berathon turned slightly, showing his disdain. "The harp holds, at the very least, a significant clue to who conspires against us."

"How do you know that?" Austin replied, meeting the angel's gaze.

"The mere fact that it was missing from the scene of the murder," Berathon answered. "That tells us whomever slew Enimon knew the harp held a clue. Harps cannot be destroyed except either in the clouds of Heaven or the fires of Hell. We believe that Enimon left us a clue in the strings of his harp."

Austin shook his head, taking his right hand off the wheel to rub his eyes. "Remember about twenty minutes ago when you couldn't figure out how to work the gas pump?"

Berathon did not respond to Austin's perceived insult.

"Well," Austin continued, "that's how stupid I feel now. Explain the harp thing to me. Slowly." While waiting for the angel to begin, he reached down to the cup holder and took a few deep gulps from his bottle of Code Red Mountain Dew.

"Angelic harps are bonded to us through the act of creation," Berathon explained.

"So no one else can use it?"

"No, others may use it, but each harp is the product of its maker. Instrument and angel are bonded together. God blesses each harp with the story of the angel's life, and as we move through the ages, we add our thoughts and prayers and deeds to the harp."

"So it's a journal?"

"Your analogy is crude, but it works," Berathon admitted.

"You're hoping there's something of his death recorded in the harp?"

Berathon nodded, reaching for his bottled water. "There is most assuredly something recorded in the harp's strings. Our hope is that Enimon had time to record some specific knowledge or thoughts." Berathon took a large sip of water, swished it around his mouth, and swallowed.

"What does this have to do with me?" Austin asked.

"Nothing."

Austin snorted. "Then why are you here?"

Berathon held the bound Mollug aloft. "Your parrot holds another clue."

"The changing message he squawks endlessly?"

"The first message he repeated was comprised of my own words."

Austin showed mild surprise. "How? When?"

Letting out a deep sigh, Berathon squirmed in his seat. "The First Night of the New World. While you were painting the hull of the *Cottonmather*, ironically. Mollug and two other parrots overheard Enimon and myself debating the merits of the alleged forgery of God's Word."

Another sip of his Code Red, then Austin asked, "And the other two parrots? What have you learned from them?"

"Nothing," Berathon said curtly.

"And that's because ...?"

"I slew them the moment I discovered their treachery."

"Their treachery?" Austin asked, dumbfounded. "They're parrots! What kind of treachery-"

Berathon held a hand aloft to silence Austin. "Our words were –
are – to many of the Host, blasphemous. To angels, there is no
greater crime."

Austin thought of the dead angel. "What about murder?"

Berathon frowned, but didn't budge. "Murder is a crime of
blasphemy."

"Thou Shall Not Kill," Austin said, shaking his head.

The angel nodded. "I believe that whomever changed the words
Mollug repeats is part of the conspiracy."

"Makes sense," Austin admitted, checking the road signs for his
exit. "Hey, can I ask you a question?"

"Of course."

"Is my girlfriend alive?" Austin asked, blurting out the words.

Berathon looked at the young man, holding a sharp reply in his
throat. He'd wanted to snap that angels were not omniscient, but the
pain that was evident in Austin's eyes caused him to soften his words.
"I do not know," he admitted. "Were I in Heaven, such an answer
would be easier to ascertain, but on Earth the vision of angels is
limited. Our eyes were created to look down upon the earth, not on
its surface."

Scratching his head, Austin said, "I understand. No problem."

"Do you really wonder about her continued existence on this
plane?"

Austin shrugged. "I don't know. Honestly, my heart tells me
she's alive, but I was told she was dead. Truth is … I don't know
what to think. I guess, I mean, I think I'm too unwilling to believe it
without seeing it, you know?"

"Is this why you travel away from your crew?" the angel asked.

Austin nodded.

"You have not looked overly concerned," Berathon added.

"No use getting worked up until I need to."

"I wish you well on your quest," Berathon offered. "Love was a
gift not given to the angels," he said solemnly, thinking of his recent
encounter with Aphrodite. He shuddered, wanting to put that
thought behind him. "Before you begin your search," he held
Mollug aloft, "I would welcome your assistance, if you have any to
give, with solving the mystery of Mollug."

Austin looked at the stilled parrot and nodded. "Whatever I can
do."

"Pull to the side of the road," Berathon ordered. "The motion of
this vehicle is making me ill at ease."

"You're carsick?" Austin asked as a thin smile spread across his face. "Will wonders ever cease?"

Berathon, taking Austin's question as literal, replied, "If God is not found, then yes, wonders will cease. It is our job to make certain that depressed day never arrives."

Austin opened his mouth to reply, then shut it. *Really*, he asked himself, *how do you reply to that?*

Parking three spots to the left of the captain's Mercedes, Carl Yesek sat in the passenger seat, too nervous to sleep. He kept wondering if it was a good thing, or a bad thing, that Austin wasn't with them anymore.

"I'm going to let you go," Captain Samuel had told him, "but I swear on my mother's grave if I don't have Austin and Hector's head rolling around on the deck of the Cottonmather by the end of the month, I will hunt you to the end of the Earth, then take you apart piece by piece by piece."

Carl nervously rubbed his temples. He didn't have to listen to Samuel, of course. He was free now, wasn't he? Couldn't he just ignore Samuel's threats?

Yeah, Carl thought. I can.

But will I?

Samuel had not simply threatened Carl, but tempted him.

"All the booze and broads you could ever want."

An empty promise. Or was it?

Glancing nervously at the driver, who was busy arguing with the man in back about whether it was more inhumane for the state to kill a man by lethal injection or the guillotine, Carl reached into his pocket and removed a list that Samuel had given him. The list was comprised of six coastal New England towns and cities. Corresponding with each city was a name.

"*Cottonmather* spies," Samuel explained. "Don't fool yourself into thinking these are all my spies, neither. You go into one of these towns, you find the man on this list. Ask him for anything. He'll deliver. You bring me Austin and Hector, you'll get whatever it is you want."

"Why?" Carl had asked. "Why do you care so much about Austin and Hector?"

Samuel had given Carl a rough smile. "I don't."

"Then why-?"

Samuel had turned and looked away. "Someone else does. Someone who scares the ever-loving shit out of me." He turned back, looking up at Carl with wild eyes. "Who just so happens to be the same person that can give me what I want. Make it happen, Carl."

Carl's memory was lost as the driver punched him in the arm. "Yo, Carl, let's go! It's time for pancakes."

"Pancakes," Carl thought, wondering who was pulling Samuel's strings.

Austin watched as Berathon said a prayer, hands moving in ritualistic arcs over the bound parrot Mollug. Mollug lay still on the hood of the A6 and Austin stood off to the side, feeling hungry. He rubbed his stomach, looking at his surroundings, wishing he'd pulled into a restaurant's parking lot instead of a bank's. They were about a half-hour north of Boston.

Probably a good time to come up with something of a plan.

"I am ready," Berathon announced. "I have used the powers granted to us through God's Word to calm the soul of this parrot."

"Animals have souls?" Austin asked, thinking of all those hours in Catechism class wasted arguing questions like this and, "If dinosaurs really existed, why aren't they in the Bible?," and "If God can do anything, can He create a rock so big even He can't lift it?" Sheer idiocy. *Like God and the angels ever sat around pondering such nonsense.*

"Of course animals have souls," Berathon replied, annoyed Austin would ask such a question at a time like this. "They are one of God's creations, are they not?"

Sensing the angel's annoyance, Austin kept his mouth shut. *Time and place*, he told himself.

"If I have performed the recreation rite successfully," Berathon explained, removing the leather bindings, "this parrot should be cured of its lunacy, and, hopefully, shall provide us with answers." Concentrating fully, Berathon removed the parrot's hood. Unconsciously, both he and Austin braced for the impact of Mollug's shrill madness.

It never came.

Instead, Mollug squawked, "Well, it's about fucking time, isn't it?"

Samantha was in the room that Frederic and Vanessa shared when Kelly awoke. Of the three, this was the last person Samantha wanted to awake first, but as her luck was running, she had kinda figured it would be Kelly.

"Hey," Kelly said, as if they were friends, as she stretched and yawned and rubbed her eyes. "Samantha, right?" she asked. "Our time together is … fuzzy."

"You were hung over."

"Yep, that about covers it."

Samantha had been so hoping that Kelly wouldn't wake up first that she hadn't bothered to prepare how she would handle the conversation. So she winged it. "He has a thing for you, you know."

"Who?" Kelly asked, moving to the sink to get a Dixie cup of water.

"Good question," Samantha mumbled, thinking of both Frederic and Scranton. Which had she meant? Which would she play? "Frederic."

Kelly downed the water as if it were a shot (which, seeing it was a Dixie cup, it practically was) and turned to Samantha. Before speaking, she took the woman in. Her hair was wet, meaning she'd probably taken a shower in one of the upstairs facilities, but she'd returned to her Princess gown. Her eyes were red, probably from the shower, but maybe from crying. It was hard to tell. The look on her face, however, told Kelly that if Samantha hadn't been crying recently, there was still a good deal of emotional turmoil beneath the surface.

God's honest truth, Samantha looked one part desperate, one part pathetic. *Go easy on her*, she heard Austin's voice tell her in her mind. *The New World hasn't been easy on many.* To the voice in her head, Kelly nodded, then continued with Samantha a few gears less than she was in the mood to do.

"I don't think so, Samantha," she said, turning away from the younger woman to refill the cup. "Frederic and I barely know each other. It was random that we even met."

"I see the way he looks at you," Samantha continued, undaunted.

Across the room, as she bottomed her second cup of water, Kelly caught the jealous edge in Samantha's voice. *She likes him.* Kelly turned, saw more hurt on Samantha's face than had been there a moment ago. *Maybe they're an item.*

Not patient enough to wait for a response, Samantha pushed forward. "I suppose right here is where I'm supposed to say that he's mine, right? That you can't take him from me, but the truth is, you probably could. Girls like you always get what you want."

"And you don't?" Kelly asked. "Give me a break."

"Then again," Samantha lied, "maybe he doesn't have a thing for you. The only reason he's been looking for you is that the King ordered him to look after you."

"What?"

"You heard me," Samantha spat, standing up. "Your ex-boyfriend, the King of New England, ordered Frederic to escort you to Kent Harbor. Wonder why he'd do that?"

Kelly was struck dumb. She had no idea Brad had done such a thing. "I can't believe Brad would do that. Why would he do that?"

Samantha started to say something, but stopped herself. Wheels began to spin inside her mind. That King Regent would see to it that his ex-girlfriend was delivered safely to her new castle wasn't, in and of itself, much of a surprise. But the King's Captain of the Guard had arranged for Samantha and another girl to have sex with Frederic. She looked over to Frederic and thought about how awful a lover he had been that night, then thought about the connection between Frederic, Kelly, and the King. Something wasn't right …

"What is it?" Kelly asked, noting the change in attitude in Samantha's facial expression.

"You were attacked and Frederic saved you," Samantha thought aloud, more to herself than to answer Kelly's question. "Then the King ordered Frederic to escort you to Kent Harbor. Why would he do that?"

"Well," Kelly said, playing along, "Frederic had just saved my life."

"But … if the King really wanted you safe, why not send an escort of his Guardsmen? Why send some ranger?"

"He had just saved my life."

"No. I didn't."

The two women turned to Frederic, laying on his stomach and facing away from both of them. "What do you mean?" Kelly asked, feeling very uncomfortable about where this conversation was headed.

Frederic rolled over, wincing as his aching back readjusted to the pressure of being on the bottom. "Might as well admit it now. I didn't save you, Kelly. Not really. The King saved you."

"But you … you caught the man who abducted me."

Frederic shook his head. "He caught himself on my sword. Truth was," he reached his hand out to take Samantha's hand in his, "when I saw that group of men pushing you around, I …" Frederic closed his eyes tight, and shook his head from side to side on the large pillow slowly. "I froze. Completely. King Regent was the hero. He dashed right in and beat the hell out of the group. Only reason I caught the guy I did was that he ran himself onto my sword."

"But …" Kelly didn't know what to say. *Just what the hell was going on that night?* "Why wouldn't Brad tell me about that? Why did he assign you to protect me?" She thought of the attacker on I-95. "Did he know someone was after me? Why would anyone want to kill me?"

Frederic opened his eyes and gripped Samantha's hand tightly. "He said you'd find some way to be angry at him, I think. I dunno … it's all in such a haze. I was so caught up in my own cowardice that the next day seems like it's trapped behind a thick fog."

The three of them stood there, absorbing what had been said. Kelly's thoughts focused on Brad – what was his angle? There was no way, she believed, Brad would care enough about her reaction that he'd deflect news that would make him look good. That just wasn't his style. So what was his game? Why did he place her under Frederic's protection if what Frederic said was true about how he captured her abductor? Was it possible Brad hadn't seen it the way Frederic had?

For Frederic, wracked as he was with pain, he squeezed tighter on Samantha's hand. There was only one question on his mind - Would Samantha leave him because of this? Because there was only one thought on his mind – he wanted to be with her, and only her.

Samantha's thoughts were with the other person in the room, the unconscious Vanessa. Did Scranton really think she'd kill this woman? What would be the result if she didn't? Frederic sees a picture of a decidedly different her? Something in the way he held tightly to her hand told her she needn't be concerned about him leaving her. And if she was wrong …?

"One thing is for damn sure," Kelly said, interrupting Samantha's thoughts. "I need to get to Boston and confront Brad over just what the hell is going on. Either of you feel like tagging along?"

Frederic nodded and Samantha watched him nod, then nodded herself. As she felt her head move up and down, Samantha began to see the benefits of getting away from here – if she was gone, then she wouldn't have to face Scranton about Vanessa.

"I'll need a few days to heal up," Frederic said.

"No," Samantha said, surprising the other two. "We have to go now."

"Why?" Kelly asked.

Samantha looked nervously to the door. When she saw that no one was there, she took a deep breath, and told Frederic and Kelly of her burden. "Because Michael Scranton wants me to kill Vanessa."

"Calm yourself, parrot," Berathon ordered as Mollug flapped out of the angel's grip to stand on its own in the middle of the A6's hood.

"Calm yourself," Mollug squawked back.

Austin and Berathon exchanged a knowing glance – Mollug was putting up a brave front but it was clear the parrot was nervous. Mollug glanced around constantly, looking up to scan the skies as it moved in a slow circle on the hood.

"Mollug," Austin said gently. "We need information."

"And I suppose you'd like me to give it to you, wouldn't you?" Mollug asked, looking behind Austin. "Forget it. I'd rather eat my own feathers than help the angels."

Berathon frowned. "Why do you say that?"

For once, Mollug eyed Berathon directly. "Because you're a bunch of bastards. You collected all of us parrots from around the world to serve as your little messenger bitches, but you only gave us limited speech."

Berathon attempted to explain. "You were a safety measure, instituted in order to help facilitate the transition from Old World to New."

"But the humans didn't need our help, did they?" Mollug asked, shuffling across the hood towards the angel. "They adapted almost instantly. And do you know why? Because that's what humans do – adapt. Most of them didn't even notice as their parrots started flying away. Austin," the parrot asked, turning to his assigned pirate, "how many parrots are still on the *Puritan*?"

Austin shrugged. "Not many," he said, not bothering to explain that the *Puritan* was now sitting at the bottom of the Atlantic.

"Mollug," Berathon pressed, "I do apologize for your ill-treatment, but these are pressing times. A traitor walks among the Host. Please help us solve this blasphemy."

Mollug thought about that for a moment. "What are you going to do for me?"

"What?" Berathon asked, his frustration growing by the second. "Do for you? Angels do not bargain—"

"Then figure out your little problem on your own," Mollug replied, flapping his wings as if he were going to take flight.

Berathon folded his arms, apparently content to let Mollug leave.

Austin couldn't believe this was happening. For the moment he was even willing to put aside the ridiculousness of a parrot arguing with an angel; it was the pettiness of the argument between them that was drawing his ire. With all that had happened – from being separated from Kelly to the sinking of the *Puritan* – Austin just wanted answers. "Enough, you two," he said, taking the tone he used when scolding talkative freshmen in his ENGL 127 class. "Mollug, what do you want?"

Mollug stopped flapping his wings and eyed Austin carefully. "You can't make it happen."

"I realize that," Austin said, wondering what the hell a parrot could want that would be so tough to procure, "but if you tell me then Berathon will hear it, too, and maybe we can come to some resolution."

"I don't know …"

"What've you got to lose?" Austin asked. "If Berathon says no, you don't tell him anything."

Berathon turned on Austin. "Are you trying to help or hinder?"

Austin ignored him. "Come on, Mollug. What is it you want?"

Mollug tried his best to look like the answer was being pulled from him against his will, but capitulated. Unable to look either Austin or Berathon in the eye, Mollug looked down at the hood of the A6. "I don't want to lose the ability to talk."

To Austin, the parrot's words made sense. "That doesn't sound so bad. What do you say, Berathon?"

"Absolutely not," the angel stated flatly. "To give in to the demands of parrots …"

"Oh, please," Austin replied. "Think of the larger picture. How can you be so petty now that you are this close to getting an answer to your questions?"

Berathon frowned, looking forlorn. His voice was low, measured. "Because it is not God's Will for parrots to have this ability. If He had wanted parrots to have the ability to speak freely, and not just base mimicking skills, He would've granted—"

"It was Gabriel," Mollug squawked, turning his back on Berathon.

"What?" Berathon asked, stunned, slamming his fists on the hood of the A6. "Gabriel is the leader of the Reorganization."

"Yeah," Mollug said, his back still turned, "that's why I recognized him. You angels all look the same to me, but then, that's probably because my brain is so small. Thanks, God."

Austin could practically see the dark cloud descend onto Berathon, so sullen was the angel's expression. "What did Gabriel do, exactly?" Austin asked.

Mollug's body shook at the memory. "Just what Berathon did just now. Used the power granted to the angels in God's Word to temporarily recreate me."

"Except where I gave you freedom, Gabriel gave you one phrase to repeat."

Mollug nodded. "At least in that way he was nicer than you."

"Excuse me?" Berathon asked.

"When I was repeating the phrase I overheard in your and Enimon's discussion, I was doing it because I was scared out of my mind." Mollug turned. "You were trying to kill me."

Berathon opened his mouth to talk, then closed it in order to reframe his statement. "I do apologize for that, Mollug, but the secrets of Heaven are more important than anyone – man, parrot, or angel. So please, I, an angel of the Host, do humbly beg of you, a parrot, to tell me everything you know about the conspiracy in Heaven."

Mollug waddled around to face the angel. The bird's words were soft and slow. "I was given to Gabriel by Ocilael," he explained, the memory of the incident unpleasant. "I was nearly insane with fear, but I was calmed by Gabriel's kind prayers. I was laid to rest on a cloud, where I drifted off to sleep. I heard voices … many, many voices, discussing the stealing of God's Word."

"Who was present at this meeting?" Berathon asked.

Mollug shook his head. "It was clear, though, that there was an argument in which Gabriel was caught in the middle. He was pressed on one side for immediate, harsh action against you."

"Ocilael," Berathon guessed.

Mollug continued. "There was another angel, with views nearly opposite to the angry angel, arguing for compassion."

"Any guesses?" Austin asked Berathon.

"Likely Raphael."

"The Angel in charge of Royalty?" the pirate asked, thinking of the first morning, when he and Kelly met Raphael.

Berathon nodded, thinking that this information solidified his feelings about the current state of the Host. Ocilael on the hard right, Raphael on the hard left, and Gabriel caught in the middle, facilitating the two positions. "Tell me, Mollug, what more information you have to share. Why did Gabriel put the new phrase into your mind? Why did he touch you with madness?"

Mollug shivered. "He excused the other two angels, leaving me alone with him. He came to me with kindness in his voice and explained that my words would cause nothing but problems for the angels. Then he took me in his hands and began to pray." Mollug looked heavenward with a heavy heart. "Then madness descended."

Austin felt the weight that descended onto Berathon, and remained silent.

"There is one question which dominates my mind," Berathon explained slowly. "Are the actions of Gabriel active, or reactive? Does he act because he drives the chariot, or does the chariot drive and he reacts to keep the peace amongst the Host? Tell me Austin," the angel asked, coming out of his private thoughts, "which mystery would you solve first? Who stole God's Word, or who killed Enimon?"

Austin inhaled deeply, then let the breath out slowly, his mind racing to figure out Berathon's question. "In truth," he finally realized, "I don't think it matters."

"It doesn't matter?" Berathon asked. "How could you come to such a conclusion?"

"Because neither will tell you who's behind the conspiracy, but both will get you one step closer. My guess is that the person pulling the strings won't have done either of the two acts." Austin tried to piece the puzzle together, but all he found were more questions. "Didn't Aphrodite say you were fighting a giant monster? Who created it?"

Berathon shook his head. "On that point, who freed Aphrodite, while leaving the remaining Olympians locked away in Purgatory?"

"You're asking me?" Austin asked. "Berathon, I'd love to help, but all of the questions you raise lead back to the angels. Humans don't have that kind of power. We can't steal God's Word or kill an angel or free Olympians from Purgatory. It has to be an angel, or angels, doesn't it?"

Berathon closed his eyes and said a quick prayer of forgiveness. "No," he said softly. "It could be someone else."

"Who?" Austin asked. "Wait, you don't mean ..."

Berathon opened his golden eyes and nodded. "I do. Lucifer."

"Who's that?" Mollug asked.

Austin frowned. "Satan."

"We're dealing with Satan?" Mollug asked.

"Possibly," Berathon answered.

"Fuck me," Mollug whistled. "This shit keeps getting worse and worse."

Austin asked, "Berathon, if we're dealing with Lucifer, where would he be? Hell? Earth?"

Berathon shook his head. "I don't know. In truth, however, if Lucifer does not want to be found, we will never find him."

As the sun poked above the horizon, Michael Scranton entered the hospital room shared by Frederic and Vanessa and instantly knew something was wrong. "Where is Kelly?" he asked the ranger.

"Gone," Frederic replied, pretending to wince in pain to hide the uneasiness he was struggling to keep inside. "She and Samantha left ten minutes ago," he lied by at least an hour.

Michael frowned. "Where did they go?" he asked, cursing himself for spending the past several hours with Enimon's harp, trying and failing to draw the harp's recollection of Enimon's death to the surface.

Frederic hoped this was convincing. "South," he said. "Providence. Kelly wants to contact Raphael, I think she said. The Angel in charge of Royalty. She wants out."

Scranton eyed the ranger carefully, then turned away. It was clear he was lying, but Scranton saw no need to call the ranger's lies into public scrutiny. "Why did Samantha go with her?" he asked, thinking of his supposed alliance with the redhead. "When will they be back?"

Frederic shook his head. "Don't know. A few days, I think. Providence isn't that far and if they can find a car to steal, they might even be back tonight or tomorrow."

Scranton was a little less certain about this lie. If Kelly was coming back, then there was no need to go looking for her. "Are you certain they will return?"

"They better," Frederic grinned. "I'd hate to think I've seen Samantha for the last time. A man can spend his whole life looking for a woman that great and never find her. She's just about perfect."

Scranton gave the ranger a half-smile, thinking of the picture of Old World Samantha in his pocket. The bigger question was what to do about Kelly and Samantha's disappearance ...

No matter, he concluded. As much as he desired Kelly Reed, she was not his priority. There were other things to accomplish with a higher priority. Enimon's harp was locked away and he doubted-

A loud ringing interrupted his thoughts. "The hospital's alarm," Scranton informed Frederic. "We have a visitor. I wonder who-"

"All who can hear my voice," a loud commanding man shouted, "assemble at the entrance to the hospital. I am Enimon's temporary replacement!"

Frederic struggled to sit upright in bed. "Who is it?" he asked, thinking there was something eerily familiar in that voice. Was it Kelly's abductor?

Scranton moved to the window, not bothering to hide his frown. A replacement for Enimon was not expected so soon; there were barely enough angels to fill all the roles the Reorganization demanded, let alone angels looking for something to do. Pulling aside the curtain, Scranton gasped in astonishment. "Holy hell," he whispered.

"What?" Frederic asked. "What is it?"

Scranton looked down. "You wouldn't believe me if I told you."

"Try me," Frederic shot back, his uneasiness gone, replaced by hatred for the man who tried to force Samantha into killing Vanessa while her body wasted away in a coma. He had to keep it together ... Kelly's plan rested on his ability to keep it together.

"Fine," Scranton replied, stepping away from the window to meet Frederic's gaze. "It's an entire battalion of orcs. Large, ugly, smelly orcs."

"Sure it is."

The voice from outside boomed again and Frederic realized it was coming through a bullhorn. "Astronauts, please exit the building! I have been sent by the angels of Heaven to lead you to safety! You are in grave danger!"

Something about that voice, Frederic thought again. "Orcs, huh?" he asked Scranton. "That doesn't sound like an orc."

"Oh, him?" Scranton replied, gazing back out the window. He figured there must be at least a hundred orcs in front of the hospital. "No, they're not led by an orc. Orcs are incredibly stupid creatures. They're led by a human."

Annoyed and needing to see for himself, Frederic pushed himself out of bed and shuffled over to the window.

"See for yourself," Scranton remarked, stepping aside.

"I will," Frederic answered, pulling back the curtain to look down. His eyes washed over the orcs, disbelieving their existence even as they stood in tight, rigid formation, until his eyes came to rest on the man at the front of the battalion. The man in charge wore a United States Army uniform – green camouflage style – and stood on top of a tank, holding a bullhorn in his hand.

"Oh, hell," Frederic blurted.

"What is it?" Scranton asked, curious.

"The man in charge," he said softly, unable to tear his eyes away. "I know him."

Scranton raised an eyebrow. "Really? Who is it?"

"My father."

Chapter Sixteen
Reunions Unpleasant

Frederic Kornell stood in a sixth floor window, looking down at the scene before him. Though the sun had risen, casting light across the nightmarish image, it was as unbelievable now as it had been hours ago, when Michael Scranton had first told him of it.

There, in the front entrance plaza before Hollis Memorial Hospital, stood a battalion of orcs – large, ugly, and nasty. Even more unbelievable than the sudden appearance of orcs was the human leading them.

Frederic's father. Or, as he was more commonly known in Frederic's mind – General Kornell, his mother's murderer.

The Old World janitor and New World ranger had escaped to the upper levels of the hospital. The General had ordered all astronauts outside, claiming he had been given orders by the angels to transport them to safety. The presence of the orc army was less than comforting, but Scranton had informed him (after talking with the General) that the orcs were humans who had, for whatever reason, dreamt of being orcs when they were children. The angels had collected them and turned them into some kind of security force to help with the miscellaneous accounts they didn't have time to handle.

At least, that's what Scranton said. Why the man was suddenly acting as if her were Frederic's friend was another matter. Then again … he'd just met Scranton. All he had to go on as to the man's untrustworthiness was Kelly's "bad feeling" and Samantha's claim Scranton wanted her to kill the comatose Vanessa. He'd no reason to doubt Samantha, but as his mother always told him-

"Stop it," he cursed himself. Back to the window, Frederic looked down to find his father and saw that the man was still in conversation with the group of astronauts.

Minus Scranton.

"Tell me, ranger," Scranton said, suddenly appearing in the doorway behind Frederic, "why you avoid your father? You say he killed your mother. Is that the truth, or just the angry hyperbole of a hurt child?"

"Go to hell," Frederic said, turning around and noting that Scranton had put his astronaut uniform back on. Seeing the bright orange suit calmed him, reminded him of his role in Kelly's plan – stay on Scranton, figure out his angle and what he was really after. And, if possible, what was going on with the angels. Kelly was adamant something was up, since they'd been completely absent since Enimon's death. They should've come to the remaining astronauts and … and something.

Frederic wondered what she would think of General Kornell and his army of orcs parked outside.

"Go to hell?" Scranton asked, smiling. "Do you mean that figuratively or literally?"

Frederic didn't respond to the question, but he got a sense of Kelly's unease in Scranton asking it. "What now?" he said finally. "Where's the General taking them?"

"Your father is taking them to a nearby train station," Scranton explained. "They're headed south, to the Kennedy Space Center in Florida, where they'll be trained and then, if that goes well, sent to space, fulfilling their childhood dream."

"You said 'they'."

"I'm not going with them."

"Why not? Don't you have a dream to fulfill, too?"

Scranton shrugged. "Dreams of a child are not always that of the man."

"Yeah," Frederic replied, disbelieving. "Then what?"

Scranton walked across the room so he could look out the window. His face grew grim as he looked down at the orcs and astronauts. "Something's rotten with that scene. I intend to find out what it is." He turned back. "Wanna tag along?"

Kelly's plan reverberated through his mind. Frederic didn't really have a choice. Besides, anything that could keep him away from a reunion from his father was a preferred road at this point. He needed time to figure out what he wanted to do; in the Old World, a confrontation with his father was the last thing he wanted. But now … with his New World body … perhaps it was time to talk to his dad in the only language his father understood – violence. "Sure," he said, pushing that thought aside and agreeing to join Scranton. "But first, I want you to tell me everything you know about Enimon's harp."

Austin was surprised to find that the New England Aquarium was still open. Most businesses had closed their doors, but the Aquarium was filled with … well, filled with ninjas, vampires, and strangely dressed female musicians. There were also men in knight's uniforms, but Austin had learned they were the King's guards. He was the only pirate in sight, a fact that got him more than one odd glance from the crowd.

"Oh wow, you're like, so groovy!" one of the strangely dressed female musicians said to him. Austin knew she was a musician because she walked around with a guitar strapped around her back. Her strange dress was evidenced by a costume that only made sense when it was drawn in a cartoon. The young woman had a beehive hairdo and was dressed as a bumblebee. "Are you, like, a wicked pirate?"

"Sort of, yeah."

"Sort of?" the woman asked, smiling broadly. "Sort of wicked, or sort of a pirate?"

"Sort of both, I suppose," Austin replied. "So, um, what are you supposed to be?"

"Me?" the woman asked, giggling. "Why, I'm a mystery-solving musician! Do you have a mystery that needs solving?"

Now that's an interesting question, Austin thought, wondering if he should take her up on it, wondering how she'd respond if he asked her to help him find his girlfriend. What the heck, he figured, and asked her.

"Wow, you're missing your girlfriend? That's so awful," she said, not dropping her smile, "but, like, so romantic that you're looking for her! Let me get my band together and we'll help!"

Austin chuckled, throwing up his hands. "No, no, that's okay. Really, it's very sweet that you're willing to help, but don't you have a concert or something?"

"Oh, yeah!" she giggled. "We're, like, playing tonight at a big festival out near the dolphin tanks! You should, like, so be there! You know," she said, dropping her voice but not her smile, "if you've found your girlfriend!"

"Gotcha," Austin nodded, wanting to be anywhere else.

"See ya, cutie!"

"Yeah," Austin replied, waving the mystery-solving musician good-bye. He turned his attention to the large circular tank at the center of the Aquarium. The tank moved upwards through every level of the Aquarium and a circular ramp led you round and round from bottom to top. Walking over to the tank, Austin wondered just how many times he'd been here over the years. Seems like every other year as a kid his school would take a field trip to the Aquarium, and he'd been here a couple times when he was dating Jessica Jenkins.

Since he'd been dating Kelly, however, he'd been here just once. It was her first date after breaking up with Brad Regent and she'd spent almost the entire time talking about the time she and Brad had their first kiss by the penguin exhibit, or how Brad (who everybody thought was a total jerk) had comforted a crying kid by the sea urchin tank, or how she had gotten completely soaked by the dolphins and Brad had given her his sweatshirt, or …

Blah blah blah.

It was almost the worst date Austin had ever been on. It was so bad, in fact, that Austin spent a good year believing the only reason he'd gotten a second date with Kelly was that she felt so bad about talking so much about Brad that she felt she owed him a second date. She offered to go to the Aquarium again, but Austin had no intention of going back here with her. That the Aquarium was a favorite spot of both his and Brad's was too much for Austin's paranoid mind to handle.

Now, despite all the craziness, it felt good to be back.

Austin scanned the tank for sharks and found two large tigers right away. To his surprise, there was someone in the tank, hand-feeding them from the large coral reef.

"Crazy, isn't it?" a female ninja said from beside him. "Heard King Regent so wanted this place to be open that he offered a half-million to the water docs?"

"The water docs?" Austin asked, looking over at the ninja. She was covered, head to toe, in a tight black outfit.

"Whatever you call them," the ninja said, smiling through her black mask.

"Marine biologists?" Austin asked.

"Sure," the ninja replied, then pulled off her mask, revealing a beautiful young woman with blond hair cropped short. "King Regent really wanted this facility open, so he paid to get a few marine biologists to stay here, instead of heading for warmer waters." She looked Austin up and down. "Pirate, huh? How's that working out?"

Austin smiled. "Not bad, all things considered. Sure, I've been separated from my girlfriend, shot at, been told by a complete stranger that my girlfriend is dead, and had my ship sunk on me, but other than that, no complaints."

The ninja laughed. "At least you're still smiling," she said, punching him lightly in the arm. "Name's Liv," she grinned, offering him her hand.

"Austin," he replied, shaking her hand. He looked around at the mass of ninjas, vampires, and what he now knew to be mystery-solving musicians. "Quite a crowd. What are you ninjas doing here in Boston?"

"Caught up in paperwork," Liv answered, frowning. She motioned to Austin that she wanted to walk, and the two began to walk around the slow rising ramp, the large circular tank to their left. "All of us New England ninjas were told to meet here, at the docks. They were supposed to fly us to Los Angeles, then send us by cruise ship to the Pacific."

"What happened?"

Liv shook her head. "We were taken to Logan where our planes were waiting, but then our angel representative, Philodael, got all uptight over something. Told us we were momentarily grounded. They put us up at the Four Seasons, but we haven't heard from him – or any other angel – since."

Austin wondered if he should tell her what he knew, but decided against it. "We experienced much the same," he said. "Lots of contact with our angel rep early on, then nothing." No need to get into last night's surprise visit by Berathon, he reasoned.

"King Regent has been great to us," she informed him, causing Austin's skin to crawl at the idea Brad could be great to anyone. "Of course," she continued, "he spends a lot more time with the mystery-solving musicians." At that, Austin smiled – *Good to see some things stay the same.* Liv motioned down to her costume, "Not as much to leer at with the ninja costumes."

"And most of you, it appears, are male," Austin chuckled, stopping to look at one of the tiger sharks that almost appeared to be following them up the ramp. "Look at that thing," Austin said reverentially. "Awesome."

Liv was nonplussed. "Fish are fish to me. Sorry. I'm only here because its better than sticking around the hotel."

Austin glanced around. "Is this an arranged trip, or did one ninja mention this at breakfast and the rest of you thought it was a good idea?"

"Arranged," Liv answered, moving forward again. "King Regent has invited us to dinner tonight at the castle to make up for our delay."

"Isn't that nice of him," Austin groused.

Liv studied Austin carefully.

"What?"

"Did the King used to beat you up for your lunch money or something in the Old World?"

Austin rubbed his stubbled chin, really wishing he could shave. "Worse. He used to date my girlfriend."

"Used to date?"

"Yeah."

"Then what's the problem?"

"What's the problem?" Austin asked, stopping in his tracks.

"You said you're separated from your girlfriend because of the Reorganization, right?" Liv asked. "And that you've been told she's dead. Do you think the King has something to do with it?"

Austin kicked at the ground. Looking past Liv, he could see into the giant tank. He watched a school of little silvery fish swim to and fro, seemingly content. "Do you know some people wished they were fish or bears or lions? And the angels, for some reason, turned them into fish and bears and lions? So unless they wished to be a talking bear or a thinking lion, they're really just animals now?"

Liv turned her head to look back at the tank, then slowly came back around to Austin. "Think you recognize someone in there?"

Austin smiled. "Not really, no."

"Then don't avoid the question. Do you think the King has something to do with whatever's happened to your girlfriend?" Liv punched him lightly in the arm for the second time. "You know, if anything has actually happened to her?"

Looking Liv in the eye, Austin replied, "I don't know. What I do know is that if anyone – other than the angels – knows what's what with Kelly, Brad is the guy."

"Why?"

"About a year ago, Kelly's dad had a heart attack," Austin said, feeling the same sick feeling in his stomach he had felt that night. "Kelly and I were at a University function when we got the call from her mom. Somehow, even though her mom swears he wasn't called, Brad was there at the hospital when we arrived. Trust me," Austin stated, looking Liv in the eye, "if there's something to know about Kelly, Brad Regent knows."

Kelly Reed and Samantha Dixon exited a designer department store, dressed in new clothes – jeans and black sweaters. Kelly had ditched her princess gown a few days earlier, but she didn't want the clothes Scranton had picked out for her now that she had an option to get something new. Samantha had given up her dress reluctantly, going so far as to try and stuff it in a handbag before Kelly convinced her it wasn't worth it.

"What, exactly, is our plan here?" Samantha asked.

Kelly looked around, amazed at the lack of people milling about the city streets. "What day is it?"

Samantha thought for a moment, then shook her head. "You know, I have no idea."

"Me neither," Kelly replied, "but I can't remember ever being in Boston at noontime and seeing so few people. I think that's weirder than seeing all the knights and royalty walking through these modern streets."

"I'm more weirded out by the fact that we just stole these clothes without blinking than anything else," Samantha remarked as a half-man, half-giraffe walked in front of them.

"Care to revise that?" Kelly asked, smiling as her eyes followed the creature down the street.

Samantha smiled, then changed her mind and erased it from her face. She was still unsure how to play this – all that petty jealousy she had worked up over Kelly was hard to let go, but she really didn't have any problems with her one-to-one. All her problems with Kelly were based on how Frederic thought about her (or, really, if she wanted to be totally honest, which she didn't, her problems were really about her own insecurity). "You didn't answer my question," she stated, trying to act indifferently but probably coming off bitchy. "What's the plan?"

"Nothing fancy," Kelly replied, eyeing Samantha carefully. *This girl changes moods more often than Austin changes t-shirts*, she mused, thinking of how Austin once packed exactly three shirts for a weeklong getaway to Maine, and all of them Boston Red Sox t-shirts. "I figure we just go knock on the castle door and ask to see the King."

Samantha blinked. "That's it?"

Shrugging, Kelly said, "Sure, why not? What else do we need to do? Brad will see me."

Well, Samantha thought, *aren't you full of yourself?* "I just figured … you know …"

"What?" Kelly asked, grinning. "That we'd have to come up with some complex plan to sneak in and see the King without anyone seeing us? Only a moron – or someone with something to hide – would do that."

Samantha forced a weak smile, thinking of Enimon's harp, thinking she did, in fact, have something to hide.

"Do you think you could sneak me into that meal?" Austin asked Liv. "I've been wracking my brain all day trying to figure out a way to get inside and I'm stumped. The best I can come up with is disguising myself as a caterer."

Liv looked at him as if he had sprouted a second head. "Do you think that would work?"

"Not really," Austin smiled.

"Why don't you just go up and make an appointment?"

"What? He won't see me."

Liv held her ground. "Sure he will."

"The guy hates me."

"Austin, if he's everything you say he is, my guess is that he thinks he's so much better than you that he'll see you just to rub it in."

"Rub what in?"

"That you've lost Kelly somewhere in the New World. Seriously, can't you just call her on her cell phone?"

Austin shook his head. "Tried that. That's when I got the message she was dead."

Liv's face grew a shade darker. "Wait, someone has her cell?" Austin nodded. "Maybe she is in trouble."

"That's why I've got to know."

"Or maybe she's having an affair."

"You're not helping."

Liv chewed her bottom lip, thinking. Her eyes took in Austin from head-to-toe as she tried to formulate some kind of strategy. "Tell you what," she said at last. "I don't see any reason why you couldn't come to the dinner with us, though I'll ask around. We might need to get you into a ninja outfit. Either way, it won't be difficult. Just, promise me one thing."

"Anything," a relieved Austin replied.

"You have got to take a shower and get that outfit washed," Liv stated honestly. "You smell like sea ass."

"Sea ass?"

"Sea ass."

"You have a very strange vocabulary," Austin joked.

"And you have a very strange smell," she smiled back. She opened her arm, pointing back down the ramp. "Come on, you can shower at my place, and we can use the hotel's laundry room to get that stank off of these clothes."

There was pain and darkness and a dream of a better world. Inside Father Otten's mind, there was peace in our time. Father Otten stood on a mountaintop and watched, joy filling his heart with song. There was no war, nor even the threat of war, anywhere on God's Earth. There was a respect for all religions, and extremists were nowhere in existence. There was no killing in the name of God or Allah or Buddha. There was neither extreme poverty nor extreme wealth. There was a free exchange of ideas, and every man, woman, and child was born into a world where they had a chance to be whatever it is they wanted to be, so long as they were willing to work for it.

But through it all, pain. Pain in the pit of the stomach, growing like an acorn, cracking open and growing outward. From this pit of pain, darkness spread out across the Earth.

Otten was horrified; the darkness emanated outward from within himself and covered the globe. The peace was broken. Skirmishes gave way to conflicts. Conflicts gave way to aggressive states. Aggressive states went to war and the world was plunged into blood and fire.

What kept the fifty-seven-year-old Catholic priest sane was the simple truth that he'd had this dream a thousand nights before. "It symbolizes the lack of power you feel in your position as priest," a high-ranking Cardinal had told him years earlier in seminary. "When you preach the Homily, you offer a view of the world as it could be, but then you retire to the rectory and are confronted with the world that is. We are eternally caught between the dream and the actuality. We offer the world God, but in the Confessional you will hear the workings of Satan thrown back at you. It will not be easy, young Thomas. It will not ever be easy."

Light.

A blinding, searing light, bringing even more pain into Father Otten's existence, this time through the eyeballs.

"Easy, Father," a troubled voice said to him. "You have been injured."

Otten tried to bring his right hand up to rub across his face, but it was locked into place. Without thinking why, the left hand came up and did the deed. Slowly, Otten opened his eyes.

He was lying on his back, in the middle of the woods, looking up at a group of scared men and women. Otten attempted to rise, but dizziness overtook him.

"Rest, Father," one of the women said, placing a hand on his chest and pushing him gently back to the ground. "You have broken your right arm, and there is a nasty gash on your head." The woman, middle-aged and motherly, reached for a cup of water and fed it to Otten slowly. "You will survive, but you need rest."

"What … what happened? My head … so unclear," Otten said, thankful the water was cold.

"There was an accident," the woman explained. "We found you and brought you back here."

Father Otten tried to look around, but his neck was too stiff to complete the move. "Where is here?"

"A transient community," the woman said, looking around.

"Transients?"

"We heard that's what the angels refer to us as," she said, wincing. "We are those that have rejected God's supposed gift."

"Why?"

"Various reasons. Some because the angels wanted to take our children. Some because they resented the forced change. Some because," she stopped herself and patted Otten kindly on the forehead. "You need rest, Father. We will care for you as long as we can."

"As long … as you can?"

The woman's face turned grim and sorrowful. "Transients live in fear, Father, of the day the angels come and force us to accept the New World. For if we don't, we face death."

Otten couldn't believe what he was hearing. "Death? My dear, I highly doubt the angels would kill someone for-"

"All respect, Father," the woman snapped, looking at him with fear-filled eyes, "but we have seen the remains of a transient settlement that has incurred the angels' wrath. When you are better, if you would like, we will show it to you."

Otten nodded once, then lay fully back. "I would very much like to see that site," he said, wondering if it was at all possible that angels would do such a thing.

The shower and shave refreshed Austin to the point of surprise. The twenty minutes under hot water had done him a hundred times more good than the quick nap he'd taken this morning after Berathon and Mollug had left for parts unknown.

Wrapping a towel around his waist (all his clothes gone, taken by Liv down to the laundry room), Austin stepped back into the spacious one bedroom hotel room to find Liv sitting on the bed. "Thanks," he said. "I needed that like you can't believe."

Liv gave him a pleasant smile. "Oh, I can believe it. You stunk."

Careful to make sure his towel didn't reveal the unrevealables, Austin took a seat in a large, overstuffed chair to Liv's right. He noted she had the remote control in her hand. "Anything on television?" he asked, pointing to the remote.

"Not really," she answered. "There's one news channel," she informed him, flipping on the TV. "It just shows notice after notice, informing us when certain events will be happening."

"Events? Like what?"

Liv shrugged, showing she either wasn't impressed or didn't care. "The professional sports leagues are supposed to start in another month – football, baseball, hockey, basketball, both men's and women's, and soccer, both men's and women's. They haven't finalized all of the locations because they're holding tryouts right now, then they'll hold a draft, then mini-camps, then get going. Everyone who wants to play gets to play, apparently, though there's so many of them that they're not taking any switches right now, and encouraging anyone who wants to go do something else to go do something else."

"Any news on your situation?" Austin asked, noticing a pitcher of water by the TV. "You mind?" he asked, pointing to the pitcher.

"Help yourself," she motioned. As Austin moved to pour himself some water into a small plastic cup, Liv added, "Nothing on my situation. Please," she said as Austin offered to pour her a cup.

"So you've just got to sit around and wait?" Austin asked, handing her the cup.

"We've got training every morning, and optional training every night," she explained, taking the cup.

"Those uniforms can't be comfortable," he remarked, hoping he wasn't staring too hard at the tight-fitting outfit.

"They're not too bad, really," Liv said. "At first it made me feel very self-conscious and restricted, but as the uniform stretches out to fit your body, it actually feels really nice. Plus, they give us a black wrap to wear as an outer costume for extra protection. Better than your costume anyway," she added, smiling.

Austin let out an easy laugh, falling back into his seat. "Surprisingly, you get used to it. Kelly – my girlfriend – told me I looked like a waiter at a fish shack, but other than the boots, it's pretty comfortable. The boots are brutal."

Liv smiled; Austin reminded her of a couple of her older brother's friends: nice, easy-going, and a bit off. "I checked with our Master Ninja-"

"Master Ninja?"

"- and he said there'd be no trouble with you coming dressed as a pirate. Apparently there's a TV journalist group coming along, too, so it's something of an open event." She motioned towards the TV. "TV news stations are supposed to be up and running by the end of next week."

"Any mention of when the angels are supposed to be back?" Austin asked, turning serious.

Liv shook her head. "Nothing. I wonder if we've been abandoned."

Austin didn't answer, but the frown that found its way to his face told Liv that he knew something he wasn't telling.

"Are you sure this is a good idea?" Samantha asked as she and Kelly walked up the front steps of Regent Castle. She eyed the throng of ninjas and men and women dressed in business suits around them warily.

"Easiest plans are the best."

"Even when you've been drugged, abducted, almost raped, then attacked on the highway?" Samantha asked skeptically. "Even when we know an angel was killed and we've seen a giant muck-and-clay monster stomping through a small town? Even with whatever plans Michael Scranton has going on? You still think walking in through the front door is the best policy?"

Kelly nodded. "I've found it's always better to be straightforward. If it doesn't work," Kelly smiled, "then we can try something sneaky."

Samantha shook her head, offering a weak smile, telling herself this was a much better place to be than back at Hollis Memorial with Michael Scranton walking the halls, trying to get her to kill someone.

The two young women reached the top of the steps and moved across a short patio towards the front doors, where two guards, dressed in shining, silver armor with no helmets, stood at either side of the large opening. "Excuse me, ladies," the guard on the right (who looked to Kelly like Burt Reynolds, circa *Smokey and the Bandit*) said, holding out his hand to halt them. "Dinner will not be served for another half-hour. Are you with the ninja contingent or broadcast journalist contingent?" he asked, looking skeptically at their jeans and sweaters.

"Neither," Kelly said, not bothering to lie and making Samantha feel a butterfly rise up in her stomach. This just felt all wrong to her, though she couldn't put her finger on an exact reason. *Must be general nerves and lack of sleep*, Samantha thought unconvincingly as Kelly continued with the guards. "I want to see the King."

Bandit Burt laughed. "I'm sorry, ma'am, but he's the King. He's busy."

"What's he doing?"

The other guard (who looked to Samantha like Johnny Depp, circa *Nightmare on Elm Street*) decided it was his time to laugh. "We don't have his schedule, ma'am, but I assure you, he's busy."

Kelly gave Samantha a look that said, "Watch this," as she folded her arms across her chest. Samantha wasn't buying it, but there was nothing to do but let Kelly play her hand. "Call him and tell him Kelly Reed is here to see him."

A look of annoyance flashed across Bandit Burt's face. "Ma'am, please move along. I cannot simply call the King and-"

Nightmare Depp, however, had already pulled his left arm to his face. Kelly and Samantha noted the guards had a cell phone implanted into the armor, and watched as the guard depressed the walkie-talkie function. "Captain O'Malley, please" he said quickly as he glanced nervously at Kelly. "Code Zero-Five."

"O'Malley here," a gruff voice replied. "You better not be jerking my chain, guard."

"I'm not, sir."

"We'll see," O'Malley replied. "I'll be right down. Take Ms. Reed to Side Entrance B5."

Bandit Burt and Nightmare Depp exchanged a nervous look; Samantha caught it and grew even more nervous, but a glance to Kelly told Samantha that Kelly didn't share her concern.

Nightmare Depp spoke again into the implanted cell phone. "Captain O'Malley, sir, there is a Zero-Zero-One attached to the Zero-Five."

O'Malley's response was instant and direct. "Entrance B5!"

"Yes, sir!" Nightmare Depp said crisply.

Nightmare Depp shook his head at Bandit Burt, looking every bit a scared kid. "I'll take them to B5, you stay here."

Bandit Burt shook his head. "We've both got to go."

"What's a Zero-Five?" Samantha asked, angry that Kelly seemed adamant about continuing.

The two guards ignored her. Nightmare Depp said, "We can't leave the front door unattended."

Bandit Burt turned around and walked through the entrance doors, and yelled to a group of interior guards to come replace them.

"Again," Samantha said to Nightmare Depp, "what's a code Zero-Five?"

Nightmare Depp looked to Kelly. "Are you really Kelly Reed? *The* Kelly Reed? Can I see some ID?"

"What the hell is going on?" Kelly demanded, not reaching for her identification because she didn't have any on her. She wondered just how many people in the New World had any identification on them.

Nightmare Depp looked back and forth between the two women. "A code Zero-Five," he said, his lip shaking, "is the highest possible priority."

Kelly looked to Samantha and smiled. "Told you Brad would see me."

Samantha smiled weakly in return, thinking that whatever Kelly had just gotten the two of them into wasn't going to be pleasant.

At that moment, at the bottom of the large stepped entrance to Regent Castle, Austin McNamara stood with Liv the ninja, waiting to get into the dinner. Something about this woman's confidence had rubbed off on Austin, and as he waited for his confrontation with Kelly's ex-boyfriend, he felt more calm than concern.

"Must be the clothes," he mumbled, thinking of how nice it was to be in clean clothes.

"What's that?" Liv asked.

"Nothing." Austin smiled. "Just feels good to be clean."

"You clean up nice," Liv said, putting a gentle hand on Austin's arm.

"Thanks." Austin took the compliment, but when Liv didn't say anything he began to feel a sense of awkwardness creep in. Talking was a good defense to awkwardness, he'd learned. "So, what did you do in the Old World?"

Liv shook her head. "We were told not to talk about it."

"Why?"

"The whole secretive ninja thing, I guess," Liv answered. She looked up the steps, wondering when they were going to be allowed inside. "So," she asked, more to pass the time than anything else (she didn't feel any of the awkwardness Austin felt), "you say your ship was sunk. Where's the rest of your crew?"

"Going to get another ship," he replied, feeling a sudden pang of emptiness at not having Hector, Carl, Mathers, and the rest of the crew around him.

"You got the angels to give you another ship?" Liv asked, disbelieving what she was hearing. "How do pirates rate a second ship while ninjas can't even get out of Boston?"

Laughing gently, Austin replied, "No, no, it's not like that. The angels haven't given us a new ship."

"Then how-?" Liv started to ask, then realized what Austin was getting at. "You're stealing one."

"Yep."

Liv felt a surge of excitement run through her. "Here? Are you stealing a ship tonight?"

"God no," Austin replied, getting serious. The last thing he wanted was Brad to think he was here to steal one of the Royal Navy's warships.

Liv pouted. "Too bad. That would've been fun. Where, then, if not here?"

"Maine," Austin replied, wishing (if only for a moment) that he was there, with them, to steal their new pirate ship.

"I don't see it," Carl sighed, looking at a large black castle. Carl and the rest of the crew of the *Puritan*, minus Hector and two others who'd gone into town on an intel run, stood on the backside of a small hill a half-mile outside of the village of Kent Harbor, Maine. Kent Harbor had been transformed into a seventeenth century village, spread out before the Black Castle, with a long winding dirt road leading into town and a short winding road leading from the village to the castle's entrance.

"It's on the other side," Aphrodite said, growing tired of Carl's constant whining. She'd almost gotten up from her table at breakfast to shove Carl's toast down his throat. "There's a cliff on the other side of the Black Castle," Aphrodite explained, "and a dock at the bottom. To get to the docks, we'll need to go through the castle."

"Sounds like fun," Captain Mathers grinned, handing her binoculars to Carl. "Check out how the terrain rolls upward. The village itself is on a rise. I want to send a small group to the water's edge, straight from here to the shore, to check out if we can get to the docks from the side."

Carl took the binoculars as Aphrodite informed them they couldn't reach the boat that way. He ignored her and brought the binocular to his face. Finding nothing at the shore (not even knowing, in fact, what he should be looking for), he moved his view to take in the castle.

Aphrodite kept talking. "There's a woman on the balcony. Her dress indicates she is the Lady of this castle. A dreadful woman by all appearances."

"Check her out, Carl," Mathers ordered. "Tell us what you see." Mathers studied Carl carefully as he moved the binoculars to try and find the castle's Lady. She knew Hector didn't trust him, didn't think Captain Samuel of the *Cottonmather* would just let him go, and she wanted to watch Carl in action. If he was here to do Samuel's bidding, Mathers wanted to figure out what that was. Hector wanted them to tall Carl to leave, but Mathers wasn't about to do that without proof. And if Carl was a spy, perhaps they could use him to learn something about Samuel's plans as they prepared to go hunting for the *Cottonmather*.

Carl couldn't find the woman, but he could feel Captain Mather's eyes on him. He ignored her, but knew she didn't trust him. Hector, too, he suspected, didn't trust him, either.

They had good reason. He had no real intention of delivering Hector and Austin to Captain Samuel, but the fact that he'd even made that deal was probably enough to get him … get him what? To walk the plank? Would these people really kill him for knowing what he'd agreed to do? And if that was the case, maybe he should keep an open mind about Samuel's-

"Sweet Jesus!" he gasped as his binoculars took in the Lady of the Black Castle.

"What is it?" Mathers demanded. "What do you see?"

"The Lady of the castle," he said, dropping the binoculars.

"What about her?"

The blood drained from Carl's face as he turned to his captain. "She's my ex-wife."

Wallace O'Malley, Captain of the Guard for the King of New England, stood just inside the B5 entrance to Regent Castle. They had labeled this entrance B5 because it was, moving in a clockwise rotation, the fifth (and final) basement entrance. O'Malley had been dreading this day since the morning after the First Night Feast. As he moved a few steps back down the corridor to stand inside a small security room, he felt that old familiar rush of excitement and fear.

It was happening. It was going down. Kelly Reed had come back to talk to the King.

"Sir," a member of his guard said, pointing to a television monitor. "This is the feed for entrance B5."

O'Malley grunted, taking in the sight of two guardsmen and two young women. He was surprised to see that the redhead was one of the women he'd arranged to sleep with the ranger Frederic Kornell after First Night Feast. Her name was Dixon. Samantha Dixon, he remembered. Total slut by the looks (and acts) of her. The secret video recording he'd ordered made of the sexual romp between Samantha, Frederic, and the bimbo blonde had made the rounds several times over amongst the guardsmen.

He had to wait for the other woman, the woman who claimed to be Kelly Reed, to turn around, as her back was to the camera. "Come on, show us your face," he said roughly, and on cue, Kelly turned. O'Malley slapped the desk, then raised his arm to access his armor-implanted cell-phone.

"Attention all guardsmen," he said into the phone, all-business. "Code Zero-Five confirmed. Blackout conditions. Repeat, blackout conditions." O'Malley let the line go silent for a moment, letting his guardsmen absorb his message. Then, to emphasize just how serious this moment was, he sent one final message to his guards. "Anyone breaks blackout, I'll drop you and everyone on your crew into a pit of dog shit, set it on fire, and watch all of you burn to ashes."

O'Malley ended his message, then turned to the guard beside him. "Get dungeon cell 42 prepped and open," he ordered.

The guard nodded and hurried out of the room. O'Malley placed his finger on the monitor, tapping Samantha's image, then Kelly's image. "These two bitches have seen daylight for the last time in a very, very long time."

Austin and Liv moved up the steps and into the main entrance of Regent Castle with the crowd of ninjas and broadcast journalists. The guards eyed him skeptically, but none made any move. As they passed a group of four guards huddled together, Austin and Liv noted that they all pressed their fingers to the ears, appearing to listen intently to a message they couldn't hear.

The ninja and the pirate glanced at each other, but said nothing.

The crowd was rustled down the hall to the left, and then turned right down a long corridor that ended by emptying into a large dining hall. Six massive tables were lined parallel with the length of the room; one end of each table greeted them and the other faced a stage where a final table sat perpendicular to the floor tables. Each of the tables held a hundred seats, but Austin wasn't interested in any of that. His eyes held one man in a very expensive Italian suit in his gaze.

Brad Regent.

"When do you want to-?" Liv started to ask, but Austin was already gone, already walking right down the middle of the large banquet hall towards the front stage. "Great," she said to herself, figuring of all Austin's options, this was the worst.

Austin didn't care, feeling a surge of adrenaline rush through him the moment he laid eyes on the King.

The King stood on the stage with two incredibly beautiful mystery-solving musicians, and six guards were on the floor in front of him. Brad didn't see the determined pirate coming towards him, but he did notice the movement of his guards before him. Seeing the guards tense, the King looked down the aisle to find the source of their concern.

At first, the King didn't understand what the worry was. It was only a less-than-menacing pirate coming towards him. But then the face of that pirate came into focus and the King forgot all about the two women at his side.

"Austin McNamara," he said, his face turning into a grimace as Austin reached the guards. "Leave him be," Brad ordered as regally as he could to the guards who'd drawn their swords. "This man is of no concern to me. Hello, Austin. What brings a common pirate to the castle of the King?"

Austin was in no mood for games. "Where's Kelly, Brad?"

Brad's face turned dark and fierce enough for the two women at his side to back a few steps away from him. "What are you talking about?"

"Don't bullshit me," Austin said, feeding on his anger. "Like you've gone ten minutes in the past two years without knowing where she was."

Brad folded his arms across his chest, looking down at Austin with as much contempt as he'd ever felt. "Go to hell."

"Not until you tell me where she is," Austin demanded. "I'm not playing, Brad. Where is she?"

The darkness that had enveloped Brad lifted slightly, allowing confusion to carve out a space on his face. "What are you talking about? I'm sure she's in Kent Harbor, Maine. That's where she was assigned, I do believe."

Kent Harbor? Shit. Shit shit shit! Of all the god-damned luck! "Are you sure?" Austin asked, feeling the slightest hint of panic creep into him. "Have you confirmed that?"

"No," he replied. "Jesus, Austin, what the hell is wrong with you?"

No time for lies. "Brad, a few days ago I called her on her cell phone and a man answered."

"Maybe she's finally seen the error of her ways and left you behind."

"The man who answered told me she was dead."

Brad felt his knees go weak, and was surprised to find himself still standing. "If this is some kind of game—"

"I wouldn't when it comes to Kelly."

The King of New England studied Austin's face, thinking hard, then slowly nodded. "Give me five minutes," Brad said, "to greet this group. After that, you and I will do whatever it takes to find her."

"If that's a game," Austin started, but Brad held up his hand to silence him.

"I wouldn't," Brad said. "Not about Kelly."

Austin nodded. If this was what it took to find out the truth, so be it.

Chapter Seventeen
These Things Tend to Sort Themselves Out

In Heaven, chaos reigned, and the angel Raphael was beginning to wonder if this all hadn't been a very terrible mistake. The Host was splitting apart. The Earth was falling into chaos. God was still missing. Lucifer, it was now rumored, had left Hell to search for God. An Olympian was free. An angel was murdered.

"Beautiful, isn't it?" the angel Azrael asked suddenly from his shoulder.

"Beautiful?" Raphael asked, looking down upon the Earth. "It's chaotic."

"Isn't chaos beautiful?" Azrael asked, smiling.

"I am in no mood for your cleverness today," Raphael said, his usually joyous face hidden behind a dark veil.

Azrael insisted. "We were born from chaos."

"We are the creation of God."

"And God was born from the chaos that marks the beginning of time," Azrael said passionately.

It was Azrael's passion that caused Raphael to choke down his retort. He studied his fellow angel carefully; rare was the time when Azrael was capable of anything but a playful cleverness. On this occasion, at the least, Azrael appeared to be completely serious. "What is your point, Azrael?"

"My point, brother?" he asked, his voice dripping with contempt. "I throw back to you the words you threw in the face of the humans on the first day of the New World, when they were panicking at the dramatic change."

"Which words?"

"Are you so quick to forget?"

"Please, Azrael."

Azrael studied Raphael carefully, then nodded. "Things tend to work themselves out, Raphael."

"More of your cleverness?"

"Look to the Earth, my friend," Azrael said, placing his hand on Raphael's back. "Order always springs from chaos; it is the way of the universe. In the beginning, chaos was ordered into two beings: Universe and God. And today, when all appears chaotic, order is already taking hold, growing out across the Earth silently, slowly, but growing nonetheless. Look to the Kingdom of New England and see order reassert itself. Austin searches for his girlfriend and they both find themselves in the same castle at the same time, separated by several floors and a few hundred meters. The ranger, Frederic Kornell, finds himself staring down at the image of his father, General Kornell, the man who murdered Frederic's mother. In Kent Harbor, Carl Yesek finds himself confronted by his ex-wife."

"Coincidence," Raphael protested.

Azrael shrugged. "Perhaps so, but perhaps it is all part of God's plan. Perhaps this is a 21st century version of the great flood, a way of cleansing the Earth, but this time not through destruction, but through *construction*. What has God done, after all? He has left us to walk the Earth as a 'normal' human. He has changed his perspective. And isn't that, in its simplest form, what the Reorganization has done? Simply changed the perspective of each and every human? And now we see all of the separate strands slowly working themselves back together – change perspective, then confront. God has confronted something in himself during his walkabout. Now, though not all at once, it is time for the humans to confront something in themselves."

"I don't ..." Raphael started, then let his voice trail away.

"Things tend to work themselves out, Raphael," Azrael said as he slowly began to back away. "If we have faith, mustn't we continue to believe this is all part of God's Plan?"

Raphael said nothing, not knowing whether there was a correct answer to that question.

"Welcome, ninjas and broadcast journalists, to Regent Castle!"

The seated crowd cheered heartily as Brad Regent, King of New England, opened the evening's festivities. He stood in a slick Italian suit on a stage at the front of a large ballroom that held six long tables, each holding one hundred seats. The ninjas and broadcast journalists had intermingled, welcoming some outside company. Both groups had been stuck in Boston since the New World began and were thrilled for the night of distractions.

Most of this was lost on Austin McNamara, who stood impatiently off to the side of the stage. He'd come to Boston to seek out Brad in order to enlist the King's help in finding his girlfriend, who he had been told was dead. Austin smirked at that thought despite the gravity of the situation; phrasing it like that made it seem all so simple. What made it complicated was that he really didn't believe Kelly was dead and that Brad was not only her ex-boyfriend, but the ex-boyfriend that immediately proceeded Austin. Even worse, in the Old World (and now presumably the New, as well), Brad was Boston's Most Eligible Bachelor and Austin had more than his share of psychological angst built up over why Kelly had chosen to be with him and not Brad.

He looked up to Brad, sitting there between two insanely beautiful mystery-solving musicians, coming to grips with the realization that he was now going to rely on all those things about Brad he hated in order to find Kelly. Looking out across the sea of people, Austin made eye contact with Liv, the ninja that had helped get him inside.

"Ready?"

Austin looked up to see Brad coming down off the stage. "Let's do this."

Wallace O'Malley truly felt like a cop for the first time in the New World as he walked down a narrow corridor in the dungeon/basement level of Regent Castle. Behind him, his guards prepared Dungeon Cell 42 for its soon-to-be occupants. Five steps before him was the door to the outside and on the other side of that door were two guards and two women. The women were Samantha Dixon and Kelly Reed.

They were destined for DC 42.

O'Malley felt nothing for Dixon; the only reason she would spend any time in Regent Castle's dungeons was her choice to come to the castle alongside Kelly Reed.

Reed was the target.

She'd always been the target. From the moment he met Brad Regent, the newly crowned King of New England had mentioned how important Kelly Reed was to him. Not ten minutes into that first meeting, Regent had let his plan be known to O'Malley. The King intended to have a buddy kidnap Kelly from the First Night Feast festivities and drag her into the woods where the King would dramatically rescue her from her "abductors." O'Malley had thought it foolish, and let the King know, but Regent was adamant that his plan be carried out. He wanted to win Kelly back from her current boyfriend, but his desire was more to prove himself the better man than one Austin McNamara than it was to reclaim Kelly.

O'Malley thought the King was asking for trouble, which is exactly what they received when the ranger, Frederic Kornell, inserted himself into the activities. Reed, in fact, believed Kornell to be her savior and not the King. That led to the King assigning Kornell to escort Kelly, Samantha, and four other New World royals to Kent Harbor, and to O'Malley sending Kelly's original abductor to assassinate Kornell on the road. If Reed happened to die during the fighting, so much the better from O'Malley's point-of-view. Kings shouldn't concern themselves so deeply with one person when they had a kingdom at their disposal. O'Malley had learned that lesson the hard way in the Old World, covering for politician after politician who couldn't stop from getting involved with people they shouldn't.

The abductor-turned-assassin, Jim Catlin, had failed. Last he heard from his angel contact, Catlin had been turned into some kind of giant creature and programmed to kill Kelly, but had failed once again. Catlin, he had been told, was likely dead.

Likely? Until O'Malley knew that for certain he considered Catlin a loose end.

But now ... now Kelly Reed had come walking back into O'Malley's arms and the Captain of the King's Guard had no intention of letting her out of his sight a second time.

Forcing his thin grin off of his grim face, O'Malley unlocked the door and pushed it open, letting a slender sliver of sunlight fall across his face as he came face-to-face with the woman that had plagued him since the New World began. "Ms. Reed?" he asked Kelly, though he knew the answer.

"Yeah," she said with a hint of annoyance, pushing the door fully open. "What's going on? Why didn't they let us in through the front entrance?"

"My apologies, ladies," O'Malley said, giving her a short bow of his head. His rough voice, however, offered no apology. "My name is Wallace O'Malley, Captain of the King's Guardsmen. There is a state dinner this evening and the King is engaged with his kingly duties. He is very interested in meeting with you, of course, and we have been instructed to make you comfortable as you wait. If you could follow me," he finished, turning around and walking down the hallway before they had a chance to respond to anything they said.

Kelly started to follow, but Samantha reached out to grab her arm. "We should go," she whispered harshly.

Kelly pulled her arm away. "And do what? Hang around the city? Might as well wait inside as outside." She started walking into the corridor.

"This doesn't feel right," Samantha insisted, but followed.

"Trust me, Samantha," Kelly insisted as the two guards behind them followed them into the corridor, "Brad and I have had some issues between us, but he wouldn't let anything bad happen to me."

Ominously (to Samantha, at least), the door closed behind them.

A few steps ahead of them, Wallace O'Malley heard the door shut and the locks click into place. Deadly serious, he turned to face the two women. "I can assure you," he said menacingly, "that there is no chance the King would knowingly put you in harm's way. Of course, the King has no idea you're here."

"What do you mean?" Kelly asked, taking a step towards O'Malley.

O'Malley stopped Reed in her tracks as he pulled a gun from his belt and pointed it at her. Samantha screamed, but when she turned to run back the way they'd come, she was similarly stilled as the two guards behind them had guns drawn as well. "If you ladies will be so kind as to follow me, I will show you to your quarters," O'Malley grunted, satisfaction evident across his rough face as his thick, black handlebar mustache twisted weirdly around a deep grin.

"I feel very uncomfortable about this," Carl Yesek said weakly. He was trapped in a situation he felt had been forced on him by Fate, trapped between the proverbial rock and a hard place. I'm stuck, he thought to himself. Now how the heck do I get out of it?

He stood just outside the village of Kent Harbor, Maine alongside his fellow crewmates of the sunken ship *Puritan*. They had come here looking for a ship to steal because the goddess Aphrodite had told them there was one here to be taken. The ship, they believed, was on the backside of the imposing castle that resided at the back of the village, in between the town and a high cliff. At the bottom of that cliff was the Atlantic Ocean and, supposedly, a dock. To get to the dock, they would need to go through the Black Castle.

A full-on raid of a castle would be difficult enough, but the Lady of the Black Castle made it even more difficult for Carl.

The Lady of the Black Castle was Sheila Watson, Carl's ex-wife.

"What do you mean you're uncomfortable with this?" Hector Ladrone asked pointedly. Around them, milling about in a grove of trees, the crew of the *Puritan* waited for its order from its captain, Mary Mathers. Mathers stood with Hector, Carl, and Aphrodite, apart from the others, to create strategy.

"That's my ex-wife over there." Carl was exasperated. Hector was just looking for a reason to have his mistrust in Carl confirmed. Carl couldn't really blame him since he had agreed to sell out Hector and Carl to Captain Samuel of the *Cottonmather*, but he'd done it only to save his own life. He didn't really believe he ever would turn them over to Samuel, but then … if Hector had no loyalty to him, why should he have any loyalty to Hector? "You can't expect me to be happy about raiding my ex-wife's house?" Carl challenged.

"Stop it," Captain Mathers ordered, wanting this discord ended before it spread throughout the crew. "Carl, I want you to be in charge of finding and neutralizing Lady Watson."

"You've got to be kidding," Carl said, and Hector agreed with the older man.

Mathers let it be known she wasn't playing games. "It's either you or Hector," she said flatly. "If you'd rather Hector be in charge of securing your ex-wife-"

"I'll do it," Carl said quickly, feeling physically ill at the thought of confronting Sheila. *But better me than anyone else. At least I know I won't hurt her.* "We should just walk in and ask her to borrow it," Carl suggested, trying to find the most peaceful way through this scenario.

Everyone around him looked at him as if he'd suggested they fly to the moon. "Carl," Captain Mathers explained slowly, as if to a child and not a forty-year old man, "we're pirates. We steal. It's what we do. Who we are."

"Perhaps love will be rekindled," Aphrodite offered as a means of changing the subject, but neither of the three pirates could tell if she was being sincere or insincere.

Mathers ignored the Olympian. "That's settled, then," she said definitively. "Hector," she said, turning to her second-in-command, "you will lead the raid. Carl, you will secure the Lady Watson."

"And what will you do?" Aphrodite asked.

"I'm taking the ship," Mathers replied, meeting the goddess' gaze. "And you're coming with me."

As Captain Mathers and Hector began to plot out the strategy of their raid, an apparition left them behind and headed for town. Lazarus, the ex-captain of the *Cottonmather*, wondered if there was any way he could help the crew of the *Puritan* procure the ship that waited for them beyond and below the Black Castle.

It wasn't that he cared about the *Puritan* crew, but simply that their goals and his goals were, for the moment, mutual goals – the destruction of the *Cottonmather*.

Brad Regent offered Austin a glass of bourbon, which the pirate waved away. Brad shrugged, pouring Austin's glass into his own. The King was purposely taking his time; he had a delicate line to walk here between what was actually known and what he intended to tell Austin. The best lies, he always believed, were those that were closest to the truth.

"During the First Night Feast," he said slowly as he walked across the massive office to look out the window at the Aquarium, "Kelly was drugged and abducted."

Austin's stomach dropped. "What?"

"She had been requested, along with all of the other royalty in New England, to report to Providence," Brad informed, not yet getting to his lie. "As King of New England, I had gone to Providence to welcome the new royalty and facilitate their new assignments. Sometime during the Feast – in which I had no contact with Kelly, though I knew she was there, of course-"

"Of course."

Brad half-turned towards Austin. "Her name was on the list Raphael, the Angel in Charge of Royalty, had given to me."

"Like I said," Austin replied, walking his own thin line between needing Brad's help and hating his guts, "of course."

Brad let it go, turning back to the window, but catching Austin's reflection in the glass and holding it. "I had received word that a young woman, apparently drunk, had been taken into the woods. I went after her. I probably shouldn't have – that's why I have a set of guardsmen, after all – but it was the First Night, and I was feeling both alive and restless."

Austin nodded, thinking of his own First Night adventure. "Lot of nervous energy floating around that night."

The King nodded to the reflection. "Out behind the Castle Providence is a large wooded garden. Deep into that garden, I found the abducted girl, surrounded by five princes."

Austin's blood was at a near boil; that Kelly had undergone such an ordeal and he wasn't around …

"While they were pushing her back and forth, I noticed it was Kelly. I couldn't believe it was her," Brad said slowly, hoping that Austin's clearly rising anger would mask any problems with the lie he was now telling. He had, of course, known it was Kelly, since the King had been behind the abduction. He'd had her abducted in order to save her, in order to attempt to win her back, in order to show Austin that he was the better man. Looking back on it, Brad realized how stupid he'd been, but looking at Austin's reflection in the glass he also realized that Kelly deserved a better man than Austin McNamara.

"Was she …?" Austin couldn't give voice to the question.

"She was unharmed," Brad said, turning around and placing his nearly full glass of bourbon down on his large mahogany desk. "Drunk to the point of near unconsciousness," Brad said, frowning at several memories of Kelly's over-indulgence with alcohol, "but still fully clothed."

"Thank God," Austin said, moving to pour himself a shot of whiskey. He downed the shot, slamming the short glass on the counter.

"I jumped into the fray at once," Brad answered. Not wanting to make himself seem too heroic to Austin, he downplayed his faked accomplishment. "The princes were drunk, as well, and it was easy to disable them. The main perpetrator, by all appearances, ran off and a ranger by the name of Frederic Kornell stopped him." Brad waited until Austin turned to look at him before continuing; he wanted none of what he said next to escape Austin's understanding. "The ranger had been assigned to bring her to Providence by the angel Raphael."

Austin nodded; he'd been present when Raphael had given Kornell that charge.

"I do not know why he was there, in the gardens," Brad said slowly, "but we are lucky he was standing off to the side."

"Standing off to the side?" Austin asked.

Brad nodded, frowning. "I didn't understand the full incompetence of the ranger until just a day or two ago, when I reviewed the full security tapes from Castle Providence. The ranger was watching the ... incident," he said, allowing his anger to grow. That much had been true, at least. "Kornell was frozen in place, overwhelmed by panic or fear," Brad said, angrily knocking his drink off his desk. "And I, like a fool, put him in charge of Kelly's protection."

"You did what?" Austin snapped, moving to the desk. "Why would you do a stupid thing like that?"

"You forget," Brad seethed, "that I didn't know of Kornell's cowardice until much later. What I saw was the ranger running his sword through the abductor. I didn't know he'd been hiding off to the side, scared stiff. If I had ..." Brad let his voice trail away as his hands gripped the back of his chair for all it was worth.

Austin couldn't believe what he was hearing. His mind raced, trying to place Kelly's timeline with his. While he was laughing it up, painting the hull of the *Cottonmather* with obscenities, Kelly was going through this ordeal. It made him angry. It made him feel powerless. *At least Brad had been around.* Austin felt his spine shrivel at that thought. *At least Brad had been around.*

"Brad, I don't know what to say," Austin said, weakly grateful.

"How about thank you?" Brad asked pointedly, asserting his control of this situation.

Austin looked at him weakly. "Thank you," he said. "If you hadn't been there ..."

Years of experience allowed Brad to smile inwardly while his outward face stayed hard and cold. "Well, perhaps Kornell would've eventually found his courage."

Kornell, Austin fumed. "Doubtful," he said, shaking his head.

"Go ahead. Say it."

"I told you so."

"Feel better?"

"Not really, no."

Kelly and Samantha sat in a padded cell, behind a closed door, prisoners of Wallace O'Malley. The room was small and bright, the padding a clean white that reflected the overhead light back into the center of the room.

"Is this a cell for a nutjob?" Samantha asked. "This doesn't look like any dungeon cell I've heard of."

"And that's a bad thing?" Kelly asked in return. "No dirty, straw covered floors, no rats … heck, we've even got two padded benches to sleep on."

Samantha shot daggers into Kelly's back. "You planning on staying?"

Kelly spun, feeling a seed of anger crack inside of her at Samantha's continued hostility. "Don't be stupid." She watched as Samantha choked down a retort, wondering whether the redhead was showing self-control or had nothing to say. "I have no intention of staying here," she said, keeping her voice hard, "but I'm not nearly strong enough to rip this door down. So unless you dreamt of super strength, why don't you do me a favor by lying down, shutting up, and getting some sleep."

"Is that an order?"

"Yeah," Kelly said, dropping herself onto one of the padded benches, "it is."

Wallace O'Malley kept his smile buried deep behind his bushy, black handlebar mustache as he entered King Regent's office. The capture of Kelly Reed, and the soon-to-be ex-problem she represented, had O'Malley feeling better than he had since the King hatched his illogical and foolish abduction scheme. He figured the King wanted a report on the scuffle that had broken out downstairs – a television reporter had angered a group of ninjas by referring to them as "agents of Satan" and the ninjas had responded by starting a brawl – and was surprised to find the King in the company of a pirate.

Regent, locked in deep conversation with the pirate, didn't turn to face the Captain of his Guard until O'Malley had coughed to announce presence. "Captain," Brad said quickly, "thank you for joining us."

"How can I be of service?" O'Malley asked, laying it on thick. "Are we expecting to be raided by pirates?" he asked, tilting his head to Austin.

"What?" Brad asked, momentarily confused. "Oh. Austin. Right."

"Austin?"

"Austin McNamara," the King explained, hurriedly introducing the two men. "Austin, this is Wallace O'Malley, the Captain of the Royal Guard."

Austin and Wallace shook hands as O'Malley felt the slightest noose begin to tighten around his neck. While he didn't recognize the face, he recognized Austin's name from all of the King's rantings about Kelly Reed. And the small fact that it was O'Malley who'd told Austin, via phone, that Kelly was dead. While he didn't fear Austin, the pirate's presence could only be predicated on Kelly, which meant she needed to be disposed of with even greater haste and caution. "I repeat myself," O'Malley grunted, now all business. "How can I be of service?"

Brad ran a hand down the front of his silk tie, getting right to it. "I want you to find Kelly Reed."

O'Malley didn't blink. "Is she not with the ranger, Kornell?"

"We think she might be in trouble," Brad snapped, angry at having to explain himself to a subordinate. "Find her," Brad ordered. "In fact," he said, an idea coming to him, "post her picture throughout every royal hall in New England. I will personally reward whomever finds her with one million dollars from the royal treasury."

O'Malley ground his heel into the carpet, a trait held over from his days on the beat when he felt trapped. "Sir, I am certain-"

Brad exploded. "Do it, Captain! Find her! Whatever the cost!"

Stiffening, O'Malley nodded. "Of course," he said resolutely, then turned and exited the room, heading straight for Dungeon Cell 42. All of the Kelly Reed nonsense would end right now.

It had taken Samantha five minutes to figure out Kelly's plan; if they couldn't break out of this cell, they'd need someone to do it for them. Or at least open the door. Pretend to sleep, lay in wait, and then when the door opened surprise whomever it was that entered. Samantha wasn't sure it was a great plan (or even a good one) but she couldn't think of a better one, so she lay down on her stomach and pretended to sleep.

Ten minutes in and she was beginning to feel genuinely tired. "Be just our luck," she thought, listening to Kelly's relaxed, even breathing and wondering if she had succumbed to sleep, as well.

Behind her, the unmistakable sound of a key being inserted into the cell door's lock snapped her awake. Her mind raced. What now? What do we do now? As much as she didn't want to, Samantha realized in that instant that her best strategy was to follow Kelly's lead. Part of her thought this was only fair; Kelly got them into this, so she could get them out of it. The other part of Samantha's mind, the part that had dominated her sullen worldview in the Old World, hated that she'd owe Kelly one if this managed to work.

"Get up!" a rough voice commanded as the door slammed open.

"Whu-?" Kelly asked, pretending to awaken from a deep slumber.

Samantha opened one eye to see Wallace O'Malley grabbing Kelly's hair roughly. "Get up," he demanded, coming at her like an animal.

"Huh?" Kelly said, trying to roll over. O'Malley slapped her in the face, knocking her back to the bench.

Samantha gasped in shock. Kelly's hands went to her face for protection. "Stop!" Kelly yelled, but O'Malley ignored her pleas, punching her in the stomach.

"You're not going to screw the New World up for me, understand?" he asked. Samantha felt her blood run cold at O'Malley's tone. Far from a raging lunatic, he appeared angry but under control. With the force of O'Malley's punch, Kelly's torso was knocked up off the bench. O'Malley grabbed her hair and tugged. "Get up," he said simply.

Samantha knew she had to do something. She glanced to the door, hoping one of O'Malley's guards would object to their captain's treatment.

There was no one at the door.

Samantha pushed herself up. Had O'Malley really come alone? She looked at O'Malley's back, then again to the door. There was no one there.

Make a decision! her mind screamed. *Stay and fight or get up and run, but do it now!*

Her eyes darted to Kelly's anguished face as O'Malley wrenched her off the padded bench with one hand. "Shit," Samantha groaned. O'Malley was encased in the shining silvery armor of a knight. All that was exposed was his hands and head. On his right side (the side with the free hand) a sword was strapped to his waist. Kicking her feet off the bench, Samantha kept her eyes on the back of O'Malley's head as she crept towards him. *Three steps*, she reasoned. *Three steps, grab the sword, then swing as hard as you can.*

Two steps away. One step away. Her hand reached out.

"Heh?" O'Malley asked, seeing Kelly's eyes open wide at something behind him. He turned his head and spotted Samantha. Letting go of Kelly, O'Malley shot his left hand behind him, connecting hard with Samantha's face and knocking the redhead to the floor. For one decisive second, O'Malley let his anger get the better of him.

He assumed Kelly wasn't a threat, and squared his body to the sprawled Samantha. Behind him, lying on her back, Kelly saw the sword that had been Samantha's target. She reached for it …

And stopped. The moment was one where perception and reality parted; lasting only a second, Kelly would have sworn it lasted longer. The cause of her stilled motion was what was strapped to the left side of O'Malley's armor.

A gun. The same gun he'd pointed in her face not an hour ago.

Kelly hopped to her feet and made her move. O'Malley, concentrating on Samantha, never saw it coming. Kelly didn't hesitate, coming up hard and fast, grabbing the gun and then stepping back.

"Eh?" O'Malley turned and found himself face-to-face with his own gun.

"Let us go or I'll shoot," Kelly said, trying to keep her hand from shaking.

O'Malley clenched and unclenched his hands; he was more concerned with Kelly's shaking hand than her intent. He didn't believe she'd shoot, but he didn't want to do anything to make her nervous enough to get that index finger to twitch.

"Try to play me like a little girl and I'll shoot."

O'Malley held up his hands as his mind raced; there was no chance that Kelly was getting out of this room without him. "Wouldn't dream of it," he said, putting a blank face forward.

"Sam, you okay?" Kelly asked, keeping her eyes locked on O'Malley.

Samantha pushed herself to her knees, then up to her feet. "Think so."

O'Malley's eyes stayed locked onto Kelly's, but his concentration was at the corner of his vision, where the young woman's hand was now stilled. Classic trap, O'Malley thought. The calmer Kelly became, the more O'Malley was certain she wouldn't shoot.

"Now, what you're going to do-"

O'Malley said nothing. His left hand shot outward to grab Kelly's arm. He connected, his fingers barely wrapping themselves around her wrist when Kelly's index finger twitched.

The gun went off like a thunderclap and O'Malley's head jerked back, blood exploding from the left side of his face. Behind him, Samantha screamed as the bullet shot past her, imbedding itself in the padded wall.

O'Malley fell in slow-motion; Kelly watched as the Captain's ass, then back, then head slammed onto the floor of the cell. A sick, plaintive grunt was forced from O'Malley's lungs as his head slumped to the left. Blood instantly pooled outward from the wound.

Kelly and Samantha stared at the body, then at each other.

"Is he …?" Samantha tried to ask.

Kelly didn't know and didn't bother to guess. Feeling a state of shock coming on, she tossed the gun to the corner and moved towards the door on shaking legs.

"Kelly." Samantha grabbed Kelly's arm as she walked past. "I have to know … did you pull the trigger on purpose?"

Something turned over inside Kelly and her legs gave out. With a thud, she dropped to her knees, then looked up blankly at Samantha. "I … I'm not sure."

Samantha looked to the unmoving O'Malley, shuddering, wondering if this scene would've played any differently in the Old World. The New World Princess shook her head, realizing it didn't matter. "Come on," she said, pulling Kelly to her feet. "We've got to find the King."

"Things tend to work themselves out."

The words of Azrael rang in the ears of Raphael; the angel watched as the adventure of two of his charges – Kelly Reed and Samantha Dixon – played out in Boston, New England. Exiting their dungeon cell, the two moved swiftly down the hallway, looking for an exit. Fortune was, for the moment, with them. Wallace O'Malley had cleared the dungeon of guards under the pretext of needing extra security in the ballroom, so Kelly and Samantha had free reign to wind their way through the uncomplicated corridors.

Several floors above and on the opposite side of the castle, Brad Regent and Austin McNamara were locked in conversation about how to best locate Kelly.

"Azrael be damned," Raphael mumbled. The world, he believed, couldn't always be counted upon to work itself out.

Kelly and Samantha moved up a set of stairs, not knowing what lay on the other side of a steel grey, metallic door. "Gotta be better than what's on this side," Samantha mumbled, her hand reaching for the door.

"Let's just hope," Kelly prayed as Samantha turned the handle, "it's not-"

"Locked." Samantha's hand didn't budge the handle. "Damnit! What now?"

To the surprise of the women, the door swung open, revealing Raphael. "Come with me," the angel said, "if you want to see the King." Raphael's eyes locked onto Kelly's. "And Austin."

Kelly blinked, unsure she had heard Raphael correctly. "Did you say 'Austin'?"

Raphael nodded.

Joy rose through Kelly as she stepped out of the dungeon corridor and into a side corridor of the castle. "Take me to him," she said, nearly overcome with emotion. "Please, take me to him."

Berathon sat in a seat high atop the high left field wall inside Fenway Park, deep in thought. A baseball stadium was not where he was accustomed to doing his best thinking, but it was close and quiet. Quiet so long as Mollug was somewhere on the other side of the stadium, at least.

The angel found the scene beautiful ... oddly beautiful.

When the Romans were building the Coliseum in the first century AD, the angels sat in Heaven and watched, marveling at the accomplishment, just as they had when the Egyptians built the pyramids. The angels were architects and engineers writ large, after all, the designers and builders of much of the Earth. God could have done it all, they all knew, but He thrilled to seeing what others could create and add to His great creation. Those were God's happiest days, the days of the early construction. In truth, Berathon knew, those were the days before he created Humanity. He'd created the Olympians first, thinking that because He was God, He should people the world with gods. They had been a miserable failure, arguing and fighting, more interested in their own self-pleasures than any kind of self-advancement.

The angels had come next, created in opposition to the Olympians, created to help God build the world. The Olympians were relegated to Purgatory while the Earth was constructed. Humanity grew outward from Adam and Eve to populate the world and as part of His apple deal with Eve and partly of natural consequence of free will, different cultures emerged. Different belief systems with them. Different gods.

Some, such as the Olympians, were created by God. Others emerged on their own. Humanity, to everyone's surprise, also had the ability to create life, to even create gods.

"In my image," God had said in an awed voice the day Heaven learned of humanity's power.

The Olympians, in due time, were freed from Purgatory, though they were ultimately no better than they had been before. Especially Zeus, who wielded his awesome power with a near total lack of responsibility. Though it was Zeus' fathering of Heracles – or rather, the greatness of Heracles himself – that gave God the idea that he should father a child with a human mother, as well.

A warm breeze moved off the ocean and over the city of Boston, drifting across Berathon and basking him in its warmth. The sun was high in the sky, approaching its zenith, and the angel's thoughts again turned to Olympus. Apollo and his chariot, humanity had decided, drove the sun across the sky each day.

Berathon allowed himself a chuckle, remembering how dismayed Apollo had been the day he learned that legend, the very idea of a daily chore (and one that consumed half the day at that) enough to send him into a deep depression.

The angel looked to the waterfront, where the angels had built the King of New England a large grey castle beside the Aquarium. He thought of Austin's mission to confront the King about his girlfriend, about how he was willing to go to the man he disliked most in the world in order to achieve a higher purpose.

Berathon rose from his seat, taking one last look at the lush green grass before him. Color. He would miss it well, for where he was going there was nothing but white, black, and grey.

Berathon had decided which mystery to solve first.

The angel was going to Purgatory to look for Olympians.

Chapter Eighteen
The Turning Home

Juramel looked down from Heaven at the activities in Boston with grave concern. "Do you see what Raphael is doing?" he asked Ocilael.

"I see him," Ocilael replied, non-plussed.

"He is interfering with the world of humans!" Juramel protested. "We are forbidden from interfering without the consent of God. Raphael commits blasphemy!"

Ocilael turned to square himself with Juramel. "You would have me arrest him?"

"I would."

"No," Ocilael replied. "There are other, more important mysteries to solve."

Juramel narrowed his eyes at his fellow angel. "If you will not act, I will."

"Be careful, Juramel," Ocilael said calmly. "If the Host tears itself apart, then-"

"The Host has already torn itself apart," Juramel declared. "The murder of Enimon, the missing harp, the alleged forgery of God's Word, the escape of Aphrodite ... confusion runs rampant in our ranks. The trust we all so recently shared in one another has been shattered."

"And your solution," Ocilael replied, anger rising in him, "is to arrest those who commit the slightest transgressions?"

"Blasphemy is not a minor crime."

"We were given orders to reconstruct the world," Ocilael reminded Juramel. "Interference in human affairs is no longer blasphemy."

A snarl, so foreign to the visage of angels that Ocilael had to force himself to stand his ground, came instantly to Juramel's face. "Then there is no crime in what I am about to do," the angel threatened. Juramel spread his wings and dove through the clouds of Heaven, headed for Earth.

"Austin?"

The heart of Kelly Reed had led the body through the corridors of Regent Castle to the upper office of the King, Brad Regent. With each step the need to be reunited with Austin grew deeper; that he was here was unbelievable. That he'd been searching for her … that he'd been worried enough to turn to Brad for help …

God help Raphael if the angel tried to keep them apart now.

"Kelly?" Austin McNamara turned away from the window to a sight he didn't think he'd see today. With the opening of the door and the image of his girlfriend walking towards him, Austin found his legs rooted to the floor. "Kelly?" he repeated, the pounding of his heart in his head making him wonder if the words had even come out of his mouth.

Austin relieved seemingly every moment of the New World since they'd parted in the ten steps it took her to get from the door to his arms. "Babe …" he said, choking up, as he wrapped his arms around Kelly.

"I can't believe you're here," she said, holding him tight.

Not five feet away, unnoticed by the woman he still loved, Brad Regent felt his own heart grow dark. *What is it*, he wondered, *that makes us want so desperately that which we can't have?*

Across the room, Raphael's thoughts mirrored the King's, as he watched him intently, wondering how Regent would react to the reunion of the woman he professed to love and the man he professed to hate. Next to Raphael, Samantha Dixon, dressed in a similar black sweater and blue jeans to what Kelly wore, was surprised that Kelly was dating a guy who looked like a cute dork. *Probably loves Weezer*, she thought, rolling her eyes.

"I can't believe you're here," Austin said, slowly regaining the ability to think and talk at the same time.

Kelly took a half-step back, allowing them to both see and hold one another. She smiled the crooked smile that caused Austin's heart to melt every time he saw it, and looked her boyfriend up and down. "I can't believe you still look an extra from *Treasure Island*. Seriously, you haven't thought once about changing your clothes?"

Austin grinned, tried and failed to think of a catchy comeback, then gave Kelly the same up-down inspection she'd given him.

Kelly noted the dumb grin on his face. "What?"

Austin shook his head. "I just can't believe you're here."

Brad could take no more, but found himself unable to muster any hatred towards the two lovers. *They are in love*, he realized, and after two years of wondering how Kelly could love Austin, Brad no longer needed the answer to that question. It was clear that she did love him; his elaborate, late night fantasy that she was simply using Austin to get back at him seemed to vanish all in that one hug. "I think we've established that, in fact, neither of you can believe the other one is here," he said almost smoothly (almost – his voice cracking slightly, giving his inner emotions away) as he moved to them. "I am feeling similar sentiments."

The reunited couple turned into each other as they opened up their embrace to look at Brad. "Hello, Brad."

"Kelly," the King nodded, smiling weakly. He might not have felt hatred in his heart at the sight of the two of them together, but realization was not the same as joy, either. "You had us worried."

"Why?" she asked, wondering if they knew of her capture at the hands of Wallace O'Malley. "What's wrong?"

"I was told you were dead," Austin said softly, turning slightly to kiss her forehead. "I called your cell and a man answered. I asked for you and he told me you were dead."

Pulling back, Kelly asked, "Who was it?"

Austin shook his head.

"Do you think it was the man who abducted me?"

"Impossible to say," Brad interjected. "For all we know it could well be a prank. Where did you lose your cell phone?"

"It must've been during the First Night Feast."

"Then there are hundreds, if not thousands, of suspects," Brad answered solemnly. Brad had no idea that it was, in fact, Wallace O'Malley that had told Austin Kelly was dead, but he didn't see any purpose in pursuing the question. "What's important, and I'm sure Austin will agree with me, is that you are very much alive."

Austin nodded in agreement; to him, now that he was back with her, it didn't matter who said Kelly was dead because they were wrong.

Kelly was unwilling to give up the question that easily. Sensing that she was about to press the issue, Brad quickly changed the subject. "The real question is where is Frederic Kornell, the ranger I assigned to protect you on your journey to Kent Harbor?"

"In a hospital," Kelly replied, not liking the insinuation in Brad's question. "He-"

Kelly was interrupted by a message that blared suddenly from the castle's speaker system. "Attention all guards and guests, this is Captain Wallace O'Malley. I have been shot."

"Oh hell," Samantha mumbled, looking to Kelly as the two women turned pale.

O'Malley continued. "My assailants are loose in the castle. They are both female, dressed in similar outfits: black sweaters and designer jeans. Guardsmen, you know of whom I speak. All visitors inside the castle are hereby ordered to remain where you are. I am authorizing all guards to arrest anyone attempting to leave Regent Castle."

All eyes in the room looked between Kelly and Samantha.

"You didn't ..." Austin said, looking at Kelly with concern.

Kelly didn't bother looking to Austin. She knew there was only one person in the room she had to convince. "Brad, listen to me," she said quickly, not liking the stern look on his face. "We came to find you."

"You came to find him?" Austin asked, feeling the old stab of jealousy rear up.

Ignoring Austin, Kelly continued pressing her case to Brad. "We came to find you, Brad, because Frederic told us what happened."

"He did?" Brad and Austin asked at the same time.

"He did," Kelly answered Brad. "He told us that it was you who rescued me, that he froze like a coward and that I would've ... well, that things wouldn't have turned out so well for me if you hadn't rescued me."

Austin hated feeling jealous but was powerless to stop it. And the more jealous he felt, the more petty and paranoid the jealousy became. "So you came to thank him?"

Kelly spun on Austin. "Jesus, Austin, shut up for ten seconds, will you? We're about to have every guard in this place looking for us."

"Big deal," Austin said defensively. "Who cares what the Captain of the Guard says when we've got the King with us."

As if O'Malley was listening to the conversation, the Captain's voice cracked again over the speakers. "One last thing, and I regret to inform the castle of this news in this manner, but … I have airtight evidence that suggests King Regent himself was behind my assault. Arrest the King at all costs."

Kelly glanced to Austin. "You just had to say something."

The stench came to them on an otherwise gentle breeze, seemingly trying to burn them from the inside out. Frederic Kornell and Michael Scranton rode two horses (Kornell hadn't asked where Scranton got his), keeping what they hoped was a safe distance from the marching column of orcs. In the center of the orcs, the astronauts from Hollis Memorial Hospital walked haphazardly as a unit. There appeared to be a hundred of the fat, foul creatures in the column, though it was the human who was sheltered in the lead tank that held Frederic's gaze more than the fantastic sight of orcs.

General Kornell. Frederic's father. The killer of Frederic's mother.

"Your father appears, so far at least, to be telling the truth," Scranton said calmly. They rode their horses several streets away from the column as it moved through the small city. They were moving out of the downtown district, toward the old rail yards. "Note the train station," he said, pointing to an unkempt building. "Perhaps they are simply shipping the astronauts to Florida."

Kornell eyed Scranton skeptically. "Thought you were the one who had a funny feeling something wasn't right."

Shrugging, Scranton replied, "It was just a feeling, ranger. I could be wrong."

Somehow, Frederic thought, *I doubt that*.

"Are you going to tell me about your father now?"

Kornell stiffened in his seat. "Nothing to tell. He killed my mother. Haven't spoken to him in years. Hoped I'd never see him again."

"And yet, here he is," Scranton offered. "A confrontation seems inevitable, does it not?"

"Seeing isn't confronting," Frederic shot back, wondering why he'd chosen to play word games with someone he was certain had a larger vocabulary.

Silence fell on the two men as General Kornell's tank slowed to a halt in front of the train station. The astronauts, marched in the middle of the column, were ushered forward by the orcs into the station.

"You could always kill him," Scranton offered.

Frederic's blood froze. He'd been thinking just that since his father had wandered back into his life. "Shut up," he said weakly, then wished he hadn't said anything. *New World outside*, he reminded himself, *but Old World inside*.

"Your life," Scranton replied, his eyes gleaming.

Frederic turned away from Scranton, looking to the rail yards simply because they were opposite from where he didn't want to look. The station was old and in obvious disrepair. Beyond the station, multiple sets of tracks stretched into the distance. The state of the rest of the yards, in fact, was worse than that of the station.

"Hey," Frederic said to Scranton, "what looks wrong about that picture?"

Scranton's eyes narrowed on the rail yards, taking in the various tracks and rail cars covered with dust and overgrown with weeds. For the first time since the birth of the New World, Scranton allowed his face to show surprise. "No engine."

"No engine," Frederic repeated, feeling edgy. "Perhaps it's coming?"

"Perhaps," Scranton repeated. "But-"

Scranton never finished the thought. General Kornell, now standing with his orcs fifty feet from the station depot, interrupted Scranton by yelling, "Fire!"

General Kornell's tank obeyed, blasting a mortar shell at the station. The shell exploded into the building with deafening force. The station, already weakened by the passage of time, was obliterated by the attack. Bricks, glass, debris, fire, and dust billowed out of the station. If any of the astronauts survived, neither Scranton nor Frederic could hear their screams.

The tank fired another round.

"There!" Scranton pointed to two astronauts moving out of the building to the right.

Their escape was short-lived. Not ten feet from the building, a cadre of four orcs moved to them and beat them down with spiked clubs, killing them in the street.

"I'm thinking we should run," Frederic whispered.

When Scranton didn't respond, the ranger turned to the older man and was surprised to find a look of utter disgust on the astronaut's face. It wasn't that he thought Scranton above being disgusted; it was that Kelly and Samantha had built up such an image of this man as a shadowy puppeteer that Kornell had doubted the man's humanity. Now ... now he wasn't sure. Was this the same

311

man that (allegedly, according to Samantha) had asked her to kill the coma-ridden Vanessa Yvgenilenko?

"Did you hear me?" Frederic asked. "I said I think we should get out of here."

Scranton had his eyes locked on the blazing, battered husk of the train station. "No," he said, his voice set and cold. "We're not going anywhere."

"We're not?"

"No." Scranton shook his head slowly, almost mechanically. "We're staying just as we are, shadows following orc."

"But-"

Finally turning, Scranton's determined face sent a shiver down Kornell's spine. "We follow. And then, when the time is right, we call reinforcements."

"Reinforcements? Do you mean Kelly and Samantha?"

Turning back to the flames, Scranton was lost in his own thoughts. "There is much at work here that I do not understand."

Frederic almost laughed at the absurd turn this trip had taken. "You ain't lying," he mumbled to himself. "You sure as shit ain't lying."

"We must get you free," Raphael announced, walking across the room to Austin and Kelly.

Kelly shot a sideways, haughty look at the angel. "Now you want to help? The angels haven't been doing squat for us in days and now, suddenly, you're involved?"

Raphael nodded apologetically. "There are things going on in Heaven that you would not understand. I trust you to believe me when I tell you that the angels have not been idle."

Noting the wrinkled nose on his girlfriend's face, Austin cut her off before she lit into the angel. "He's right, Kelly," he said quickly and firmly. "It would take too long to explain, but trust me, he's right."

Wanting to argue, Kelly spun her head to Austin. The look on his face told her to drop it; this was a discussion they could have later.

"I'm not going anywhere," Brad said simply. "I'm still the King of New England. I will not be run out of my own castle."

"Don't be stupid, Brad," Kelly snapped. "O'Malley's up to something bad." Inspiration flashed in Kelly's brain. "Maybe," she said, excited but low, "he's got something to do with my abduction. Why else would he have arrested us?"

Brad blinked. "What? He arrested you?"

"Yeah, then tried to … I don't know," Kelly said honestly. "He came for us. That's why I shot him. He'd just hit Samantha and … bang."

"Bang?" Austin asked.

The King glanced to Samantha; the two exchanged a glance that conjured images of tangled webs woven together. They both knew O'Malley had propositioned Samantha and another Princess to spend the night with Kornell. Neither had any love for O'Malley, but neither wanted certain truths uncovered, either.

A knock on the door stilled the room. "King Regent, open this door!" a guard called. "By orders of Wallace O'Malley, you are to be placed under arrest. Please, sir, come quietly and we can resolve this peacefully."

Slamming his fists onto his desk, Brad wanted to scream. How could this be happening? He was King of New England … King! He'd been appointed by the angels! He looked to Raphael. "Can't you do something?" he asked, seething.

Raphael nodded. "I will help you escape." The angel moved to the window and looked over and down at the Aquarium. "You can hide there," he said, pointing. Putting his back to the window, Raphael faced the room. "I can carry two at a time. Stand back while I-"

Raphael never finished the thought. Catching him by surprise, the window crashed inward as another angel dove through the glass, wrapping his hands around the wings of Raphael and tossing his fellow angel across the room. Raphael hit the far wall with a sharp thud, then crashed to the floor of Regent's office.

The four humans watched, stunned and horrified, as the intruding angel Juramel turned to face them. Locking his silvery eyes on Brad, Juramel unsheathed his golden-flaming sword. "Abdicate your throne and spend the rest of your days repenting your sins, or be sent to Hell in this, your final moment."

Brad stared the angel down, his face an unflinching mask of anger and confidence. "Go to hell."

Juramel cocked his head slightly to the side and offered a wicked smile. "In another day, I won't have to."

"What's that mean?" Austin asked, fearing the answer.

Juramel's eyes appeared to flash silver flame. "In the morn, Hell is coming to Earth."

One hundred miles to the north, the village of Kent Harbor, Maine was overrun with pirates.

Mary Mathers, captain of the sunken ship *Puritan*, strode through the small village that lay before the Black Castle. Her crew made its way steadily forward. They had yet to face any security force, so the pirates were free to scare the villagers as they marched forward. She had given them strict orders – incite panic, not destruction. This cruddy village, perched at the top of a steep cliff, held only one object worth stealing – a Spanish galleon, the king of pirate ships. Docked at the bottom of the cliffs, hidden from their sight, the crew of the *Puritan* aimed to get themselves a new ship right now and be after the *Cottonmather* by nightfall.

"Forward!" Mathers yelled, her long blonde hair waving in the sea breeze. She thought of her life in the Old World, modeling for a shopping channel, and felt joy rip through her. How could the Old World have gone so horribly wrong? Truly, she felt with an unwavering sense of knowing, she was born to do just what she was now doing.

Not thirty feet ahead, her second-in-command, twenty-year old Hector Ladronne, led the way. He moved confidently towards the front doors of the castle. She saw his hand reach for his wireless phone and a moment later heard his voice crackle from the phone in her own hand. "No sign of any defense," the younger man said confidently. "This will be a piece of cake."

"Do not get overconfident," Mathers shot back. "We've seen security. We know they're in there somewhere." Raising her voice to her crew, Mathers shouted her next order. "Draw pistols!"

Hector sent two pirates (Mathers didn't know their names) towards the two large doors. With some effort, they managed to pull them open. Hector stood dead center, his eyes locked onto whatever would be revealed.

"'Bout time," he said with a cocky grin as the castle gave up its security force at last. Six men, dressed in black armor with sea green trim, roared from the doorway, swords drawn. "Time to live out a fantasy," Hector grinned, raising a Glock 9 he'd stolen from the hunting store several days back at the center guard. The guard kept coming, raising his sword to an offensive position above his head. He would never get the chance to strike.

Hector fired.

The bullet slammed through the guard's skull just above his left eye, battering flesh, bone, and brain. The impact jerked the guard's face backward, then his entire body dropped, lifeless, to its right. "Thank you, Indiana," he whispered through a smile.

Around Hector, the other four armored guards fought hand to hand with twice as many pirates. The C.O. turned to the pirates coming up behind him. "Storm the castle! Go!" His eyes searched back, finding Mathers, then skipping past her to the Olympian goddess Aphrodite, then past that vision to the man who trudged a few steps behind.

Carl Yesek. The New World friend that Hector no longer trusted. The fortysomething biochemist that had somehow escaped from the clutches of Stocky Samuel, the pirate that wanted them both dead. Inside this castle, the Lady in charge of this village waited for them. As Fate would have it, the Lady of the Black Castle was Carl's ex-wife.

Across the small, grassy rise that bridged the village and the castle, Carl's eyes locked onto Hector's and he felt trapped. From someplace unknown to him, a vicious hate consumed Carl. The hate was reserved not, as he would have expected, for his ex-wife, but instead for the younger man he had considered a friend as recently as yesterday.

Sworn as an oath in the exchange of glances, both Carl and Hector knew only one of them was making it to the stolen ship.

Neither intended to miss the launch. Which meant, someplace and sometime between now and the boarding of the galleon, one of them was going to do something very, very bad to the other.

Lunging forward, Raphael hurled his battered body at the legs of Juramel. "Escape!" he commanded the moment before impact.

The four humans watched Raphael's shoulder drive into the back of Juramel's knees, sending them both to the carpet. Though commanded to flee, the sight of two angels wrestling and clawing at each other on the floor kept them rooted to the spot. Juramel, caught off-balance, was struggling to right himself, but Raphael had jumped on his back, gripping tightly to Juramel's wings. "Escape!" he shouted again.

The humans looked at each other. "What's the best escape route?" Kelly asked Brad.

"I'm not leaving."

"To hell with you then," Austin spat. "Tell us how to get out of here."

Brad's face, hardened in anger, stared daggers at Austin. "I do this for her," he said, glancing to Kelly.

"Fine with me," Austin said.

Samantha, trapped on the opposite side of the angels, screamed as the door to the office was smashed in by two of the King's guards. Whatever the two were expecting, it wasn't two angels wrestling on the floor.

"Anytime, Brad," Austin said, trying not to panic.

"Did you ever have Castle Greyskull?"

"What?" Austin asked, his mind racing. "You mean that He-Man castle?"

"Yeah."

"No," Austin said, his mind racing back to his youth. "I hated the He-Man toys. They were all out of proportion with the other toys. I mean, what were they thinking when-oof!"

"You're such a dork," Kelly snapped, elbowing him in the ribs. "Brad," she said, turning to glance at the two guards who were trying to navigate past the brawling angels, "get us out of here."

Brad let out a smile; he was surprised to find he was enjoying this. That this scenario was a chance at redemption – allowing him to actually save Kelly – didn't escape him. "Greyskull used to have a trap door."

"Did it?" Austin asked skeptically. "I don't think it did."

"Trust me, it did," Brad grinned. "I love trap doors, secret passages, all that stuff."

"Point?" Kelly asked, her eyes darting to a frozen Samantha. So far it appeared the guards hadn't noticed her.

"Watch this," Brad grinned, reaching towards the conference phone on his desk. The King punched a series of numbers, then pointed to the corner of the room nearest him where a portion of the wall slid away, revealing a set of descending steps. He turned back to Kelly, his face grinning but serious. "Get moving."

Austin and Kelly nodded their thanks and moved quickly past Brad to the doorway. Austin stood to the side to let Kelly move past him, but she stopped. "Come with us," she said to Brad.

The King shook his head. "I will not surrender my kingdom."

"Brad," Kelly insisted, noting that Raphael was now the angel taking the severest beating, "this is silly. *You're King of New England*. Think of how stupid that sounds. This can't last. Why risk your life over a kingdom that didn't even exist two weeks ago?"

Brad was surprised how much he meant what he said next. "I'm not risking my life for my kingdom, Kelly. Now, go, get moving. I've got to stay behind to close the door."

"But Samantha-"

Brad shot across the room, grabbing Samantha. His actions drew the interest of his two guards. "Get going!" he ordered Samantha, shoving her to Austin. "Get them to safety, Austin."

Austin nodded his thanks, sending Samantha into the winding, stone staircase which Kelly was already descending. Stepping inside, he watched Brad punch one of his guards in the face, then jump back to his desk, quickly and assuredly punching in the code that sent the wall panel sliding shut.

The last image Austin saw was Brad Regent, up until today the man he most personally hated in all the world, take the butt-end of the second guard's sword directly in the face.

The door shut, plunging them into total darkness. Austin let out a deep sigh, his hands touching the now shut panel, wondering where the staircase would lead them, but hoping it meant to safety.

Even if that meant owing Brad Regent a very large chip.

Entering the Black Castle, Carl Yesek and Aphrodite in tow, Mary Mathers allowed her eyes a moment to adjust to the low light of the interior. The sight before her thrilled and shocked her. All around the floor, pirates and armored guards were locked in bloody combat. The sound of gunshots and screaming filled the room and the unmistakable smell of blood soaked their senses.

Carl felt the urge to vomit.

The pirates had the advantage at a distance, relying on their guns to mow down the guards. At close quarters, however, the advantage switched to the men of the Black Castle. In tight, the guards held the advantage as their swords dug deep into the flesh of the pirates, whose costumes offered no protection against strong, steel blades. Bodies of both groups littered the wide stone entryway.

Aphrodite shook her head. "Men," she said disgustedly.

"You don't approve?" Mathers questioned.

"Battle without love is a wasted enterprise," the goddess remarked.

Mathers eyed Aphrodite carefully, but detected no irony in the Olympian's face. Somehow, it made her hate the goddess even more. "Then take Carl and find his ex-wife," Mathers ordered. "Maybe that'll satisfy you."

Without questioning the mortal, Aphrodite nodded and took Carl's hand in hers. "Come, Carl," she said solemnly. "None will harm you while you walk with me."

The two walked directly through the middle of the battle. True to her word, none of the combatants did anything but stare at her as she led Carl towards the large staircase at the opposite end of the room. As they moved up the large staircase, Mathers' eyes shot up the stairs ahead of them to see Hector waiting at the top. She keyed her wireless.

"Hector, move ahead and secure the ship."

From across the expanse, Hector looked down at his captain as he keyed his own wireless. "Doors to the docks are locked. We're going to need the Lady of the castle to get them for us."

Mathers frowned. Was Hector playing her? "Do you really think the Lady Watson is going to have the keys with her?"

"No, but she'll know where to get them."

"Get it done quickly. And painlessly."

"I still think Carl presents too high a risk," Hector repeated, his eyes moving to his right where Aphrodite and Carl were now reaching the top of the staircase.

Mathers silently fumed at this growing feud. "And I still think I'm the captain, and I say we do nothing. We're not going to toss every man overboard that presents the hint of a problem."

Hector's eyes left Carl and refocused on Mathers. "Aye, aye, sir," he fumed.

Two seconds after being plunged into total darkness in the staircase that led away from the King's office, a set of rectangular, dull lights hummed to life on the floor of the staircase. Every four steps, all the way down, the light allowed them to see where they were going.

"Where does this lead?" Kelly asked, coming back up the steps to place a comforting hand on Samantha's shoulder.

Shaking his head, Austin moved down the steps to meet them. "You okay?" he asked Samantha.

The redhead let out a few deep sighs, nodding as she attempted to regain her composure. "Think so," she said. She offered Austin her hand. "Samantha Dixon."

"Austin McNamara," he replied, shaking the young woman's hand. Glancing back towards the door, Austin was surprised how quiet it had become. Was the tunnel soundproof? Or had the fighting stopped? "Let's get moving," he suggested. "I don't know where this staircase goes, but we've got to trust Brad." The words had barely left his mouth when his lips turned into a frown. "God, I can't believe I just said that."

Kelly smiled, taking a step up to kiss him on the cheek. "Me neither. Must be a sign you're maturing."

Samantha rolled her eyes; this was the guy the great Kelly Reed chose to be with? "C'mon," she said, moving down the steps, "we're not out of this, yet."

The three of them moved quickly and silently down the spiraling tunnel, thankful for the lights that lit their way. They hadn't descended for more than a minute when the staircase dropped them onto a landing, from which a straight tunnel herded them forward for another minute. The passageway was narrow enough that they had to walk single file. "I should probably be in front," Austin suggested from the back of the line, causing both women to stop and turn around.

"Why?" Samantha asked.

"Because we're poor helpless women?" Kelly asked, punching him in the arm.

Austin threw up his hands. "Hey, we're in a castle, ain't we? If you can't be chivalrous here …"

Kelly turned away from him, rolling her eyes to Samantha. "Don't mind him. He's afraid of mice. Probably heard one coming up behind him."

Samantha looked Austin up and down. She wasn't surprised. "Mice?"

"Elephants are afraid of mice, too," he answered weakly. Samantha arced an eyebrow at him. "Can we just move along, please?" Austin implored.

Smiling despite the gravity of the situation, Samantha started moving down the tunnel again. In another two minutes they stopped at a shut, steel door. "If this is locked…" Samantha whined, saying what they were all thinking. Figuring if this was a dead-end she wanted to know as soon as possible, Samantha reached for the door handle and pulled. To all of their relief, the door swung open, revealing a sight none of them had expected to find at the other end of the secret passageway. This time, it was Austin who gave voice to what they were all thinking.

"Penguins?"

"Hector, she's in here!"

Hector nodded to his fellow crewman, then motioned for Aphrodite and Carl to follow him down the hall. "Status?" Hector asked, stepping over the bodies of three fallen castle guards and two pirates.

"She's in here," the pirate said, blood running down his left temple.

"You okay?" Hector asked.

The pirate frowned as he looked down at the dead bodies that littered the hallway. "I … I don't know…"

Hector nodded. "You did what you had to do. Find a bathroom and clean yourself up, then come back and wait for me here." As Hector watched the pirate head down the hall, he realized he knew neither the name of the wounded pirate nor the names of the two pirates at his feet. His face set in stone, the Old World auto mechanic turned to Carl. "Don't fuck this up."

Carl's face was pale and ghost-like. "What are we doing?" he asked, staring at the bodies. "Jesus Christ, why couldn't we have just asked for the ship?"

Hector ignored him, turning the handle and entering the room. The Lady of the Castle, Sheila Watson, a heavy-set forty-year-old with curly auburn hair, sat on the bed. She held a linen cloth to her forehead to stanch the flow of blood. Her bottom lip was busted open. Hector used that to his advantage. Storming across the room, he removed his Glock 9 and pointed it in Sheila's face.

"We're taking your ship," he said flatly.

She looked up at him as if he'd just asked to borrow a bowl of sugar. "You want my ship?" she asked, stunned. "All this bloodshed … for a ship? Why didn't you just ask for it? I've got no use for a blasted ship!" She rose to her feet, pushing Hector's gun to the side. "I didn't even know the damn thing was there until three days ago! I … I …"

A wave of nausea overcame Sheila and she dropped to a knee. Carl, who'd slunk into the room and stayed by the door, rushed forward to keep her from tumbling to the floor. "Sheila!"

Having dropped the linen, blood dribbled from her forehead and down her nose. "Carl?" she asked. "What are you doing here?" The look of surprise changed to one of disbelieving anger when she saw Carl's uniform. "You're with these people?" she asked, slapping him in the face.

"It wasn't supposed to be like this," Carl said quickly, rubbing his face. "I told them all we needed to do was ask! I told them, I swear it!"

Sheila pushed him away, then fell back to sit on the floor, her back resting against the large bed. "Too bad," she said maliciously. "You want the ship," she said to Hector, "it's yours. Just make sure you take this son-of-a-bitch with you."

"We need the key," Hector demanded.

"The key?" Sheila asked, confused. "There's no engine on that boat."

"To the docks," Hector said, relishing the look of anguish on Carl's face. "The big doors leading to the docks are locked."

"And you thought I'd have it on me?" she asked. "I have no idea where it is."

Hector rolled his eyes. "You must know where it is. You're the Lady of the castle, aren't you?"

Sheila looked to Carl. "Nice friends. Smart."

"Just give us the fucking keys," Hector sighed.

"I told you, I don't know where they are."

Hector looked to Carl. "You were married to her?"

Carl nodded.

Hector looked back to Sheila. "No keys, the son-of-a-bitch stays with you." He called to the hallway, "Aphrodite, come in here."

"Watch your tone, mortal," the goddess reprimanded the young pirate. "I am not one of your crew."

"Sorry," Hector said without feeling. "I need a favor. Work your magic, will ya? Turn these two back into lovebirds."

"I will not," she said flatly. "Love cannot be forced."

"Can't you shoot them with your little arrows or something?"

Aphrodite folded her arms under her breasts.

"Can you rip the locked door down?"

Aphrodite nodded angrily.

"Well, then," Hector said, feeling the burn of shame as Sheila looked at him with disdain, "I guess I'll have to shoot Carl instead." Before anyone could act, Hector pivoted the Glock to Carl and pulled the trigger.

Carl screamed in agony as the bullet ripped through the wooden floor. He looked to Hector with fear in his eyes. "You almost fucking shot me!"

Hector slowly backed away. "You should thank me, Carl. You're not made for this life. Whatever you did to get away from Samuel ... you paid some price. I wasn't willing for that price to be my head. Stay here. Mend the fences with the old lady. Your pirate days are over."

Austin, Kelly, and Samantha made their way through the basement of the aquarium and up onto the main floor. "Penguins," Kelly chuckled. "Brad always loved penguins."

Austin grunted. "Filthy birds. Smell worse than your Uncle Teddy's gas."

After everything that had happened, Samantha was glad to be with Kelly and Austin right now. They kept it light, diffusing fear with gentle barbs. "What's the plan?" she asked as they kept their eyes peeled for the king's guards.

"Hopefully by now my fellow pirates have stolen a new ship," Austin replied. "We should move north. Stay to the coast. We can rendezvous with them after I've made contact."

"I don't think so," Kelly answered as they came in sight of the large circular tank that dominated the center of the aquarium. "We've got something of a base camp set up south of here. A group of astronauts are holed up at Hollis Memorial. Frederic's there, too."

"Frederic?" Austin asked, stopping suddenly. "You want to go back to the guy that almost got you killed?"

Kelly stopped and turned back to him. "It wasn't his fault, Austin. We all get scared sometimes. What's important is that he's been there for me since then."

Austin didn't want to argue, but couldn't help himself. "Unlike me, right?"

"Relax, Austin," Kelly snapped. "Stop reading something into everything. Suddenly you're acting like you did the first couple of months we dated. Not everything is a veiled shot at your manhood."

"Fine, I'm sorry," Austin said disgustedly, throwing his hands up. "Wait," he corrected himself, "was that a veiled shot at my manhood?"

"Get a grip. If I thought that you-"

Samantha, only half-hearing the content of their spat, interrupted them. "Um, you two might want to stop arguing and come take a look at this."

Austin and Kelly gave each other a glare, but stopped arguing long enough to walk the ten steps it took to get to Samantha. "What is it?" Austin asked, then stopped dead on his feet, as if running into a brick wall. His eyes were locked onto the sight they could now see through the front doors of the aquarium. "That's ... that's ... I mean, it can't be … can it? I mean, he wouldn't really look like that, would he?" Pause. "Would he?"

"Maybe you should stop talking," Kelly whispered, "before he hears you and comes inside."

All three began to slowly back away from the line of sight of the horrific being they had spied. Tall and ripped, skin of dark crimson, radiating power … the being standing in front of the aquarium brought many names to mind, but all of them represented the same creature of Christian legend.

Satan had come to Boston.

Chapter Nineteen
Lucifer Comes to Boston

Austin, Kelly, and Samantha slowly backed away from the front doors of the New England Aquarium, moving deeper inside the building. They had, it seemed, avoided the boiling pot of water only to find themselves face-to-face with the fire. Regent Castle (the boiling pot) was under attack, but thanks to the assistance of King Regent, they had escaped through a secret tunnel that let into the next-door aquarium, which led them, it appeared, directly into the path of a being that looked an awful lot like they imagined Satan would look (the fire).

Tall and toned with dark crimson skin, Satan stood at the front of the Aquarium, looking around to take in the New World. His clothes were reminiscent of the angels in that he wore little beside sandals and what Austin had taken to calling "angel diapers," a wrap that covered the groin area but little else. Black leather bands at his wrist and around his thighs replaced the angelic belt, but held no weapons. His hair was black, curly, and short and his eyes were a glistening gold. While Satan (they had each decided on their own that this being could be no other) had neither horns nor tail, Austin, Kelly, and Samantha did not find themselves anything but impressed. The being, even from this distance and through the plexiglass doors, radiated a palpable power.

"That can't be Satan, can it?" Samantha asked in a near-silent whisper.

"Do you want to find out?" Austin replied.

Their voices, barely audible to one another, succeeded in doing what they had hoped it wouldn't: drawing the attention of Satan.

Outside, Satan turned, his glowing eyes freezing them in their tracks. Too stunned/scared to move, the three were rooted to the floor as Satan casually opened the door and walked inside.

"I swear to God this is the single weirdest moment of my life," Austin muttered.

"Even weirder than what you saw during the Primus set at Lollapalooza?" Kelly asked, referring to one of Austin's most oft-told adventures.

Austin thought for a moment, then nodded. "Okay, this is the second weirdest moment of my life."

Satan came to stand before them. He was, they all agreed, an impressive figure. To Kelly, it was the natural grace of his movements, the casual but assured way in which he walked and held himself. Samantha found him almost … beautiful. Almost. Not that she'd ever spent a lot of time thinking about what Satan would look like, should she ever meet him, but now that he was here, she thought he should look more like he did in that crappy Tom Cruise movie (*what the heck was that called?*), and not like … not like … Josh Hartnett, maybe?

Wow, she thought, frowning, *that's … disappointing. Shouldn't Satan look more like … I dunno … Brad Pitt in Troy?*

Satan turned his golden gaze upon the shorter Samantha. "I can hear you, you know."

Samantha stopped breathing.

"It's okay," Satan sighed. "When you're the source of all evil in the world it's hard to live up to people's expectations." He cocked his head to the side, as if he were a bird of prey studying a potential meal. "But *Legend*? Really? You think I should look like Tim Curry in make-up?"

Austin was having a hard time. "I think I just shit my pants." He turned to Kelly, a blank, pale look on his face. "I think it happened when Satan said, 'Tim Curry' for some reason. This is definitely weirder than Lollapalooza."

"Mortal," Satan snapped at Austin. "Do not refer to me as Satan. The name is Lucifer. Satan is so … childish."

Austin turned back. Slowly. "Sorry."

Lucifer waved the slight away with the swipe of his hand. "I'll let the transgression pass."

Of the three of them, Kelly had managed to stay the most composed. It wasn't so surprising to her that Satan - *Lucifer*, that is – would appear on Earth, just that she'd get a chance to talk to him. Up close, however, he looked almost normal. Or at least what passed for normal in the New World. But only almost normal. And only then if "normal" meant "angelic," for that's what he most looked like to her, the more she studied him. Like an angel, stripped of his wings and painted a dark red. Kelly began to feel something as she looked at him, something deep and ... primal. It reminded her a bit of how she had gotten lost in Michael Scranton's eyes, only where Scranton's look made her feel a bit light and giggly, Satan's golden eyes made her feel warm and alive.

"Ahem," she pretended to cough as Lucifer appeared lost in thought, staring over at the large, circular tank at the center of the Aquarium. She felt a strong desire for him to return his glance to her. "What, um, what do you want with us?"

Lucifer ran a hand through his curly hair and brought his golden eyes to bear on her. He started to answer, then stopped, a curious look coming over his face. "My God," he said in a rich tone, almost breathless, "you are exquisite."

Kelly found herself blushing like a schoolgirl as a wave of warmth rippled through her.

"Figures," Samantha mumbled, not at all surprised.

"Heh," Austin said. "Satan just said, 'God.' Kinda funny when you think about it." He stopped, the latter half of the sentence now penetrating his mind. "Wait, did you just say she was *exquisite*? Who says exquisite?"

Lucifer nodded, his eyes seeming to radiate. "For truth, one of the most beautiful women in all of history."

Austin blinked. He looked to Kelly (who was still blushing), then back to Lucifer (who was still gawking). Suddenly, Brad seemed like much less of a threat to steal his girlfriend away. "Just flippin' great," he mumbled. "Satan has the hots for my girlfriend."

Without turning, without losing the pleasant smile that played out across his crimson face, Lucifer said, "Mortal, if you call me by the name Satan one more time, you will spend eternity watching a continual loop of *The Prince of Tides*."

"Just so long as it's not *Friends*."

"I wouldn't dare let you watch *Friends*," Lucifer replied, somehow making a putdown come off as charming. "You have always taken far too much enjoyment in Jennifer Aniston's breasts, which, and I believe this is correct, you find to be the most perfect breasts in the world."

Austin opened his mouth, but had nothing to say.

"I do not know why," Lucifer continued, taking a step towards Kelly, "you would find any part of any woman more perfect than the woman who now stands before me."

Austin winced. "Was that a line? Are you using that cheap-ass line on Kelly?" Austin shook his head. "Listen, I don't care if you are, what, the second most powerful being in the universe? That line isn't going to work on Kelly Reed unless your goal is to get knocked on your ass."

"Austin?"

"What is it, babe?"

"Shut up for a moment, would you?"

And then, in what was both the weirdest and worst moment in Austin's life, Kelly Reed and Lucifer lost themselves in each other's embrace, coming together in a lengthy, smoldering, passionate kiss.

"Um … what?" Austin managed to ask, feeling the world drop away from him. The moment had only been humorous until now because he didn't think anything would come of it besides flirting. He was used to guys flirting with Kelly and used to her rejecting them cold. But this …

Samantha moved to stand next to him. "Um … wow," she said, watching the two slobber over each other. "That is one hell of a kiss."

Austin glanced at her. "Hello? I'm standing right here."

"Hey," Samantha replied, grinning wickedly, "if Kelly doesn't care, I don't care."

Brad Regent spit blood onto the floor of his office, the only pleasure coming from hitting the damaged phone that doubled as a remote to the escape route. With the phone damaged, there was no way for anyone to go after Kelly. He spit more blood. This was *his* office. In *his* castle, he reminded himself, staring daggers across the room at Wallace O'Malley. O'Malley's head was wrapped to stem the flow of blood from the gun shot he'd taken from Kelly. The entire left side of his body was stained with blood. Brad ran his tongue around his bottom set of teeth, feeling for any looseness. The last backhand from the angel Juramel felt like it had dislodged something, but he could find no weakness amongst his teeth.

Plenty of blood, though.

The King of New England leaned back against the glass wall that overlooked the Aquarium, his hands tied together with the telephone cord from his desk phone. The same phone he'd used as a remote to open, then close, then smash against one of his guard's heads. Beside him, the angel Raphael stood without bonds. He looked to the angel with something akin to sympathy. It was Raphael, after all, as the Angel in Charge of Royalty, who had served as his angelic liaison. Raphael looked in worse shape than himself; gashes were splayed across his skin and a silvery liquid oozed from the wounds. His left wing appeared to be broken. Feathers littered the floor of the office, though some of them, at least, were Juramel's.

"Juramel," Raphael admonished, "I do not understand your actions. You have betrayed the Host, betrayed God."

Juramel folded his arms across his chest, breaking off a conversation with O'Malley to answer his fellow angel's accusation. "God broke the sacred covenant. He abandoned us."

The words were like daggers to Raphael's ears. "He left us so that he could walk amongst the humans, for they are also his children."

"As were the Olympians," Juramel spat back. "And the Asgardians and Egyptians and Martians and on and on. Do you not understand, Raphael? In the end, all God's children are abandoned."

The words hit Raphael like a thunderbolt, physically knocking him back into the wall. "He is still All Father. His is still the Creator."

"And all children," Juramel seethed, "grow to one day replace their father. We are no different. This is the way of the world."

"The other angels will stop you," Raphael protested.

"The other angels?" Juramel replied, a look of gleeful satisfaction coming to his face. "Most of them side with me."

Raphael shook his head, not wanting to believe. "How did you turn them?"

Juramel laughed. "Me?" He shook his head. "Me? It was not I who turned them, as you put it. I am one of the turned, not the orchestrator."

A look of anger now made its way to Raphael's face. "Was it Lucifer? Was it he, after all these ageless years, who finally corrupted the Host?"

A twinkle so malicious that had Raphael a heart it would've stopped sprang into Juramel's silvery eyes. "No … no, my brother," the angel said softly, coming over to place a hand on Raphael's shoulder. "Lucifer is not the one behind it all. Lucifer has grown soft over the ages. Like God, he is also in need of replacing."

"Then who?" Raphael pleaded.

Juramel withdrew his flaming sword and pressed the flat of the blade horizontally onto Raphael's chest, causing the angel to scream in agony. "A name for another time," Juramel whispered, "for it is not my place to reveal the Grand Design."

Brad winced as Juramel held his sword across the chest for what seemed like an eternity. When he was done, the flaming broadsword had left a thick line across Raphael's chest.

Juramel wasn't finished. Giving his "brother" only a moment's respite, Juramel turned the sword vertical and pressed it back against the flesh.

Brad turned away; he didn't need to see the design of the scar to realize what Juramel was branding onto Raphael's skin.

He was marking the angel with a crucifix.

After five minutes, Austin had taken a seat at the edge of the penguin pool. Behind and below him, a set of penguins went about being penguins, skimming through the water, then propelling themselves up onto solid ground. Austin had always found penguins to be miserable creatures, but now he felt a kinship with them. Or rather, he felt a kinship with the quality he'd attributed to them; he doubted the penguins thought themselves as miserable, smelly beasts.

"Seven minutes," Samantha said, now coming to join Austin as she looked from the kissing couple to the clock on the wall and back. "This qualifies as a make-out session, I do believe."

"You're not helping."

"I wasn't trying to." She grinned. "I did figure out who he reminds me of, though. At first I thought it was Brad Pitt in *Fight Club*, but it's not; it's Brad Pitt in *Thelma and Geena Davis*."

"Thelma *was* Geena Davis," Austin grumbled.

"Whatever," she grinned.

"This only happens to me, you know," he said, pointing to Kelly and Lucifer. "I mean, not that I've ever lost a girl to Satan before, but if you'd told me someone I knew was going to have that happen to him, I would've bet my house that it would've been me."

"Ah," Samantha said, oddly enjoying what was happening even though her problems were with Kelly and not Austin, "but would you have bet your soul on it? Get it? Lucifer … soul?"

"I get it," Austin grumbled. "I do teach literature, you know."

"As a matter of fact," Samantha said, "I didn't know that. I really don't know anything about you except you're Kelly's boyfriend. Man," she said, "they're really going at it. Wow, is she licking his nipple?"

"Shoot me," Austin groused. "Somebody shoot me. Where's Mollug when I need him?"

"Does she do that for you?"

"Do you not have a gun?"

"I do wonder," Samantha thought idly, "just what he's doing here. On Earth, I mean. In general. Not right at this second. We can see what—"

"Just stop," Austin pleaded, burying his head in his hands, really not liking the way Kelly's hands moved slowly up and down Satan's back.

Mollug, at that moment, was in Purgatory. The parrot sat silently on the shoulder of the angel Berathon as they traversed the limbo world of the Olympians. "Time passes differently in Purgatory," Berathon explained as they walked through a thick, swirling fog. "It is a realm of non-time, as it were. Like Heaven and Hell, time simply does not exist here. I shall let you in on a secret, Mollug; angels are not immortal. Neither are the Olympian gods. It is simply that we exist in a place where there is no time. Were we to move to Earth, we would age. Not as fast as humans, of course, but we would age, grow old, and eventually die."

"Fascinating," Mollug dead-panned, not really caring.

"Here we are," Berathon announced, pointing through the dense air to what looked like an oasis. Green grass, as far as the eye could see, appeared as if out of nowhere to dominate the landscape; even the swirling fog dissipated. Berathon stepped onto the grass and Mollug could feel the angel's body tense. "I must warn you, Olympians are not fond of angels. We are rivals, as it were, the first two of God's creations."

Scanning the rolling green hills, Berathon spotted an Olympian laying in the grass to his left. Making his way across the thick lawn, Berathon could see that it was Apollo who lay before him. "Fortune is with us, parrot," he explained. "Apollo has always been among the most level-headed of Olympians. Ho, Apollo!" he called at twenty paces.

At ten, he called again.

At five, he frowned.

At one, he could see that Apollo's head had been severed from his body, then replaced to look, from a distance, like the body was whole.

The dullness of the timeless centuries had slowed Berathon's senses a fraction of a second. That was all it took. Sensing a trap, the angel spread his wings and leapt into the air. His leap saved his sight, but not his shoulder. Berathon screamed in pain as a trident imbedded itself hard into his shoulder, knocking him backwards and to the ground.

At impact, Mollug spread his much smaller wings, lifting off Berathon's shoulder. He tried to feel bad for the angel, but then, Berathon had tried to kill him a scattering of days earlier, so it felt, to Mollug, more like the universe balancing the scales. Still, the parrot realized he, too, might be a target, and his eyes peered into the distance to view the attacker.

A tall, muscular man with flowing white hair and beard came walking towards them with malice etched across his face. "Taken down by an old man," Mollug mumbled, then changed his mind as the man drew closer. Mollug had guessed the attacker was old because of the white hair, but at close range he could see that the man, while aged, was not old. More like middle-aged with prematurely white hair. The beard, too, added to the aged appearance.

"Berathon," the attacker declared in a booming voice as he stepped on the angel's chest, stilling the squirming angel. "Let me get that for you." The attacker grabbed the handle of his trident and pulled, ripping angelic flesh and silvery blood from Berathon's body. "Welcome to what God calls Purgatory and I call Hell."

Berathon grimaced, staring up into the eyes of an old enemy. "Go jump in a lake, Poseidon."

The Olympian let his sandaled foot slide up Berathon's chest to apply pressure to the throat. "If only I could. But, you see, there is no water in Purgatory."

Mollug flapped in close to Poseidon's face, startling the god. "I think that's why he said it, dumbass," Mollug squawked.

Poseidon waved his arms at the bird. The movement brought his foot off Berathon's throat, allowing the angel to roll free and get to his feet. Mollug, seeing Berathon was up, glided out of range.

"I'm here to talk," Berathon said, holding up his hands to show Poseidon he would make no move to attack.

"About what?" Poseidon grumbled, eyeing Mollug with hatred.

"About how Aphrodite was freed from Purgatory," Berathon explained, ignoring Apollo's dead body for the moment. "None of you could escape from Purgatory without the assistance of an angel. That was written by God into your punishment."

Poseidon flipped his trident upside down and planted it into the soft grass. The god of the seas sighed, rubbing his eyes with his muscular right hand. "It wasn't an angel," he informed Berathon, turning to look wistfully into the distance. "It was the son of an angel."

"Angels cannot have children," Berathon snapped.

"No," Poseidon mumbled, "but ex-angels can."

"Ex-angels?" Berathon frowned, realizing the Olympian could mean only one person. "The son of Satan freed Aphrodite? Why?"

Poseidon slapped Berathon with his glance. "Not even a cockless angel is that stupid. Why do all men seek Aphrodite?"

Berathon thought of his own encounter with Aphrodite and with the kiss they had shared.

"Just like his father, he is," Poseidon grumbled. "Willing to do anything for a woman." The Olympian shook his head. "At least Lucifer only brought sin into the world of man; the hellspawn's plans are much worse."

"And what are those plans?" Berathon demanded.

The Olympian smiled maliciously, glad to see the high and mighty Host taken down a notch. "Damien plans to bring sin to Heaven itself."

"Austin, I'm so sorry … I … I don't know what happened." Kelly pleaded the truth with Austin; she didn't know exactly what had come over her. "That's never happened before."

"I don't want to talk about it," Austin replied. The pure strangeness of the situation lessened the impact of what he was feeling only slightly. He'd just seen his girlfriend, the woman he deeply, truly loved, kiss another man. That it was Satan really didn't matter when it came right down to it.

For his part, Lucifer stood to the side, looking more depressed than anything else. "I, too, apologize, Austin McNamara. I have problems controlling my emotions. Always have, always will. I see something, I want it, I take it. Doesn't really matter if it's the throne of Heaven or a craving for roasted duck. I have no impulse control. It won't happen again, I swear it."

"Just … stop," Austin begged. "Just stop, would you? I mean," he said, rising to his feet, "what are you trying to do? Be a nice guy about it? You just made out with my girlfriend! In front of me! That's uncool, dude. I don't care if you are the most evil fucking being in the whole goddamned universe, what you did was seriously fucking uncool!"

"Austin," Kelly said, embarrassed, "please … it meant nothing. Really."

Austin spun on his heels. "That's supposed to make me feel better? You sound like every cheating husband in every fucking stupid Lifetime movie!"

Lucifer placed a strong hand on Austin's shoulder. "You have no right to yell at her, Austin. It is true. It meant nothing to her. Yes, there was a momentary spark of brief, uncontrollable passion, but by the end … nothing. It's my lot in life. Women love the bad boy only for the briefest of moments."

Austin just stared. *Love lessons from Satan*, he cried to himself. *What next?*

"Please," Lucifer reminded him. "Remember, I can hear what you're thinking. It's Lucifer. Not Satan. Satan is the name the propagandists gave me." Lucifer removed his hand and walked over to a small, blue bench against the near wall and sat down. "Story of my life, really – not that the true story ever gets told. You're all familiar with the sordid tale of Adam and Eve?"

The three humans nodded.

"They blame me for tempting Eve with the apple." Lucifer threw his hands up in disgust. "And yes, I did bring sin into the world, I will admit that, but the idea that sin was trapped inside a damned apple … preposterous." He looked at them almost desperately. "I was in love with Eve. And she loved me, too. That was the sin between us – love. Not wickedness. Not evil. Love." Lucifer glanced quickly to Kelly then turned away. "If only for a moment."

Samantha wasn't buying the story. "So you didn't turn yourself into a snake and seduce her with your forked tongue of lies into taking a bite of the apple?"

"Please," Lucifer fumed. "Damned propaganda!" he swore adamantly. "They took a story of love and changed it into something … something rotten and wicked. A parable. Or metaphor. Whatever it's called," he spat, waving his arms in disgust. "I suppose I should be thankful they left out the tryst with Mary. Adam was a buffoon and look how the Church came to his side. Can you imagine what the propagandists would do to me if they knew about that? Stealing Adam's mate is one thing, but attempting to steal the betrothed of Christ … Mary took the worst of that, though she doesn't deserve to be called a prostitute. I can assure you the man responsible for that addition is not enjoying his afterlife."

Samantha looked from an ashamed Kelly to a fuming Austin to a perturbed Lucifer. "Explain it to me." She raised her hand. "Not the Jesus bit. The apple thing."

Lucifer took a deep breath, sizing Samantha up with his golden eyes. "Do you really believe the Bible is wholly factual?"

"Well, no," Samantha admitted. "But almost completely factual, yes."

Lucifer rose to his feet, adrenaline running wild within him – the Bible was one of his pet peeves. "Think about how silly it sounds … I was a snake? An apple contained the sin of man? Why would God put evil into an apple?"

"Er …" Samantha said, looking to Austin and Kelly for help and receiving none.

"The propagandists did that, in part, to humiliate me, and, in part, to snub their noses at the Olympians and their legend of Pandora's Box," Lucifer explained forlornly.

"Can you please explain the snake bit to me?" Samantha asked, noting how Austin and Kelly kept stealing glances at one another.

"The snake?" Lucifer continued in a somber voice. "Did you never see it for what it truly was, Samantha? There is no more phallic a creature than a snake. Return to the apple. What do apples contain? Seed. And what are apples? Round. It wasn't that the apple contained the evil which I tricked Eve into letting loose upon the world. The apple was the sin made real. They even made it red, an insult to my scarred skin," he explained, absently holding up his arms. "We were in love," he frowned, repeating, "if only for a moment. Adam was wholly unworthy of her love. Do you know how he spent his time? He walked Eden, naming everything he came across when he had the most wonderful companion anyone could ask for waiting for him at home." Lucifer shook his head. "He did not deserve her, and after the hedonistic Olympian nightmare, God refused the Host companionship." Lucifer's eyes bore into the circular tank, focusing on a distant memory. "The apple contained sin, but it was a sin born of love. The propagandists twisted my love into lust, turned me into a 'vile' creature. They took Eve's pregnancy and concocted that ridiculous apple tripe. It's all symbolism for the purposes of conversion. Keep it safe for kids and easy to swallow for adults. I never was allowed any credit."

"Credit?" Samantha asked. "You're, like, the most evil being ever."

Lucifer's back straightened. "If only that were true," he groused, staring hard at Samantha. "Answer me this, Samantha. If I were truly that evil—the balancing evil to God's good—then why did I slum around Mississippi bartering for the souls of blues musicians, or carousing in the English countryside and Los Angeles to accumulate heavy metal souls? Does that sound like the work of an all-powerful being?" Lucifer paced back and forth, holding court, his anger rising. "How does one define evil? It was not me, Samantha, who flooded the Earth in a fit of anger. It wasn't me who refused my son's offer for help." Lucifer stopped at the reference to Christ, wincing. He shook his head, calming visibly. When he spoke next, it was in a somber, controlled voice. "The Old Man was teaching me a lesson there. I gave my son everything, helped him however and whenever I could and look what's become of him."

Samantha had to ask, "You have a son?"

"I do," he said, frowning. "Damien."

"And this son," Samantha asked, almost too afraid to let the words out, "is ..."

"Yes," Lucifer nodded. "The apple. Damien is the son of Eve and I."

Samantha shook her head. "That's ... that's just not ... possible."

Lucifer returned to the bench near him and sat down, slumping back against the hard blue plastic. "That's why I have come to Earth. To search for him. To stop him, as it were, before he makes a terrible mistake. Sins of the father relived in the son. Not my son. Not this sin."

Father Thomas Otten awoke with a start, not knowing where he was.

"Easy, Father," a kind female voice said to him as she placed a hand on his chest.

Otten looked to the woman, realizing he knew her, remembering he was among the transients somewhere in western Massachusetts. His mind swirled. He couldn't remember her name, or why he was here ... or much of anything. "Did I pass out?" he asked the woman.

"You did," she replied. "Twice last night, as a matter of fact. What do you suffer from?"

"I have ... blackouts," Otten admitted. "They have been happening with a greater frequency of late. I ... aaaaarrggghh!" The priest screamed in agony as an unimaginable pain seized his brain.

The woman tried to comfort him, but the crazed priest knocked her away. For nearly a minute he screamed, attracting the attention of all the transients in this small community.

Then, as quickly as it started, it stopped, and Otten found himself on his feet. Breathing hard, sweat dripping off of him, he had gained an understanding. He looked at the people around him. "I need to get to Regent Castle."

Without questioning why, he knew in his heart that God had called him to that location. With a certainty so powerful Otten believed it had to be a direct message from God, Father Thomas Otten knew that he would find God at Regent Castle.

Lucifer looked to Austin, Kelly, and Samantha. "My son, Damien. Have any of you, by any chance, seen him? I have been told he is in these parts."

The three of them shook their heads.

Nodding, Lucifer rose from the bench. "The seat of power in this region is here," he explained, referring to Regent Castle. "He is attracted to power. Before long, he will make his way here."

Austin threw his hand up, simulating a wave good-bye. "Yeah, well, good luck with that. Well see you when we see you."

Lucifer made no move to leave. "He sometimes goes by other names. Have you, by any chance, run into a man named Russ Clefion? He is rather fond of anagrams, as embarrassing as that may be."

"Russ Clefion?" Samantha asked.

"A rearrangement of Lucifer's Son," the devil explained. "Perhaps he has taken the name Stan Oafson? Del Kidiv? Brad Seavest?"

"Brad Seavest?" Austin asked.

"Eve's Bastard," Lucifer answered, frowning. "Damien and his mother do not get along."

"Haven't heard of any of them," Austin answered, shaking his head. "Well, we're gonna just get going now-"

Lucifer folded his arms across his chest, when inspiration came to him. "Trick Name Son," he said, nodding. "It's his screen name," Lucifer explained though Austin hadn't wanted one. "At least the one he uses in online poker games, which is where he's been spending most of his time lately."

Austin shook his head. "Haven't heard of him. Try New Amsterdam," he said, glad this was about over. "That's where all the superheroes are hanging out, I've heard. Trick Name Son sounds like a superhero name, doesn't it?" he asked, looking around for support.

He didn't receive any. Samantha looked at him as if he'd sprouted a second head and Kelly didn't look at him at all. At first, he thought it was because of her shame over kissing Satan, but then he saw her lips moving, realized she was trying to spell something out.

She had it. Gasping, "Oh, God," Kelly took a step and placed her right hand on Lucifer's left arm. "I've met your son."

Lucifer smiled warmly, bringing his left hand up to touch Kelly's right arm. "You have?"

"You have?" Austin repeated. "You've met a guy named Trick Name Son and you haven't told me about him?" he asked, hating the way the slightest touch of Kelly's hand on Lucifer's arm had stirred up all those old feelings of jealousy.

"Not Trick Name Son," Kelly replied, looking to Samantha. "But we have met Michael Scranton."

"There's no 'k' in Michael," Austin protested, wondering who Michael Scranton was and whether Kelly had made out with him, too. *Stop it*, he scolded himself, knowing he couldn't.

"But there is in Mike," Kelly answered. "Mike Scranton." She looked back to Lucifer, hating how good it felt to simply touch this man. "And we know where he is."

Not thirty miles to the south, Michael Scranton and Frederic Kornell rode their horses in the shadow of the orc army. The orc army was traveling along the highway route, leaving the two horsemen to the woods from which the highways had been cut. Kornell felt lost and tired, feelings made worse by the intense pain that wracked his body. He was still a long way from being fully healed and the pursuit of the orc army, languid as it was, still caused him to be bounced on the back of his horse, Alfred.

Scranton's face showed a deep concern. Kornell was still trying to figure out exactly what Mike meant when he referred to "reinforcements" he would call when the time was right. What reinforcements? The orcs, led by Frederic's father, General Kornell, had just slaughtered the astronauts they had been sharing time with at Hollis Memorial.

"What we saw should not have happened," Scranton said, as if reading Kornell's unasked questions. "The world has been reorganized by the angels. But there is no room for orcs in that world, not orcs that would do murder like that."

Kornell asked, "How do you know that?"

"What have you seen in the New World, Frederic? Or rather, what haven't you seen?"

Frederic nodded. He'd noticed the lack the other day. "Kids," he said. "I haven't seen anyone younger than, I dunno, fourteen or fifteen, I'd guess."

"True, but I was not thinking of the children at this time," Scranton answered, maneuvering his horse around a fallen tree. "I was thinking of the, for lack of a better term, bad guys. Not all childhood dreams were of pirates and astronauts. Some children dreamt of wickedness – of being wicked people doing wicked deeds. They have been absent from the New World."

Kornell shook his head. "I disagree. There was the abduction of Kelly during the First Night Feast. And the man who attacked us on I-95. And that swamp and clay creature. That's three instances right there."

Scranton shook his head. "On the third, you may have a point, but in the other instances the guilty party are normal people. Normal people sometimes commit wicked deeds, but they are not, in and of themselves, evil. What we witnessed with the slaughter of the astronauts was evil."

The New World astronaut did not reveal to Frederic his role in the creation of the muck-and-clay monster that was formerly Jim Catlin.

They rode in silence for several minutes, losing the army for a time as the woods grew thick. "Evil," Scranton explained, "was not supposed to play a part in the New World. Someone has changed the rules before they were meant to be changed."

Kornell studied his companion. Kelly had wanted Frederic to stay close to him, to try and learn what his game was, but after a day's ride the ranger believed he was even more confused about Scranton's intentions than he was before.

Chapter Twenty
A Cold Morning Sweat

Summer turned to autumn.

In all parts of New England there were those up with the break of the morn who noted that the warm days were now gone for the year and the slow descent to first snow was upon them. The leaves had already begun to change, of course, but now the weather had made the turn, as well. Winter, most of those awake at this early hour would agree, was going to be long and cold and white.

In Kent Harbor, Maine, Carl Yesek stood on a balcony of Black Castle, looking out over a small village and sipping a cup of coffee. Sheila, his ex-wife and Lady of this castle, was furious with him for bringing the pirates of the *Puritan* to her door. Carl had tried telling her that it was random luck, but she didn't believe it. She believed he had done this to get back at her for the end of their marriage, and for blaming her for the death of their only child. As punishment, she had placed him under house arrest. Glancing behind him, Carl smiled at the large, four-poster bed.

Some punishment.

He wasn't so foolish as to believe he was in the free and clear, but at least he was off the *Puritan* and away from the life of a pirate. Too much hassle, too much work, too little reward. He cared nothing for gold or adventure; a comfortable bed and warm coffee was all it took to keep him happy. It was the height of irony, Carl believed, that while Hector had acted out of malice, in the end the young, Old World mechanic and done him a very large favor.

Behind him his door opened, and Carl turned to see Sheila, dressed in a very sharp black business suit that nonetheless made her hips look too wide. Not her best look, Carl thought, but he was in a good mood this morning and decided she looked plenty attractive enough for an overweight forty-something with a very mean disposition who also happened to be his ex-wife.

"Good morning, Carl," she said pleasantly. "Did you sleep well?"

"I did," he replied. "Thank you."

"You're welcome," she said, snapping her fingers. From the open doorway a stream of five villagers (dressed as if they were straight out of seventeenth century colonial America) entered and moved directly to Carl.

"Sheila? What's going on?" Carl asked as the villagers began to measure his arms, leg, chest and in-seam.

"Your measurements were perfect, ma'am," a bookish young woman reported.

"Of course they were," she replied, then turned to the door to see a nervous man, fifty-ish with tousled grey-black hair, enter the room, holding a large rectangular box. He walked to Sheila and held the box out for her inspection. "May I present to you my finest work?"

Sheila ripped the top of the box off, tossing it to the floor. Carl, shielded from viewing the box's contents by Sheila's back, began to feel like this was going to be bad for him. "Sheila, what is this about?" His ex-wife turned to him, holding aloft a very long, very luxurious coat. Vibrantly red, offset with white trim and gold buttons, Carl thought it monstrous in its extravagance. "What is it?" he winced.

Smiling, Sheila Watson said, "It's a captain's coat."

"For what?"

"For the captain of my naval vessel," she replied, deadly serious.

"Naval vessel?" Carl asked, confused. "I thought the pirates stole your ship."

"They stole a ship," Sheila answered, a cold edge coming to light in her voice. "I have three. Why do you think I was so willing to let them steal from me?"

"But ... I only saw one."

Sheila's grin widened; Carl half-expected her to start rubbing her hands together and cackle. "The King has given three ships to every castle up the coast as part of his Royal Navy program. We don't even have crew enough for one ship here, so the other two are kept in a secure port down in Portsmouth, at the old naval shipyards." She tossed the heavy coat to her ex-husband. "Assemble a crew, drive to Portsmouth, captain the ship ... and get my galleon back."

In Boston, Austin McNamara stood out behind the New England Aquarium, on the side opposite from Regent Castle, looking out at the Atlantic Ocean. Inhaling deeply, letting the salt air penetrate deep into his lungs, he wondered how Mary Mathers' quest to find a replacement ship was coming along.

He really wanted a doughnut. *When,* he wondered, *is the world going to get back to enough normalcy that there's stores selling fresh doughnuts and hot coffee every morning?*

"Morning, Austin," the world's most beautiful voice said from behind him.

"Morning, babe," Austin replied, turning to see Kelly coming towards him. Her hair was tousled and her eyes red; she looked terrible, but then, all three of them looked terrible this morning. Lucifer had made Austin, Kelly, and Samantha sleep in the Aquarium overnight. They'd managed to find some netting in one of the storage rooms and made three hammocks, which they'd hung up in one of the display rooms upstairs. Austin had awoken in the middle of the night and looked around at the eerie tanks, filled with fish from all over the world, and had the curious sensation that he was sleeping on the bottom of the ocean. It was eerie, but not unpleasant.

"I feel like crap," Kelly said, moving to stand next to Austin by the metal railing. Like Austin, she kept her eyes glued to the ocean.

"Yeah," Austin agreed. "Those hammocks weren't the most comfortable, were they?"

"That's not what I meant."

"Oh." Pause. The morning was deathly silent, an ominous sound in a city no matter the time of day. Austin wondered how Brad was doing and figured the intense silence was likely not a good sign for the King.

Kelly waited for Austin to say something, but, as usual, it was she who had to confront what they were thinking. Austin, unfortunately, came from a family that believed problems did not actually exist if they were not discussed. "About last night ..."

Inhaling deeply, Austin closed his eyes, remembering the sight of Kelly kissing Satan. He exhaled, wondering why the image didn't hurt like it should. "Listen, Kelly ... if you say it meant nothing ... if you say you don't know what came over you ..." Austin closed his eyes tight and shook his head. "If you say that ... I ... well," he opened his eyes, saw the hurt in hers and almost broke down.

"Austin, I'm so sorry," Kelly said. "I feel terrible. It's just ... I don't know. I mean, he's Satan, right. The devil. But when I looked into his eyes ..." She felt a dangerous thrill run through her, thinking of Lucifer's sparkling gold eyes.

"I can't be mad at you," Austin said, surprising her as his gaze returned to the ocean. "I ... I went through the same thing, felt the same feelings as you."

That surprised Kelly. "You did?" she asked, confused.

"There's something about being around them," Austin continued, unaware of Kelly's confusion. "Maybe it's because we've heard stories of them are whole life, or maybe it's something more. Maybe it's ..." Austin shook his head. "I don't know." He scratched the back of his head as he turned to face Kelly. Looking at her the only thing he really wanted to do was take her in his arms and not let go. But he didn't. Didn't feel he had that right this morning. *Time to get honest*, he thought. "Few days ago, I went through what you went through last night."

Kelly blinked. "You made out with Lucifer?"

"What? No. No."

"Then what do you mean? Who's the 'them' you're referring to?"

"I ... God, why is this so hard?" he asked himself, gripping the rail tightly.

"Just say it."

"Easy for you," he said flippantly, "since I saw you do it."

Kelly took a step backwards, getting what he meant. "You mean, you ... you cheated on me?"

Austin hung his head, confirming Kelly's question without giving voice to the answer.

"Who ... who was it?"

"Aphrodite."

"Afro-who?"

"You heard me. Aphrodite. Goddess of love and all that." Austin hated himself. "I don't know what happened. It's just ... you're around them and they look at you and it's like ... I don't know.

"You feel warm," Kelly said, hugging herself. "You feel special and you know it's them that makes you feel special so you run towards it."

"Like a moth to a flame," Austin frowned. "All those ancient tales I've read and I never really believed that hearing a woman's voice could make you run your ship aground. But now, now I believe it."

Kelly took two steps towards Austin and placed a hand on his arm. "What do we do? Where do we go from here?"

Austin looked down and saw his leather pirate boots. Just seeing them made him feel twice as foolish. *Damned costumes*, he cursed inwardly. *That's all we're doing. Acting. Pretending. I'm no more a pirate than-*

"Austin?" Kelly asked again, her hand rubbing up his arm.

"I love you, Kelly," he said, nearly blurting the words, "but ... even if they're gods ... we kissed other people. That has to be bad, doesn't it?"

Kelly nodded. "It must be."

He turned to her, placing his hands in hers. "I don't want to lose you, Kelly, but it just doesn't feel right to simply push past what we've done."

Squeezing his hands tightly, she stepped into him, leaning her head down so that her forehead rested on his chin. "Austin, I-"

The voice of Lucifer interrupted them. "Austin, Kelly, you are needed inside."

"We're a bit busy," Austin said, eyeing Lucifer angrily.

Lucifer's eyes flared angrily, but he caught his anger before it erupted. He realized that the struggles Austin and Kelly were living through at this moment were, in a very real way, his fault. "Very well," he said reluctantly. "But come inside at the earliest convenience. There is something you need to see."

Unlike Lucifer, Austin saw no need to check his anger. "The only thing I need to see is in my arms."

Lucifer held the human's gaze, feeling his back tighten at Austin's insolence. "Humans," he said disgustedly. "God's greatest creation. The intelligence of angels and the passion of Olympians, yet you still cannot differentiate between want and need. Kelly is all you *want* to see, but she is not all you *need* to see." Lucifer turned away in disgust, a voice in his head wondering if, just perhaps, his anger wasn't fueled over an envy of whom it was that was holding Kelly Reed. "When you are ready, come to the roof and look to the south. Pieces are in play."

Just as Lucifer's hand reached to pull open the door, a large, darting shadow passed over him. Drawing his hand back, he looked to the sky and felt an intense dread rise within him. Somewhere in the city behind him a thunderous crashing noise broke the silence of the morning.

"What was that?" Kelly asked, gripping Austin tighter as her own eyes turned skyward. "That shadow? What was that shadow? Because it sure as hell looked to me like it was a big wooden ship."

Lucifer pointed above them, back out over the water. "Pieces," he said flatly.

Kelly and Austin turned to look out over the ocean, and it took a moment for their brains to process the images their eyes captured. "My God," Austin said breathlessly, looking out at the surface of the water where four human giants (two male, two female) strode towards the shore. One of the giants held a clipper ship above his head, ready to hurl it into the heart of the city. In the center of the four giants, a large, Tyrannosaurus-Rex-like creature walked with them. One of the giants tugged the dinosaur along by a large chain that connected to a collar around the great beast's neck. "Are those ...? Is that ...?"

"They are," Lucifer confirmed, a deep sense of dread enveloping him. "The Titans once again walk the Earth." Somberly, he stated, "I do not need to tell you that this is a very bad development, but mark my words well. Before this day is out you will come to realize that the creature that walks with them represents a far, far greater threat. That the Titans are loosed bodes ill for humanity, but that creature ... that creature is humanity."

Austin thought he detected a trace of fear in Lucifer's words. "What do you mean?"

Lucifer shook his head. "What is it that differentiates humanity from angels and Olympians?"

"This isn't the time for twenty fucking questions," Austin snapped.

"Souls," Lucifer explained. "For angels and Olympians, the body and soul are one, but for humanity God chose to prioritize the soul over the body. Bodies have finite existences for humanity, souls do not."

"What does this have to do with that Godzilla-slash-*Jurassic Park* reject?" Austin asked.

"That creature has a human soul," Lucifer educated them. "That creature has undergone the same transformation as yourselves."

Kelly was beginning to understand Lucifer's point. "You mean he was changed into that during the Reorganization?"

Lucifer nodded, coming to stand by them at the rail, his eyes locked on the giant beings that were far enough towards shore than they were practically waist-deep in the ocean water. "*She* was changed into that creature," he corrected. "Which means an angel is blatantly disregarding God's Word."

"How do you know that?" Austin asked, thinking of the possible forgery that Berathon had explained to him.

"I know that," Lucifer said, "because I helped God write the New World Order. And that creature," he seethed, "has no place in the New World."

"So his presence means what?" Kelly asked, feeling as if she were fighting a losing battle with understanding. Why was Lucifer assisting God with anything?

"It means that someone has let loose the Nightmares," Lucifer explained. "God help us all." In his mind, Lucifer knew who was responsible – his son, Damien.

Or, as he was known to the humans, Michael Scranton.

On the outskirts of Boston, Frederic Kornell (dressed as a middle-ages ranger) and Michael Scranton (in an astronaut's orange jumpsuit) shadowed the orc army. The orcs had marched quickly and, surprisingly for their massive size, efficiently. They were seemingly tireless, marching all night without rest. Frederic had been more interested in the changing attitude of Scranton, moving from supremely confident at Hollis Memorial, to confused at the train station massacre, to determined in the here and now. There was obviously something unrevealed about him; Frederic could not shake the feeling that he was nothing more than Scranton's sidekick at this point.

For another hour they followed the column of marching orcs, making their way into the heart of the city, then down towards the pier district. "Look at that," Frederic said, pointing to a large wooden ship, mostly smashed apart and lying in the middle of a city street. "How did a ship get here?"

Scranton frowned. "Things are moving too quickly," he mumbled as he looked skyward to see where the Titan had hurled the ship into the building.

"What is it?" Frederic asked, seeing the deep frown settle onto Scranton's face.

Scranton tore his eyes away and changed the subject back to the orcs. "Their goal appears to be Regent Castle." He pointed to the towering stone building, simultaneously majestic and out of place.

"Do you think they're working for the King?" Frederic asked, desiring to go back and search the land-wrecked ship.

Scranton shook his head. "I doubt even the King has the ability to call the orcs forth. Look, the leader leaves his troops." At the front of the column a modern military tank that held the leader of the orcs, General Kornell – Frederic's father – took a turn to the right while the column marched straight. Frederic and Scranton stopped their horses as the hatch atop the tank opened and General Kornell emerged.

The General addressed his troops. "To the Aquarium," he ordered. "The building is as open as your mothers' legs. Take all the fresh fish you can eat. We fight in the morning!"

Scranton watched the column walk in its entirety past the General, then turned to Frederic. "We must part ways here, Frederic. Follow your father," he ordered. "This is your opportunity."

"Opportunity for what?"

Scranton gave a half-smile and the old, mischievous look came to his face. "To kill your father. To balance the scales for what he did to your mother."

On the deck of their new ship, officially rechristened as the *Puritan*, Mary Mathers looked around at her crew with pride. They'd suffered heavy casualties in the fight at Black Castle – of the ninety or so pirates that had gone into the Black Castle, twenty-three hadn't made it out the other side. Of the rest of the nearly seventy men, roughly half of them had suffered some form of injury. Most of the wounds were cuts from the castle's guards, but there were also broken bones, cracked ribs, a few missing eyes, and one case in need of an amputation. Despite all of this, however, the crew of the *Puritan* took to their new ship. Bigger than the clipper, the Spanish galleon was a massive craft. Too big for a pirate ship, Mathers realized, the galleon was more like a floating military base of operations than an attack vessel in its own right. There would be no sneaking up on anyone in this craft. What it lacked in speed and maneuverability, however, it more than made up for in raw power. Mathers envisioned the *Puritan* as an ancient aircraft carrier, as the main ship in what she hoped would become a fleet of pirate ships, all sailing under her command.

"Captain, here is the information you requested."

Mathers nodded her thanks to Hector, taking the yellow, legal notepad from him. Her eyes glanced over his official casualty numbers that dominated the first two pages and flipped to the third page, where the statistics on the ship were held. "Seventy cannons?" Mathers asked, impressed.

"Spread out over three decks," Hector responded with a smile. "No one will be able to outgun us."

Mathers agreed with Hector, but frowned. "We are incredibly understaffed."

"We are. Even barring the casualties from the Black Castle we would have been short of men. Just by counting up the beds in the sleeping quarters we could use up to two hundred additional men, maybe more." Hector looked around, proud that the men were working... But it was all too evident that there were simply not enough of them to adequately do the work that the ship required. "Captain, I hate to bring this up, but ..."

"This is not the best ship for us," Mathers finished. "Galleons, from what little I remember, were mostly naval ships, used to transport large cargo and treasure. They were most typically a target of pirates and not pirate ships themselves. Once we have defeated the *Cottonmather*, we can find a sleeker vessel, but for now," she grinned beautifully under her long-flowing blonde hair, "I'll take raw power over maneuverability. The *Cottonmather* thinks us finished, so that alone will serve as our cover."

A voice from the crow's nest of the ship called down to Mathers. "Captain! Captain! There's ... something in the water!" the pirate called, panic threatening to overcome him.

Mathers and Hector rushed forward to the bow of the ship, their eyes looking off the starboard bow, in the direction the pirate in the crow's nest was pointing. Mary's hands had reached to the binoculars around her neck, but when she reached the ship's railing she realized the binoculars weren't going to be needed. "My God," she said, fear rising within her. "That can't be real."

On her right, Hector felt his jaw drop and his stomach tighten.

Across the calm waters of the Atlantic Ocean, sitting in the docks of a small New Hampshire village, ten ghost ships rocked gently in the water. Massive and a pale, ghostly white, the ships, all East Indiamans, seemed to fade in and out of existence before them. Mathers hoped that was just an illusion of the early morning fog that rolled in off the land.

"What are they?" Hector asked. "Are they pirate ships? Ghost ships?"

"They look like both," Mary answered, "but ... those don't look like pirate flags they're flying." Reaching for her binoculars, Mary focused the glasses on the red flags that flapped lazily in the inconsistent breeze. Her heart froze.

"What is it?" Hector asked, seeing her body tense. "What flag do they fly?"

Mathers lowered the binoculars. "Those aren't pirates ships, Hector. They're naval vessels."

"The King's ships?"

"Not unless King Regent is a demon."

"What?"

"Take a look," Mathers ordered, handing Hector her binoculars.

Hector took the glasses and focused in on the black design that sat in the middle of the red flags. "Pentagrams?"

"Now look to the decks."

Hector lowered his gaze. "Christ," he mumbled, his eyes locking on the red-skinned figures that walked the decks of the ghostly ships. "Are those really demons?"

"What else could they be?" Mather asked rhetorically. "Just what the hell is going on here?"

"Do you want us to stop and ask?"

Mathers was adamant. "What I want is to get past here as fast as we can." Turning back, the Captain noticed that many of her crew had come to the side of the ship to view the nightmarish scene. "What do you think you're doing?" she berated them. "Full sail ahead!"

"And God help us," she mumbled to no one but herself.

In Boston, Juramel stood in the office of Brad Regent, looking out through the glass wall to gleefully take in the sight of the Titans and giant dinosaur heading for the coast. At his feet, Raphael and Brad Regent knelt, taking in the sight with revulsion and horror. Their hands were chained behind their backs and Wallace O'Malley stood at their side, watching them intently, his head wound seemingly forgotten despite the copious amount of drying, sticky blood that ran down the left side of his body.

"Madness," Raphael accused. "This is madness. Who is responsible for this, Juramel? Who has freed the Titans?"

Juramel grinned. "I did."

"So it was you who are behind all of this?"

"No, brother. I am but a cog in the greater machine."

"Why?"

"Why do you think? God abandoned us. We must rise up and take control of our own destiny. What right does God have to create life, then selectively remove it from the world? It is unnatural."

An unexpected voice answered Juramel. "Well said, angel. The Nightmares have just as much of a right to a place in this world as the Dreamers."

Juramel turned to welcome the man behind the treachery, Michael Scranton. "Damien, welcome to Regent Castle." The angel beamed with pride. "The King has been captured," he said, motioning to Brad's bound body.

"As has Raphael," Scranton remarked, coming to stand before the angel. "The heart of our opposition amongst the Host. Well done, Juramel. But tell me, what of the Host as a whole? Have our actions been revealed to them?"

Juramel smiled. "After I stormed from Heaven yesterday, making clear my intent to interfere with humanity, Ocilael, as predicted, called a meeting of the Host. Gabriel was only too willing to take the Host into closed quarters. There is much confusion in our ranks."

Raphael wheezed, "You will never-"

Scranton silenced the angel by kicking him violently in the stomach. He reached down to grab the angel by his hair and jerked his body back into a kneeling position, then turned back to Juramel. "What of the mysteries? Do they know who killed Enimon?"

Juramel shook his head. "They have no idea it was you who orchestrated his death by using a Nightmare Fire Angel. And now, with the death of the astronauts from the other bus, there is no witness to the Nightmare's actions."

Scranton frowned, eyeing Juramel suspiciously. "Then you were behind the freeing of the orcs and the order to assassinate the angels in the train station?"

Juramel beamed proudly. "It was I, Damien. I did what you have always said; I took the initiative. I noted how you tried to trick the redheaded Princess into killing the coma-ridden astronaut and knew they would all have to die."

The son of Satan's eyes narrowed. "Tell me, Juramel. What is our goal?"

"To claim Heaven. To break the barrier between Heaven and Hell and let each soul choose his own eternity."

"What is our Earthly goal?"

"To free the Nightmares," Juramel answered enthusiastically. "To make the world a place for all to inhabit. To return the

Olympians to the Earth and free them of God's banishment. To give the Nightmares the same equal right to walk the Earth as the Dreamers."

"So if our goal is to give everyone the right to walk the Earth," Scranton asked slowly, "why do you think I would approve of the slaughter of twenty innocents?"

Surprise came to Juramel's face. "I … I don't understand. You're angered by their deaths?"

"I am angered," Scranton seethed, "that my orders to send them to Florida were disobeyed."

On the floor, Brad and Raphael watched in awed horror as Scranton's entire body seemed to ripple in waves. It was as if his flesh were a body of water and someone had dropped a stone in his center. Instead of slowing, however, the waves increased in speed and intensity. "Avert your eyes," Raphael whispered to Brad. "You do not want to view what is happening."

"Bite me," Brad shot back. He found himself fascinated by the almost hypnotic transformation that was taking place. The waves began to jump and fall unpredictably. They began to bubble right off his flesh, causing the astronaut's jumpsuit to literally melt off of Scranton's body. The skin melted away next, dripping to the floor in large, gooey chunks, like sauce and cheese falling off of a pizza. "That's sick," Brad grunted, watching blood and flesh fall off until it was gone, replaced by a muscular, middle-aged man with bright red skin, no hair, small horns, and a lashing tail.

"Damien, please," Juramel begged, taking a step back. "I was only doing what I thought was right."

In a flash, Damien lashed out at Juramel, knocking the angel back against the glass window with a thundering backhand. "You ordered the deaths of my pawns!" Damien roared, stepping over the angel. "You let loose the Titans a day early! You took Regent Castle ahead of schedule! You put my entire operation at risk for your own selfish needs! Tell me, Juramel," he said, reaching down to grab the angel's short, wavy hair, "why I should trust you now that you have disobeyed me?"

"I …"

"Tell me!" Damien roared, slamming his other fist into Juramel's face, shattering the angel's nose.

"Because there's no one else who will have me," Juramel whined. "I have turned my back on the Host, on God, to serve you. Without you, I am nothing but a wanderer!"

Tugging hard on Juramel's hair, Damien jerked the angel backwards, letting him fall pitifully onto his back. "At least you know your place, Juramel," Damien laughed. "Your place in New Heaven will be prominent indeed. But still," he declared, "you have disobeyed me and need to be punished. To your feet."

Juramel weakly rose to his feet. "What would you have of me, Damien?"

"Do you see the two Titans on our left?" Damien asked, pointing to the ocean. Juramel turned and nodded. "Oceanus and Tethys. Water gods. Take my order to them. I want this city flooded. Do you understand, Juramel?"

"I do, Damien."

With movements almost too quick to follow, Damien reached in and grabbed Juramel's sword, unsheathed it, and sliced it hard down Juramel's back. The angel screamed in pain as both of his wings fell to the ground.

"Let me revise your orders." Damien grabbed Juramel by the back of the neck and shoved him forward, pressing the angel against the glass. "Take the King and Raphael to the dungeons. By the time your wings grow back let us both hope that your insolence is cured. Just because I want to open Earth, Heaven, and Hell to all does not mean I believe in complete freedom."

Off to the side, Wallace O'Malley had watched the events of the past few minutes with acute intensity. This Damien fellow was apparently the man behind the scenes, the one Juramel was taking orders from. After what he'd just seen, O'Malley could see why. The cop held his ground as the son of Satan turned his silvery eyes on him.

"You are O'Malley?" Damien asked.

"I am," O'Malley grunted.

"You have served me well," Damien said, coming to stand before him. The devil's son offered his hand and O'Malley shook it. "As I have promised through my agent Juramel, you will be given control of New England. You have always lusted for power, even as a young child. That dream is now fulfilled, by the grace of the devil's only son. Congratulations, O'Malley, you are now King."

O'Malley nodded, smiling roughly down at a grimacing Brad Regent. "Thank you, Damien."

"Get your guardsmen prepared," Damien ordered. "The Nightmare's gate has been opened. After the Titans thrash this city, your men will be placed in charge of the next wave of attack."

"I understand, sir," O'Malley nodded, "but who will the Nightmares fight against? With the kingdom under our control, is there any need to fight a battle it appears we have already won?"

Damien was not to be deterred. "We have won the throne," he explained, "but we have not yet won the populace. There are always those who will rise up to resist their rulers. We will fortify the city, then let the Nightmares loose on the rest of the kingdom. We do it not to win battles or win wars. As you noted, we have already won."

"Then why do we do it?" O'Malley asked, feeling slightly light-headed from the loss of blood.

Damien smiled, placing a hand on the new King's shoulder. "Why do criminals commit crimes?"

"Because they think they can get away with something," O'Malley answered.

Damien shook his head. "They do it because it is who they are. We will let the Nightmares look to do what they dreamt of doing. It is the arrogance of God that I rebel against – the idea that peace on Earth can be achieved artificially, by removing the bad seeds and letting the good grow wild over the Earth. It is a false assumption; create a world with nothing but good people and good people will turn bad. Likewise, create a world with nothing but the wicked and some of the wicked will turn pure. God created this paradise of dreams made real called the New World, yet he locked away those whose dreams did not fit into His plans. We free them. We are the side that lets us be who we are." Damien removed his hand from O'Malley's shoulder. "Any questions?"

"None."

"Then get it done," Damien replied. "And send your most trusted man to Hollis Memorial Hospital. Bring me Enimon's harp." And then, as an after-thought, "And kill anyone on sight you find. Even," he smiled, "if they happen to be in a coma."

"Contrary to popular belief," Lucifer explained, "God and I have a good, professional relationship. Which is not to say we are friendly, of course. Merely that, as the leaders of Heaven and Hell we have come to something of an understanding over the years." The devil stood with Austin, Kelly, and Samantha on the roof of the Aquarium, watching as the Titans and giant dinosaur stopped walking forward, apparently waiting for some sign indicating when to continue their march towards the city. "I have long since lost my desire to rule Heaven," Lucifer explained.

"And God has forgiven you for that?" Samantha asked, finding the fallen angel's story hard to swallow.

"God forgives all of His creations, so long as they seek forgiveness with a pure heart."

"And you did that?" Samantha pressed him. "Had a pure heart?"

"For what I did? Yes," Lucifer answered somberly. "I am not a good being," he informed them. "From the moment of my creation I had urges and desires my fellow angels did not. I desired ... what is the Earth saying ... wine, women, and song. I was attracted to the darkness in life. I was restless, bored. While the other angels spent their days in quiet contemplation or debating philosophy, I was less interested in why we were here as I was in what we could do. I accused God of creating the angels as a slave labor force. I raged against him for keeping from us that which he had so willingly given the Olympians."

"So you tried to claim Heaven for your own?" Samantha challenged.

Lucifer nodded. "I did, and for that I was cast into Tartarus to spend eternity with the disgraced Titans. God changed his mind, however, as He was wont to do in those days, and freed me from Tartarus and placed me in charge of Hell. Christians have the concept of the afterlife wrong," he explained. "They have framed Heaven as a reward and Hell as punishment, but that is not always the case. Mortal life is a test, but to see Heaven as the ultimate reward is more propaganda. Judgment day is more akin to ... to ..." Lucifer searched for an example they would understand. "Have you read the Harry Potter books?" he asked.

Austin and Samantha nodded, while Kelly rolled her eyes. Austin had been trying to get her to read those books for years, but she couldn't get past the first chapter of the first book. She found it mindless.

"Being placed in Heaven or Hell is much like the Sorting Hat Ceremony, only with a stricter judge."

It was Austin's turn to challenge Lucifer. "You have got to be kidding."

"Not an exact match," Lucifer backpedaled, "but close. Mortal life is more about deciding where you would most enjoy spending eternity."

"So there's no punishment in the afterlife?" Austin asked.

"Oh, there is punishment," Lucifer clarified. "Christianity has always been a hierarchical organization. Hell is no different. Dante had it mostly right, you know. Nine levels, each succeeding level containing more and more vile beings, but the upper levels aren't so bad. Humans simply have taken the concept of Heaven and Hell, reward and punishment, too far. Not everyone is 'condemned' to Hell. Some are, but some are there because they are more comfortable there than they would be in Heaven. Think of it this way," he tried again. "Where would you rather vacation, in Vatican City or Las Vegas? In the course of your life, how do you view vacation time? As a chance to relax and pray, or an opportunity to consume alcohol and chase sexual partners? For most of humanity, this is the choice you are asked on Judgment Day. You are given the right to choose where you desire to spend eternity. Some are not, but they are the minority."

Austin raised his hands, stopping Lucifer. "Enough," he implored the devil. "Let's get back to the issue of God's Word," he demanded, thinking of his conversation with Berathon. "You co-authored the document that issued the New World Order?"

"I was in consultation with God on that letter, yes," Lucifer admitted.

"So you know where He is?"

Lucifer shook his head. "He spoke to me as he communicated with mortals in the old days, through spiritual contact."

Austin rolled his eyes. "What's that mean? You had a vision?"

"No. He spoke to me as He spoke to Moses and Noah."

"You do know He's considered lost, correct?"

Lucifer nodded somberly. "He walks the Earth in a mortal guise, hidden in plain sight. Not even He realizes who He is. He must do this, you understand, or else the knowledge He gains would be tainted. That is why He sent His son to live as a mortal; it was the only way for Jesus to truly understand humanity."

"So is Michael – Damien," Kelly corrected herself, "a mortal?"

"No."

"Why not?"

"Because I am not God," Lucifer smiled. "Because I cannot create life with the snap of my fingers. My ways of impregnation are much more … physical."

Samantha wrinkled her nose as a foul stench drifted across her path. "Ew, what is that smell?" she asked. "Gross."

Concern came to Lucifer's face. "That is an unnatural odor."

Each of the four moved to a different side of the rooftop to peer over the edge. Fate chose Kelly to have the side that contained the answer. "Guys, over here," she called, looking down at the marching column of orc. "We have company."

"Come on, you two, keep it moving."

Brad and Raphael exchanged a glance as Juramel shoved them in the back, herding them forward. Brad sensed a trap; a wounded Juramel was the only guard with them and he was clearly distracted by the oozing wounds on his back. Either that, he reasoned, or Damien had so little concern over what they did that he didn't really care if they escaped.

"Juramel," Raphael pleaded, "this is madness."

"Shut it," Brad snapped. "He's not buying what you're selling, angel."

"We must try," Raphael urged Brad. "I must return to Heaven and warn the Host."

"They will know soon enough," Juramel promised. "Once Gabriel lets them out of conference, they will see it for themselves."

"I must know," Raphael said, stopping his walk. "How deep does the conspiracy go? How many in the Host are sided with Damien?"

"Almost half," Juramel grunted, leaning against the wall for balance as a wave of nausea passed through him. "And more will join once they- urgh!"

Brad and Raphael watched the angel's hands snap to his neck. He was being choked by a small wire, but by whom they couldn't tell until Juramel's body convulsed to the side and they saw a lithe ninja strapped to his back. The ninja leapt back, releasing her grip, and Juramel's body lurched forward. Reaching to her side, the ninja pulled two sai from her belt. With shuddering accuracy, the ninja drove both sai into the exposed, bony stumps that once held his wings.

Juramel screamed in pain and his body fell to the floor. Flailing helplessly, the angel tried to reach back and pry the weapons from his back but was unable.

"You boys gonna stare all day or do you wanna get out of here?" the ninja asked, stepping on Juramel's back to pin the angel to the cement floor.

Brad and Raphael tore their gaze away from Juramel to witness the ninja remove her mask, revealing an athletic young woman with cropped blonde hair. "Name's Liv," she said casually. "Hell of a party you're throwing, King," she remarked to Brad. "Where's Austin?"

Brad didn't bother asking how she knew him. "He escaped."

Liv nodded. "Good. Now, you boys ready to get lost?"

"Absolutely," Brad nodded.

Frederic followed his father back to a luxury hotel. In the distance he could make out five giant beings walking towards the shore, but his mind was so enraptured by being this close to his mother's murderer that they didn't even register. The General moved to the front desk of the hotel to talk with a member of the King's guard. Frederic watched as he received a room card and headed to the elevators.

The moment of truth, Frederic realized. *Do I follow or stay?*

He followed, moving quickly around a fern display to enter the elevator bank just as his father entered an open door. Without thinking, Frederic leaped into the elevator just before the doors slid shut. A cold sweat soaked his skin as he realized he was alone in an elevator with his father, a man he hadn't seen in years, a man he swore would pay for murdering his mother. Drawing forth every last reserve of courage he could muster, Frederic turned to face his father.

And came face-to-face with a handgun.

"Hello, son," the General sneered at the taller ranger. "Damien told me you'd be coming. I didn't think you had the balls, but the New World is just chock full of surprises, ain't it?"

Chapter Twenty-One
Blood

Father Thomas Otten pulled the bright red 2002 Corvette he'd taken from the western part of the state before Regent Castle in Boston. The transients that had nursed him back to health had given the car to him. Though Otten knew the car was not theirs to give, he took it nonetheless. He needed to get to Boston, to Regent Castle. A few days (weeks? Months? Otten could no longer tell the passage of time for some reason) ago, one of his blackouts had caused him to drive off the road. The blackouts, with him all of his life, had become a more frequent affliction in the New World, but they had mercifully let him alone in the drive to the castle.

Stepping out of the car, Otten felt a deep shudder run through him, visibly shaking his entire body and causing him to lean on the low roof of the car for support. God, he believed, had sent him a message. That message had told him to come to Regent Castle.

Otten believed he had been sent that message for one reason.

Somewhere inside these stone-walls, God was present, and He wanted Otten to find him.

The muzzle of General Kornell's gun pressed into the temple of his son, Frederic Kornell. Frederic felt a cold sweat envelop him and despite his athletic, muscular New World body, being in the presence of his father made him feel like the shy, awkward teenager he'd been the last time he saw the man who had murdered his mother.

"I'll say this," the General sneered, "you sure don't look like my boy." The General leaned in, making a show of sniffing loudly.

"Smell like him, though. Just like pussy." The General laughed at his own joke and stepped back, sliding his gun back into his holster at the side of his camouflaged uniform. "Hit button 21, boy. I'm staying in a penthouse suite."

Feeling small and meek, Frederic leaned over and pushed the desired button.

"Yeah," the General grinned as the elevator began to ascend, "Damien – you knew him as Michael Scranton – told me you were coming. Didn't believe it. So at least you've grown one of your balls. I supposed I should give you credit for that. So tell me, son, just what the hell are you doing here?"

Frederic's heart was beating wildly, wondering exactly the same thing. *I'm here to kill you*, he wanted to say, but didn't for two reasons. One, he didn't know if it was true, and two, he doubted he could get his sword out faster than his dad could get the handgun.

So instead, he said nothing, which is exactly what his father figured he'd say.

Berathon stood before an assemblage of Olympians in their Elysian Field sanctuary somewhere deep in Purgatory. Mollug the parrot sat on his shoulder. He had journeyed here days ago to learn the means by which Aphrodite had escaped the netherworld prison in which God had locked the Olympians centuries previous. The truth of that escape troubled him greatly; it was Damien, the son of Lucifer, who had freed Aphrodite, apparently in a bid to win the beauty's heart.

"Is this all?" he asked, disappointed in the small number of gods that stood before him. "Seven of you? Seven?"

"It is," Poseidon replied, sensing the angel's disappointment. "Demeter, Artemis, Hephaestus, Ares, Athena, and Hera. A proud collection of gods."

"Y'all look like yesterday's lunch," Mollug squawked.

Berathon shot a glance to the bird on his shoulder but he couldn't disagree with Mollug's assessment. The Olympians assembled here before him were a rather pathetic lot. Hera looked worse than a beggar woman living off the streets. Artemis, the proud twin of Apollo, had wild, unkempt hair and glanced around nervously. Her eyes darted everywhere and nowhere, seeing everything and nothing, unable to focus on any object for more than a moment. Hephaestus had grown fat and lazy. Demeter stared blankly at the grass, mumbling, "Why won't the pretty flowers grow?" Ares looked like a hermit. It appeared to Berathon as if the Olympian hadn't cut his hair since the Olympians were condemned to Purgatory, his black mane flowing down below his waist where it seemed to merge with his scraggly beard.

Only Poseidon and Athena looked close to their former selves. Poseidon had clearly assumed the mantle of leadership among the gods; his eyes were bright and muscles sharp, and the trident he had used to attack Berathon still sharp and shiny. Athena, for her part, was ever-vigilant, alert and at the ready. Her white tunic and pastel sashes looked worn but not dirty and when she spoke it was the voice of a god that Berathon heard.

"The rest have succumbed to in-fighting," Athena explained in an accusatory tone, "or fallen to despair and madness. We have been the victim of our own kind. Hermes runs wild through the swirling fog, coming around only to kidnap one of our kind and deliver them deep into limbo. Apollo lies slaughtered before you, a victim of Hermes, who tore through these fields with a sword born of Hephaestus' forge extended outward, cutting the sun god down where he stood."

Athena strode forward to stand in Berathon's face. "Whatever your game, angel, we are not interested. You are not the first, nor likely the last of your kind to come offering temptation. We rejected Damien. We rejected Azrael. We reject you."

"Azrael was here?" Berathon asked. "When?"

"Just after Damien made his offer to Aphrodite," Athena replied. "Azrael came to collect her and shepherd her to the outside world."

"Azrael works with Damien?"

Athena shook her head. "It is my feeling, angel, that Azrael works only for himself. Now go, leave us to our damnation. We would not whore ourselves for Damien, nor humiliate ourselves for Azrael's amusement. Whatever it is you want, we are not interested."

"Athena," Berathon bowed, "I came here only seeking answers. Answers that you have provided. I ask nothing of you, but instead offer my services. Is there anything I can do for you?"

Athena looked to Poseidon, then around to her fellow gods.

Poseidon made the request. "We want to go home. To Olympus. Can you offer us freedom, Berathon?"

Berathon thought for a moment, then nodded. "I cannot guarantee God will not force you back. Nor can I guarantee that my fellow angels will not come to Olympus to do the same, but I will show you the way out."

"To do so is to risk being cast out of Heaven," Athena reminded him.

A sad expression made its way to the angel's face. "Athena, I fear that Heaven is a place I no longer wish to reside. Now, come, gather your fellow gods and walk with me to your freedom."

"So … what do we do?" Kelly Reed asked from atop the New England Aquarium. She stood on the roof of the building with Austin McNamara, Samantha Dixon, and Lucifer. Austin was her boyfriend (at least, she thought he was still her boyfriend), but yesterday, in front of him, she had kissed Lucifer. Satan. She'd kissed Satan. She still couldn't get her head around why she'd done it other than it was simply intoxicating to just be around him. When he looked at you … she shuddered, pushing the image of those sparkling golden eyes out of her head.

"Nothing we can do," Austin replied, looking down as the last of the orc column marched into the building. "I've checked for an easy way down off the roof but there's nothing. If we took a running start we might be able to jump into the ocean, but I'm not sure how deep it is there." Pause. "I'm also not sure if we can all make it. So unless you want to fight your way through fifty or so orcs, or hope they're friendly and will let us waltz out of here, I'd say we're stuck."

He pointed to the ocean, where four giants – original Titans, according to Lucifer – had paused their march in from the sea and waited. In the middle, a large dinosaur-like creature roared impatiently. The beast – Austin had taken to calling him G-Rex, a combination of Godzilla and Tyrannosaurs Rex – was kept in check by a large leash connected to a large collar around its neck and held fast by one of the female Titans. "Might as well enjoy the show," he said dourly, "and hope they don't come after us."

Samantha ran a hand through her long red hair, sighing angrily and looking to Lucifer. "Can't you do something?" she asked. "You *are* the devil."

Deep in meditation, Lucifer had barely heard Samantha's words. Somberly, he answered, "As I have told you several times, I have no great power. I am an ex-angel. My wings," he turned to show them the two blackened small stumps that protruded from his upper back, "have been taken from me, the very marrow of my bones burned so that they may never regrow."

"Well this just beats all," Samantha said, her hands flashing to her hips in what she hoped was proper Southern belle irritation. "We're stuck with Satan and he can't do anything. If I offered you my soul could you get us off this roof?"

Lucifer's face flashed anger at Samantha. "Stupid human," he scoffed. "Do not mock the traffic of souls."

"Why not?" she asked. "After what you told us earlier, Hell doesn't seem like such a bad place."

"For those who choose to spend eternity there, it is not," the devil answered. "But for those who foolishly consign themselves to an eternity within its gates for milliseconds of mortal joy, it is a place most dreadful."

"Cut it out you two," Kelly ordered, stepping to move between them. She looked to Lucifer, feeling the primal pull towards him she hated. "Do you have any suggestions?"

Lucifer turned away, feeling a primal pull of his own every time he looked at Kelly. "You could jump."

"I don't think that's viable," Kelly snapped. "We must be a hundred feet off the ground, at least."

"You could jump," Lucifer repeated, "and I could catch you."

"No deal," Austin interjected.

Lucifer shrugged, "The decision is yours. I could leave at any moment."

"Then why don't you?" Samantha asked, looking to Kelly. "Oh, wait, I think I can guess."

Lucifer clenched his fists tightly. "You'd better pray Heaven is your destiny, Ms. Dixon. I stay because you and Kelly can bring me to my son. Nothing more."

Samantha looked to Austin. "Do you believe that?"

"Shut it, Samantha," Austin answered.

"We cannot wait," Lucifer snapped. "My son's plans are in motion. We must find him and stop him before he can see his plans to their end."

"We don't even know what his plans are," Kelly replied, hating that Lucifer was the most sensible one on of the roof.

"All the more reason we need to find him quickly," Lucifer replied grimly. "If you will not jump, then we must fight."

"Fifty orcs against four of us?" Austin asked. "Somehow I don't like our chances."

Lucifer glared at the New World pirate. "I may not be God's equal, Mr. McNamara, but I am willing to be the equal of fifty orcs. I have fended off more would-be conspirators to my throne than days you have lived. Follow me," he said, extending his hands outward and calling two flaming scimitars out of the void and into his hands. "But not too closely. I will need room to work."

General Kornell opened the door to his penthouse suite and ushered Frederic inside. As his son passed him, the General took a moment to eye the young man's strong frame. "Ironic, isn't it?" the General asked. "That all your life you hated me for wanting you to be more of a man and yet when you are remade by the New World, you have turned into exactly the man I wanted."

"This is the dream of a ten year old," Frederic snapped. "When I was ten I didn't realize a son could want to be anything but what his father wanted."

The General laughed, shutting the door behind him and moving into the interior of the luxurious suite. "My, my, look at this place." He waved his arms around, taking it all in. "This living room is bigger than our old apartment, never mind the two bedrooms down that hall. Yes, sir, your father is living the high life."

"So you're working for Scranton?"

The General shrugged. "Guess I am. Says he's the son of Satan, if you can believe it. All I know is he pays well. I gotta tell you, though, I've never actually met him. All of my orders come from my direct superior, the angel Juramel."

"What's your mission?"

"National security."

Frederic blinked, annoyed at the breakdown in logic. "National security? For the son of Satan? Which nation, Hell?"

General Kornell shook his head, sitting his middle-aged body down on an overstuffed couch. "For this nation. The United States. God, or the angels, have taken our land from us. I aim to help us get it back. I've been in touch with several of the 142 Presidents and they're gearing up to take the nation back. All of the little kingdoms that have sprouted up thanks to the Reorganization will need to be reclaimed. We're talking more than just New England. The former state of New York has been transformed into New Amsterdam; it's where all of the superheroes are hanging out. Actually," his mood lightened, "you could provide a valuable service in that area. You were into all that fag superhero stuff. It seems the entire state has been transformed into a series of interconnected cities that resemble Metropolis, Gotham, Marvel Manhattan, and places I've never heard of." The General eyed his son carefully, the luster fading from the idea. He doubted Frederic would help his old man, no matter what the benefit.

The ranger felt tired, having been pulled in too many directions the past few days. His ribs still ached, and the ordeal of the all-night march following the orcs was taking a toll on his body. What he wanted more than anything was sleep. Knowing that wasn't possible at the moment, he slumped onto a large sofa cattycornered with the sofa his father sat upon. "So the entire nation has been transformed?"

"The entire world," the General replied, "if our intel can be believed. I still don't trust the angels that are working with us, but they haven't lied to us, yet." Pause. "As far as we can tell, at least."

"So there are angels working with you against God?"

General Kornell nodded. "Some of them. They're not happy with God's order."

"And the son of Satan?"

"The money man, I think. He's got the finances to pull this operation off so he gets to call the shots. He's got big plans," the General grinned. "Huge. It'll make D-Day look like a picnic."

"Care to share them?"

"Ha," his father laughed. "Good one. Needless to say, it's big. Like I was saying, the whole country has been reorganized into separate kingdoms. Florida is a swamp. The Carolinas, Virgina, and southern Pennsylvania are busy re-fighting the Civil War. The Southwest is the Wild West. And on and on." General Kornell shook his head. "These lands need to be reclaimed. Armies are massing all over the country. Tobias, my angelic superior, informs me that Damien has a secret army in hiding, but I'll worry about them once I start needing to. I've got my orc army. That's who I'll worry about."

"Country before family," Frederic said sadly.

"Sacrifice makes you strong," the senior Kornell said unapologetically. "Look at you. A ranger. I've received reports you saved a young woman's life." The General looked Frederic in a way Frederic had never seen before. "I'm proud of you, son."

Emotions erupted inside of the ranger and he had to choke down tears. He raged at himself: *Why does it mean so much what this bastard thinks?*

Hating it didn't change the fact that it did matter. Surprisingly to Frederic, it seemed to matter a great deal.

"Is the ship ready?" Damien asked Wallace O'Malley, the new King of New England.

"It will be ready by the time we reach the docks," O'Malley assured Damien as the two men stood in the center courtyard of Regent Castle. The courtyard was roughly the size of a baseball infield, cluttered with trees, hedges, and statues of Brad Regent. O'Malley planned to have them replaced as soon as this business with Damien/Scranton was complete. In each corner of the courtyard, a guardsman stood at the ready. "My men have worked all night readying the ship for battle."

"Battle?" Damien asked, waving the thought away. "We will not see battle."

"Doesn't hurt to be safe in case you do," O'Malley countered.

"I have nothing to fear from attacks angelic or human," Damien boasted.

"Maybe, maybe not," O'Malley argued, narrowing his eyes, "but that ship will be crewed by the men of my Navy. I don't intend to see them sacrificed unnecessarily."

"A wise King," Damien said without feeling. "I trust you have enough of those men guarding the cargo?"

"Only the one I trust most," O'Malley answered, moving to one of the statues of Regent. In this statue, Brad stood on a platform, and was posed in a business suit. He stood straight with arms outstretched and his head pointed towards Heaven. In his left hand he held a globe four times the size of his head; in his right a thunderbolt.

"Hideous," Damien commented.

"Not much of an art critic," O'Malley replied, "but then, neither was Bradford. What the former King was, I learned, was paranoid." O'Malley climbed onto the platform, gripping Brad's arms for support. To Damien's momentary confusion, O'Malley pressed his finger against Brad's left eye, then his right, then both buttons of his suit coat.

O'Malley jumped down as the large globe cracked and swung open, from right to left. In the interior of the globe was a lock box and two large, clear bottles. One bottle contained a thick red liquid and the other a liquid as equally clear as the bottle. The new King reached in and took all three in his hands, then turned to offer them to Damien. Damien took the box and opened it, revealing a hundred thin, white wafers. "The body of Christ," Damien said with a smile. "They have been blessed by a priest?"

"Of course," O'Malley nodded.

"There are not many priests left," Damien said skeptically.

O'Malley shook his head, hating the words he was forced to say. "We'd been looking since yesterday without luck," he admitted, "and then, just this morning, a priest pulled up in front of Regent Castle in a bright red Corvette."

Damien eyed the ex-cop carefully. He did not believe Wallace O'Malley was a man to jest, yet such a coincidence seemed unlikely.

"I know, I know," O'Malley admitted. "If I hadn't seen it, I wouldn't have believed it, either. My guards, knowing we were looking for a priest, brought him into the small chapel on the western side of the castle. I told him – his name is Father Thomas Otten, and, it gets better, he was a priest in the Old World as well as the New - we were looking for a priest to perform mass. I brought my guards in and after he'd consecrated the water, the wine, and the Eucharist, we arrested him and placed him in the dungeons."

"Well done, King," Damien nodded, then turned to the large glass bottles. "The blood and water?" he asked.

"They are."

"Excellent," Damien enthused, feeling a surge of power tingle his flesh. "Take them to my ship. I sail at once, for Nantucket Island."

"Sir," O'Malley said, proceeding cautiously. All his years as a beat cop had honed his ability to spot weaknesses in the plans of superior officers.

"What is it?" Damien asked. "You have my permission to speak freely."

Wallace resisted the urge to tell Damien to go fuck himself, and said, as politely as he could, "I do not understand why you want to retreat to Nantucket. It is a small, pitiful island. Difficult to defend. One of those Titans standing offshore could destroy the island by itself. Better to move inland for safety."

Damien laughed. "Safety? I do not go to Nantucket for safety. I go there, with those three sacred objects you have procured for me, because that is where the Gate resides."

"The Gate?" O'Malley asked, hating to be out of the loop.

"The Nightmare Gate," Damien smiled broadly. "Nantucket became one of a hundred Nexus points between all of God's worlds during the Reorganization. It is where Juramel loosed the orcs and Titans from. Like a fool, Juramel risked detection by opening the Gate. Now, it no longer matters. Unfortunately," Damien frowned, "I cannot open any of the Gates without Holy Water and the body and blood of Christ because I am only a half angel. A half ex-angel at that."

"Why not have Juramel open the Gate?"

"Because as you will learn, King O'Malley," Damien sneered, "an effective ruler does not leave his most important deeds to underlings. Now, ride with me to my ship. Tomorrow, I open the Gates and flood the Earth with Nightmares."

"Kelly!" Austin whispered harshly. "Get back here!"

"She listens well," Samantha replied through a smile.

Austin ignored her, watching Kelly move ahead of them with great concern. They had followed Lucifer back down into the Aquarium, a move that made all of them feel uneasy. While neither Austin nor Samantha trusted Lucifer, Austin was particularly bothered by the idea of following him on a path that led down. Didn't matter that the Aquarium was mostly above ground to Austin at all; the simple move from sunlight down into a darkened interior creeped him out.

Kelly was uneasy because she thought they simply should've trusted him and leapt off the side of the building, letting him catch them. Austin believed she ran ahead of them now simply to protest Austin and Sam's refusal to jump, but he was wrong.

Ahead of him, Kelly just had to see Lucifer in action. She realized it was wrong, that the feelings that were threatening to envelop her were unnatural, but she could not control herself. It was akin, she felt, to her relationship with alcohol. She rarely drank, but when she did she found it hard to stop. The warmth and buzz the alcohol generated in her was too enjoyable to be denied.

And what she wanted now was to see Lucifer in action against these orcs.

The upper levels of the Aquarium were free of orc, but as she descended to the floor beneath, an acrid smell washed over her. Moving quickly and recklessly, Kelly entered a section of the building that contained a jellyfish exhibit. The sight stopped her cold. Four orcs lay dead on the floor, their throats slashed and oozing a thick black liquid. It looked like oil, but she knew it to be blood.

Nearly vomiting from the stench, Kelly rushed forward just as she heard Austin and Samantha come up behind her. She ignored Austin's pleas to stop and ran down a short tunnel that opened up into a larger room. Tanks again lined the walls, containing fish from around the world. Many of the tanks had been smashed open and from the half-eaten fish that lay scattered about the floor, she guessed the orcs had come here to dine.

Those facts barely registered with her as ahead she heard the sounds of orcs screaming. *I'm coming*, her heart cried as she rushed through corridors containing more dead bodies to come to a long, descending walkway. The walkway was lit from above by a dark light, causing all white objects to glow eerily. Halfway down the walkway, Lucifer danced.

There was no other way to put it.

Both of his flaming scimitars flashed and swirled around him in a dizzying display. Each orc he met lasted no longer than ten seconds as the blades sliced the fat creatures open at the belly and throat. Between her and him, another dozen dead orcs already lay on the ground, but her eyes were locked onto his graceful form.

She thought him invincible, but then in the shifting rhythms of his movements, she saw that his body was glowing the same eerie white as her white sneakers always used to glow.

Lucifer was bleeding nearly everywhere, the silvery blood glowing under the lights. *He needs help*, Kelly's mind screamed.

"Kelly!" Austin screamed, grabbing her by the arm. "You've got to- oh my God." Austin's eyes went wide with equal parts awe and revulsion as the sight on the walkway overtook him.

"He needs help!" Kelly yelled at him, pulling her arm free.

"How are you going to help?" Austin asked. "You've got no weapons."

Kelly wanted to punch him. Instead, her brain processed that the dead orcs at her feet held large, spiked clubs. She bent down to pick one up and nearly wrenched her shoulder out of its socket as she pulled the heavy metallic weapon off the cement floor.

"Oh for crying out loud," Austin mumbled. "Remember when I promised you I'd do anything for you?" he asked her. "Well, I never thought 'anything' would mean helping Satan kill a bunch of orcs." Austin pulled out two guns that he'd stolen in Maine from inside pockets. "I just want you to know that."

Kelly smiled. "I love you, babe."

"Yeah, well, *mmmffff!*" She had interrupted him with a kiss. While Austin knew he should thrill at the moment, his paranoid heart wondered who she was thinking about when she pressed against him. Pulling off him, she whispered, "I love you, Austin. *You.* I just want you to know that."

He said nothing as he moved past her down the walkway and raised his gun. The devil on his shoulder wondered why he didn't just bury one of these bullets in Satan's back, but then remembered Lucifer could hear what he was thinking and ran away to hide himself deep in Austin's subconscious.

Mary Mathers stood at the back of the *Puritan*, staring North, waiting for the demon ships to come sailing onto the horizon after them. Night had fallen and a cool sea breeze wafted over the decks of their new galleon. That the ghost ships hadn't come didn't ease her worry. That they had let the *Puritan* sail by without so much as a glance didn't ease her concern.

"Captain," Hector said, coming up to stand beside her. "I don't mean to sound like a broken record, but you need to see this."

"What is it?" Mathers asked.

"We've got Boston Harbor within sight," he informed.

"Then why aren't we dropping anchor?" Mathers snapped angrily. "You know the plan, Hector," she reminded him. "Drop anchor once the Harbor is in sight and send a crew ashore to make contact with Austin."

Hector shook his head. "Plans change."

Mathers back stiffened. Was Hector challenging her Captaincy? "Why aren't we stopping?" she asked icily.

Hector shook his head, a look of disbelief on his face. "The crew is afraid to stop."

"Because of the demon fleet?" she asked.

Hector had given up trying to get her forward with his voice. Grabbing her by the arm, he dragged her to the bow of the boat and pointed straight ahead. "No one wants to be caught with the anchor down with those things out there, waiting for us. In fact, we're thinking of turning this boat around and getting the hell out of here. I suggest," he said, leaning in close to whisper in her ear, "that you take this idea to heart before you have a mutiny on your hands."

Mathers said nothing, her voice caught in her throat as her eyes tried to focus on the sight of four giants and one very large dinosaur standing near the shore of Regent Castle.

Hector removed his hand from her arm and stood back. In a voice loud enough for the crew gathered around them to hear, he asked, "What are your orders, Captain? Do we drop anchor, or do we head out to sea?"

Rage caught hold of Mathers' brain. Angrily she spun on her crew. "We drop anchor. We send a crew ashore and make contact with Austin. Anyone has a problem with that, they can take it up with me right here, right now."

The crew of the *Puritan* mumbled, none wanting to be the first to challenge their captain, but none too happy about her plans. One of the crew dropped their head behind another's shoulder and yelled, "To hell with Austin!"

All it took was one voice of dissent for courage to grow in others and soon Mathers had thirty angry pirates challenging her orders.

"I thought we were going after the *Cottonmather*!"

"Giants? I didn't sign up for giants!"

"She's lost her mind! She means to kill us all!"

"Enough!" Mathers yelled, firing a pistol in the air to silence them. "You crew a Spanish galleon now," she reminded them. "Let those giants come at us. We have enough firepower to send them all back to Hell!"

"Actually," a voice called from the back, "you don't." The crew parted as Aphrodite made her way casually forward. "Those are Titans, Captain Mathers. The original Olympians. I don't know what that beast is with them, but I would not take it lightly."

"I take nothing lightly," Mathers answered, her gaze matching the Olympian's, "but we promised Austin we would connect with him. He has as much right to seek revenge on the *Cottonmather* as the rest of us! Besides, we don't even know where the *Cottonmather* is."

"Actually, we do," Aphrodite smiled. "May I introduce you to the former captain of the *Cottonmather*, Captain Lazarus."

The crew backed away in fright as the ghostly image of Captain Lazarus shimmered into existence at the goddess's side. "Greetings, all," Lazarus grinned, looking very much the stereotype of a pirate's captain. "I can bring you to the *Cottonmather*, Captain Mathers. It is why I have joined you. I want revenge on that ship as well."

"Then where is it?" Mathers asked, feeling her control on this ship coming loose.

"Right now she's moored on Nantucket. Just down the coast and around the bend, as it were."

Mathers was trapped and she knew it. She hated abandoning Austin like this, but she wasn't about to lose her ship. "Why should we trust you?" she asked the obvious question to buy herself time, half-hoping Lazarus would hang himself with the answer.

Lazarus' answer never came. As the crew turned to the ghost, a cannonball smashed onto the deck of the Puritan, exploding at the feet of a handful of pirates, killing them all instantly. "What the hell?" Hector asked, putting himself between the explosion and Captain Mathers.

Mary knocked him aside, rushing to the ship's stern. "Oh, hell."

Hector was on her hells. "Where did they come from?" he asked.

Behind them, the first ghost ship cut hard and swift through the ocean, glowing a deathly white in the night. The distance between the two vessels seemed impossible to traverse with a cannon. But that, Mathers realized, was only true for one of the ships. Again the ghost fired. Mathers and Hector could do nothing but watch it come hurtling over their heads and splash harmlessly into the water.

Mathers eyed Hector harshly, deciding to take her anger out on him. "Devils behind, giants in front, Hector. Your preference?"

Hector said nothing, his eyes locked onto the ghost ship that sailed in their wake. "I ... I ..."

"Exactly," Mathers groused. "Remember that if you ever conspire mutiny aboard my ship." She turned to find the crew awaiting her command. "Move this ship forward as fast as she'll sail," she commanded confidently. "Aim for the open seas beyond the rear of the Titans. Let's see if we can't get giants and demons fighting each other instead of us."

As the crew jumped into action, Mary caught the eyes of the goddess Aphrodite. The Olympian smiled, nodded slightly, and made her way to the bow to view her own personal nightmares, the Titans.

Mathers looked around for Lazarus, but the ghost (as ghosts were apparently wont to do) had vanished.

For the first time in his life, Austin was doing more than pretending to have a grand adventure. Dropping himself behind a large display advertising the COMING SOON sea turtle exhibit, Austin released the ammo cartridges from his handgun. He didn't even know what this kind of handgun was called, he realized as the spent cartridges clacked onto the floor. Putting the guns down for a moment he reached into his vest and pulled out the last two full cartridges he hand, hoping they'd be enough.

Slamming the ammo in place, Austin rose to his feet and spun around the corner of the display. Alone for a moment, he counted seven orcs left. All of them surrounded a fading Lucifer. The devil had killed most of the orcs they'd encountered, but Austin had done his part, killing a handful with his guns. It had been too easy on the walkway; the orcs were crowding towards Lucifer and had herded themselves into a tight, unmoving mass. Austin simply pointed and fired at the middle.

Now, however, they were in the open and the orcs roamed freely. Moving across the forty-foot gap between himself and Lucifer, stepping over and around several dead bodies, Austin leveled his gun at the orc the furthest distance from the devil. At twenty feet he stopped, took a deep breath, and fired a shot from each gun.

One bullet missed everything, slamming against a concrete wall and ricocheting off to the side. The second bullet tore into the orc's shoulder, causing the fat creature to roar in pain.

"Fall down, fall down, fall down," Austin prayed, but the orc wasn't willing. Turning to Austin, the orc roared a challenge, raised his giant pike and charged. Ten minutes ago, Austin would've froze in fear at the sight, but now …

Now, he realized, he felt nothing.

Drawing a bead on the center of the orc's body (a lesson learned from a friend who was a cop years ago; aim at the center, not at the head because you're more likely to hit something), Austin fired another shot from each gun. One bullet connected with the orc's belly; another tore through his right bicep. Still the orc came. Two more shots. One missed, the other shattered teeth.

Still the orc came forward.

Again, Austin squeezed his fingers. The first hit the orc in the throat, staggering him. The second sliced passed the orc's neck, tearing both flesh and artery. Blood spurted instantly and wildly from the neck of the orc and he dropped to the ground, his pike smashing against the floor. Austin watched the orc struggle to avoid death, feeling nothing.

No, he thought, shivering at the realization. It felt good. He had killed this orc and it felt good.

"What's wrong with me?" he whispered to himself.

There was no time for an answer. Another orc had peeled off from Lucifer's attack and made Austin his target. Without another thought, Austin raised the two handguns again and fired.

On the walkway far to his right, Kelly watched him and felt something break inside of her. Austin, one of the kindest people she had ever known, was killing without hesitation. This was the man who would see a spider on the wall and capture it in a cup so he could bring it outside. The guy who didn't even like to kill ants or

371

rats was now emptying bullet after bullet into living beings. Orcs or not, the sight unnerved her.

How could any of this, Kelly wondered, *have been God's plan?*

General Kornell snored loudly from the couch, his body sitting but slumped backwards. His head rested on the back of the couch, leaving his neck exposed.

For twenty minutes Frederic had watched his father sleep. For twenty minutes he realized he could make his childhood threat a reality. His hand rested on the hilt of his sword.

I'm not a killer, he argued inwardly.

Not even for mom? he argued against himself.

Back and forth the debate raged inside of him. His father deserved to die; the courts had sided with him, acquitting him of murdering his mother. It was bullshit and Frederic knew it. He was needed to run a mission for the government overseas and he believed with all his heart that the government had stepped in and gotten his father off.

It's not revenge. It's justice.

Isn't justice revenge?

Is it?

You tell me. But first take out that sword and cut this bastard's head off.

Frederic felt his hand move up, pulling the sword out.

It's time.

It's time.

"No," Frederic said aloud.

Pussy.

Mama's boy.

"I don't care," Frederic said, slamming his sword back down. "I'm not a killer."

Moving before he convinced himself to stay, Frederic ran to the door and left his father behind. When he hit the elevator bank, he vomited as he hit the down arrow.

But he did it with a clear conscience.

The elevator door opened and Frederic launched himself inside, wanting only to escape.

Chapter Twenty-Two
Convergence

Somewhere ... beyond the sea ... somewhere ... waiting for me ... my lover stands on golden sands and watches the ships that go sailing ...

The son of Satan stood on the deck of the *USS Constitution* feeling better than he had ever felt. All around him, the dulcet tones of Bobby Darin poured from the speakers he'd ordered installed on this old wooden war ship, bathing the crew of smallish demons as they crewed the vessel that would carry them to Nantucket Island. He chose to make his move in the skin of his birth – the pale crimson frame of his mixed demon/human parentage. His father's frame, like that of all angels and ex-angels, was perfectly sculpted flesh, muscle, and bone and filled in with a silvery bloodish substance to give them form. Damien's frame, in contrast, was a head too tall and a shade too thin, giving him an awkward rather than threatening appearance.

His body used to bother him, but now he saw it merely as the container that held his brain, a weapon far greater than any physical body.

Damien loved to frustrate the expectations of his father. Lucifer went hard for the hard stuff – Black Sabbath, Iron Maiden, Megadeth, Queens of the Stone Age – but Damien found it all so ... emotionally infantile. Lucifer's plans never came off, his own emotions getting the better of him time and again. Damien, by contrast, had found his musical niche with the Rat Pack Movement: cool, efficient, emotional but thoughtful, playful until you pushed them. Let his father have Dio, Damien would fill his days with Sinatra and Dean, Sammy and Darin, Nat King Cole and Tom Jones.

Better for morale, as well, Damien mused, looking around at the sons and daughters of angels who had been cast out of Heaven and lived their eternal lives under the rock and too close to the constant flame. The heat and fire of Hell had burned their wings when they'd sprouted at puberty and turned their skin an ashen crimson. They had all been so easy to turn; all Damien had to offer was a way out of the caverns and into the light. His father, he'd realized long ago, could have done this at any moment. Whatever faults Damien placed in his father, stupidity was not one of them. Why, the younger child had wondered, had Lucifer stayed below, consigned to a darkness kept at bay solely by the eternal fire?

He claimed it was a lack of power to stand up to God and that much, at the least, was true, but Damien thought there was more with a fervor that defined his teenage years.

There was, indeed, more.

Eve. The first woman, the first wife, the first mother, the first whore.

Damien's mother.

When Lucifer had laid the truth before his son, Damien knew somehow that it was Eve that kept Hell at bay.

On that day the plan that was now playing out across the Earth had been hatched. Damien glanced to the box that one of the female demons held not more than ten feet from him. Inside that box was water and wine and bread, all blessed by a priest. They were the key to opening the gates that held the Nightmares at bay. The world was filled with Dreamers and the Nightmares had been locked away from sight.

Would God never learn?

He gave the world free will and demanded obedience. He created the Olympians, the angels, and the humans and waited for their "flaws" to reveal themselves in order to lock them away.

Damien would undo all of that. He would smash all the walls and let all God's children free. The good, the evil, the moral, the corrupt, the righteous, the wretched … what Damien understood and God either did not or refused to acknowledge was that change was the true nature of the universe. Life was not static. Life changed.

And not in any controllable manner; sure, God could turn everyone into what they thought they wanted to be but that would not bring eternal happiness. It would only encourage the change that so frustrated the Father. In earlier days, God had responded to this frustration by flooding the Earth with water, killing most of the world, and starting over.

By nightfall Damien intended to flood the Earth with life, not death.

Glancing to the receding distance, Damien noted the four Titans standing in Boston Harbor. Two of them held a Godzilla-esque monster on a leash. A gift of his father's genetics allowed Damien to see not only the physical surface but the spiritual soul held within all bodies. The Titans had no differential souls, coming from a time when God had treated soul and body as one. The fairy-tale T-Rex dinosaur had a soul, however. The monstrous creature that waited impatiently for its chance at destruction was, just before the Reorganization, a fifty year old insurance salesman from Connecticut who, as a ten year old, had so hated the paralyzed left arm he had been born with that he'd fantasized endlessly about being able to turn into a monster and take his revenge on all the playground kids who'd teased him.

Why, Damien thought, should not this man have the same chance to fulfill his dream as anyone else?

"It is time," he said in a low voice, speaking to the Titans and T-Rex and though anyone on deck standing more than three feet away from Damien could not hear what he said, the giants across the waters heard him clear enough. Having stood waiting for hours, they began to move towards the city of Boston, determined to destroy all in their path.

Kelly Reed walked across the blood and guts-covered first floor of the New England Aquarium, stepping over dead and dying orcs. The odd orc would make a half-hearted lunge for her leg, which received a half-hearted (but effective enough) kick in the face in return.

Ahead of her Lucifer and Austin waited by the front door of the Aquarium. Both were bloodied and gasping for breath. Lucifer's crimson skin was covered with a slick mixture of his own black blood and the greenish blood that had exploded from the orcs that he'd hacked open. Austin, by contrast, had only a brief splattering of his own blood thanks to Lucifer's having cleared the way, but was winded to a far greater extent.

Behind Kelly, Samantha Dixon followed closely, too stunned to do anything but numbly follow along.

"Well fought," Lucifer said to Austin.

"Bite me," Austin shot back, bent over at the waist, his hands on his knees.

Lucifer said nothing in reply, and meekly turned to push open the door and walk outside.

"Maybe you could be a bit less of an ass," Kelly said as she approached, placing a gentle hand on Austin's back.

"You can bite me, too," Austin snapped, rising up quickly. "The whole world can bite me."

"Hey," Kelly said gently, moving to him to lightly take hold of his arm, "it's okay."

"Is it?" he asked without turning back, his eyes locked onto the back of Lucifer who walked to the edge of the pier.

Kelly rested her head on his wounded left arm, slipping her hand around his waist. "I don't know," she admitted. "You're scaring me."

Austin stiffened. "Really? I thought I was finally being the guy you always wanted."

"What are you talking about?"

"C'mon, Kel," he said, turning to her as she took her head off his shoulder to look at him. "Bradford, Lucifer … that's the kind of guy that you want. Not me."

"Austin…" Kelly started to disagree but the words failed in her throat. She held him tighter. "Truth is, I don't know what I want anymore. I've wanted you and no one but you for so long… but earlier, when Lucifer kissed me … and now, after watching you kill all those orcs … I've got doubts. I just don't know and I hate that feeling more than anything. I'd rather tell you straight out I don't want you than to stand here and say I don't know." She brought a hand up his back to caress the back of his sweaty, blood-stained head. "I'm sorry."

Nothing had ever felt better to Austin that her hand on his head. "Let's just get through this madness," he said, determined to choke all of his emotions down. "Then what will be, will be."

And without waiting for a reply he stepped away from her and walked outside towards Lucifer.

"What've we got?" he asked when he stood alongside Satan.

Lucifer answered through a frown, pointing out to the open waters.

"Fuck," Austin said, his mind taking a moment to wrap itself around what he was seeing.

The late morning sky was a brilliant blue speckled by magnificent white clouds, yet Austin couldn't imagine a setting more out of place for the scene that played out between him and the horizon. Four giants and a Japanese monster dinosaur were walking towards the city. Their bodies were roughly half-submerged by the water. One of the two female giants roared at a ship to her left and broke off from the rest of the giants. Austin flinched when he saw the Jolly Roger flying above the crow's nest – it was a pirate ship. Somehow he knew it was the new *Puritan*. "That's my ship," he said softly, pointing.

"And those are mine," Lucifer beamed, pointing in the other direction. "A marvelous sight, are they not?"

Austin turned to the opposite side of the scene before him to see three ghostly ships bearing down quickly on the male giant at the far end of the line. Without a warning, they opened fire, sending nearly a dozen large balls of fire hurtling towards the figure. A handful of them connected and the giant roared in anger, spinning towards the ghost ships. Parts of the his wild hair and loose-fitting rags flickered with the remnants of the cannonballs flame.

Lucifer watched the three ghost ships turn their sides towards the approaching giant, the better to hit him with their side cannons. Another volley erupted, slamming into the giant's face and chest. In a brone-crushing roar, the giant bellowed across the water, turning his head toward the shore. Austin and Lucifer watched as the giant's left eye-ball caught fire and exploded out of his head.

Austin let out a whoop of joy at the sight of the staggering giant.

"Fools!" Lucifer spat in disgust.

"What?"

"The three ships continue to batter the wounded giant instead of breaking off to attack the others. We've only minutes before the middle two giants and the nightmarish dinosaur reach land," Lucifer explained. "And if you hadn't noticed, the male giant on our left is headed straight for us." Lucifer gripped the railing before him hard enough to crush it in his hands. "And your ship runs away instead of fighting."

"They are humans," Austin replied defensively. "What fear do ghostly demons have of dying?"

Lucifer pursed his lips as his eyes drifted further down the coast. "A fate worse than death, Austin."

"What could be worse than death?"

"Eradication," Lucifer said somberly. "When the body dies, the soul moves on to the afterlife. But when the soul dies, the energies dissipate back into the Void where the next Chaos cloud forms, waiting God's Divine Spark to form a new universe, a new planet, a new species … whatever moves the Creator to create in that moment."

"Reincarnation?"

"Of energy only," Lucifer said somberly. "Your individualism dies."

"That ... that sucks," Austin said dumbfounded.

"It does," Lucifer nodded. "And God wishes it were not so, but there are rules even He must foll..."

Lucifer's voice dropped away as his eyes widened in horror. "Of course," he whispered. "Of course."

"What?" Austin asked, looking in Lucifer's direction, but not seeing anything.

"My son, Damien ... he sails to yonder island ... he means to break the gates."

Austin wanted to ask what that meant, but Kelly beat him to it. As she asked Lucifer what breaking the gates meant, Austin turned to see her and Samantha come to stand with them. Kelly's face was hardened; whatever emotions she was feeling at the moment were buried beneath the surface.

"Damien seeks to break one of the gates that separate this world from the others," Lucifer said anxiously. "If that happens all of God's worlds will suddenly have access to one another – Heaven, Hell, Earth, Olympus, Asgard, Purgatory ... in the name of the Father, Damien seeks to loose the Nightmares."

"Do we even have to ask?" Samantha asked, rolling her eyes. The sheer absurdity of the experience was keeping her wits intact as a defensive mechanism.

"The Nightmares," Lucifer explained. "You do find it odd that on this reorganized world there are neither children nor monsters, do you not?"

"Have you looked out at the ocean?" Samantha asked. "Do you not remember the angel getting killed? Or the orcs back in the Aquarium? Or-?"

"Individual instances," Lucifer said quickly as his mind raced through his options. "Surely you have noted how few people walk the earth. God's Word removed the Nightmares from this plane in order for the Dreamers to have room to realize their innermost wishes. Damien wants nothing less than to level existence." He turned away from the horizon to the three humans, "We must stop them. The fate of your world is in our hands."

A voice from behind them said sarcastically, "That's a bit dramatic, ain't it?"

The group turned to see the ex-King Bradford Regent, the angel Raphael, and a female ninja approach them. Brad and Raphael were in terrible shape. The ex-King was bruised and bloodied, his business suit tattered and soaked in blood. Raphael fared worse, his left wing tilted at an odd angel, obviously broken, and his alabaster flesh was scarred with a crucifix that had been burned into his skin.

The ninja appeared unharmed. "Hey Austin," she said, offering a crooked smile. "Found some friends of yours."

"Hey yourself, Liv," Austin half-smiled back.

"Lucifer, your son …" Raphael started, but stopped when the ex-angel raised his hand.

"I know, old friend," Lucifer assured him. "He must be stopped."

"The Host has been poisoned with his plan," Raphael admitted bitterly.

Lucifer nodded and motioned to Austin, Kelly, and Samantha. "We are going to stop Damien before he can break the gates. We welcome your help."

Brad stood silently, watching Kelly and Austin not look at each other. Part of him saw the opening and wanted to jump in, but he resisted. His feud with Austin felt silly now, as did the idea that Kelly was a prize to be won. He felt a deep shame at his earlier plan to "rescue" her from an attacker he had unleashed on her.

"I'll do whatever you need," Brad heard himself announce, his eyes moving to Satan. "Those fuckers stole my kingdom."

"Right," Austin said, his voice chillingly without emotion. "Let's do this." He turned to Lucifer, "What's the plan?"

And Lucifer, for the first time in a long time, felt the weight of the world on his shoulders.

Lost in contemplation, Frederic Kornell strolled into Regent Castle without realizing where he was. He wanted nothing but to crawl under his covers and sleep; or rather, to fantasize his problems away. Under the cover of covers he could rewrite reality however he needed to make himself feel better – if he'd been rejected by a girl, he would fantasize about a more attractive woman (or two or three …) throwing themselves at him. If he'd been bullied or beaten up by the schoolyard bullies, he'd fantasize about taking them all out in order to save the school. If his dad hit him, he'd fantasize about …

The New World ranger stopped in his tracks, feeling the weight of failure once again come crashing down on him.

When his dad hit him, his fantasies usually involved one outcome – his father's death.

Yet earlier, when he'd had the chance to end his father's life, he didn't take it. Why? Did that mean his fantasies were full of shit, too?

Confusion turned to anger and his consciousness spiraled upwards, bringing the world to life around him. In a moment he was aware he was standing inside Regent Castle with the King's guardsmen standing around him in metallic armor, swords and guns drawn.

"By the orders of King O'Malley, you are under arrest," one of the guardsmen announced, drawing the hammer back on his revolver.

They made their way across Boston Harbor in a small motorboat they'd stolen from the Aquarium, heading for Nantucket Island. Austin had the wheel and Lucifer stood beside him. Behind them, Raphael bled silvery blood onto the seat and floor from his broken wings.

"He's in it bad," Austin said to Lucifer over the roar of the engine, nodding to the angel.

Lucifer nodded, more concerned with the male Titan looming above them. "Oceanus," he murmured, pointing upwards. "The oldest of the Titans." They were within a hundred yards of the Titan, attempting to cut between Oceanus and the male Titan currently under attack by the demonic-crewed ghost ships.

Austin didn't need the history lesson. "Does that make her Tethys?" he asked, pointing to the female Titan on the other side of the dinosaur monster.

Lucifer nodded. "Sister and mate of Oceanus." Lucifer eyed her carefully. "She will reach the shore first."

"If we don't stop your son," Raphael added, "it will not matter. If he lets loose the Nightmares, the World is lost."

Lucifer turned, annoyed. "Don't be so fatalistic, Raphael." Then, as an aside to Austin, "Arc towards Oceanus."

"Why?"

"Please do it."

Austin bit his lip and followed Lucifer's order. A moment later a fireball splashed down into the water to his left. Austin grunted his thanks, hoping Kelly was having better luck.

"She'd better," Lucifer said, reminding Austin that Satan could read his thoughts, "because that dino-monster is already ashore."

"We should help them," Austin said, though he knew it was neither possible nor practical.

"We should stick to the plan," Lucifer countered. "We stop Damien, they stop the new King. We'll need control of the King's resources if Damien unleashes the Nightmares."

"Wait," Brad said, sticking his arm out to halt Kelly and Samantha's advancement. Ahead of them Liv held up her hand for them to stop. The four watched the dino-monster stomp between them. All felt numb to its passing – in the Old World such a sight would've been too much to comprehend; in the New World it was merely another happening.

They let the monster bash and roar for a half-minute, allowing it to put some distance between them. Liv motioned for them to come towards her and they dashed across the open street. Kelly still wasn't sure why they had to circle around the castle to approach from the back but Brad was so confident in his plan that she agreed through sheer force of his will.

"We'll head four blocks into the city and enter the castle through the underground tunnels," he'd announced. "I had them built as an escape route. Never thought I'd use them in reverse."

And then he grinned, she remembered as they crossed the street; not the phony grin he'd developed over time but the open, warm, mischievous grin that Kelly remembered from the day she fell in love with him. Confident, but not cocky. Open, not calculating.

"Stop it," she admonished herself.

"What's that, K?" Brad asked, stopping in his tracks to turn back to her. Samantha kept moving forward, joining Liv on the opposite side of the intersection.

"Nothing," she mumbled.

Brad nodded, starting to turn away when he caught himself. "You okay?" he asked gently.

"Of course," she snapped. "Let's get going."

Brad put up his hands, "Sorry. I just- what the hell?" The ex-King looked down to see a stream of water running over the blacktop. The water began to pick up speed and weight. The stream was now high enough to run over their shoes.

From the dry space ahead of them, Samantha yelled for them to hurry. "The city's flooding!"

Kelly looked back to her left, towards the docks, to see Tethys, the large female Titan, rising onto dry land. She called the ocean to her and directed it down the street that Kelly and Brad were caught on. Quickly the two tried to make it to Liv and Samantha, but the water came faster. It was now up to their knees and the force of it drove them to the right. Both of them knew they'd never make it to Liv and Samantha if they kept trying to go straight.

"We've got to move to the left!" Brad yelled over the rising roar, starting to walk up-stream.

Kelly reached out to grab the back of his shirt. "No!" she yelled. She'd been caught in suddenly raging rivers twice. The first time she'd panicked and lost all of her camera equipment. The second time she'd kept her cool and moved with the river. She grabbed Brad's shoulder. "Aim there!" she yelled, pointing to the next street to their right.

They locked arms together for support and carefully moved diagonally forward, moving more with the water than against it. By the time they'd reached their destination, water was beginning to slide down that street as well, but the sheer force of the water and the angle it moved kept it mostly behind them. Moving quickly they circled the block, reuniting with Samantha and Liv.

"Good call," Liv said, nodding to Kelly.

"Thanks," she said, breathing hard.

Aboard the *Puritan*, Captain Mathers wiped blood from her cheek as Hector reached down to help her up. Mary swiped Hector's hand aside, picking herself off the deck that was now slick with blood and seawater.

"You okay?" Hector asked.

"How many men have we lost?" Mary asked, ignoring Hector's question. Around them men struggled through their wounds, climbing over fallen bodies to fix the rigging and work the sails. Below them their crewmates worked the cannons. The thrill that had run through them when they realized the ghost ships were after the four giants and not them was wearing off as casualties mounted.

"About twenty dead, Captain," Hector answered.

"What happened to your hand?" Mary asked, noting the blood-stained wrap on her second-in-command's left hand.

"The last fireball that hit us, the one the giant swatted aside," Hector explained. "Tore through the port railing when I was standing next to it. Splinters tore through it."

"Look out!" one of the crew shouted as a female Titan reached forward towards the sails.

"I was wondering when she'd try that," Mary grumbled. Until now they'd been able to keep the giantess at bay by concentrating their fire at her mid-section. While their new galleon wasn't as swift as their previous ship, they were far enough out into the bay that the giantess was slowed down by most of her body being submerged. The Titan would get close, the *Puritan* would open fire, stunning her, then run away. Now the giantess was going to try and damage their sails, making the *Puritan* dead in the water.

As a shadow fell across the deck, the cannons roared to life beneath their feet, pelting the Titan with ten direct hits. Most exploded onto the Titan's chest and arms, causing the skin to puncture and the Titan to be stunned, but it was clear they were not making a lasting impression. Following almost immediately on the heels of the first wave, another wave of cannon fire blasted the Titan from the secondary cannon-deck. One of the cannonballs got lucky, slamming against the Titan's eye and exploding, rupturing her eyeball. The Titan screamed in pain, clutching both hands to her face.

"Get out of here!" Mathers yelled, guessing the victory was only temporary. An enraged Titan would be a hell of a lot more difficult for them to handle. "Head to deep water!"

The crew jumped to their captain's command, several of them wondering why this hadn't been their plan all along. Mathers could see it in their faces, yet despite this questioning, they had kept their mouths shut and followed her orders. The realization sent a wave of power and weight through her – the *Puritan* was undoubtedly hers, but a responsibility came with that power. Mary wasn't certain she was entirely ready for it, but she wouldn't have it any other way. All those years in the Old World where she was "just a pretty face" could stick it, she thought, a wide smile playing out across her face, and she realized she'd fight God himself if he tried to put things back the way they were.

In Heaven, Gabriel released the clouds that held the Host in private session. He'd revealed himself to his fellow brothers, telling them that he had assisted Damien in an attempt to allow all angels and their fallen demonic brothers to come together again. The Host had a mixed reaction. Ocilael wanted him arrested. Others wanted him saluted as a hero. As the clouds parted with the Host threatening to erupt in chaos, Gabriel realized he had failed. It was foolish, he now understood, to side with Damien, but-

"I am going to kill you, Gabriel."

Silence rolled through the Host as the deranged angel Azrael floated just above their heads, flaming sword in hand.

"Azrael, I didn't know Enimon would be killed. That was a mistake, I swear it!"

"Was it?" Azrael asked, screaming. "I loved him!"

"We all-"

"You've betrayed God, Gabriel," Azrael accused, pointing his sword at Gabriel.

"I stopped a demon revolt!" Gabriel protested.

"Did you?" Azrael asked. He swung his sword to the side, pointing towards Earth.

As one, the Host turned to see Damien exiting off the *Constitution* at Nantucket Island. Ahead of him, not fifty yards from shore, a set of large black doors stood ominously.

"The Gates?" Gabriel asked, stunned at their appearance. "But ..."

"But you thought Damien simply wanted to open the doors between Heaven and Hell?" Azrael asked, his voice rising in righteous anger. "That all he wanted was a chance for the demon spawn to come to the home they were denied simply by their birth to our fallen brothers? That for all of God's talk of penance and forgiveness He denied that to the residents of Hell?"

"Azrael, please ..."

"Damien's intent is to break the Gates that keep all of God's worlds at bay, Gabriel. He will let the Nightmares loose upon the world!" Azrael rose his sword high above his head. "And you allowed this to happen!"

"Azrae-uuurrkkkk!"

Gabriel's words were choked down as Azrael tossed his sword through his fellow angel's throat. Gabriel staggered backwards, silvery blood spurting from the wound. Desperately he tried to pull the sword out, but Azrael had driven it too deep.

At the last, Gabriel realized he would fail to save himself just as he had failed the world. Dropping his hands to his side he dropped to his knees. Mustering the last of his strength, he tried to choke out two last words, but it was not to be. The words died inside him and so he offered them only as a prayer.

"Forgive me ..."

Gabriel's eyes rolled back in his head and his body slumped to the ground, still and dead.

"Is that … is that Austin?" Hector asked, pointing across the waters to the powerboat that raced across the Harbor.

Mathers looked through an eyeglass and nodded. "It is," she said. "It appears he rides with Satan."

Hector snorted, but quickly saw that Mary wasn't laughing. "You're serious?"

"I am," she said. She pocketed the glass and looked to Hector. "What do you think it means?"

Hector shook his head. "No idea, Captain," he whistled. "No flipping idea."

"It means the Day of Reckoning is at hand."

Mathers and Hector turned to find Aphrodite standing in the midst of chaos, half-smiling at them. "Sorry," she grinned, "but I do love the dramatic. Day of Reckoning and all."

Mathers gritted her teeth and kicked away a severed arm that bled at her feet. "Tell us what's going on, Aphrodite." Mathers pulled her pistol and pointed it between the goddess' eyes. "Now."

"Or what?" the Olympian asked, her eyes sparkling.

Mathers fired, the bullet slamming into Aphrodite's skull and bouncing off to the left, clanging harmlessly across the deck. "Ow!" she yelled, rubbing her head. "That hurt!"

Mathers cocked the pistol a second time and Aphrodite threw up her hands, "All right. I was going to inform you anyway." The goddess regained her composure and moved to the deck. "Lucifer and the one you know as Austin are making their way to Nantucket, to attempt to stop Lucifer's son, Damien, from breaking the gates that hold the different worlds at bay. If he is successful, Captain, the Nightmares will be let loose upon the world."

Hector scratched his head, "Um …"

"It means the bad guys win," Mathers spat, staring at Aphrodite.

"So the question you have, Captain," the goddess replied, moving to stand in Mathers' face, looking slightly down at the human woman, "is whether you want to take your crew to the safety of open waters, or head to the island where your world ends."

Mathers could feel what was left of the crew stopping in the tracks to stare at her, waiting upon her answer. She knew what the majority wanted – these men weren't pirates, she reminded herself. They were schoolteachers and businessmen and pharmacists. What they wanted was to be back in their homes or apartments, with their wives or their porn, not trapped in some supernatural battle between the forces of good and evil.

Aphrodite grinned slightly, applying pressure.

Mary turned away from the goddess and her eyes found Austin's boat, zooming across the ocean. "That's a member of this crew out there," she said confidently. "We sail for Nantucket."

"I thought you might say that," Aphrodite answered. When Mary turned around to see what the goddess intended to do about it, she caught the Olympian's fist with her face and went down hard.

Chapter Twenty-Three
Breaking the Gates

Hector looked at Aphrodite in stunned silence. A second earlier the Olympian goddess had just punched the captain of the Puritan, Mary Mathers, in the face, knocking her unconscious. Mathers lay on the ground, out cold, blood dribbling out of her nostrils, down the sides of her mouth, and to the deck.

Aphrodite looked around at the crew of the pirate ship, a group of men who already looked defeated. She doubted they'd be any trouble at all. "Your captain," she announced, "desired to take you to the isle of Nantucket, where Damien is, at this moment, readying to break open the Gates that restrict access between all the worlds of creation. If he is successful, all denizens of Earth, Hell, Heaven, Limbo, and Olympus will have access to each other. Captain Mathers wanted to stop this; I could not allow that."

"Why?" Hector asked, his hand twitching towards the pistol he wore at his waist. "Are you in cahoots with Damien?"

"No, I- wait, did you just say 'cahoots'?" the goddess asked.

"Just answer the question," Hector said, clearly agitated. His mind flashed to the image of Austin and Lucifer

"No," Aphrodite said, shaking her head. "I want what Donald wants," she said, pointing to an overweight pirate breathing hard by one of the long boats. "And Thomas," she said, raising her voice. "Who has been loading cannon balls for the past twenty minutes with a left hand that he already knows he will lose, wants what I want. As do nearly half the men on this ship."

Hector was growing tired, impatient, angry – they'd spent the better part of the last hour fighting giants, and now this. He just wanted all of this to be over. "Answer the damn question," he said, reaching for his pistol. "Why would you want the Gates broken when that means the Nightmares would come pouring through?"

Aphrodite stared at him with soft, almost pleading eyes. "It's not only the bad people that have been removed from Earth, Hector. When I was freed from Limbo, it was done so that I may take back what was taken from me - the same thing that has been taken from Donald and Tom and forty-three other men on this vessel. I want my son."

The clouds above Nantucket were dark and rolling. Flashes of lightning streaked through the billowing mass as Damien stood before a towering black arch known as the Gates. The world held many Gates, but they were all as one, united in a connecting circuit. Breaking one would break them all, and the barriers that held God's worlds at bay from one another would fall. The Nightmares that the angels had locked away in Purgatory would come rushing into this world, drawn to their place of belonging like a starving animal to the scent of blood. The children would come forth, too, Damien knew, as would the Olympians and angels and demons.

A horde of demons thirty strong mulled around the base of the Gates, watching Damien, the son of Satan and Eve, lead them into a future without boundaries. "Are you going to give us a speech, Damien?" a demon asked, smiling.

"Speeches are for those who want others to do the work for them," he replied. "I am willing to do it myself."

Damien reached into the shoulder bag at his side and removed a small golden bowl from a box. The black gate hummed with energy, its smooth, slick surface slightly vibrating. Damien moved to the left column. Opening the box, the son of Satan removed a handful of thin, white wafers and tossed them at the Gate, where they stuck to the surface.

"The body of Christ," Damien said, smirking, placing the bowl back into the bag and removing a bottle of blessed wine.

"The blood of Christ," he intoned, popping the top off the vial and shaking the wine onto the Gate, the liquid sticking to the surface and vibrating into small, shifting pools. Damien exchanged the wine for water. Removing the top of the vial and tossing it onto the ground, Damien held the Holy Water aloft, pausing for the briefest of moments. Damien was nearly overcome with what he was about to do and the surge of emotions that ran through him gave him momentary pause.

He was about to undo what God had done, to break down the walls between all of God's worlds and create an open, free society.

And then he went and got shot in the left shoulder.

Damien grunted in agony as the burn from the bullet seared his flesh. He knew who had done it without turning. He would have known it even if the demons of his crew hadn't started backing away from the man who'd shot him.

"Hello, father," he said, turning around. He turned over the wounded shoulder, shielding the vial of holy water in his right hand.

"Son," Lucifer replied, his hands behind his back. Satan noted the surprised look on his son's face and cocked his head towards the man who stood beside him. "If I had shot you, Damien, your head would be in pieces on the ground."

Damien grimaced as he eyed Austin McNamara. Austin stood on Lucifer's right, the smoking pistol still pointed at the demon. Part of Austin wanted to run and hide, but the boat ride to Nantucket with Lucifer had solidified the desire in Austin for all of this to be over. His mind shut off the questions and fears of working alongside Satan. Truth be told, he was more upset about Lucifer's make-out session with Kelly than the fact that he was the Prince of Darkness. Double truth be told, he'd much rather none of the "breaking the gates" nonsense was going on so he could put a bullet in Satan's head for making a play at his girl-

"I can still read your thoughts," Lucifer whispered.

"Right," Austin replied. "Sorry."

Lucifer turned his full attention back to Damien. "You cannot do this, son," he said quietly, his voice barely audible over the rolling storm clouds above them. "To give all of God's worlds full access to each other is to court a danger like the world has never seen."

"You're wrong, father," Damien snorted. "The worlds have had access before – the angels have long walked the Earth. So have the Olympians. All I am doing is giving the neglected children of God – the humans and the demons – a chance to experience what God has kept from them."

Lucifer took a step forward on the wind-blown grass. "Humans were not built to sustain in those worlds, and those worlds were not built to hold the mass humanity that you risk sending to them."

"I despise elitism."

"It isn't elitism," Lucifer snapped, his anger becoming harder to control.

"With humans," Damien sneered, "God built a lower class of being. A class that would populate the Earth and serve as the eternal amusement for the angels and Olympians."

"That's not elitism, Damien, any more than it is elitist God made fish to populate the waters and insects to populate the land."

"So fitting you should choose insects to illustrate your point."

Lucifer took another step forward and Damien flashed his left hand forward, ordering him to stop. With his right hand, Damien raised the Holy Water above his head. "It is going to happen, father. All I need to do is pour this water across the threshold and I have won."

Lucifer ceased moving forward. "Then why do you hesitate?"

Damien smiled. "There is one thing you can do to stop all of this."

Thoughts ran wild inside Lucifer's head as he wondered exactly what Damien could mean. After a thousand possibilities proved fruitless, he relied on Damien to administer his demand. "Go on."

"I want God."

Austin cocked back the hammer on his pistol. "You want to be God? You're nuts."

Lucifer frowned. "He doesn't want to be God, Austin. He wants God brought here, before him."

Damien's smile showed true madness. "And why do I want God brought here, father?"

Lucifer took a deep breath before answering. "You want to kill Him."

"Find Him, father," Damien ordered Satan. "Find God. Kill God."

"No one knows where He is," Lucifer answered.

"If there is anyone who can find Him, it is you."

Lucifer shook his head. "I won't kill God."

"Then what happens next is on your conscience, old man," Damien announced.

Behind Lucifer, Austin was done weighing his options. There was some truth, he had to admit, in Damien's observations, but they were a twisted truth and his response went well beyond reasonable.

Austin took a step to the right to clear Lucifer from his sightline. "Screw this," he said as he took aim on Damien. "I'm ending this right now," he whispered, and pulled the trigger.

"No!" Lucifer screamed, hearing the hammer drop on Austin's gun. The first traitor spun his body and lunged, trying to jump in the bullet's flight path.

He missed, the bullet whizzing between his outstretched fingers as the entire world seemed to move in slow-motion. Austin wondered why Satan wanted to stop the bullet. His eyes refocused from Satan to Damien, and he was equally confused as to why Damien was cackling with glee.

Austin watched Damien shift his body, moving the vial of Holy Water forward, putting it right in the bullet's path. "Not good," Austin mumbled, knowing he'd screwed up again. His bullet slammed into the vial, shattering the glass and causing the water to explode outwards then down, like a mini-fireworks display. With a concussive series of splats the water slammed into the ground.

The world paused.

Damien shouted and ran to the left side of the arch. He cocked his right hand back and brought it forward hard, slamming his fist into the black, vibrating surface. A visible crack began splintering upwards, snaking across the surface. The vibrations increased ten-fold and the humming became deafening. The centerline of the crack moved quicker, reaching the top of the gate then down the other side. As it hit the Earth the world began to shake and the black and grey cloud rolled inward on itself, then flashed outward, expanding rapidly from horizon to horizon.

Damien took several steps backwards, his eyes on the sky above, waiting for what all seemed to know was coming. The cloud dropped. "Do it," he whispered.

As if in response, a massive crack of lightning shot down from the clouds, slamming into the Gate, the white-hot energy pouring through the crack as if it were transformed into liquid. The vibrations reached a crescendo then instantly dropped into a powerful low hum for several seconds. Austin moved to Lucifer, who remained on his stomach, his head twisted around to watch the Gate.

All went silent.

The world held its breath.

The Gate exploded.

Shards of black rock were blasted outward, sending everyone diving for cover as the Gate that held God's worlds apart became a gateway. In place of the black arch was an arch of liquid white and yellow energy. The energy arch buzzed with what seemed thousands of self-contained lightning bolts swarming over one another as they moved up and down across the Gate.

Damien laughed.

Austin was the first to his feet and his brain, so accustomed over the past few days to translating the unimaginable images brought to it by his eyes, nearly shut itself down. Looking into the Gate Austin saw the other world, a gray, swirling mass of shifting clouds, not unlike a fog that was both translucent and impenetrable. For one moment Austin thought he could see for miles; in the next he could not see more than a foot. The swirling mass made Austin lose his sense of balance, but Lucifer was there to steady him.

"We must leave," the devil said softly, placing a hand on Austin's shoulder.

"Why?"

Looking at Austin as if it were obvious, Lucifer answered, "The Gate is open. We have no idea what will come through the other side. Or when. But that is Purgatory, or Limbo, if you prefer, and there are many horrors held within its nearly limitless borders."

"Couldn't the missing children be held there?"

"They likely are, Austin," Lucifer nodded. "I have heard it whispered they are in the Missing Lands or the Hidden Lands. Both are names for Limbo."

Austin looked around at the demons and saw them celebrating. He shook his head, "We can't leave, then. We cannot be responsible for delivering the children of the world into the hands of Damien and his minions."

Lucifer cocked an eye at the New World pirate. "This is hardly the time to grow a backbone, Austin."

Annoyed, Austin shot back. "I earned your respect back in the Aquarium, Satan. I'm not afraid to fight."

Lucifer's response was overwhelmed by a loud *snap snap snap* of electricity from the Gate. "Something is about to come through," the devil said, his eyes searching the swirling mass of Limbo for a sign.

"Is it the children?" Austin asked, glancing towards Damien only to find him and most of the demons missing.

"I don't know," Lucifer replied just before his eyes went wide. "Run," he said, backing away. "We cannot be here, Austin!" The sheer panic in Lucifer's voice gave Austin pause even as he knew it should bring the exact opposite reaction. "Now, Austin!" Lucifer demanded as he turned and ran back towards shore where their speedboat waited for them.

Austin began to back away, his eyes still glued to the Gate when a figure exploded out of the swirling mass, headed straight for him. "Holy shit," Austin whispered. "A werewolf." His brain screamed to his legs to run but he couldn't move, so it tried sending an order to his arm to fire. Slowly, too slowly, Austin's right hand raised the pistol but the werewolf was on him before the gun was level and Austin fired harmlessly into the grass.

The werewolf knocked Austin to the ground and leapt on top of him, pinning Austin's rather thin arms to the ground. Austin could feel the hot breath from the beast wash over his face, as the werewolf's head descended towards his own. "Uncool," the beast said.

"Um ..."

"Where are we?"

"Um ..."

The werewolf's right claw dug into Austin's left shoulder. "Where are we?" he asked again, his snout pressing dangerously close to Austin's face.

Austin nearly gagged as drool from the beast's mouth slobbered down on him. "Nantucket."

"An island?" the werewolf asked, his head snapping up to take in the sights. He could see the beach in the distance. "Then there's hope."

"Hope?"

"Of containing them here."

"Them?"

The werewolf leapt off Austin in the direction of the beach. "Is that Satan getting into a powerboat?" he asked Austin, turning back to face the pirate.

"Yeah," Austin said, moving to his feet. "Um ..."

"You talk too much and say too little," the werewolf smirked. "You want to know what's coming through that Gate?"

"I do," Austin said, brushing grass off his clothes. "I'd also like to know why you're not trying to kill me. And why you talk. And-"

A low, menacing rumble of thunder stopped Austin's words. He looked back to the Gate to see bolts of lightning flying in all directions.

"The Nightmares are about to break through," the werewolf revealed. "Come, we must hurry."

"How do you know?" Austin asked, his feet finally moving as he and the creature ran towards Satan's powerboat.

"Because I'm one of them," the werewolf replied.

"Then why aren't you trying to kill me?" Austin asked, now running at full stride. "Not that I'm not grateful and all, but, I mean—"

"I was ten," the beast snapped, his head turning to look at Austin. "I'd just seen *Wolf*."

"The crappy Jack Nicholson movie?"

"Yes. I—"

A massive shockwave blasted both of them onto the sandy beach that had been a good ten feet still in front of them. Austin tried to move to his feet but doubled over in pain – the wind had been knocked out of him. "Hells bells," the werewolf grumbled. "The Nightmares are here."

Austin felt the beast's front claws dig into his shirt and drag him forward. As his body was jerked across the sand his head was pointed back towards the Gate and what he saw numbed him. From out of the Gate poured monstrosities of his childhood – werewolves, vampires, orcs, dinosaurs, assassins, Nazis, robots, Frankensteins, insects grown to massive proportions, aliens … there were hundreds of Nightmares and they just kept coming, spreading outward with a speed and ferocity that terrified him.

A tiger as tall as an elephant charged towards them and Austin knew he wouldn't be granted a second reprieve. The werewolf's pace was slowing in the thick sand and the tiger's massive stride combined with its momentum closed the gap in seconds. The tiger leapt at Austin's chest, but before the strike could connect Austin's body was flung forward into Satan's powerboat.

"Oof!" he gasped, his body slamming hard onto the front of the boat (which still pointed inland), then tumbled over the windshield as Lucifer dragged him backwards. Austin's body slammed into the seat and his eyes locked on the sight ten feet away of the werewolf slashing at the tiger's back legs, using its speed advantage to circle the giant beast.

It almost worked.

The tiger's tail was also of massive proportions and it swished hard at the werewolf, who leapt high to avoid it, just as the tiger planned. As the werewolf's body descended, the tiger's tail swiped again, this time connecting and hurling the werewolf into the shallow tide. Before the werewolf could right himself fully the tiger was on top of him, its massive jaws snapping at the werewolf's twisting head.

"Get the boat turned around!" Lucifer ordered, leaping into the water towards the dueling animals. Austin obeyed without hesitation, but as he moved towards the controls he looked to the back of the boat and saw that Raphael was missing. The former professor pushed the question aside and concentrated on the boat – the angel would have to take care of himself right now.

The werewolf was in the position Austin had been in minutes earlier, trapped beneath a more powerful creature. The Atlantic Ocean turned red as the tiger's claws slashed at the werewolf's flank. The counterattack of clawed slashes and snapping bites the pinned werewolf unleashed would have been enough to kill Austin, but it did little against the gigantic tiger. Bits of flesh and fur tore away from the big cat, but no significant damage was inflicted. The werewolf knew he was going to die unless he got away right now.

Lucifer had reached the beasts and did not hesitate. He was not a being of raw power as some envisioned, but rather an angel. Powerful but not unstoppable. His power lay in the tempting of others who exchanged their souls for his gifts. Satan could inspire and trick but he could not take the world by force, and he sincerely doubted whether he could survive an attack by this horrific creature if he engaged it in single combat. Drawing all of his energy reserves into what he hoped was a killshot, Lucifer leapt out of the water towards the tiger's flank and slammed his right fist into the tiger, puncturing fur, flesh, and bone and grasping the hot, pumping heart.

The tiger roared in pain, whirling on Lucifer, but the animal's own movement ended his life. Its eyes locked on Lucifer as the devil held the tiger's heart in his hand, then fell into the ocean, gushing blood.

"Move," Lucifer ordered the werewolf, dropping the tiger's heart and offering a hand.

"Hurry!" Austin yelled from the boat. Nightmares rushed down the beach towards them and another attack was only moments away. The pirate's eyes washed over the oncoming horde, trying to discern whether a 1950s-styled thirty foot high robot (how the hell did it even fit through the Gate, he wondered) or a swarm of flying monkeys was the greater threat.

"Hit it!" Lucifer yelled as he and the werewolf pulled themselves into the boat. Austin slammed the engines forward, zipping out and away from the shore.

"He's mine!" he heard the werewolf yell and he glanced back to see the creature hold a flying monkey by the throat. Looking up at the swarm of five monkeys who were conversely looking back down at them, the werewolf placed his second clawed hand under the monkey's chin and pulled its head from its body.

The swarm left them, veering off ahead of them and towards the left, where Damien was just now pulling himself back aboard the *USS Constitution*.

Frederic Kornell sat against the wall of a cell in the bowels of Regent Castle. His cellmate sat in the opposite corner, convulsing and babbling incoherently. The ranger had tried to ignore the disheveled old man but there wasn't anything else to do so he sat and watched and listened, trying to discern either who the man was or what he was prattling on about. To this moment he had enjoyed little success. Every now and then he would pick up a word or phrase, but it was jumbled and incoherent.

"I told them to fruttle the tuttle but they magumbled the unmagumable!"

"Apples and oranges are both tasty mctasty!"

"Kangaroos are the whores of dissent!"

Kornell sighed, leaning his head back against the cold stone wall. He'd been captured by King O'Malley's men but had been told nothing else in the few hours he'd been down here with Old Man Looney. The ranger closed his eyes, thinking back on the past few days and all that had happened; he was just about to start feeling sorry for himself when the old man was suddenly on top of him. Frederic started to move but the old man was surprisingly strong and held him in place.

"My name is Father Tom Otten! You must get me out of here!"

"Why?"

"Because I can stop everything!"

Kornell played it cool, readying his body for a strike at the old geezer. "You can stop what?"

"Everything!"

"You're pretty powerful then, huh?"

"The most powerful mcmuffin you've ever seen!"

Sucking on his teeth, the ranger nodded toward the bars of the cage, "Then why don't you free us from this cell, Mr. Powerful?"

Father Otten screamed and fell backward onto his back, "I am the forsaken!"

"Crazy bastard," Frederic sighed, wishing he was elsewhere.

Damien landed on the deck of the Constitution with a thud, looking back towards the Gate with a grand smile on his face. "Look at my legion!" he yelled triumphantly. "All over the world, thousands of Gates have been unlocked. Nightmares rush forward into this world, demanding the same access to life occupied by the Dreamers. We have done it! We have won! We have- arrgghhh!"

The son of Satan looked down to see a sword run through his stomach.

"You speak too frequently," the angel Raphael said from behind him.

Damien's demons were shocked at the sudden appearance of the angel, who had been hiding in the upper rigging of the ship as they had made their way to break the Gate. They were frozen for only a second. Before Raphael could so much as twist his blade the demons jumped him, pulling him to the ground where they beat him with fists and feet. Silvery blood spilled onto the deck of the Constitution as Raphael was pulped towards death.

Damien slumped to a knee. The angel's sword had been ripped from his stomach and his own red blood also dotted the deck. "Kill him," he rasped towards the demons, but didn't know if they could even hear him. Not that it mattered. Raphael looked to already be unconscious. Death was minutes away. "I'm going to enjoy this," Damien wheezed, leaning back against the side of the ship.

"So is Mollug! Squawk!"

Damien looked up to see a parrot flapping its wings.

"What?" he asked, when the parrot's dropping splattered onto his face. Damien roared in disgust, his hands moving to clear his face. Focused on his own cleanliness, Damien didn't see the parrot drop down and dig its claws into the scalp of the devil child.

"Stupid bird!" Damien roared, jumping to his feet. Looking around wildly for Mollug, Damien was knocked back onto the deck as a fist slammed into his nose, shattering it and several teeth. "What duh fud?" he roared, blinking through pain to see a huge figure standing above him. "Bedafon! I wid kid woo!"

"No more killing," Berathon announced, moving forward to put his boot on Damien's throat. "That is," he announced his change of mind, "no more killing after you are gone."

The angel put all his weight onto his foot and crushed Damien's windpipe. His world going dark, Damien could barely make out a horde of angels overriding his ship, saving Raphael and murdering his demon army en masse.

Damien's world turned black, but did so with the knowledge that he had won. He had defeated God. It was not Satan, after all these eons, but the son of Satan that had crushed God's plan.

Already unconscious and slipping towards death, Damien's body smiled.

Chapter Twenty-Four
What Are We Fighting For?

"Jesus Christ!" Austin yelled from the passenger seat of the powerboat he and Lucifer had stolen from the Boston docks. The New World pirate was pointing back across the water to the *USS Constitution*, which they had sped past minutes earlier.

"Not possible," Lucifer replied calmly, the adrenaline of their escape from Nantucket wearing off. "Jesus has gone into the-"

"Figure of speech," the werewolf corrected.

"What do you mean then, Austin?" Lucifer asked, half-turning his neck to look where Austin was pointing, but not wanting to surrender control of the boat. "What's going ... on?" Lucifer's voice trailed off and he turned away from the controls, leaving the boat zipping forward on its own. The sight that was taking place behind them stilled the angel who had led a rebellion of Heaven.

All around the deck of the *Constitution* a massive battle ensued between angels, demons, flying monkeys, and one monstrous bat. The sight, shocking enough, wasn't what gave Satan pause, but rather it was the viciousness of the angels' attack that caught him by surprise. "I have not seen angels fight with such hostility in all my years amongst the Host," he said, his voice low and somber.

Austin winced, knowing from Lucifer's words he hadn't seen what had caused his own original pronouncement. "Look to the top of the main mast," Austin said quietly.

Lucifer's eyes traveled up the mast and the psychical punch delivered to him caused him to fall back into a seat. A deep, pained burst of emotion ripped through him and he began to tremble. "My son ..."

Atop the mast of the *USS Constitution*, the body of Damien, son of Satan and Eve, hung limp in a noose, flying monkeys pecking at his eyeballs.

"What happened?" Kelly asked, yelling above the roaring swarm of shrieking giant vampire bats that darted between the buildings of downtown Boston. Around her, Brad Regent, Samantha Reed, and Liv the Ninja ducked as the bats circled around the Prudential Center and dive-bombed back at them. Kelly shivered as the Nightmares rolled past, the flapping of a hundred wings and the shrieking of fifty mouths causing her whole body to shudder involuntarily.

"Lucifer and Austin must have failed!" Brad yelled, running to her. Behind him, Liv shook her body to try and regain composure while Samantha was staring towards the corner of a nearby building.

Kelly shook her head, "No! They couldn't have!"

"They must have," Brad said, his voice reverting to normal as the bats were out of range. "These are Nightmares, Kelly. They have to be."

"But Austin ..."

"I'm sure he's fine," Brad said quickly, not bothering to figure out if he believed it or not. He wanted Austin to be fine, however, and that surprised him. It was only days ago that he had plotted to steal Kelly from Austin and now he was hoping the jerk was okay. Why? Because he wanted to see them together? Because he wanted to win her honestly? "Maybe they never even reached Nantucket," Brad suggested. "It's not exactly a stone's throw away."

Kelly nodded, taking a few deep breaths to re-center herself. The city was no longer quiet – all manner of sounds, from human to monstrous to alien, were echoing off the glass buildings around them. The sky was dark and ominous. Storm clouds flashed lightning and rumbled thunder as all manner of winged Nightmares flew across the sky. Kelly remembered seeing a documentary as a child about hammerhead sharks congregating at one particular spot in the ocean every year; the camera was on the ocean floor, pointing directly up. The sun radiated light through the water and hundreds of sharks moved back and forth, back and forth, back and forth. Through the years that image had stayed with her, fueling her own paintings. She had never seen anything that was, in the same breath, so beautiful and terrifying.

Until now.

An aviary of horrors flew above the city of Boston: bats, griffins, hawks, creatures that looked like stingrays and sharks, aliens with wings, pigs with wings, cats with wings ... it went on and on. Everywhere Kelly looked there was another creature she'd never seen before. In another context, some would surely have caused her to laugh or be inspired, but in this context they brought nothing but fear and doubt. She turned to Brad, who was equally shaken by what was happening, and thought of Austin's words from earlier. Did she really prefer men like Brad and Lucifer to Austin?

Brad felt her eyes on him and turned to her. He smiled. "You look like hell."

She couldn't help but grin. "We all do," she said, looking over to see Liv staring hard at the buildings around them, and Samantha walking to the corner of an office building. "What the heck is Samantha doing?"

"Sam!" Brad yelled. "Let's go!"

"Go where?" Kelly asked. "We lost. The Nightmares are free."

Brad whipped his head back to his ex-girlfriend, "I still want my kingdom back. I still want O'Malley to pay for what he's done. This isn't over."

Kelly started to snap back at Brad when she noted Samantha disappear around the corner of the building. "Where's she going? Liv, what's with Sam?"

"She's gone," Brad said. "What the heck's going on?"

Kelly took off for the corner where Samantha had walked and Brad followed instantly behind. Ten strides later they rounded the building and stopped dead cold. Samantha was in the classical grasp of a Dracula-looking vampire – he held her in his arms, her head tilted back to expose the neck, fangs bared and moving in for the kill. Brad shouted at the vampire, and the pale-white being looked up momentarily from his descent onto Samantha's neck to offer a brief smile.

A moment later that smile was replaced by a gasp and a widening of eyes from the vampire, who let Samantha slip from his grasp. The redhead slumped to the ground, unconscious but alive and unbitten, revealing a large silver candlestick sticking through the vampire's throat with Liv on the delivering end. Now that Samantha was clear, Liv jammed a second candlestick through the vamp's heart, then a third.

"Just to be sure," she grunted as the vampire fell to his knees.

"Will that kill him?" Kelly asked, moving to Sam's shivering body.

"No idea," Liv replied, shaking her head, "but this buys us time to get away." She kicked the vampire to the ground, where it spasmed uncontrollably.

"Get away to where?" Kelly asked from the ground. Samantha appeared physically unharmed, but she was still out of sorts. "Seriously, what are we going to do now? The Nightmares are out. Even if it were possible to put them back where they came from, do any of you know how to do it? Because I don't." She looked to Liv. "Brad wants to take back the Castle. What do you say?"

Liv shrugged. "I have no idea. Look around at all of this," she said, motioning to the madness in the sky with all the flying Nightmares. "It feels like we should be fighting someone, or something, but ..."

"Let's stick to the plan," Brad urged. "Take back the Castle."

"So you can be King, again?" Kelly asked.

"So we can organize a defense," Brad replied. "So we can have a base of operations."

Kelly looked to Liv, who shrugged for what seemed like the tenth time in the past hour, then down to Samantha, who was conscious and rubbing her head to clear the cobwebs. "Fine," Kelly said, getting to her feet. "But we need to find a place for Sam to recover."

"Not a problem," Brad said, smiling at Kelly's decision. "We'll sneak into the Castle through the underground passageways that lead through the cell block. We can put Sam in a cell to rest."

Kelly shook her head. "Forget it."

"But you just said-"

"I know, but I don't like it."

"Kelly, please."

"Forget it, Brad," she said in a tone that Brad knew meant that Kelly had reached her decision. "You and Liv can storm the Castle, but I'm taking Samantha and getting out of here."

"No, you're not," Samantha said from the ground. The redhead pushed herself to her feet and leaned on Kelly for support. "You're taking me to the top of the Pru," she said, pointing to the tallest building in the center of the city. "I want to find Frederic and that'll be our best chance to spot him. And Austin," she added. "Or Satan, whichever one you've got the hots for. Look, we know Austin and Lucifer didn't get the job done, that the Gate was opened, but we don't know what happened to them. They are our first priority."

Kelly chewed her bottom lip, but nodded. "Brad," she said, turning to the ex-King, "you take back the Castle and we'll head up to look for Lucifer. We can't do anything without him, anyway. I hate to say it, but he's the only one with a clue as to how to stop this."

"I don't know how to stop this."

Lucifer pulled the powerboat into the dock in a coast town in southeastern Massachusetts. He didn't want to take the powerboat back up and around Cape Cod at night - especially with the sea battle that he could see was still raging.

"What?" Austin asked. "You're kidding, right?"

Lucifer frowned, "No, I am not. I do not know how to stop this because there is only one being who can stop this."

"Who?"

"God."

"Oh," Austin remarked smartly, "is that all we need to do? Just find God." He glanced over to the werewolf, "This should be no problem."

"Convincing Him to do what must be done will be a problem. Finding Him will not be the problem."

"Why not?"

"Because I know where he is," Lucifer said, jumping from the boat onto a wooden dock.

Austin blinked. "You do?"

"I do," Lucifer said softly. "I have known all along."

Jumping out of the boat, Austin felt his anger rising and didn't bother to check it. "You've known all along? What the hell, Satan? Why didn't you say something? We could've avoided all of this nonsense!"

Lucifer crossed his hands over his chest. "I didn't say anything because He didn't want me to." The devil sighed and suddenly looked to Austin and the werewolf like a very old man. "When God decided to walk the Earth He entrusted His secret identity to me."

The werewolf's claws clicked on the dock as he rose from the boat. "Why you?" he asked, his voice gravelly and rough. "No offense, dude, but you're the devil. Lord of Lies and all that."

Lucifer rubbed his eyes. "That's exactly why He told me, Wells. And yes, before you ask, I know who you are. God entrusted me because He knew no one would think to ask me of His whereabouts. Now, come, we must find a car and return to Boston."

"And?" Austin asked.

"And hope we can convince a man He's God so that all of this may come to an end."

The three men moved down the dock and towards a parking lot full of cars. As they moved forward Austin wondered about Damien. While their goal was to stop him, he was still Satan's kid. You'd think he'd show some sign of remorse, some outward-

"He's not dead, Austin," Lucifer whispered in response to the pirate's thoughts. "He was born to a mortal woman, so his soul and body are uniquely joined. For angels, the body is the soul given form. For humans the soul is held within the body. But for demi-gods like Damien and Jesus, the body is a by-product of the soul. Think of it," he explained as he opened the driver-side door to a Porsche Cayenne, "as a protective layer for the soul. When Christ died, what happened? His physical body was taken down from the cross and entombed. Three days later, he arose from the dead and ascended, body and soul, to Heaven. Damien will do this, as well."

Austin thought of the flying monkeys tearing into Damien's flesh. "But what if there is no body? What if it was burned to ash or beaten to a pulp?"

Lucifer frowned, his eyes glancing back across the waters to where Damien's body now swung limp on the *Constitution*. "Then he is reborn into the world in the form of a child. His soul will literally kill another's soul in the womb and come back to Earth, hidden from sight until he acts. We cannot let this happen."

The devil climbed into the SUV and slammed the door shut. From outside the front passenger's door Austin shook his head at Wells.

"Always this fun?" the werewolf asked.

"You've got no idea," Austin sighed.

On the deck of the *Puritan*, Mary Mathers pulled herself to her feet, wiping the blood from her face and spitting out a copious amount from her mouth. "The hell?" she asked Aphrodite.

The Olympian didn't hear her. Her eyes were locked in a search for the missing children. "Azrael said they were being kept in the Caring Lands," she said to everyone and no one. "But that tells us not where they will emerge," she whined. A dozen members of the crew had gathered around the goddess, hanging on her every word, but she gave no indication they meant anything to her.

"What's her deal?" Captain Mathers asked Hector, who was leaning against the rail, tired and exhausted. The Titans were now on shore and Lucifer's ghost ships simply sat unmoving.

"Her child was stolen by Damien and hidden away with all of the other kids in the world," the Old World mechanic explained. "Her best chance of getting him back was to let Damien break the Gate." Hector sipped water from a tin cup and shook his head. "We're dead in the water, Cap. Aphrodite has made sure of that – all the masts are broken, all the oars tossed overboard. On the plus side, the Titans are gone and the aerial Nightmares haven't made their way out here, yet. They're concentrating on the city. Lucky us."

Captain Mathers spit more blood onto the deck; she looked around at a ragged crew and a crazy Olympian who was holding them hostage. "Tell me something," she said to Hector without taking her eyes of Aphrodite. "You ever get the feeling you're about to enter the shit?"

Hector smirked, "Hells yeah. The way I figure it, we ain't getting off this boat."

"There!" Aphrodite yelled, pointing to the distant southwest. "The children!"

"Where?" The crewmen who'd been hovering around her sprang to their feet, demanding to know if their children were safe.

"I must go," she announced, and her flock responded by begging her to take them with her. "The children are in Baja California, so I must go there." She ignored them and took to the air at a diagonal angle. The goddess moved at a good clip, but she didn't move fast enough. A bolt of lightning disguised as an angel shot down from the night sky above and grabbed the Olympian, slamming her under the surface of the ocean.

"What was that?" Hector asked, running to the opposite side of the ship.

"An angel," Mary answered, more interested in the condition of her galleon than whomever attacked the goddess. Spitting out what she hoped was the last of the blood from her mouth, Mathers moved gingerly to the starboard wall to look out across the waters. There was a massive battle raging, though she wasn't sure whether there were actual opponents or just random chaos. It was mostly flying Nightmares that attacked Boston, though there were several Titans, dino-monsters, and giant robots, as well. To this point the city was mostly free of the smaller, land-based Nightmares.

A thud on the deck caused Mathers to turn around. Berathon landed on the deck alongside Aphrodite; both were soaking wet though neither showed any indication of being cold despite the cool night air.

"You have no right to hold me!" Aphrodite snapped at Berathon, sounding to Mathers more like a spoiled child than a regal goddess.

"I have every right," Berathon snapped, alighting his flaming sword. "Your very presence outside of Purgatory is reason enough for your arrest."

Aphrodite rang water from her long, flowing blonde hair. "Are you Ocilael's errand boy now, Berathon? Put away that sword," she snapped. "You're not going to use it."

Berathon's face gave no hint to his intent as he moved his sword quickly to her belly. Aphrodite jumped back, startled, her hands moving to her stomach for protection. The angel nodded, "It becomes clear now, doesn't it, goddess?"

Aphrodite cracked, dropping to her knees, "Please, Berathon! Do not harm me! I had no choice! You don't know what it's like trapped in Limbo!"

The angel put away his sword but advanced on the goddess. "You're blaming boredom for your infidelity?" The Puritan's crew was completely focused on the argument, unintended witnesses to one of the opening moves of Damien's gambit.

"You would deny me physical pleasure?" Aphrodite spat back at the angel. "So typical of your kind."

"I would deny you pleasure with the son of Satan!" Berathon roared. "Especially when he's willing to break God's law and traverse into Limbo!" He turned away in disgust. "You probably thought it romantic."

Berathon took several deep breaths he didn't need to take to calm himself, then turned his attention to Mary. "Apologies, Captain, for the use of your ship."

"Not the weirdest thing that happened today," she added without humor. "Want to tell us what's transpired?"

"Aphrodite is pregnant with the child of the son of Satan," he explained. "It is his, to use your words, insurance policy."

"For what?" Hector asked, moving to stand beside his Captain.

"At this moment," Berathon explained, "Damien's body is hanging from the upper rigging of the *Constitution*. He is dead, his body beaten severely by the angels and now being pecked apart by various aerial Nightmares." He turned back to Aphrodite, who sat slumped against a broken mast. "Were you aware, Aphrodite, that you were a pawn in Damien's game?"

The goddess said nothing, staring down at her stomach.

"Damien is dead, but death to a demi-god is naught but a temporary condition," Berathon explained. "Death in this realm for him leads to rebirth. The only means of eliminating him from existence is to kill him in Heaven."

Hector scratched his head, "And this has what to do with Aphrodite being pregnant, exactly?"

"When Damien dies, his soul retreats inward, protected by the outer shell that is the body," Berathon explained in a tired, worn-down voice. "Left on its own the body will regenerate instead of decaying."

"So you're going to let the, uh, flying monkeys eat him to nothingness?" Mathers asked.

"That is the last thing I will allow," Berathon said harshly. "Ocilael watches the body as we speak. Our plan is to rip Damien's body down as much as possible, forcing his regeneration to last for months instead of days. If we were to cleanse this world of his presence through fire and make regeneration impossible, Damien's soul would be reborn into this world as the child of another." The angel turned to look at Aphrodite. "That would be his prime target. If he were reborn as a mortal child he would become mortal. But by impregnating Aphrodite he guaranteed himself a rebirth as a god."

Mathers was shocked. "That's … disgusting. He was going to be reborn as his own son? Where would he get such an idea?"

Berathon waved a hand in disgust. "Comic books. He gets all his ideas from comic books."

One of the crew shouted from the back, "*Avengers* 200," but no one paid him any attention.

"So," Hector asked, "what now? Is it over?"

"Not even close," Berathon frowned. "The Nightmares must be contained. We will gather all our forces and smash them back through the Gate. We cannot close the Gate, but we can make them not want to come through."

"A fool's plan," Aphrodite accused. "There are hundreds of Gates. You will never force the Nightmares from this realm."

"Yes," Berathon said, his tone dark and menacing, "we will. We're talking open warfare, goddess." He turned to Captain Mathers. "And we could use your help."

"Pirates like a world of chaos, Berathon," she said. "It is more profitable."

Berathon's demeanor turned even darker, "It is time to advance beyond your costumes, Captain. God's gift of Reorganization is a chance for you to become what you want to be in the here and now.

The change to reconstruct you into your childhood dreams was merely God's version of a reset button. You are not trapped by your designation."

Mathers nodded, "I understand what you're saying. But I like being a pirate."

The angel mulled his options. "We'll pay you."

"In gold?"

"If that's your choice."

"Deal," Mathers grinned. "But it better be enough to make us all stinking rich. Now we just need to repair our-"

"You will start now."

"Look at our masts," Mathers said, pointing around them. "We're stuck in the water. Unless we can do whatever you want from right here, we're not going to be of much use."

Berathon allowed himself a smirk. "I'll bring you to the battleground."

"What about Aphrodite?" Hector asked.

The angel flapped his wings and elevated a few feet off the deck. "Now that I know she is pregnant, I no longer care. She can be watched wherever she travels." He spun gently, looking down and taking some measure of pity on the goddess. "Go to the children, Aphrodite. They are mostly alone and afraid. You can bring them some measure of comfort, I suppose."

Without another word Berathon swooped around the deck, picking up every spare piece of rigging that had fallen from its perch, then began to pull the *Puritan* to Nantucket where it would do its part to save this small portion of the world.

New World ranger Frederic Kornell sat in a cell in the bottom of Regent Castle with a priest who'd lost his mind. Father Thomas Otten had blacked out an hour earlier, though he continued to mumble mostly incoherent words over and over. In the Old World, Frederic had been a janitor at a high school; though he preferred to stay out of the way, there were times, at night, when he'd read through teachers' plans and search through their desks.

He'd had a crush on the Spanish instructor because she reminded him of Marissa Tomei, so it was often her classroom where he'd choose to have his midnight snack, and often her shelves and drawers and plans he'd read. While she taught 5 classes of Spanish each day, every spring the school board would let her teach one half-year of Latin. Frederic didn't begin to understand the language, though he could sure as hell recognize it when he heard it or saw it.

As he waited for someone to come either rescue or torture him, Frederic was comforted by this priest's ramblings in a dead language for a reason he could not understand.

But when so much that happened in the world didn't make any rational sense, relying on feeling and emotion worked for him just fine.

"Look at you," a voice he didn't want to hear came from the doorway to his cell. "Not even trying to escape."

"Hello, dad," Frederic said without opening his eyes. "Working for King O'Malley now?"

"Guess I am," his father replied.

"Life of a soldier, huh?" Frederic asked, looking to the door. "Good at taking orders, good at giving them, but unwilling to think for yourself."

His father laughed. "After all this time, you're still a mama's boy."

"Have you thought about why I wanted to be this?" Frederic asked, rising to his feet. "Why I dreamt of being a ranger like Aragorn and not a soldier like you?"

General Kornell chewed his lower lip. "Can't say I have."

"It's because rangers get to make their own choices," Frederic replied, his anger rising but under control. "I never doubted you were a good soldier, dad. Never doubted you were good at barking orders or training recruits, or even killing. But you did all of it for someone else. You didn't do it because you believed in it. You did it because you were told to do it by your superiors, and when you came home to me and mom, you tried it out on us. Take orders, give orders … for you it's all about the chain of command. Whomever has the most stripes gets to make the orders and never be wrong."

"Been practicing that speech long?"

"I respect the abilities you possess, dad," Frederic said, standing right up against the door. "I just wish you had a fucking clue."

"Careful, boy," General Kornell threatened. "Don't forget who's in the cell and who isn't."

"Good soldier, lousy father, criminal husband," Frederic challenged. "You killed mom on the inside long before you killed her body. I want to kill you."

The General laughed. "You can't. You ain't got what it takes to kill me."

"I said I wanted to kill you. I didn't say I was going to," Frederic continued, not backing down. "But if I get out of this cell, I am going to hunt you down and give you the beating of a lifetime."

"Why don't you do it right now?" the General fired back. "I came down here to offer you a position in the army. King O'Malley's got me in charge of defense for the Kingdom of New England and I thought, with all your gifted abilities, you might like a place in that army in exchange for letting you out of that cage, but I can see you'll never reach your full potential. You've always lived inside of books, Freddy. Your outside has changed but inside you're still that weak little fatty you were in the Old World. So why don't you say I open this cell door and kick the shit out of you, just like old times? That work for you?"

"Do it," Frederic seethed.

Frederic took a step back as his father reached for his key to the cell and unlocked the door. With a grunt, the General kicked the door in and charged Frederic, knocking him to the ground beside Father Otten.

"Get up!" General Kornell screamed. "Get up, you goddamned coward! Get up!"

The General's words caused Otten to snap awake. His body went rigid and flat on the floor but his eyes went wide with awareness. "Thou shall not take thy Lord's name in vain!" he roared. Both Frederic and his father stopped at the priest's words, waiting for a second outburst that wasn't coming. Otten's face turned a pale white and his body slumped. The only sign he wasn't dead was the skittish jumping of his hazel eyes.

"Nice company you keep, boy."

Frederic slowly rose to his feet and he and his father began circling one another. The General threw a punch and missed, then a second that Frederic deflected. Frederic went on the offensive next, firing two quick punches that both missed. His father was thirty years his senior but the more experienced fighter. "I will come down here once a week and beat the piss out of you, son. Just because I can." Frederic answered by landing his first punch, a hard but poorly aimed shot that hit his father's shoulder. "That all you got, Freddy?"

The two men continued to punch and counterpunch each other for five minutes before they noted the floor of the cell was covered in water. The General was the first to notice and his momentary distraction allowed his son to smash his large fist into the father's gut. The General fell to one knee and Frederic fired again, knocking him to the ground. It was only then the ranger noted the water. "Where's this coming from?"

The General laughed, "Whole city's about to flood. Damien has let loose the Nightmares and the waves around the city have been coming higher and higher with all the turmoil in the oceans around the world." For the first time in his life, the father was looking up at the son. "Take the priest and go. I won't have your death on my hands."

"One death in the family too much for you?"

Leaning back, Frederic saw the water had risen nearly to his knees; it was high enough that Father Otten's body was floating precariously on the surface.

"Listen, son," the father explained, "I ain't asking for your forgiveness because it don't mean shit to me. And I ain't trying to taint the memory of your dear old mom because I couldn't. Like I said, you're a mama's boy."

"Now's not the time," Frederic said, staring down his father.

"Now is the time," his father insisted. "I wasn't a good father or husband. So what? You know why I married your mom? I was stationed at Fort Bragg after Grenada. Drill instructor. Your mommy was a stripper at one of the local establishments. Placed called Hot to Trot. She was a terrible dancer but she had the biggest titties in the place."

"I don't want to hear this."

"You're going to," the General answered as the water moved up to his chest. "Being a stripper ain't easy, especially around a base. We tear these kids down to build them up, but when they're raw like that our job is to put them through a cycle of two states – containment and release. Firing guns can do only so much. A man has needs, especially when he's being jerked around. That's why we give them a release pass every so often. These kids, they head to town and tear the place up. Every pass some local punk says the wrong thing and the soldier boys kick some ass, letting off steam. Normalizing themselves, the psychs say. Some of the boys hit the dance clubs and boogie their woogie. Others hit the strip clubs or the whorehouses. We know this so we go out and watch them, make sure they stay in line. One night, I'm at the Hot to Trot, watching the recruits ogle women who barely rate a seven and toss their pay away to see some tit and pussy. Strip clubs are a waste of money, you ask me. You'd like them because they're for guys not man enough to go get a whore and do what they can only think about at the club. Well, your mom comes on, starts to do her number and two of the boys get a little frisky. A punch is thrown by one of the guys and your mom kicks him in the face. I jump in and break it up, send the kids back to the barracks. Next night, there's a knocking at my door. Your mom wants to thank me, so I let her thank me, but only after telling her a lap dance ain't the only thing I want. She didn't want just that, either. We fucked. She got pregnant. Her father, get this, is some hotshot corporate exec who happens to be a golf buddy with the fucking Vice President. I'm ordered – fucking ordered – by the VP of the United States to marry her. So I do. She loves the idea of marriage; turns out she'd been trying to get knocked up by an officer for over a year. I was the unlucky winner."

"Stop it!" Frederic yelled.

"No," his father continued. "Understand I know you don't want to hear this, Fred, but your mom … she had needs no one man could satisfy. Remember your Uncle Jackie, your cousin Matthias, our 'financial adviser,' the constant problems with cable, and all the other men who would hang around the house when I was gone?"

"Don't you fucking say it," Frederic raged, tears starting to run down his face.

"I don't have to," the General shrugged. "You already know. You've always known, and that's why you can't kill me. Because in some small part of that over-sized imagination, you know your mom doesn't fit the fairy tale image you've constructed. You want her to be, what, Snow White? Cinderella? She ain't. And you might not like what I did to her, but some part of you understands that a wife ain't supposed to cheat on her husband. Even if he is a heartless bastard."

Tears flowed freely down Frederic's face now and his father turned away. The water was up to his chin now, forcing him to rise to his feet. "Come on, let's get Father Otten out of-nnnnhhhhhh …"

Frederic couldn't see where he hit his father or how hard he was hurt. The tears in his eyes made all the world a blurred image of shapes and colors that barely resembled anything concrete. Using the water to help him, the ranger grabbed Father Otten's feet and pulled him along. He moved Otten into the hallway and saw that the water was at a slight angle, mirroring the slight tilt of the hallway. Right meant back into the Castle. Left meant out to the street.

He wanted to risk going left, but knew he'd never make it. Pulling Otten along the water's surface behind him, Frederic made his way to the Castle, leaving his father behind in the cell. He left the door open.

Let Fate decide this one.

"Samantha, this isn't going to work," Kelly said from the floor as she slumped against an interior wall of the Observation Deck of the Prudential Center. All around them (though luckily all outside the building) the aerial Nightmares continued their fight against anyone and everyone. "We'll never find Frederic in all that craziness."

"I know," Samantha said, though she did not sound disappointed to Kelly. "I knew we wouldn't, I just had to get away from Brad and Liv. I wanted no part of fighting when there's nothing to fight for. Come up here," she suggested. "Look at all this craziness. I can see ninjas fighting orcs, guardsmen fighting vampires. There's an army of giant ants on Route 2 heading for the interior. Who are we supposed to fight? What are we supposed to be fighting for?"

Kelly moved to the window, looking out at a city under siege, wondering if anyone knew why any of them were fighting. The Nightmares, at least, seemed bent on destruction.

"Do you love Austin?" Samantha asked.

Kelly hesitated. "I'll always love Austin."

"But …?"

"But I don't know if I'm in love with him anymore," Kelly admitted.

"How do you know?" Samantha asked. "How do you know when you're in love?"

"You just … you just know," Kelly answered, looking to the redhead. "Haven't you ever been in love before?"

Samantha shook her head slowly and sadly. "In the Old World … I didn't look like this, Kell. I can't ever remember not being the fattest, ugliest girl in any room I walked in. Even when I was a child … I escaped into books and cartoons and movies. I wanted to be like Sleeping Beauty but look like Red Sonja." She glanced down to her breasts, smiling weakly, "I guess that's where these came from."

"Do you love Frederic?"

"Yes," she said, not paying attention to the griffin that buzzed the window before them, "but I'm scared I'm not good enough for him. I'm scared he won't turn up alive after all this. I'm scared he'll find some flaw in me he can't get over. He's the first man I've ever slept with. It was during the First Night Feast. Brad came to me and another girl, told us to seduce Frederic."

Kelly blinked several times, trying to absorb the words. "What?"

"Oh, he told us Frederic was some hero and one look at him and I knew I wanted him more than I've ever wanted anyone," she said, tears forming. "What makes me feel worse than anything isn't the sex, but that Brad paid us to do it. He paid us, Kelly. When we left Frederic that night and returned to our quarters there was a huge pile of gold coins waiting for us." Samantha pounded her fist against the glass. "I'm a whore, Kelly. My first night in the New World and I turned into a whore. How can Frederic ever love me? How can anyone?"

Kelly wrapped a hand around Samantha's shoulder. "Did you know Brad was going to pay you?"

"I ... I guess I did," she admitted, "but the second I saw him, I didn't even care. I just—whoa!"

The griffin charged straight towards them, then dove just before hitting the glass. Samantha and Kelly pressed their foreheads to the glass to see what happened. The griffin flew back into their sightline, a spider the size of a large dog in its beak. "That's so disgusting," Samantha gagged, stepping back from the window.

"That isn't the half of it, Sam," Kelly gasped, moving away from the window. "Look."

The two women watched several more large spiders climb the other side of the glass, then what seemed like a million small spiders push up past them. There were enough that their view of the sky was cut in half. Moonlight flashed in the room as a constantly changing movement of spiders stopped and allowed light in at a different spot every second. "We need to get out of here," Kelly said, moving to the elevator. She pressed the button but the door didn't open. "Oh, hell, the elevator has moved," she said, trying not to panic.

"It better get here fast," Samantha gasped, her eyes locked onto the griffin beyond the shifting wall of spiders.

Kelly looked up, intending to reassure Samantha everything was cool because the spiders couldn't get through the glass. The words never came. The griffin was flying madly, having been bitten by a poisonous spider, and in its dementia smashed into the glass wall, putting a massive spider-web crack on its surface. "Please tell me there's no opening," Kelly murmured.

"There's no opening," Samantha prayed, her eyes locked back on the griffin who raged across the sky. The impact had caused the death of one large spider and a hundred smaller ones, their crushed bodies oozing back down the glass as other spiders either moved around or over them.

Kelly saw the trouble spot first. "There's an opening." The two women watched as one small spider, then another moved through a break in the glass not much larger than a quarter. "Come on, come on," Kelly urged the elevator that seemed determined to not arrive.

"I hate spiders," Samantha moaned.

"Everyone hates spiders."

"Not by the look of them," Samantha replied. "These are all people who wanted to be a spider, remember?"

Kelly didn't answer. There was a steady stream of spiders coming in now, but they were all small. With revulsion, she asked herself if she'd rather be consumed by a small or large spider? Small spiders seemed to be the only option until one of the dog-sized spiders accidentally placed one of its legs through the hole, getting stuck. The spider tried to pull its leg out, but it was stuck so it began a sawing motion that shook the entire cracked web of glass. "That is so not good," Kelly grimaced.

"Why isn't that elevator here, yet?" Samantha panicked, as the glass web was pulled outward from the force of the dog-spider. A section the size of manhole cover was pulled loose. Neither Kelly nor Samantha took any pleasure in watching the offending spider fall away from the window. Spiders by the hundreds began pouring in and they both knew it was only a matter of time before one of the larger spiders found the hole too enticing to pass up. The two women huddled back against the elevator door. The roof of the Observation Deck was now a completely swirling mass of black. The walls were half-covered and the floor was covered by nearly a third.

The women figured they had less then a minute before they made contact.

And still the elevator hadn't arrived.

At the base of the Prudential Center, impatiently hitting the up arrow was Father Thomas Otten. He paid little attention to anything but the button as Frederic rushed into the building, a full thirty seconds behind the Catholic priest. "Hey," the ranger called, covered in spiders, "what's going on? What are you doing?"

"I must ascend!" Otten screamed. "Stupid button! Stupid stupid button! I damn you, you stupid button! I damn this whole elevator!"

Brad Regent and Liv the Ninja stood across the street from Regent Castle, huddling in the doorway of an abandoned Dunkin Donuts.

"Forget it," Brad said, shaking his head.

"It's possible," Liv suggested, looking at the mass of guardsmen that were defending the castle from a legion of multi-colored robots. "The distraction will actually help."

Brad shook his head, "It's not that. I know we can do it. I just don't want to do it anymore."

Liv looked at him sideways. "Your call."

Brad's head continued to shake. "Not worth it. Everything that's happened … being King just doesn't seem that important anymore."

"You doing this for you?" Liv asked. "Or Kelly?"

"For me," Brad said resolutely. "I'm doing this for me. She showed me the error in the Old World me over the past few days, but I'm doing this for me. Let O'Malley have the kingdom. For the first time in my life, I don't want power or money or responsibility."

"O'Malley's still an evil guy."

"So what? You want to kill him, he's all yours. Heck, you could be the Ninja Queen or something." Brad offered a friendly smile, "It's all yours for the taking, babe."

Liv laughed. "The last thing I want to do is rule a kingdom. I'll tell you a secret, Brad Regent," she said softly. "The night before the Reorganization I was with this great guy. I have no idea what happened to him, but I aim to find him. Our paths part here."

"Understood," Brad said, shaking her hand. "I'm headed for Sam and Kelly over at the – holy hell! Look at that!" His eyes opened in horror at the sight of the building being overrun by spiders. "Come on, we've got to go help them!"

When he turned around, Liv was gone.

Lucifer sped the Porsche SUV into downtown. A thin layer of water covered most of the road; in spots there was none and in others it ran as high as the top of the wheels.

"Where do we look?" Austin asked, shuddering at the sight of the spider-infested Prudential Center.

"We don't have to look," Lucifer replied. "I know exactly where God is."

In the backseat, Wells the werewolf groaned through his fanged teeth. "Are you heading for that building with the spiders? I hate spiders. I mean, I really hate spiders."

Austin answered, "We're not headed there. Satan here just wants to scare us a bit. Right, big guy?"

Lucifer laughed and punched the accelerator.

Berathon flew high to look down at the battle beneath him. The *Puritan* and the three demon ghost ships were locked in battle with various sea creatures, from killer whales to piranha to sharks that swam on top of the water. Surely, he wondered, there is something majestic even to humanity's Nightmares. Such a wide selection of ideas ... truly, they were the greatest of God's children, the closest to being a mirror to God himself.

Ocilael flew up to join him, silvery blood marking his skin. "We need to get Damien's body out of here. He's lost one leg up to the knee and the other halfway up the shin. One arm is gone completely. The other is hanging limply, all but torn away. His face is mush. Ribs are missing as the woodpecker swarm feasts on his entrails."

"Give them time, Ocilael," Berathon ordered. "So long as there is a handful of flesh and bone left, Damien is tied to that body."

Captain Mathers had to admit this was all starting to seem like a great bit of fun. The *Puritan*, unable to move and thus a sitting target for the sea Nightmares, was more than holding her own. Her crew was busy firing cannons at anything that moved. Berathon had pulled them close enough to shore for their cannonballs to reach and they were busy smashing and pulverizing the land-locked Nightmares that were trapped on the small island. Some were getting off, of course; she'd noted several of the sentient Nightmares tearing away from the island in boats carrying other Nightmares with them. On the way to Nantucket she'd noted a huge yacht swarming with spiders that would cause her own bad dreams the next time she slept.

For now, though, it was wanton destruction. She looked to her second-in-command to see Hector firing his pistol at the surface sharks. The night sky was practically on fire thanks to the never-ending volleys of fireballs from the ghost ships.

The *Puritan* suddenly seized up, its rocking in the waves brought to an abrupt stop. Mary's first thought was that they'd run aground, but the large tendril that rose up suddenly before her made for an even more horrific truth.

They were being attacked by a giant octopus.

Less than a mile away, the dread ghost Lazarus smiled to Captain Samuel from the deck of the *Cottonmather*. "There she is," he laughed. "The *Puritan*, in the grasp of a Nightmare, just ready to be cut to pieces. If you want to be the one that drowns her, you'd best hurry."

Stocky Samuel set his face, then roared to the crew, "Full steam ahead!"

King O'Malley watched the battles unfold from a window in his tallest tower. How had it all gone so wrong, so fast? It was those damned angels, he knew. Damien was at least honest, but he knew the angels had to be somehow responsible for-

"Urkkkk!" he gagged, a knife shoved through the back of his throat.

He turned, his body reeling, to look into the cold, deadly eyes of a beautiful ninja.

"Not your kingdom," Liv said simply. "Not even close."

She left quickly, leaving O'Malley to die alone.

The elevator door finally opened and Father Otten stepped inside. Behind him, Frederic wasn't sure what to do, having no intention of moving up into a building with all of these spiders. He looked to Otten, who stood with his hand on the "Open Door" button.

"Well?" the priest asked. "Don't you want to see how this ends?"

"How it ends?"

"No? Well, don't you want to see Samantha?"

"Of ... of course."

"Then get in," Otten demanded. "She's up there."

"How do you know?"

"I know everything," he announced. Frederic believed him and jumped into the elevator.

The *Puritan* began to crack as the octopus tightened its grasp. From out of nowhere a mad, raging white whale was now smashing into the opposite side of the vessel.

"We're going down!" Hector yelled.

Captain Mathers nodded. "It all fell apart so quickly."

"Want some even worse news?" he asked. "We've got a gallery come to watch us die." He pointed out beyond the octopus to where the *Cottonmather* bared down on them at an angle prime for firing.

"Great," Mathers sighed. "This is definitely not how I wanted to go out." She raised her voice, imploring her crew. "Fire with everything you've got! I'm not headed to the bottom without taking some flesh with me! I don't care if it's whale, octopus, or *Cottonmather*!"

The crew roared and increased their output as Lazarus appeared on the deck beside Mathers and Hector. "You might want to revise that last option," he said, clearly disappointed.

"Why?" Mathers asked a moment before the answer became clear. The *Cottonmather* was in shouting range.

"Fire!" Samuel ordered his crew as the gun deck was set ablaze in cannon fire.

"I'll be damned." Mathers couldn't believe her eyes – the *Cottonmather* hadn't come to sink them but to save them. All of their guns were aimed at the octopus and volley after volley of cannonball and musket fire pulverized the slimy hide.

Hector laughed crazily. "Look to port! The ghost ships are taking care of our whale problem!"

Mathers shook her head and turned to Lazarus. "Why?"

The ghost sighed. "Captain Samuel said he wants to be the one to kill you, not some, *ahem*, ass-fucking octopus."

Mathers chuckled. "Good enough for now! Tell him we'll be waiting!" She looked across the water to Captain Samuel and pointed her finger as if it were a gun and smiled broadly.

Brad arrived at the Pru just as Lucifer's Porsche slammed on its brakes. The three men inside jumped out and exchanged brief greetings with Brad as they moved through a mass of spiders towards the door.

"Can't you do something?" Austin asked Lucifer, motioning to the ankle-high swarm of spiders.

"Yes," he smiled, "I could."

But he didn't.

The ride to the Observation Deck seemed to Frederic to take half his lifetime. When the door finally opened he wondered if his life was about to end. The spiders on the deck were waist high and as the door opened, the spiders stacked against the door fell inside, bringing Kelly and Samantha with them. Both of the women were shocked to see the two men and screamed variations of, "Hit down! Get us out of here!" Samantha's arm shot for the control pad, but Father Otten stopped her.

"It is okay, my child," he smiled.

Samantha, seeing that Otten was a priest but not caring, asked, "Are you fucking nuts?"

Otten's smile widened. "Not anymore."

The priest waved his arms and the spiders parted before him. He walked into the Observation Deck as if contained in a protective bubble a foot wide. The spiders simply avoided him.

"What's going on?" Kelly asked, unnerved at this simple but unmistakable sign of power more than anything she'd seen yet in the New World.

"It's time to end all of this," Father Otten said softly.

"How?"

Without turning back to them, the priest simply said, "Because I'm God and I want it to end. And so it shall."

Chapter Twenty-Five
New World Sabbath

From the Journals of Austin McNamara

With the snap of His fingers, it was over.

It was a little unnerving to have God turn out to be hiding on Earth as the priest from your hometown, but even more unnerving that He hand't known who He was for forty years. Turns out it was all part of His plan – He wanted to live close to a full life as a human to gain the experiential knowledge of what it was like to be human. Things went wrong, though, as they often do. From what Berathon has told me, this all started a few centuries ago when God tried to create a rock so heavy that even He couldn't lift it. He lifted it, then it crashed down on His head, so I guess his brain isn't working at full-steam.

Kinda scary, but He seems like a good dude, so I'm willing to cut Him some slack.

And yes, I realize I'm talking about God. Strange world.

When Lucifer, Brad, and I reached the Observation Deck atop the Prudential Center God was just starting his pronouncement. Kelly tells me that whole deck had been covered with spiders, but I didn't see any. Not saying she's a liar, of course, just that God had cleared things out by the time we arrived on the scene. Story of most of my life, I suppose, always showing up too late to see the show.

Anyway, it ended something like this: God snapped his fingers, said "Stop," and the world stopped. All of the fighting, here and everywhere, ended with people frozen in place. Then slowly, like ice melting on a warm day, everyone just sort of ... relaxed. God spoke to the world directly from His location here in Boston. He didn't have much to say, but it was pretty heavy:

"People of the world, I am sorry. In my desire to experience life as a human, I unwittingly allowed myself to become a pawn of those who would seek to do harm in my name. It is not the first time this has happened, I am sad to say, but it is the first time I played a direct role. I will not bore you with the details ..."

As if hearing God talk about anything could be boring ...

"... but I have been living among you for many years. For the past four decades, I have hidden myself away from even myself, living as a priest. I have had ... spells, you would call them. Moments of blackness as my omnipotent soul struggled to stay contained in your Earthly frame. During one of these blackouts, I sent a letter to my angels in Heaven. As many of you are aware, there have been ... issues with the abuse of children throughout the world. After a particularly angry meeting between myself and my priestly superiors in which they decided it was better to protect the Church than the individual, I feel into a deep and unsatisfactory slumber. I dreamt of the terrible crimes perpetuated on these innocents and wished that we could all go back and experience the innocence of childhood. I directed a letter to the angels, asking them to Reorganize the world based on those dreams. Perhaps because of my state, I asked that the so-called Nightmares be removed from the world until they had a chance to repent their nightmarish wishes. It was not my intent to keep them there in perpetuity, but only for a short time. Unfortunately, there were those around the globe who chose to rush mayhem back into this world. Those threats are now over, but the Nightmares will remain among you, as will an open passage between all of my worlds. I have returned to every living being the freedom of will, so any Nightmares trapped to act in villainous ways in accordance with their childhood dreams are no longer bound by those early conclusions. This means everyone will be able to decide whether to act for good or ill. I have also ordered the angels to grant everyone a new chance at a desired profession, so those currently in forms they disagree with will be quickly changed to their new bodies and roles. There is more to say, but I will end my talk here. It has never been my intent to lead an army of mindless followers, but to give you the tools to lead a good and honest and moral life. I wish you all the very best. You will not hear from me again."

And that was that.

DREAMER'S SYNDROME

God ordered today to be a day of peace. No one was allowed to do anything harmful to anyone or else God would personally interfere. My watch says it's almost midnight so I guess we're almost ready to start the rest of our lives. Let me rundown what I know ...

The Nightmares aren't going anywhere. God is giving everyone a chance to start their life over with a clean slate, so long as they're genuinely interested in forgiveness and redemption. It's got people nervous, but a lot others are glad that their loved ones won't remain trapped as a fifty-foot tall robot or giant dinosaur.

The angels will remain mostly on Earth, serving as an oversight committee of sorts. God has made it clear that each domain remains the domain of its created host—so Earth remains under the control of humanity, Heaven of the angels, Olympus of the Olympians, etc. Earth is going to remain segmented as it was by the Reorganization, so it will still be the Kingdom of New England, the six states all decked out as a romantic Middle Ages, mixed with the roads and buildings of pre-Reorg.

Frederic and Samantha were married this afternoon. God performed the ceremony, which I guess makes them a pretty unique couple. Kelly thinks it's a mistake, but she didn't tell Sam that. I wish them well, of course, and they'll need it. They've been installed as the new King and Queen of New England.

Brad gave them his blessing; he was actually offered his seat of power back, but he refused it. Said he wanted to see the world. Good for him. He's still an asshole, but after all we've been through, I'm willing to give him a chance.

Liv has disappeared. Wish I had the chance to say goodbye to her but I know she's got people she wants to find.

God's cessation of time (I don't know what else to call it) last night saved some bad folks, too. Frederic Kornell's dad and ex-King O'Malley both survived, though they will need some time to recover. Both are being held in jail for their actions, however. I know Fred was glad to see his father make it out alive, even though he clearly hates him. Lot going on there I don't know about and I'll respect Frederic's wishes to keep that backstory buried.

Lucifer took his son's body and went home. Berathon, Ocilael, Raphael ... heck, most of the angels weren't pleased, but God's Word wasn't to be questioned. Didn't get a chance to talk to Lucifer except to thank him for his help. He apologized again for making out with Kelly, then apologized to her. I don't know what to think. When she looks at him there's a definite magnetism there on both of their parts, but they didn't act on it. A win for me that didn't feel like much of a win.

We heard from Berathon that Aphrodite is with a large portion of the world's children; God has placed His trust in her to help care for them until they can be reunited with their parents.

I got a chance to see the Puritan *today. Ship's in bad shape but they're staying in Boston Harbor for repairs. I was glad to see Hector again and shocked to hear the* Cottonmather *had helped the* Puritan *out. Strange bedfellows when it looks like the fate of the world is on the line. They've asked me to come along with them, but I told them no.*

"That's it, then?" Kelly asked, entering Austin's bedroom inside Regent Castle. "No more pirate business?" she asked, looking at the pirate clothes on the bed and the Red Sox jersey and jeans on Austin.

"No more pirate business," he said, rising from his journal to move to the woman that was still, technically, his girlfriend. His heart started to pound; he figured his odds were no better than fifty-fifty for her to be his girlfriend by the end of this conversation. He looked at her lack of a Princess costume and smiled. "White blouse and jeans doesn't scream 'Princess' to me."

"I'm done with that, too," she said as they moved to each other. They stood about a foot apart, holding hands between them. "What are you going to do?" Kelly paused to choose her next words carefully. "You know that you can't just follow me around, right? We've got to talk about—"

"I'm not going to," he said quickly, biting down the hurt as he turned his back to her and moved to the work desk. A journal lay there and he picked it up.

"The Journal of Austin McNamara?" she asked, taking it from him. "What's it mean?"

"It means I'm going to write in it," he said, forcing a smile.

"Be serious," she said, punching him lightly in the stomach.

"We're living inside a book now," he said confidently. "I figure I'll travel the world, see what there is to be seen, and write it down. Someone's got to do it, and I'm hoping there's a lot of people like me who will step up and write down whatever it is they see in their corner of the world." He reached out to take her hand, but stopped himself, forcing it back to his side. His voice was low and thoughtful. "You? What are your plans?"

Kelly felt a flash of anger rip through her, but kept her voice low to match his tone. "Is that how it's going to be? We're not even going to discuss what's happened to us? You're just going to—"

"A book like this … it could use some, uh, illustrations," he said, scratching his head and alternating his gaze from her face to the floor and back again.

Kelly blinked, her anger gone in a flash and replaced by uncertainty. She stuffed her hands into the back pockets of her jeans. "Are we just going to pretend that Aphrodite … that Lucifer … never happened?"

"I kissed Aphrodite because I've never felt that I deserved you," he said resolutely. "And when *you* feel that way… you revel in anyone's affection or attention." He kicked at nothing on the floor, "But that's not why you and Satan …"

"No," she said, "it's not."

"Do you—?"

"He's asked me to go with him," she said quickly. Folding her arms in front of her, she locked her eyes onto Austin's face until he pulled his eyes off the floor. "Lucifer," she clarified, even though there was no need for it.

"To Hell?"

"To Rome."

"Oh."

Silence hung between them as Austin waited for her answer.

"I told him no," she said quietly, after a few moments more than Austin thought she'd needed, and he could hear the unease in her voice over the decision. Was it regret? The words seemed to reset Kelly's resolve. "I hear there's a dragon up in Maine. Maybe we could … check it out?"

"Yeah," Austin said, his heart in his throat. "I think we could. And if … you know, along the way … we figure out where we are …?"

Kelly nodded, offering him a wry smile underneath reddening eyes. "Duh. We'll be in Maine."

Austin smiled, the first honest smile, it seemed, he'd had in weeks. "Do you really think I'm in an emotional state to handle that kind of humor?"

Kelly shook her head, then both of them took a step forward to hold each other close.

"You're not staying," Berathon said to God as they stood outside the Gates of Heaven. The Gates had been smashed into little gold pieces that littered the ground made of cloud, and where they had once stood, a humming mass of electricity danced in the shape of the Gates.

"No, I am not," God said softly.

"Some will say you have abandoned us," Berathon pointed out carefully.

"Some have always said that," God answered. "It was never my intent to control the world, Berathon. You know that."

The angel nodded. "What would you have us do?"

God smiled and placed a gentle hand on the angel's shoulder. "It is time for you to make your own path, Berathon."

"Where are you going?"

"Into the Holy Lands," God answered. "I want to see my son."

Berathon smiled, "Tell Noah he still owes me a herd of elephant."

God rolled His eyes, "He owes everyone a herd of something."

Mollug had the hots for a dove. The parrot had spent the better part of the Sabbath following her around, flirting and laughing, dancing and diving. He was pretty sure the dove was flirting back, but it was hard to tell.

She was a dove, after all.

"Hello, Mollug," a voice said from below.

The parrot looked down to see a wounded Raphael waving up at him from a park bench, and dove to sit on the bench beside him. The dove followed.

"A friend?"

Mollug shrugged.

"Then I am truly sorry," Raphael frowned, sprinkling dust on the back of the dove.

The dove began to shimmer and when it unfolded its wings a twenty-something woman emerged. "What happened?" Jessica Jenkins asked, shaking her head. "I think I'm going to be sick," she gagged, then did just that onto the grass before her.

Mollug groaned. "Am I the only one in this blasted World who got screwed? Where's my second chance?"

Jessica spit out a vomit filled with worms. "Yuck," she said. "I remember being on an island … and now I'm here." She looked at Mollug and blushed. "And why am I attracted to this bird?" She slapped her hand over her mouth. "I didn't just say that," she mumbled.

Raphael rose to his feet. "This is Mollug, Jessica. He is your handsome prince in waiting, though, of course, he's not really a prince. But you have grown fond of him."

"I have."

"You totally have," Mollug replied.

"All that you need to do to free him from his imprisoned state is … well, you know how the fairy tales go."

With only the slightest hesitation Jessica moved forward and kissed Mollug on the beak. As both human and parrot closed their eyes, Raphael sprinkled some dust onto Mollug's back. Before Jessica could open her eyes Mollug's small frame transformed itself into human form.

Jessica opened her eyes to find a handsome young man sitting next to her on the bench. He wore a light armor of green. On the chest was a crest with a parrot's beak, the only sign of who he used to be. "I am so confused," she whispered.

"Roll with it," Mollug whispered back, leaning in for a kiss.

"Second chances," Raphael smiled, then turned and walked away.

Mark Bousquet is in the American Studies PhD program at Purdue University, studying the relationship between water, literature, and culture. He is currently working on his dissertation, an examination of nineteenth century whaling narratives. *Dreamer's Syndrome* is his first novel.

www.ingramcontent.com/pod-product-compliance
Lightning Source LLC
Chambersburg PA
CBHW020927020726
47495CB00002B/377